Princeton Theological Monograph Series

Dikran Y. Hadidian

General Editor

26

JESHUA

NAZARETH TO JERUSALEM

JESHUA

Nazareth to Jerusalem

Moelwyn Merchant

☙PICKWICK *Publications* · Eugene, Oregon

Pickwick Publications
An imprint of Wipf and Stock Publishers
199 W 8th Ave, Suite 3
Eugene, OR 97401

Jeshua
Nazareth to Jerusalem
By Merchant, Moelwyn
Copyright©1987 by Merchant, Moelwyn
ISBN 13: 978-1-55635-010-8
Publication date 7/9/2015
Previously published by Christopher Davies Ltd., 1987

CONTENTS

Prefatory Note

It was one of those unexpected revelations. The five of us, relaxing after dinner, in an Edinburgh drawing-room, included two Jewish friends, Joseph and Elaine Gerber. We had been talking of the Messiah and of Nazareth and, after a long silence, Joseph turned to me: 'Tell me; if you and I returned to Nazareth over nineteen hundred years ago and stood on the village square, would you take me by the arm and, pointing, say to me: 'You see that young man over there – he's God, you know.' Is that what you're seriously saying?' 'Yes, that's what I'm *trying* to say.'

Now, there's a real human problem here. 'The Doctrine of the Incarnation', latinate in language, learned, and of profound abstraction, is one thing; 'that young man over there, he's God', is another thing, striking very different resonances. We approach 'The Incarnation' with the profound respect we accord to any deeply argued and elegantly resolved intellectual problem, but the paradox of 'the Divine made Flesh' remains to tease us and in the dramatic form 'that young man – God!' it affronts us by its remoteness from our day-to-day experience.

This book is my attempt to be honest to my conviction about 'that young man' and his Godhead. The process of writing it has raised in bewildering variety the aspects of the one stark problem: If Jesus of Nazareth was 'Very Man', then he had human problems, dilemmas, aspirations – and a daily human context fascinating to explore. For his first thirty or so years we have little evidence beyond the assertion that he grew in knowledge and favour even as he grew in stature. For the final brief period we have the complex evidence of four of the most remarkable literary works in man's history and the countless libraries of comment they have propagated.

And in all this time he had a physical context, the land of Judah and Israel. The drawings which accompany the text here are not mere 'illustrations'; David Roberts and Edward Lear, in the nineteenth century saw a landscape which was almost Jeshua's.

Over the years – more than four decades – in which I have hoped and prepared to write this book, my debts have been countless: to the Church (the Cowley Fathers, Exeter Cathedral and Salisbury Close and the parishes of Llanddewibrefi and All Saints, Leamington Spa); to academic life here and in the United States; above all to those who have listened patiently to my gropings, and especially Ruth Hook, Lynne Brown, my son Paul and my wife who have read each stage in the writing; to Josef Herman, his astringent creative mind interpreting the tragedy of modern Jewry even while his paintings transcended it; and to Rabbi Tony Bayfield of the Manor House Centre for Judaism who has commented so charitably on my searchings.

Commentaries have been inescapable, from the magisterial Cassuto, *Book of Genesis* (Jerusalem, 1961) or the equally splendid Soncino Edition of *The Pentateuch and Haftorahs* (1962) to Denis Nineham's stimulating *St*

Mark (Penguin, 1963). Four books demand my especial gratitude: Geza Vermes, *Jesus the Jew* (1973), the two superbly argued studies by Edward Schillebeeckx, *Jesus* (1974, E.T. 1979) and *Christ* (1975), and again at the Manor House Centre, Hyam Maccoby's gracious gift to me of the Singer bilingual *Daily Prayer Book* which stands so harmoniously alongside my *Book of Common Prayer*. Jews and Christians share a noble heritage; I hope *Jeshua* may be seen as a humble part of this long inheritance.

W.M.M.

Acknowledgments

I give my thanks to the Librarian, University Library Edinburgh, and the Director and Trustees, Tate Gallery, London, for the reproduction of the engravings by David Roberts and Edward Lear, and my gratitude to Josef Herman for designing and drawing the dust jacket.

JESHUA

Prologue

The sombre faces were deeply troubled, the two pharisees pausing in what was clearly a potentially tragic discussion. Joseph, the younger of the two, was a vigorous man in early middle age. The elder, Nicodemus, was spare, grave and grey-bearded, his face bearing the look of authority long-exercised and of scholarship pursued for pleasure.

'How many more Messiahs must we endure? Their ill-considered dreaming pollutes all thought and weakens our fibre.' Joseph was patrician in his fastidious distaste for excess and his rejection of these false dreams of a holy revolt which would rid his people – poor deluded people – of pagan oppression. His features sharpened to the argument, his nostrils tightly compressed. In his friend's silence, his expression softened, grew brooding:

'And yet, one of them will, in God's good time, be He – and we shall know Him.'

'Shall we, indeed?' Authority and profound scholarship had not quenched the amused irony which came so readily to Nicodemus's eyes; he had seen so many turns of fortune for his people, so many hopes raised and dashed. Day after day he had dealings with corrupt Herodians, austere Romans and the equivocal, sceptical house of the High Priest; irony was a necessary weapon, if his soul were to remain tranquil, his hands clean.

Joseph was not to be quenched, failing to see that Nicodemus had withdrawn from argument, his gaze inward and pondering.

'And what does the Sanhedrin, our reverend peers and elders do? Debate endlessly on relations with Rome, trim over taxes, bicker about Temple boundaries and the propriety of trade in the outer Court and of proper space for the Gentiles. But the Law, the radiance of the Law, beloved Torah –'

Nicodemus looked up at him, the irony in his eyes deepening and his half-smile deprecating:

'And what of the countryside? How are the crops in Arimathea? Do you stay long in Jerusalem?'

The questions assumed no answer; they were mere diversions, an attempt to calm and deflect Joseph's increasing emotion. He stood and looked over the balcony-rail into the enclosed courtyard. 'Come; you have told me that we should explore your garden. I envy you this cool, scented place so near the heart of Jerusalem; even its sounds are only a murmur here.'

They went down the shallow stairway and, through an arch, entered a second walled court. The centre was paved with water-worn cobbles, smooth to the sandalled foot. On three sides there was a narrow bed of herbs, thyme in all its wilderness and upland variety of leaf and flower; three pungent species of mint, moss-mulched to hold the moisture; sage-bushes bearing the distant hint of desert heat; saffron, crocus and a patch of onions and leeks.

'Your kitchen and your dye-vats are well supplied.'

Joseph drew Nicodemus to the shaded corner, more deeply shadowed by the broad leaves of a mature and unpruned fig-tree; at its trunk, a crude bench had been made. They sat in silence until Nicodemus felt he could speak more directly to his younger friend.

'We pharisees carry a double burden, live two lives; sometimes they come together but for the most part they must be held in a delicate balance. On the one hand we strive with all our worldly wisdom to preserve the very life of our people, threatened by the might of ruthless Rome and the humiliating deviousness of Herod's house.' He held up his delicate hand to still what threatened to be another outburst from Joseph.

'The other side of our life is full of light; in it we have the prayers, the psalms and the feasts; through it there rings out the wonder of the Word.' Their eyes met and soundlessly there seemed to pass between them a ritual response, an echo from the Temple.

'We tend a deep river, longer and deeper than Jordan. It flows out of Eden, it was crossed by Abraham, deepened by David and the heroes who followed him and purified by the noble company of the prophets. At those waters we make our lives, Joseph; whether in the rural quiet of your home in Arimathea or here, when you join us, your friends, in the turmoil of Jerusalem, you, with us, tend the waters of that river.'

Joseph responded to the words as he would to prophecy; his restless, so mobile hands were still, clasped at his knees; his eyes had lost their haunted fever and looked to Nicodemus for their direction.

'The stream, that current is often fouled, and it is our task – our privilege – to clear the burden of weeds, to have the waters flow swift and pure, so that the strong, the heroic may drink and be renewed in strength, and the humble little ones take their rest on its banks.'

Joseph had never heard Nicodemus in these tones before. He knew the depths of his searching scholarship and had guessed where his learning had led him, into worlds were few would venture to follow him. He understood in part the wit and the defensive irony with which Nicodemus parried the cruder words of his fellows. He wished to respond to all that he had heard in this last hour but fell back upon the splendour of familiar words:

'He maketh me to lie down in green pastures,

He leadeth me beside the still waters.'

The smile of Nicodemus was a sufficient response and there was a flash of the customary irony as he replied,

'Would that they were always 'still waters'!'

They remained silent as the afternoon's heat eddied around them. There were dark shadows about them and from their seat at the fig-tree they could see the even deeper shadows of the inner court and, opposite its archway, the dark green way to the lower garden.

'Your plans for the next month; they are made?' The two friends had returned to the quiet courtesies of conversation.

'I stay until the great heats come and the crowds grow intolerably restless. Then to Arimathea for the first harvest.'

'You will stay there whatever the rumours and stirrings?'

'No. My true place is here. Here I shall argue and plead my way through life.'

'To an early grave?' Nicodemus's tone was light but the question was wholly intended.

Joseph rose from the bench and with no more than a gesture of invitation to his friend, passed through the arch into a wilder garden, seemingly overgrown but leading by a winding path to a more formal grove. Rocks encroached on the way and at the end a shallow cave, the entrance closed by a rough-hewn circular rock. In the heat the wilder scents were heady and oppressive. The city, masked by the slope, the trees and the shrubs, was scarcely audible.

BOOK ONE

Nazareth

ONE

Nazareth was a paradox. A little township (neither town nor village) it was built on the slopes of a hollow within the hills above the valley of Jezreel. Supplied with water by the one meagre spring from the limestone rock, it had its own self-sufficiency, its craftsmen met its dwelling and social needs, the fields and gardens on the slopes about it supplied all its food. Marriages caused its social structure to revolve about some half dozen large families. Very few were rich, fewer knew the depths of poverty, none lived in humiliation; it was an 'island', sufficient to itself, isolated, conservative, passionately aware of its past.

Herein lay the paradox. Sheltered and aloof, it yet looked out from its height on one of the great highways of the ancient world. The Esdraelon plain, deep soiled and fertile, was a principal traffic route for pilgrims, merchants and invading armies; here the heroes had fought; Gideon and Sisera prevailed under God and Josiah tragically lost his life. On the aloof mount of Carmel, away from the battleground, Elijah's mightier struggle with the forces of Baal still stirred the memory. From the hillside above Nazareth and from the steep escarpment below, could be seen the greatest land masses of Galilee, the waves of hills in Samaria, the Carmel barrier before the sea and far to the north the permanent snows of Hermon. Remote and aloof, Nazareth in its eyrie commanded ter-

3

rain which was the history of a nation and it was only a good day's journey north to Hellenised land, to Tiberias, to Capernaum or Bethsaida; another day's journey and you reached Carmel the country of the prophets in the west; southward Jerusalem itself was but three or four days' journey distant. Aloof as a hermitage, its vigorous inhabitants could if they wished overlook all the action of the Hebrew, Greek and Roman world.

Within an hour after dawn at a turn of the month Tebet and Sheba, a straggling file of women, water pots aslant on their hips, climbed towards the spring; streaming down through the limestone fissure into the basin built in the shade of a rock; the heavy rains which that year had followed the planting of the grain gave ample water. The pastures were unusually green and the barley shoots promised a heavy harvest. One woman, taller than most of the others, walked with a swift grace to the water basin. She filled the water pot, balanced it carefully for her return and with no more than a smiling greeting to the others at the spring, walked swiftly back to her home. Some little distance from the path a child of about four years, face and eyes as still as the woman's, watched her walk to the house and then turned, as though reluctantly, to the little knot of children playing noisily the dancing round game of 'Weddings and Funerals.' He stepped quickly into the weaving pattern, choosing partners and relinquishing them to the next in line and then slowing to the statelier dance of the funeral procession. Whether in laughter or gravity, the children moved instinctively to the old ritual, almost wordless, with smiles and mock tears in the childlike parody. Jeshua danced the complete round, grave and gay, and then stepped quietly away from the group over a hillock into the first meadow, the home pasture. A few flowers were showing their buds, some, anemones and flax, about to open. He plucked a handful, the grey dusty hairs of the anemone stems contrasting with the tough resilience of the flax, arranged them with surprising deftness in a posy, the blue of the flax flowers against the patterned hues of anemone and walked gravely home.

'For you, Mother; I'm sorry my fingers couldn't make a coronet.'

She took the flowers placed them in a small pot and set them in a cool niche by the side of the window.

The following morning the petals had almost all fallen and lay like a wreath about the water pot.

'I'm sorry they're dead, Jeshua; they were beautiful.'

'Dead? but they're still springing with life'; he pushed the petals around to a different pattern, their colours fresh and their texture still resilient with sap.

Since Joseph was a jobbing builder (the skills of mason and carpenter commanded all the simple village materials), their house, without ostentation, was bigger than most, built carefully to a plan which allowed the family to expand into increasing space. The ground floor was airy and cool, with a low table surrounded by stools; above the upper chamber was the flat roof with some herb pots sheltered by a parapet from the greatest heat; from the roof there was a view over the whole village to the plain below the escarpment; a walled courtyard separated the house from the buildings where Joseph did a substantial part of his work and here materials were stored. It was the natural playground for Jeshua and for young Jacob, a year his junior. Here with enough disarray to flatter a child's needs, they hid behind work benches and doors, gathered heaps of the shavings and chippings of wood, some of them aromatic, all of them varied in colour, in the corner by the brick moulds, or watched quietly while Joseph prepared planks with the adze, sorted nails and dowels for the next building job or set out bundles of osiers or small mounds of tile, to dry slowly in the warm air. It was a secure and mysterious place to which only a few particular friends were invited.

But for Jeshua the rabbi's house held greater and more mysterious attractions. Rabbi Lazar, though a native Galilean, had gathered his learning in Jerusalem but had returned to the back-water of Nazareth to pursue in quiet his trade of scribe and maker of parchment and his vocation as rabbi to his people. His house had always the faint flavour of the tanyard, at which Jeshua's nose wrinkled until he got used to it, for in the outhouse, which Joseph had built for the rabbi as an extension of his home, there were skins and hides in various stages of scraping, stretching, bleaching and curing; it was without the stench of slaughter – to which the rabbi was also not unaccustomed – but the skins had a strong animal odour to which the fastidious boy grew only slowly accustomed.

One afternoon in his fifth year he slipped into Lazar's living-room out of the increasing heat of the sun (it was late in the month Nisan; Passover had gone with its solemnity and barley harvest was drawing to its height); the rabbi was half reading half nodding over a newly written roll and barely noticed the eager boy.

'Please, rabbi, show me!'

It was, as Lazar knew a reminder of his promise to show him the mystery of the parchments, those rolls which came out of the synagogue's ark with country ceremony each sabbath; he wanted to know their substance, wanted to see the scribe at work.

'Into the workshop, Jeshua.'

Pegged out tight on a high bench was an almost cured lamb skin, fell-side upward.

'It's rather more than half finished. Do you see the little bristles where the wool came away? They have all to be rubbed and cleaned away. Take this stone – it's pumice – perhaps you know, eh? – and rub where I've put this little dusting of lime.'

The two worked in silence, a smile from the rabbi as Jeshua sneezed away the fine dust, lime and skin fragments, as the work came to an end.

'It will need a little scraping and polishing and this side will be ready for the larger rougher writing if it's needed. But now the other side.'

The skin was unpegged and turned from the fell- to the flesh- side. Here in its natural state it was almost ready for the pen. Carefully they rubbed away the very small particles of flesh, dried almost to dust and then with a tacky slurry of lime, rubbed and polished until the skin was smooth, a cream colour so pale as to be nearly white.

'In a day or two that will be ready. Come in good time before Sabbath and you shall see a little more.'

Two days later Jeshua was ready for more initiation into the scribe's mystery.

'You see I always carry my inkhorn at my belt – old habit from Jerusalem days – the ink looks sadly dry today and you must cut me more reeds, young Jeshua! These pens look worn and frayed at the tip.'

Lazar took a small patch of prepared skin.

'Two things to learn at the same time today – this piece of skin will do – cut from the top of the thigh and too small for a roll – yes, two things, ink and the letters! You've heard the Torah every Sabbath. Words, Jeshua, words of such power! but the words are gathered together from fragments by those of us He has called to be scribes, fragments which we love and cherish and form; letters, Jeshua, the very bones and sinews and flesh of those words we speak so reverently.'

Jeshua wondered at the childlike intensity and eagerness of the rabbi's looks and gestures, so like Jacob and Miriam and the others at the height of their play in the square.

'And so you must respect this craft, Jeshua. The scribes are a noble people, handing on the word.'

He took the skin fragment and placed it ready for writing and placed the ink beside it.

'This colour shines a little – just water with fine resin and lamp-black which I make myself from smoking, burning oil; mixed, they give me this rich black colour and if I make a mistake' (a smiling conspiracy boy to boy) 'I can wipe it away from the skins with a wet rag and pumice it clean – but that mustn't happen too often.'

'And that ink then on the full parchment?'

'That is a nobler colour and fast in the surface of the skin. I gather oakgalls on the hillside trees and I pound and boil them with copperas, sent up every year from my friend Imri in Alexandria – he who sends me these papyrus sheets.'

He spoke with the expert authority of the craftsman; Jeshua listened and watched without a word, scarcely a movement.

'Now your first letters – the single 'first and last!" Swiftly the reed pen traced the letter: 'Aleph; it almost takes flight like a bird; and now the last, Tau, it rests comfortably like a stool at the end of the alphabet!'

Jeshua smiled tentatively, not sure whether it was entirely joking.

'Aleph, Tau, first and last, beginning and end; remember them as your fragments of the Word.'

'Can I see some of the others, Rab Lazar?'

Murmuring them to himself as his reed moved rapidly over the surface: 'Beth, Gimel, Daleth, He – see how it wants to sit as comfortably as Tau! and shall we run on? Heth, Teth; Kaph, Lamed – and look, Ayin – isn't that a dancing shape? and the most beautiful of all, Shin, who dances in two forms – they dance across the skin, these little ones of mine – see how they dance!'

He paused as if he embarrassed himself in his laughter and his eyes met the grave, smiling eyes of Jeshua.

'There will be more to learn soon – another day, child;

soon after olive harvest and before the shofar sounds the New Year you, and three or four others, will begin your schooling. Until then remember 'the first' and 'the last' and all that danced between.'

Olive harvest had passed; the fruit had gone to the press and from the light golden liquid there was a gently cloying hint in the air of its rich warmth. Jeshua was both eager and apprehensive at the thought of school, that brief daily discipline which in six years would lead him to Sonship of the Law, and he would be deemed a man. It was an oppressive day in Nazareth and he wanted none of the laughter and play in the square. He walked slowly past the last houses on the hill to the north, and to the pasturage beyond the thorn bushes, the sage scrub and the tamarisks which masked like a fence the lower sheep-run. Silhouetted like a frieze against the sky as the hill curved away westward, a shepherd boy, little older than he, walked ahead of a straggling line of sheep. He scrambled on nearly to the crest and sat on a boulder, to find his breath, absorb some of the sun and feel a momentary pang of envy at the shepherd's freedom in the hills. The last of the sheep passed over the edge of the pasture and, acknowledging the strange tug of schooling, he walked almost eagerly back to the rabbi's house.

'Aleph, Beth, Gimel, Daleth – now say them after me: Aleph, Beth, Gimel, Daleth, – again and again! Coniah, will you repeat them?'

'Aleph, Gimel, Beth -' There was a little laughter.

'It is unseemly to mock! You and he will know them soon from Aleph to Tau.'

The hour was soon over and they ran to their play with the others in the square; today it was to be 'Chariots and Riders' and in the boisterous war game, all raiders into

Galilee soundly trounced, their first fragment of ancient learning was quickly set aside.

Lazar had been invited to Joseph's house for the Sabbath meal. The candles were all lit, the prayers had been said, the food finished and they all sat in the twilight in the courtyard. At one end an almost unpruned vine turned a corner of the yard into an arbour and there the three sat, Mary and Joseph with Lazar between them. The scents of the evening came in lightly from the hillside and the children – Miriam almost ready for bed – squatted before them, expecting one of Lazar's stories. He seemed to the children to be teasing them, as he questioned their father about building materials; building materials! in the quiet holiday hour of the warm Sabbath evening!

'That splendid, squared up piece of limestone, from some distance, Joseph? and quarried not from the living rock but from a building?'

'Yes, half way between us and Sepphoris; it seems it was to be a grand house – more than could be afforded!'

'Ah; did you hear' – the children sat more alertly, for this was the familiar prelude; 'Did you hear of the stone rejected by the builders?'

Joseph looked sceptical, not quite sure whether this was to be a rabbinic tale with a moral or a subtle reproof for his quarrying methods.

'Well, this builder – he was making a modest four-square house on a southern slope – just the setting for a vineyard and a little olive grove. The stone was good and well hewn and the building going along nicely when a travelling quarryman, his cart drawn by two mules, passed the front of the plot, stopped and offered him a handsome well-hewn block, of the weight of two men. A bargain was struck – an expensive bargain but the stone was handsome – and rested in the space before the building.'

10

Lazar paused, still teasing the children with their expectation of laughter, of catastrophe – you never knew with Lazar!

'There the stone lay for many weeks and the ground floor of the house was complete. A little party was called one evening to celebrate it and so very unhappily a guest, leaving the house, stumbled over the stone and broke his leg. No one was very pleased with the owner of the house. He gazed at the stone – it was so very handsome – and he came to a decision: it should be built into the very front of the house immediately above the main entrance. It looked very good but – some thought – not very secure; and they were right. A week later it fell on another visitor, this time breaking his shoulder with a glancing blow.'

The children looked very sober, how was the story to end?

'It was now time to take a real decision. He was not going to give up his handsome stone and he liked the site of his house. So he and his workmen tore down a major part of the building, that which faced the steep slope of the hill and there they bedded in the large stone, a corner stone and a buttress at the same time.'

'And so you see –' 'Oh no!' said Jacob quietly to himself 'it *was* a parable after all just like synagogue'; he sighed as Rabbi Lazar went on.

'Torah can't be ignored, and it's not a decoration; it's the corner stone or nothing else.'

And it was time for bed.

The olive harvest was almost over; a few late fruits remained on the trees, seen between the rippling green and silver of the leaves. Joseph took Jeshua to the top of the grove where the oldest trees formed a sculptured group below the hill top. One patriarch among them dominated the grove, gnarled and misshapen with only two or three branches bearing leaves and a few small fruit. Jeshua caressed the contorted trunk, straight for a few feet above his head, and then leaning away from the line of the prevailing wind and convoluted like a wilful architectural fantasy.

'It has had its living, fruitful day; now it must live its next course – the most valuable timber growing about our house.'

Jeshua looked troubled; to cut down this tree was to remove a precious landmark, to alter the very structure of his little universe which had seen scarcely any change in his seven years of life.

'We must go carefully about it, for we want all the timber we can save from it.'

With a short-handled mattock Joseph hacked away the earth between the half dozen large roots which anchored the tree. Each was severed by blows from a sharpened adze and then, with a space cleared, an axe was used for the bole, now revealed several inches below ground. Jeshua watched fascinated as the stream of wood chips flew from the axe blows. He had seen Joseph many times at work but this was true expertise, no wasting unnecessarily any of the precious wood.

'Shall I be as handy as you with the axe, father?'

'It will need a lot of practice on smaller boughs; you shall try in an hour or two on some of the these old branches.'

The sun was uncomfortably high as the olive tree rocked in its hollowed- out site. A half dozen blows with a sharpened adze and the tap-root gave with a final tearing of sinew, the old tree, ('Ancient when the Maccabees came north and in its youth when Elijah prophesied on Carmel') lay on its side, surrounded by a tangle of brittle twigs and a few branches still green with sap. Two large boughs prevented the convenient handling of the trunk.

'These need removing. Here's a smaller axe. Now, a

blow here, through the bark and biting the wood, and then a blow above it, meeting the first cut – and you see a little wedge of wood flies out. Just try!'

Jeshua aimed tentatively at the bough, alongside Joseph's first cut, clumsily enlarging the space. But soon they had circled two-thirds of the bough, revealing the dark heartwood. The adze cut through to the sapwood below and a few hard strokes with the axe severed it from the trunk.

'We shall leave the other large one as a handle for dragging. But first to clean up the smaller branches.'

Working now in concert they severed them, gathered them in bundles and stood back from the main tree, a crudely fluted pillar on the hillside.

'It can stay there today. Tomorrow we must ask Reuben and Ezekiel for an hour's help to drag it to the work yard.'

They sat together on the main trunk, master and 'prentice warmed by the other relationship and Jeshua had some moments to survey the new landscape. Above them he could now see with a more tutored eye the cluster of hewn stumps from an earlier, less economical felling, pillar-bases some eighteen inches high invaded by the thorn scrub and in smooth, conical tumuli, the termite heaps patterning the sage brush which was trespassing upon the neglected upper grove.

'Now you must see what this trunk will become.'

They walked a few hundred yards to the outhouse where so much of the work was done. Piles of oak and plane, with pine and a few valuable older balks, were piled in order about the roofed yard. From one smaller pile Joseph drew three rough planks evidently wedged and split from one trunk.

'This is a smaller olive tree than the one we cut down' (That 'we' was very precious) 'and the planks we shall have will be finer than these. You see that delicate yellow colour, like rich cream, and those fine bands of reddish brown? Those are the colours that make this such a noble wood.'

He drew out one of the rough-hewn planks and placed it across two trestles. Carefully grinding down and sharpening a finer, smaller adze and beginning at the broader end of the plank, he delicately chipped away at the shallowest of angles, each stroke overlaying the previous bite of the blade, until the whole plank, refined and smoothly revealing its coloured texture, invited Jeshua's delicate, caressing hand.

'Always work with the grain, in the direction the tree has grown and it will never resist you, never splinter.'

The surface of the plank, which appeared so plain and smooth, had, to Jeshua's finger-tips, the true undulating ripple of a living surface. Polished with wax it would be a noble texture.

'This adze and those axe-heads have lost their tempering. Reuben needs to handle them and we can ask him at the same time for help with the other tree tomorrow.'

They walked across the square to the smithy where Jeshua saw the glow of the charcoal; the muffled roar as the goatskin bellows raised the glow to a working heat recalled his long childhood feeling, half awe, half fear, of the work of the smith; for he knew the tradition of Tubal-Cain, knew in his blood the old mystery.

TWO

There were now three more brothers: to Jacob were added Joses, Simon and Jude, and Miriam had a sister as companion, gentle Ruth.

'Were you proud of my birth, your first born?' They had been gathering wild flax in the cool of the evening in the meadow below the town. Mary, though above average height for a woman of Galilee, was now scarcely taller than her ten-year-old son. His hair, of an auburn so dark as to be almost black, hung to his shoulders as he walked ahead of her and looked back eagerly at the question.

'Were you proud?' She walked a little faster, gaining the square and then the cool of their home. Jeshua found the silence constraining; rarely could he fail to talk to his mother but now he sat quietly on a stool as she moved over to the window ledge.

'You were having your first sleep.' She broke in without preamble. Her hands folded gently in her lap. 'After the wailing you were quiet in your swaddling clothes. Shepherds had come to the door, speaking of the song of angels and now there was quiet again. Joseph was tired from the journey and the anxiety – another command from those men of Rome.' She neither gave explanation or expected any questioning – the fact was peripheral, almost irrelevant. 'Was it that night or some time later? It was all of such wonder. A man entered our sleeping-place, tall, with dignity in spite of the dust of many miles. With no word beyond 'Greeting' and 'Peace', he gave me, placed at your feet, gifts.'

'I seem to remember incense, as fine as the finest in our temple worship; and myrrh – I have seen it strewn in the folds of a winding-sheet. The incense and the myrrh were given you by the two companions of the tall stranger. They were dark, fatigued, but their eyes were wise with the wisdom of learning and suffering. Their journey had been long and they waited only an instant.'

He was enveloped by it and questionless. 'It was like another country, a world of light, of music; and then a world of darkness, of exile, of Herod and Egyptian bondage. And out of that too we were delivered, Joseph and I and you, my firstborn.'

There was no call to break the silence; he gravely accepted the woman's mystery and pride, half-understanding her half-smile.

'I am only a woman but I knew in my heart that day that

15

the power of light had been with us. Herod eclipsed it with his darkness and 'Rachel wept for her children' for you were born in light and shadowed darkness.'

She had no more to say and Jeshua accepted the tone of prophecy and the words to be pondered when he came to greater stature. He looked about the room, the curtained sleeping-alcoves, the eating space, the cushioned corner where the busyness of the square could be watched. The room looked new, 'another country' and the greater part of his childhood had sloughed away.

The winter figs had been gathered and there was the rejoicing of the Feast of Purim. Miriam took a special pleasure in this celebration of Esther's triumph over Haman and the happy ending of her marriage.

'But would you really, you, Miriam, would you really have wanted Haman's sons hanged?' Jeshua's question was half-serious banter. Quiet Miriam, almost as demurely gentle as her sister Ruth, would scarcely summon the fierce words to frighten the goat-kids from the best of the lamb's pasturage.

'Yes, they deserved it!' – and cathartic Purim, its tale of another deliverance of God's people, was celebrated and set aside.

Rabbi Lazar was hurrying past the house and saw Jeshua in the doorway. 'Your friend Reuben has died.' It was Jeshua's first death, his first loss and of one whose mysterious trade had held for the boy a mystery beyond his reach. No week had passed without his standing a while at the entrance to the smithy, to savour the heat, the harsh bell tones of the hammer on metal, the malleable fruit-red metal and the drowning plunge of its tempering. Every movement was a token of urgent life, and death seemed now an absurdity.

He took the rabbi's hand as they crossed the square and went into the smith's living room. Jeshua had never been in this dark and solitary place, a mere annexe to the smithy but clean in its spare austerity. The women had been about their work and Reuben lay bound in his linen – 'Eternity's swaddling clothes', murmured Lazar – the least flavour of spices rising from the folds. The cheek-bones, the eyelids and the forehead were unbound and gave a semblance of sleep to the still form. Jeshua approached the body and placed his palm on the fore-head; it seemed for the briefest moment to stir but a cold inertness checked the caress of his fingers. 'This is not Reuben,' he said and walked out into the sun, aware of his deprivation. He felt he saw the square for the first time, the hot limestone gravel under his sandals, the brilliant white of the buildings and, across the corner where two buildings made an angular recess, a vine-arbour gave the old men a little shelter as they drowsed and murmured through the quiet evening. The familiar square was changed, translated to an alien place where the ringing of the anvil would no longer carry the old assurance.

'Today we shall 'lift up our eyes to the hills' and go quite a journey together. Bring some barley cakes, a handful of figs and a little relish and we shall spend the day in the outer country.'

As they set out north of Nazareth, Lazar seemed the younger of the two, revelling in the day's freedom. The scents of the fields began to rise in the morning air and into the silence after the dawn chorus, the birds began again the full daytime song.

'Little wonder the Lord God thought it all 'very good', all things of the light and the wonder of the dark, the stars and the variable moon.' Jeshua remained quiet, rejoicing in the boyish pleasure of the ageing rabbi.

They reached the highest peak above Nazareth and

from the purposeful lowering of Lazar's satchel and the care with which he chose two boulders for their rest, Jeshua knew they had reached the mid-day destination. Lazar closed his eyes, savouring the warmth and then turned to Jeshua. 'You have learned your letters, joined Aleph to Tau, seen how they danced from right to left and back to dance again from right to left. Here, though we can't see the dance of the words on the sheepskin, here, in the warmth, the colour, the sounds of the world about us, the rich words march back from those Jerusalem days when I probed their meaning.'

The boy had matured enough in his friendship to know that silence alone would draw out the recollections which he knew to be the rabbi's intention.

'I was a country boy like you; quite young – I was barely nineteen and longing for a craft which would discipline my hands and the learning which would tell me the truths. I was sent to Jerusalem to the schools and debates in the Temple precincts. I was lucky, so very very lucky.'

He paused as the years turned back their memories.

'I attached myself – we all made our choices – to those who crowded about Shammai, the most austere rabbi of them all. There I learnt the full rigour of the law, the definitions, the distinctions, the very function of each syllable and I questioned every jot of every reading and interpretation. I felt my mind to be a tempered tool, burnished copper from the coppersmith!'

He laughed with the old mischief. 'But it seemed a fruitless work to absorb my life, yes fruitless – like gathering stones in a wilderness. The stones were precious enough but the wilderness became drier and drier – and I turned to an oasis!' His raised eyebrow questioned quietly the boy's understanding of his story; Jeshua had only to nod his assent.

'The students about the feet of Hillel, at one end of the Colonnade, were a happy crowd; there was a lot of laughter, the questions tumbled in with the excitement of disorderly debate. I felt there that I could breathe again and after the tangled argument we looked to Hillel's calm and often radiant face, and the answers came, with wisdom and all compassion. This was bread and fruit – not a stone. I too grew in stature and they wished to make me a scribe, to live in Jerusalem. I was destined, so they said, (I never quite believed them!) for the inner sanctuaries of the wise, to write in the Temple, to inscribe, indelibly for those who should follow, the wisdom and judgments of the rabbis. But I loved the Torah too deeply to administer her; I was no government servant; I needed a clearer air, Nazareth in the hills. I wanted to hear, along with the song of the birds the words of Moses on the heights, to hear Elijah on Carmel and to hear routed the hosts of Midian, but above all the still small voice. I needed a clearer, fresher air about me and I came to Galilee to this little quiet bowl in the hills. I still carry my scribe's inkhorn at my side (the water flask takes its place today!) but I am no longer 'scribe' and if you, my people, call me rabbi I am much more than content.'

They ate in silence, sharing the wheaten bread, the fragment of cheese and dried dates which Lazar had brought with him, the barley cakes and figs which they had prepared for Jeshua. The water in the flask was slightly tepid, but refreshing in the intense heat of noon, their rock niche casting a sharp shadow on the parched hillside.

'But I didn't come to gossip about my past, though I confess I am happy to have told you of Jerusalem and of my choice in coming to Galilee. As the sun loses some of its heat I want you to share my landscape with me.'

They walked away from the rock boulders to a small open plateau. With his whole arm extended Lazar pointed southward, across the valley and the plain to the heights above Megiddo and then his gesture bore eastward.

'There – only about sixty miles away as the eagle soars, but a long and uncomfortable journey – is Mount Nebo in Moab, the most tragic mountain in our history. I sometimes fancy I see it looming out of the haze on a clear day (I expect it's my imagination feeding on its desire) and there I see Moses ('our teacher above all teachers – Moshe Rabbemu') still with his strength undiminished after the cruel journey of deliverance. And there he stands, on the mountain of dereliction. Since he has endured and conquered, though the Lord had descended in fire, though the peaks smoked like a kiln and the mountain quaked with the majesty and awe of the voice, yes, Sinai he conquered but Nebo was death – not simply the death of his body – it was the death of his vision to lead his people across Jordan. The land was promised, it lay before him from the waste of the Negeb to the snows of Hermon, from Jordan to the sea – and he was not to enter.'

The boy (in his twelfth year on the brink of manhood in his community) felt the sombre tone, understood little but knew in his intuitive sympathy that here was the heart of tragedy, the unfulfilled vision, death before the task was finished.

'It wasn't all pitiful sorrow, Jeshua.' The rabbi moved to the sombreness of the boy's look 'Already the future was secured. Eleazar (my namesake!) was High Priest and he, with Moses, consecrated Joshua (your namesake!) to fulfil the work, to make complete the will of God; the Law, the commandments of Sinai, were carried over Jordan. Torah was our heritage forever.'

The sombre trouble had not wholly left the eyes of Jeshua; they seemed to question the sure certainty of Lazar's last words. 'But Rabbi Lazar; I have heard you read in synagogue – and have heard you repeat the words as you wrote with your reed that 'the Lord would speak to Moses face to face, as a man speaks to his friend.' Wasn't this end of Moses a cruel end, undeserved by 'the Deliverer'?'

'It was cruel as we see it but it was no more than one moment in his long walk with God the Lord. And the Law – Moses will always be the Law.'

Mind struggled with compassion, as Jeshua sought to take the irreconcilable to himself; but his mind was given no respite: 'Look westward, seaward. Thrusting out before us is the shoulder of Carmel.'

'The drought and the prophets of Baal', said Jeshua, repeating the long-learnt scripture task.

'Yes and Elijah's conflicts didn't end there on Carmel. Below us, in the plain of Jezreel was a humble but coveted vineyard, Naboth's you remember. And it was coveted by King Ahab, for Mammon always covets Mammon. Naboth's vineyard, a peasant's livelihood, was no more than a fragment of desired wealth to that man of evil power. And Elijah prophesied, as he had prophesied on Carmel and the words had power.'

There was silence for a while, then Jeshua spoke, brooding. 'A strange thing, this prophecy. The breath of God seems sometimes to blow fitfully.' Lazar caught his breath at this venturesome blasphemy. 'I speak only as the scriptures speak. In the days of Eli, highpriest in Shiloh, there was evil in the land and a silencing of the word and it was to a child, the boy Samuel, that the murmur of the Lord's command came; for, it was written 'the word of the Lord was precious (precious in its tragic rarity) in those days; there was no open vision' and so it was in the days of Elijah; and so it has been in these last days, since the Maccabees 'waited for a prophet.' There have been many words, but the trumpet-call, 'Thus saith the Lord,' has been silent to our ears. We have hoped and heard no answer.'

The sun was westering, poised above Carmel, turning to plates of gold the cloud-strata at the horizon. Lazar changed his stand to the south, to the lands beyond Samaria.

'The Law and the Prophets are loved and cherished in memory, their words proclaimed in the synagogues but what power, what sovereignty have we? You are newly moving out of childhood, Jeshua but you are not too young to have heard the legions and heard tell of their eagles, poised on their standards, which so nearly polluted our sacred places.'

'Yes, I have heard of it at Dedication, when we thank God for the Maccabees and their cleansing of the Temple which Antiochus had fouled. But those eagle-standards never entered, and they never shall in our generation.'

It was the quiet of prophecy, not a child's defiance, and fear for a moment shadowed Lazar's eyes. 'It will be God's hand not ours which restrains them; we no longer bear sovereignty in the city of David. You, Jeshua, have always spoken with love of that shepherd, sweet-singer, warrior and king; since Moses there had been no man like him and since David no man his peer.'

The sun was now a sliver of fire on Carmel as Lazar, so quietly as scarcely to be heard by the boy, spoke the words of David.

Why standest thou afar off, O Lord?
    Why hidest thou thyself in times of trouble?
    In the pride of the wicked the poor is hotly pursued
    Let them be taken in the devices that they have imagined.
    Lord thou hast heard the desire of the meek
    Thou wilt prepare their heart,
    Thou will cause thine ear to hear:
    To judge the fatherless and the oppressed,
    That man which is of the earth,
        may be terrible no more.

In the silence that followed the psalm, the rabbi turned to the north. The valleys below their ridge on either side were long streams of mist; to the north-east a bluer haze marked the sea of Galilee.

'Isn't that a glory? – the last sun's rays on the snows of Hermon, majestic Hermon, 'Hermon the unassailable'?' The subdued landscape showed now only those two washes of rose-gold light above the purple shadows of Carmel and the fluted snow slopes of Hermon. Jeshua had never seen such majesty or such loveliness. The awe and the adoration compassed themselves in a whispered word, 'Abba, Father.'

Again Lazar broke the silence. 'You will see why I cherish the tranquillity of Nazareth. North, south, east and west we see the turbulence of history, the whirlpool; here we are at the still centre of the storm, apparently unharmed, unaffected. At least we can draw breath, think a little. Here history seems to have passed us by, yes, passed us by. We have no noble buildings – but we have no ruins; we have had no prophets – but nor have we had martyrs; we have known no kings – but we have grieved for no traitors. Yes, happily, mercifully, history has passed us by?'

Jeshua had never heard these deeper tones in the rabbi's voice before; his eyes seemed remote, unseeing, as with habitual affection he pressed the boy's shoulder:

'History may not pass you by, Jeshua.'

Joseph's family had known only one Passover in Jerusalem in the first eleven years of Jeshua's life. Child-bearing and rearing had occupied Mary; Joseph was the busiest craftsman in Nazareth. There had, then, been only one escape, with three of the children, from the pressing round of the town's life. Now, as Jeshua approached his adult state, a Son of the Law, there seemed the certainty: 'Next year in Jerusalem.'

Rabbi Lazar had no worried concern for Jeshua; the

23

acuteness of his intuition, the flashes of imagination, were things he had met in no other boy, indeed, had not truly met even in the Jerusalem schools. But there were formal questions to be asked.

'Have you understood the great divisions of the Law? Have you accepted what they command?'

'I don't always feel them as 'commands,' at least not all of them. The words trouble me in their great differences: 'Thou shalt,' 'Thou shalt not.' Why should 'Thou shalt' with its encouragement to worship, adoration and love, be turned always in the direction of God, our Lord? and why should 'Thou shalt not' be the command about our friends, our neighbours, those closely about us? We love them too and I long to say of them 'Thou shalt'!'

The rabbi was content to be quiet, knowing the answer to reside in the question.

'And sometimes 'Thou shalt not' troubles me in other ways. Moses sang out for joy when our people were taken out of Eygpt:

> The Lord is my strength and song,
> And he has become my salvation.
> This is my God and I will praise him

and when the Law was enclosed in the Ark, it is written: 'Then the cloud covered the tent of meeting and the glory of the Lord filled the tabernacle.' It seems to me that that is the language of the acts and laws of God rather than 'Thou shalt not'.'

'Yes,?' Lazar was content to let the argument grow in the boy's mind.

''Thou shalt not' is too cold, too rigid and I'm not sure I always know what it intends. 'Thou shalt not make to thyself any graven image' – 'any graven image'? A few weeks ago, I had picked up a small piece of olive wood which my father had discarded. I was whittling away at it, scarcely knowing what I was intending to carve; soon I realised that I had shaped roughly the form of a woman,

24

tall and graceful as my mother, though just held in the palm of my hand. One or two more touches of the knife and the figure would have seen – perhaps with her eyes; breathed – perhaps with the sweetness of her breath; smiled – perhaps with the gentleness of her lips. Was this, would it have been a 'graven image'? I didn't wish to worship it! – it was after all the work of my hands. It was to have been a gift of love to Mary my mother. But 'Thou shalt not' held me. One day I should like to ask the Doctors of the Law about this!'

Again it seemed to Lazar that he needed no reply. The silence lay between them, a tranquil pride in his pupil on the rabbi's part, a ferment of questioning for Jeshua. At last Rabbi Lazar spoke.

'A week ago we stood on the hilltop and looked towards Nebo, grieving with Moses, turned towards Carmel, rejoicing in Elijah, peered south into the distance for the City of David. I say to you, Jeshua, Moses shall be your shoulder-companion and his Law your love; with Elijah you shall declare prophecy and raise up your people; and with David shall be your sovereignty.' The intoned words were a mystery incomprehensible to the boy, their manner so unaccustomed; but they stirred in him like leaven.

THREE

He scarcely remembered the road to Jerusalem for this was only his second visit. There had been the final instruction from Rabbi Lazar, the preparation of the *Tallit* for his praying and a gift from his neighbours of the phylacteries to be bound on forehead and forearm.

'Remember the thongs, Jeshua, to bind the phylactery to your arm – seven turns about your forearm and then the letter Shin on the palm of your hand – that loveliest of all the letters.' Jeshua would not forget; the ceremonial had been his dream all the weeks before the approach of Passover.

And there had been the annual family conference concerning the route and the anxious consultation with the neighbours.

'No exciting treks through noble valleys and rocky passes, Joseph!' (Simon, their gentle neighbour, was inclined to distrust the ambitions of Joseph to lead them and to show them the grandeurs of the countryside. For Simon and most of the others the one aim was to reach Jerusalem in swift safety and to return rejoicing). So for all the eager discussions, the route south was predictable. There would be no picturesque perils, like the fearful road from Jericho to Jerusalem; Joseph would have to content himself with proud talk of Megiddo's history, of blessing and cursing at Gerizim and Ebal, of the distant glimpse of tomb, well and battlefield and the joyful ascent to Jerusalem itself. It was a passage through time, history measured out by their sandals; and the neighbours were sure that Joseph would allow them to miss nothing of the events built into the very structure of their lives, their toil and their imagination.

It was of course not just the route; their pace and the duration of the journey was determined by the endurance of the aged, the infirm and the very young. A powerful young man could cover the distance with but two overnight halts. But for Nazareth's pilgrimage it was a slower matter – six, perhaps seven modest stages. Lodging had to be secured ('My cousin at the edge of Esdraelon...' 'My brother-in-law, uncomfortably alien in Shechem, will be delighted to see us'), food and water planned for the people – there would of course be wells and some purchases possible, but prudence was necessary with such a mixed multitude – and fodder had to be thought out for the donkeys and mules. It was a garrulous planning to which the older children listened in the sure belief that this was the happiest part of the feast.

All was at last ready, the journey planned to end at Jerusalem no later than the ninth day of Nisan, with time to purchase the lamb and the herbs on the tenth day, the preparations to begin for the fourteenth. Each family had ensured its sharing of the Passover with some relative or friend in Jerusalem. Jeshua knew that Mary's uncle Judah, whose house lay near the garden to the west of the Temple precincts, had his upper room ready prepared for their feasting.

Two moments on the journey especially moved the boy. They had come down from the higher hills into the valley of Esdraelon. They were now in the fertile, busy plain. The land had been ploughed and reaped for centuries and, with the intersection of trade, marauding and invading routes, it had been for all those same centuries the cockpit of his people. Megiddo lay ahead, the focus of a score of battlefields; from south, north and east, imperious armies had invaded his land and along its plain heroes, both noble and dubious, Barak, scourge of the Cannanites, Gideon, hammer of the hosts of Midian, and Saul the haunted and treacherous king, had moved with their forces. But one of these ghosts of history haunted the young mind more than all the others; for Josiah had been noble, a man after his own desire, a seemly ruler who had begun his reign as a boy of eight years, who had trusted carpenters, builders and masons with the task of restoring the Temple, asking them no reckoning 'because they dealt faithfully.' Then had come from the high priest Hilkiah the startling words, 'I have found the Book of the Law in the House of the Lord.' And according to its commands, Josiah purified all Jerusalem from all its abominations, ordained the reading of the Law and commissioned a Passover. Jeshua murmured to himself the words that had formerly so moved him, as he now went with his people to Passover in Jerusalem.

> Surely there was not holden such a Passover from the days of the judges that judged Israel, nor in all the days of the kings of Israel, nor of the Kings of Judah.

And yet to this noble King Josiah had come tragedy in his thirty-eighth year; for Pharaoh-necho of Egypt invaded the land and slew him here at Megiddo. Along the same road they took his body to bring him to Jerusalem. For Jeshua the Passover was wholly darkened until they came to their sleeping-place in Samaria.

The straggling caravan was now approaching the heart of Samaritan country; ahead of them was the valley between the twin peaks of Ebal 'of the Curses' and Gerizim 'of the Blessings'; here there pressed in on him the solemn demand of Moses as he gazed in longing over the land and ordained these peaks to be the symbols, the altars of choosing:

> I call heaven and earth to record this day against you, that I have set before you life and death, blessing and cursing; therefore choose life, that both thou and thy seed may live.

It moved Jeshua not a whit that Joseph drew their attention to the ancient sites — 'there is the well of Jacob and here the prophets took their rest' — for about them were the villages of the Samaritans, the averted eyes and the hostile mutterings of those who saw Jerusalem as no lodestone, the Hill of David as inferior to their Gerizim. It was an oppressive journey and the past bore down its shadows on his shoulders.

Another two nights' rest and in the early sun of the final day's journey they saw the walls of Jerusalem, the Temple of such purity of stonework that it borrowed every tint of the sun's radiance, pink, pure white and honey-coloured as the day moved on to evening; and through all the gleaming of the walls, the deeper tones of gold. They began in the twilight the Songs of Ascent:

I will lift up mine eyes unto the hills
From whence cometh my help.

I was glad when they said unto me
Let us go unto the house of the Lord

They that trust in the Lord
Are as mount Zion which cannot be moved
but abideth for ever
As the mountains are round about Jerusalem
So the Lord is round about his people.

The young architect in Jeshua felt a surge of recognition as he looked at the huge dressed stones, locked together by the friction of their massive weight.

'It really is foursquare! It truly stands unlike any other!' and with a new sense of fulfilment he joined in the song as they halted where the countryside met the first walls of the city:

I was glad when they said unto me
Let us go unto the house of the Lord
Our feet shall stand in thy way
O Jerusalem.
Jerusalem is builded as a city
That is compact together.

'Compact together!' He had never seen such strength, such security.

Before nightfall they were 'at home.' There was so much to tell, such questioning of Jeshua about his new manhood's threshold, his prayer shawl to be admired, and the prayers, to be said for the first time, now rehearsed as they were to take their evening meal together. The next three days, while their elders were about Passover business, the lambs, the herbs, the bread to be prepared, the wine to be brought out, the younger pilgrims were sight-seers in the city. It was a place of mystery: venerable men as withdrawn as the dark courtyards within which they sat; steep cobbled streets that led to the tortuous old town; the mockery of the Roman garrison-tower standing guard over the Temple, Rome's might protecting the Almighty. And there were gardens to be explored, some open to their play, others secret and enclosed within walls, the merest glimpses of their courts, steps and terraces through their iron gateways. But the magnet which drew Jeshua to a solitary contemplation was the lower wall of the Temple, those massive blocks of stone on which his palms rested, to feel the stirring of their warmth, the rough movement of the chisel-marks on their surface, the sharpness of their corners. He realised, as he had never felt in Nazareth, the power of 'living rock.'

On his second day of wandering with young Reuben, his cousin some years his senior, he ventured into the Temple precincts, entered the Court of the Gentiles and hesitated, despite Reuben's superior counsellings, before the pillared colonnades which surrounded each court. There the sages, the contemplative Pharisees and the rabbis of note, gathered to garner the Law and its mysteries. From a distance Jeshua could hear only the murmur of dispute, rising and falling with the intensity of argument or dissent. Reluctantly he turned away and walked silently with Reuben to their home.

Tomorrow was the Passover. The children had played tumultuously their game of seeking out every fragment of leaven and of leavened bread, no crumb of which should defile their feast.

It was no longer play; even over the youngest of the family the mantle of gravity had fallen, enhanced by the clean austerity of the room in which Passover would be celebrated. When these preparation were finished, water-pots, and basins were placed near the door and towels arranged on a stool for the final ablutions before the feast.

In silence they entered, Mary and Joseph to the head of the table, Miriam gently taking Ruth by the hand, and Jeshua, with Jacob at his side, standing between his parents and the younger children. Silence was held and in the tense expectation of the feast Jeshua's voice rang out with the ancient ritual.

'What mean ye by this service?' and Joseph solemnly and quietly replied:

'It is the sacrifice of the Lord's Passover who passed over the houses of the children of Israel in Eygpt, when He smote the Eygptians and delivered our houses.'

The silence descended again and Joseph intoned their prayer:

> Our God and God of our fathers, may our remembrance rise and be accepted before Thee, with the remembrance of our fathers, of Messiah the son of David thy servant, of Jerusalem thy holy city and of all thy people the house of Israel; bring deliverance and well-being, grace, loving kindness and mercy, life and peace on this day of the Feast of Unleavened Bread.

There was no movement even from the youngest until the blessing of the bread and wine had been pronounced, and in the same solemn stillness they ate the lamb, the unleavened bread and tasted the harsh, bitter tang of the herbs. As they ate, Jeshua, in the silence, felt the years roll away, knew the fearful pressure of 'the Deliverance' and the testing flight into the desert.

On the morning after Passover, the hour before dawn had the glowing presence of a spring day. Jeshua slipped out quietly – they would not be worried or offended, being long used to his solitary wanderings – went out through the main gate of the city, across the Kidron valley and walked quietly up towards the Mount of Olives. It was an ancient place (hadn't David fled this way out of his city away from the anger of Absalom?) and many of the olive trees were older even than those of their grove in Nazareth. Many had overseen the prophets; some had been saplings in the harassed history of the monarchy. But there had also been a rough care for its continuity; among the 'patriarchs', groups of younger trees had been planted and protected against grazing sheep and goats by projecting triangles of stakes. One large group had been tended with such special care as to merit the name of 'garden'; within its crude, dry-stoned wall the Garden of Gethsemane faced the nobility of the Temple. Jeshua climbed about and beyond the Garden to the upper slopes of Olivet and, choosing a gnarled trunk, twisted like the arms of a chair, he sat at its base, his arms about his knees. His mind seemed to him almost empty of thought, absorbing only sensations, the first sounds of morning, cockcrow, the faint stirring of metal on metal as the watersellers prepared their round, the trumpet blare as the Roman guards were roused for the day's watch, with the faintest beat of armour, like cymbals across the valley.

It was all so changed. At yesterday's dawn he had been a child, with a fearful happiness anticipating his part in the Passover, that had been the first step to a new awareness and he was perplexed and disturbed by his new sense of maturity. Until yesterday he had been a child in pupillage, learning submissively and only occasionally aware of powers, physical and intellectual, stirring to birth. He knew he had still years 'in bond', a ward to his apprenticeship both to his craft and to the Law; but today he was – before the Law and in the sight of men – a man; he smiled with a moment's wry comment; manhood at twelve years was no light burden. It was a responsibility all boys assumed in his nation; he reminded himself that he was now formally one of the Minyan, the statutory quorum to permit synagogue worship; but at this new dawn his mind groped beyond mere formality.

The day lay all before him, full of exploration. For Jerusalem this time had stirred and disturbed him profoundly. All the tumultuous history he had learned from Rabbi Lazar: its first wresting from the Jebusites; the growth of the city of David; the heroic tunnelling of the water-course to resist the thirst of sieges; the glory of Solomon and the shame of his alien shrines; the conquest and destruction and renewal and destruction again; the hatred and betrayal of the prophets; the cleansing fury of the Maccabees and the purifying of the Temple and its worship; that panorama of time had been his intellectual heritage since early childhood. But there before him were the very stones of Jerusalem; this was actual, today and here. There before him was the glory of the Temple, its declaration that within, above and beyond was Adonai, the one Lord God. He spoke aloud the 'Shema Israel' and as he spoke those noblest words he knew also, with the first bitterest irony of his new manhood that the present shrine of that One Lord God was the Temple, built in ostentation by the unseemly Herod, and still a-building as he fraternised with the Roman powers.

The discipline of the patient schooling at Nazareth asserted itself, the insistent demand of Rabbi Lazar that all perplexities, all contraries and ambiguities, be brought in humility before the Law and the resolution brought to the test of worship. The childhood puzzles and bewilderments had taught him his gentle and secure casuistry, the testing of all difficulties by the tradition of the Law. But that had been the skill of a precocious child; now he knew that the exercize of manhood would be sterner, the struggle of man with man and of man with God as great within him as he saw it without in the paradigm of Jerusalem.

He stood up and, lest he be late for the morning prayers,

said aloud as the sun brought a radiance to the white and gold of the Temple:

> Hear O Israel, the Lord your God is one Lord
> You shall love the Lord your God.

He walked down through the olive groves; indeed, the day lay all before him.

The family was garnering all the pleasures of Passover; there were to be seven days of unleavened bread and of rejoicing and the older children were left much to themselves and to their explorations of the city. The pilgrim crowds were a jostling, noisy and kindly people, patient with the children under foot. Jeshua by mid-morning had entered the Temple again, walked across the Court of the Gentiles, withdrawing a little into himself from his countryman's distrust of the prevailing smells of slaughter and of burnt flesh, reminded himself that this too was within the embrace of Torah, and came to the first colonnade. A group of men, very still and silent, listened to a rabbi who fluently and surely dissected the laws of tithing. This group failed to hold him but a little further along the court a larger and more intent group sat about the feet of two older men who gravely and courteously responded to each others exploration of the 'Days' of creation.

'It was such a period of time as the Lord God required.'

'How then is it called 'day'? Was there dawn and dusk, awaking and sleeping?'

'Surely it was as God the Lord willed, such lengthening of dawn and arresting of dusk as brought the firmament, the spread of heaven, all creatures, into being.'

'And the Lord God created much before the sun and moon were set in the heavens; how then, my brother, can you speak of dawn and dark, when there was no sun to mark the day, no moon to temper the darkness of night?'

There was a murmur of approval, almost of applause; had not the old man over-reached himself? The connoisseurs of argument among them recognised it as an age-old conundrum of the learned but they still waited for the new twist which would now surely be given to the debate.

'You much mistake, dear brother, in equating illumination with sun, moon and the stars of heaven. Did not Adonai say, at the threshold before time was, 'Let there be light.' Sun and moon, the planets and the stars, move through the heavens, eagerly seeking that radiance which He alone gave and they reflect that divine radiance in such measure as our poor eyes can tolerate.'

The nodding was eager and appreciative, the old man had given the time-honoured answer but with such deftness, such quick grace. This move in the game had true elegance. Through the murmurs of approbation, a young voice cut in from the back. Jeshua leaned diffidently on a pillar of the portico, not wishing wholly to associate himself with the older listeners.

'May the youngest and humblest among you ask a question, reverend rabbis?'

'But of course, young man. You are a Son of the Law?'

'Indeed, sir. This is my first Passover of manhood.'

'Then ask your question and we shall hope to answer.'

There were indulgent smiles from the older doctors of the Law as this young man, little more than a child, eagerly stood as if on tiptoe and smiling, to ask his first question.

'You have spoken, reverend doctors, of the creating of light and of darkness, of day and of night. But the first book of Moses begins yet earlier in words that fill me with wonder: 'In the beginning Elohim created heaven and earth and the earth was without form and void.' Tell me sirs, if God the Lord created, is not that to give form and shape? How then could it be 'without form, void of substance and shape'?'

'You must understand' – the grave voice took the question with due seriousness, as though propounded by an elder of the people – 'you must understand that 'to create' is to bring into being that which was not before.'

'That I understand; it is a 'making' unlike any that we know as men. But something in me longs to know that God made with form, beauty, craft.'

'Perhaps you have not understood the words 'formless and void.' The two words which our father Moses wrote can be likened to something you know very well. It was as if God presided over 'an empty wilderness' and by its side 'a wilderness of waters,' 'the deep'.' The troubled young eyes probed the similitudes, not wishing to reject the elder's assistance; the latter went on.

'You have seen – perhaps you have walked – the empty, barren wilderness; it too is 'void', without living water. But you have seen the merciful rains, and the empty wilderness blossoms like a garden.'

'But the word does not speak of rain, nor of cultivation. I can understand these wonders in the world about us but here I find another mystery, and it also troubles me. My rabbi at home taught me that the next words were these: 'And the spirit of God hovered over the face of the waters' and that that word 'hovers' could be like the fluttering of a caring bird over the nest of its young or even the brooding of the hen upon its nest of eggs. But I have also heard tell that the 'Spirit' of God is like the breath of a mouth or the winds of heaven and that what Moses wrote was truly, 'A wind, the spirit of God, sweeping over the waters.' Now, reverend sirs, – and forgive me that my troubled thought gropes so slowly – 'hovering,' 'fluttering,' 'brooding,' 'sweeping like a mighty wind,' how are we to understand these strangely different words? Have we really understood what Moses wrote?'

The indulgent smiles had ceased, especially among those who dared not participate. But the rabbis darted severely on the problems raised by the tentatively spoken questions.

'We must certainly reject 'brooding' if it implies hatching from a cosmic egg; the waters were not waiting for incubation, as our backyards produce chicks!' It was a rare irony from a doctor of the law and the audience fumbled for their response.

'The *ruah* of God, your breath, child, or the winds of heaven, this spirit can be as gentle as the breath of an infant or as mighty in its force as a storm on the seas. God used its force in parting the waters above and below the firmament; he used all gentleness in stirring the dews of morning and evening and the formless and void earth became fruitful and comely.'

The words seemed like – were intended to be – a final benediction; they had been spoken gravely but with a smile and an older rabbi took Jeshua by the arm.

'Are you content, my son? It is good to ask questions, the right questions.'

'I am very content, reverend doctor.'

'Keep asking the questions, young man; only so will you grow in wisdom.'

Jeshua left the Temple precincts and returned across the Kidron to his olive grove. He had brought with him some fragments of the unleavened bread and, full of the day's debate – so full that the departure for Galilee that morning had wholly fled his mind – he took shelter in an abandoned hut and set himself to sleep.

Morning was sharp but invited to wandering on the hillside. He went from tree to tree, fondling the bark with his hands and imagining the deep pattern within, the wood's response to his carpentry. But his eyes were turned to the Temple and its activity and as if without his will, he found himself crossing the court to the porticoes and the pillar where he had stood on the previous day. Many of the men and almost all the rabbis of yesterday were already gathered and they turned to look as he crossed the paved courtyard.

'Ah, the young rabbi! And what questions today?'

Jeshua stood by the pillar, smiling and relaxed as an athlete before a race but on other faces there was tension, the expectations of a contest, as though young David stood poised with his sling.

'On this new day of the Passover feast I wish to talk to you of Sinai, the words of Elohim after he had drawn us out of bondage and the angel of death had hovered over our doors.' The old rabbi of yesterday's discussion had chosen the word 'hovered' with a smile towards Jeshua; it was like a formal salute before sword-point crossed sword-point.

'His words were commands: 'Thou shalt,' 'Thou shalt not;' but they were commands not of majestic compulsion as of a master to a slave, but of compassion as of a father to a son.' The company settled to their listening, acknowledging that this was to be a rabbinic teaching, exposition and not debate. But the old man paused, drawn by the rapt look in Jeshua's eyes.

'You love and worship the Torah, my son?'

'I love and adore it, reverend doctor.'

'But if you had 'troubles' with Creation you must have troubles with the Law!'

It was banter but strangely – and disturbing to the onlookers – it seemed almost banter between equals; to many of them it affronted the proprieties.

'I am indeed troubled, sir, and troubled where perhaps I ought not. It is that word on Sinai, 'Thou shalt not make to thyself any graven image, nor the likeness of any form that is in heaven above, or that is in the earth beneath or that is in the waters under the earth.'

A shuffling among the elders showed their unease, 'troubled?' by one of the clearest prohibitions in the Law? Quietly the rabbi responded as though to diagnose a sickness or draw out a thorn:

'And what troubles you there? The words are clear and we can scarcely mistake their meaning.'

'Reverend father, I am a worker in wood and a mason; I am the son of a master-craftsman; carving and shaping is my vocation and whittling with a knife at wood fragments is my leisure. One day I was shaping a cast-off but beautiful piece of olive wood. It was to be a gift at Purim for my mother and scarcely knowing what I did I was echoing in wood the beauty and the stature and the grace of my mother. As I held it in the palm of my hand I knew that a little more, a cut or two with my knife and she would have smiled at me. I stopped — but would that have been 'a graven image,' 'an idol?' Was this gift of love a blasphemy?'

On the flank of the gathered listeners a pharisee of some forty years, tall, assured and bearded youthfully, watched the narrative intently. He would make no intervention but waited for the rabbi's reply.

'You were right to stop. It was indeed a graven image and would not have graced your mother even in love.'

'But Moses seems not always to have forbidden this craft. With the deepest respect, my father, if we read in the second book of Moses we learn that Moses called by name Bezaleel of the tribe of Judah, and Oholiab of the tribe of Dan to construct the tabernacle.'

'True; like you they were craftsmen and laboured for God's word.'

'But God said to Moses that Bezaleel was skilful in gold, silver and brass, in cutting stones for setting and in carving of wood; doesn't this exceed the carpentry of the ark?'

'True also, and God respects the work of an elaborate craftsman.'

'But father, and with respect I say it, Moses goes on to record that the wise-hearted men among them made the tabernacle 'with ten curtains of fine twined linen and blue and purple and scarlet, with cherubim, the work of the cunning workman.' Were not these cherubim 'of the heaven above' and sometimes by the grace of the Most High, 'of the earth beneath'?'

Their consternation was palpable and mixed with some resentment. The old rabbi sought for gentle words with which to turn aside the dilemma when the pharisee broke in.

'Cherubim are indeed the servants of God in the heavens but here their likeness on earth in the woven hangings of the temple are wholly for the glory of God.'

'But in the sight of men! And they were not only fashioned for that first tabernacle. Do we not read that when Solomon built his temple – would he were standing within it today! – he caused to be carved two cherubim of olive wood, each ten cubits high, each overlaid with gold. And not only cherubim;' his voice rose in a craftsman's exulting:

'And he carved all the walls of the house round about with carved figures of cherubim and palm trees and open flowers, within and without.'

'Honoured and revered father, were these things not from heaven and from earth? Were they not likenesses? And do not our priests at the very altar of incense bear at their fringes the likeness of bells and of pomegranets? Is not the menorah itself, the candles of which we light in the shadow of God's light, itself an image of the Tree of Knowledge? Are not the very cases of our Torah rolls surmounted by rich gold crowns in honour of the Lord of Hosts?'

The pharisee waited in smiling silence while Jeshua recited his craftsman's litany. Then with complete courtesy he deflected the argument.

'We would know more about you, young man. Your accent is not of Judah?'

'I am called Jeshua of Nazareth in Galilee, the son of Joseph, a craftsman in wood and stone; I have been pupil to Rabbi Eleazar' (giving the name, with pride, its full formality) 'he was once your colleague here in the Temple; he teaches with great patience.'

'And with great success, for which I am glad. I too am called Joseph and remember Eleazar with affection and profound respect; he ought still to be with us.'

'He will rejoice in your greeting, sir.'

The old rabbi who had been silent throughout this exchange, looked with affection and not a little wonder at the two before him, the pharisee in the authority of his learning and his wealth, the very young man with the eager look and stance of one embarked on a quest of peril and profound resolve.

'We shall have to look to this young man, Joseph. It would seem that Judean Arimathea will be hard pressed in prophecy by Galilean Nazareth!'

The three were now alone in the portico, the watchers and listeners having drawn away, bewildered at the turn the speeches had taken. Joseph the Arimathean turned to Jeshua.

'You, the craftsman, have spoken today of making; yesterday you spoke of creation and the work of the Most High. You were troubled in your mind concerning idols and you were rightly troubled. Remember, Jeshua ben Joseph' (the formal address, so far from distancing them, drew them into greater intimacy) 'remember that every image is not an idol. It is said, that God the Lord made man in his own image, as if in some sort, a humble and miniature sort, we are self-portraits of the Most High! But God does not worship us! We are not idols!' There was laughter between them, the laughter of joy in absurdity.

'My Greek friends have a useful word, 'ikon', an image. I

41

ask you, carpenter, when does an artist's ikon become an idol? The commandment which Moses recorded, the very commandment which so troubles you, gives you the answer. 'Thou shalt not make a graven image, thou shalt not bow down *and worship it*.' An image can be loved, enjoyed for its own sake; it can lead to the worship of Adonai – Isaiah saw the six-winged seraphim and they abased him to the ground until their fire touched his lips to prophecy – and yet all images, all ikons may become idols, worshipped in place of God the Lord, thrusting Him into a corner. All things, all people may become idols.'

His voice stumbled as he sought for words which would express his meaning and yet not offend the young mind before him.

'But have no fear of your craft, Jeshua; have no doubts about the skill of your hands or your mind's imaginings. Your making will be great and in your work and words I would have you remember those words of Isaiah the prophet.

Have you not known, have you not heard?
It is He who sits above the circle of the earth,
and its inhabitants are like grasshoppers.
Who stretches out his heavens like a curtain,
and spreads them like a tent to dwell in.

And, carpenter, craftsman in stone and wood, remember this: He, on High, works in the likeness of your craft; he deigns to use your language of measurement and marking:

Who has measured the waters in the hollow of his
hand and marked off the heavens with a span.

You will need compass and rule in your craft; He, at the beginning of time, needed no compass but the span of His hand, no rule but the tips of His fingers. All 'making' was to Him as swift as a potter's skill with clay. At one moment it is a formless, oozing lump; the next it whirls and lifts into shape.'

Jeshua remained silent, accepting this grave conclusion of the rabbi's talk. They were now alone, the older man having withdrawn in turn from this small intimate world.

'And before you sleep tonight, let your meditation before prayer be the words of the Lord to Job – the language again is yours, you builder of houses!'

They faced each other, the tall youth shoulder high to the pharisee. Again with the intonation of Temple worship Joseph spoke:

> Where were you when I laid the foundation of the earth
> Tell me if you have understanding.
> Who determined its measurements – surely you know!
> Or who stretched the line upon it?
> On what were its foundations sunk
> Or who laid its cornerstone?

With laughter in his voice, the joy of sharing, Jeshua gave the response:

> When the morning stars sang together
> And all the Sons of God shouted for joy!

There was a moment's silence between them, as the shadows lengthened in the Temple Court. With a grave tone Joseph repeated the question:

'Where were you when I laid the foundation of the earth?'

Jeshua's heart stirred, he was poised again like an athlete. Was this a question, a rebuke, a challenge? Scarcely breathing the words, he replied, 'Where was I, indeed?'

There was further silence between them, then Joseph put his hand lightly on Jeshua's shoulder. It was like those moments with Rabbi Lazar in the Galilean hills. Without a word he allowed himself to be led out of the Temple and in the vine-arbour of a courtyard above a terraced garden, they broke bread together, savouring the Passover.

The Nazareth pilgrims had gone a day's journey since their night's rest beyond sight of Jerusalem. The oldest among them spoke quietly of Passovers in past years, of regret at the Legion's presence and of the overwhelming beauty of the feast. Friendships had been renewed, gossip exchanged and family histories knotted together for one more year. The children skirmished around the long-drawn procession of man and beasts, like Bedouin out-riders, their laughter and their anguish when rocks proved tougher than knees or ankles, a constant chorus like the cries of migrating birds.

'Miriam, I want to speak to Jeshua. Did he bring those loaves, the olives and the relishes for our evening meal?'

'I haven't seen him, mother. Isn't he with the older boys, back at that bend in the road by the stream?'

Anxiously they questioned the neighbours; it was clear that Jeshua was not with them; placing Miriam and the others in the care of friends, Joseph and Mary returned with their one riding mule, to Jerusalem. Though the pilgrims were thinning in the streets it was no easy search and it was twilight when they came to the Temple court. There, solitary and walking slowly along the length of the portico, was Jeshua who greeted them with a smile and a wave of his hand. Mary almost ran to his side.

'Jeshua, son, hadn't you any thought for us? Your father and I have looked for you so fearfully!'

'Mother, here in the Temple, wasn't it right that I should do my Father's work in my Father's house?'

He had never before been wholly incomprehensible, for all his solitariness in the Nazareth hill-meadows. Silently they began the return to Galilee.

FOUR

There were family decisions to be made at Nazareth. Jeshua at fifteen years was no longer in any way an apprentice but a partner with Joseph; Jacob now shared with the two of them the distinction of numbering among the minyan, the quorum for synagogue worship, while Jude and Joses were sturdy boys, 'day labourers' when they were needed; Miriam now rivalled her mother in height and shared with Jeshua Mary's rich auburn hair, so dark as to be black in the shadows; Ruth, the child of glancing mischief, stood high as Miriam's shoulder – it was a strong-knit, inquisitive, industrious clan.

And of course the home was too small. The site, facing south, was attractive and open, commanding both the village and the hills beyond; there had already been extensions to it, in the workshop, outhouses and yard and in a further sleeping-room at the back of the main house. Now they faced their first choice, to extend their house still further or start afresh with a new site. The growing things about them settled the question. The enclosed courtyard to the south-west had become a place of great beauty. One corner was completely roofed in by a mature fig tree (as though nature intended a permanent arbour-booth for the Feast of Tabernacles); across the opposite corner a well-tended grape-vine extended over twenty feet at the level of the outer wall and completely shaded and cooled the entrance from the court to the inner room; against the sunniest wall, a peach-tree – the pride of the youngest children – took advantage of the warmth to give a glory of blossom in the spring sunshine and almost too sensuous contrast of smooth leaf and velvet fruit in the later summer, textures which drew Ruth to caressing them – 'If only cloth for my dress could be woven like this!' An almond tree was the centre of the herb garden, Mary's especial care, a constant reminder to the whole family of the Benediction for the scents of growing things.

The workshop courtyard would have been almost as difficult to replace. The oak and sycamore work-benches had become bedded in and established with years of labour, the tool-racks had their lay-out of long custom, set from long habit in exactly the place for every process; still more important, the stacked timber, both cheap and rare, stacked with precision to mature for every demand, would be cumbersome to move, and movement would disturb the maturing and drying. So extension it had to be.

Here was the first great challenge to Jeshua's craft. From a position on the slope above their home, as dusk simplified the volumes of the building, Joseph threw the problem to Jeshua.

'We need at least twice the space, if your brothers and sisters are to have room enough and your mother and I to know a little peace! There are many ways of solving our needs but which one would you choose?'

'To add another structure to that which now extends towards us on this slope would be ungainly and would mean cutting two doors through the old and the new walls. Our mother would have less light than she needs and the whole house would lose its decent and happy proportions.'

They both looked out over Nazareth, satisfied and happy in the simple harmony of sharp rectangles and flat roofs which gave the township geometric symmetry and grace. No clumsiness or ostentation in their new structure should mar this gracious place. As the sun sank to the hilltops, the shadows, deep mauve and blue, sent a pattern of dark triangles and squares from the base of each home, a rhythm of light and dark which gave the unfettered growth of the trees and shrubs an even greater vitality. It was a restful setting for unassertive life.

'I think we shall have to get rid of our last extension.

That room has always seemed a make-shift and it would hamper any real changes we want to make.'

Jeshua now saw their problem as one of simple volumes and access.

'Why not a substantial room in its place, an upper room to take more than half the whole roof span, old and new, and a flight of shallow steps to reach the upper room from the inner wall of the courtyard?'

'Our present roof would never bear the weight'– Joseph knew the old construction, that it was little more than stout boughs, reed plaiting and mud – 'but of course the old and the new roof could be strongly raftered and I believe we have the wood, oak and some precious cedar which we shall have to use very economically.'

The light was now too poor for an accurate assessment of the wood piles but the following morning the oak and cedar balks were drawn out and measured. Joseph had already decided that the old roof should be kept with no more disturbance than deep ridging into its outer hard shell of mud, the ridges to bed down the new rafters. These, either in oak or cedar, would be less than half the length needed to span the new stretch of roofing and Jeshua was set to precise calculations of the lengths, the jointing, and the pegging needed to produce fifteen long joists to traverse the whole length of roof, from the front balustrade, which protected the present roof space, to the far edge of the new wall which would bound the extra living room. They had adequate oak-beams for this stage and some well-hardened plane-tree heartwood for pegging the joints; the cross-rafters, tying the main joists and let into grooves, would be of cedar. Since these would be the flooring also of the upper room, they planned to leave the rich cedar exposed, making of the floor a diaper patterning, richly coloured and aromatic; 'the scent of Lebanon.'

This carpentry would be the work of many weeks; meanwhile, before any work could start in good earnest, other calculations had to be made: what foundation stones would be needed, what lintels were to be cut from the limestone rock in the hills, what brickwork had they to prepare? The preparation of the mud and lime walls and the lattice and mud roofing of the upper room could be left to the month Tishri in mid-autumn, before the first rains made the work both difficult and impermanent.

They began immediately after the feast of Purim and since it was either preparation of the beams, in the shelter of the workshop, or the hauling of the stones from the quarry, they were scarcely troubled by the few showers from the 'latter rains.' Jacob, Joses and Jude joined with enthusiasm and variable usefulness in the visits to the quarry and the hauling to the new site. Four large corner-stones were needed of some four hundredweight each; two to be butted against the existing walls, and set some inches into its outer structure and bedded down to the gravel layer below; the other two set firmly at the two outer corners of the new building. The youngest boys were both fascinated and dismayed at the strength and apparent wildness of the quarrymen. They were 'aliens' from the hills of north Judah, bearded, formidably mus-cled but very ready to smile through their silence. One boulder they had ready for carting, left over from a former project this side of Carmel. Joseph agreed that it could be a pattern for the other three.

The quarrying had reached the lower bedding of lime-stone which was exposed to a breadth of over six feet. The three new foundation-stones were marked out in the bed and outlined with fine chisels. These were followed by broad-bladed heavy chisels driven down by iron-bound wooden mallets until the next bed was reached, deep enough to give the weight of the cornerstone needed. From the front edge, wedges were driven in, fine steel slivers, followed by thicker iron bolts and finally broad, triangular oak wedges which lifted the massive weight; three of the quarrymen, two in front to draw the mass outward and one at the back to lever it forward until all three could lift it on to the sledge, gave the two youngest boys the excited pleasure of a success which seemed their own.

The sledge was a primitive affair on two broad runners of oak smoothed by the abrasion of the rough ground they had to cross and by the constant greasing it received before and after each trip. Joseph and Jeshua did the dragging, Jacob corrected the course from behind the limestones slab, while Joses and Jude ran alongside with stout sapling trunks, to slip as runners under the tracks if the going got too rough. Each stone cost a full day's work.

When the four boulders had been set in position and the shallower stone placed in its bed to mark the outer doorway, the bricks had to be prepared for the inner core of the three walls, now to be built. Jeshua had never faced a task of such sheer size, for many hundreds of bricks had to be made and ready before any further work could begin, for the brickmaking would be continuous as the building went on. And Joseph was a perfectionist as director of this new operation and demanded of them three kinds and qualities of bricks. For the lower levels of the walls which would take the greatest weight, the bricks were to have an aggregate of small pebbles from the river bed; the next stage of building would have bricks with a small mixture of gravel in the mud and bound together with small quantities of chopped straw and the coarser, waste hairs of the sheep and goat combings; the third stage which would be capped with burnt tile in a single layer and 'bought in', was simply of mud with some chopped straw or stubble, bricks of Egyptian memory which ran deep and bitter in their blood.

Jeshua had prepared from the oaken offcuts, left over from the great beams, a large extra store of uniform brick-moulds and had beaten out and smoothed an open space in the warmth of the sun, before the outer yard of the workshop. The mud was hauled from a pit near the river – Joses and Jude 'helped' in this process with the greatest of pleasure – and dumped into shallow vats for the mixing. At the right tacky consistency it was slapped into the moulds as they stood on the hardened floor; the moulds were then withdrawn and the bricks left standing in neat rows. The children had brought light branches of willow which were held by stout stakes over the rows of bricks, to shade them from direct sun and to allow for the slow drying which made for the hardest texture.

The building went on swiftly, the thin slurry of mud holding the bricks in a strong structure and within the week one wall was ready for the corner post of stone on the foundation and within another week the work had reached the fine stone facings and the lintel of the door. Here Jeshua was again given the craftsman's final 'master's test', this time in stone in which he had little of the practice which wood had given him. Before they lifted the lintel into place in the jambs, he had delicately chamfered the lower edge with a fine chisel and when the shallow block was in place, had carved above the chamfer a delicate frieze of interlocked wedges; it was the simplest motif he had remembered from a Jerusalem synagogue and he was glad it could be part of their home.

Passover had been a generous break in the labour and before harvest had begun in fullest pressure they were ready for the walls of the upper room, for its roofing and for fetching and placing the stonework for the stairway from the court to the roof balustrade. The new roofing echoed the old: long, stripped boughs of willow, narrow osiers plaited between and bound with tough flax cords, the whole plastered with mud used for brickmaking and, like the bricks, allowed to bake slowly in the sun. The steps for the ascent were more difficult. A triangular buttress of square-trimmed stones was built against the wall, extending outwards some two feet, the steps left in the long sloping side then faced with their slabs of limestone. Along its foot was planted a row of vine-shoots, which by the autumn of the next year would clad the whole face of the ascent with its leaves.

Now came the final pleasure, plastering the walls, within and without with a lime-plaster which seemed so miraculously to capture the light, giving the room a glow even in the darkening evening and the outer walls an intensity of light which gave to the whole township its clear patterning.

The lime had been slaked and from the heap in the yard some had already been taken to strengthen the bricks. The rest was now divided for making into plaster and the outer walls were soon covered and smoothed by hand. The inner walls were more carefully treated, the lime sieved and ground finely to make the thick, creamy plaster. It was applied swiftly with a flat trowel, the shaping and the smoothing of the surface being left entirely to the palms of the hands. As it slowly dried the surface became increasingly white and caught every stream of light from the doorway or the curtained window openings. The subtle undulations in the plaster recalled for Jeshua his first pleasure in smoothed wood refined by the adze and rippling with a surface life of its own. So the walls of their home in all lights from gloaming and rush light to full day had the vitality of delicate shadowing which gave intensity to the grain and colour of the oak, chestnut and cedar chests, table-top and stools with which the principal room was furnished. Rich in its austerity, it was a lively setting for the food, leisure and rest which punctuated their lives, a setting won, shaped and maintained by their own labour.

Other tasks had been set aside whilst this heavier work was in progress; ploughs, yokes, mattocks, all the implements needed after harvest, had now to be repaired and new ones set in train. It was exacting work, needing precision in the shaping and a careful choice of wood for each job of work.

One task had for many weeks perplexed Jeshua's thoughts. The water-spring from which the village drew its supply was some little distance from the centre and while this was no trouble to the able bodied – they carried their waterpots with equal grace whether balanced on the crown of their heads or slanting away from their hips – but for the disabled or crippled women or girls it was a sorely hard task. One of these, Hannah, the misshapen daughter of Martha the widow, struggled her two or three journeys each day with a small waterpot precariously balanced on her right shoulder, for her left arm and shoulder twisted and fell away, crippled from her birth. If only he could devise a yoke, the journeys would be halved. He had been working in these last weeks in sycamore and admired its strength and comparative lightness; it would be precisely the material he needed.

He opened the subject gently with Martha – poverty and a crippled child soured so many relationships and words had to be chosen with care.

'I am sorry Hannah has to make so many journeys to the spring; the path is so rough for her feet. I believe I can help.'

'No man shall labour for us at this woman's work, not even her betrothed – if betrothed she will ever be.'

'I was not offering to carry but to make carrying easier for her. If I shaped a yoke to her shoulders, then she could take two waterpots with greater ease than she now struggles with one.'

'She is no ox to be yoked' – there was a venomous determination not to understand his compassion and with a smiling apology he turned away and went back to his work at the bench. But he had watched Hannah carefully as she walked and with an eye trained for calculation of this kind, estimated the wider curve needed for the left shoulder if a water-carrier's yoke was to balance truly. He shaped and smoothed it with care, fashioned chains and a leather strap at each forward projection which overhung the carrier's upper arm and fastened two waterpots in place. Finally, on the smooth back of the wide shoulder curve of the wood, he stained a pattern in vermilion which took away its associations with labour in the field and gave it something of the appearance of a fringe or collar to a garment. Padding his own right shoulder to compensate for the thicker left side of the yoke he balanced it below his neck, drew the two vessels forward in the crook of his elbows and walked down to Martha's house. His smile and the gentle question, 'May I, please?' drew no more than a grudging nod from Martha and Hannah stood bewildered by the strange gift. Carefully he placed it over her shoulders, drew the vessels forward to her hands, first the left and then the right, in perfect balance.

'Away you go!' Tentatively at first but then with increasing assurance she walked out of the village to the spring pool. The transformation was amazing; the careful shaping of the width of wood on left and right wholly masked her deformity; her shoulders now appeared straight and with the balancing of the weight, her walk itself became suppler, more assured. Twenty minutes later she was back at her home, proudly, with two waterpots filled and with no drop spilt. 'And I carried them easily, more easily than with one on my shoulder and it will be lighter work every day. Jeshua, thank you! You are so very kind.' The radiance in her eyes moved even Martha to a whispered 'Thank you.'

One other immediate request had to be fulfilled quite urgently. Silas, the son of Simeon the potter, who now did most of his aging father's work, had broken his wheel, cracking the plate to the centre. He asked Jeshua if he would fashion him a new one and Jeshua asked his father if he might have a small square of acacia wood from their carefully preserved supply. It was their hardest and finest wood, fit for the most delicate of carving, whether on the side or the end grain and Jeshua shaped it carefully to a perfect circle about two inches thick. At the exact centre he fitted an inch-long cylindrical boss and bored out from another small piece of acacia a thick collar which would take the boss with the least play as the wheel turned upon it. The two portions of the wheel and especially the boss and its collar, he waxed thoroughly and took them across to Silas. They scooped away the hole in which the broken wheel had turned, fitted the collar within it, and spinning the wheel, saw that it ran true and smoothly.

'Now you must try it wet and with the weight of clay; if it then runs true, that wheel of acacia wood should last you many years.'

Simeon threw the fistful of clay on the centre of the wheel and, cupping his hands about it, his thumbs pressed into the heart of the clay, drew up a thick-walled vessel; with his moistened fingers he drew the clay upwards and fluted it out until a graceful vessel turned slowly on the wheel. With a cutter of sinew he severed the pot from the wheel centre and placed it gently on a shelf to the side of the wheel.

'It runs true.' he said.

'I have never tried my fingers in clay' said Jeshua.

'Then try!' Silas threw another lump of clay on the centre, whirled his wheel about and gave his place to Jeshua. He cupped his hands about the clay as he had seen Silas shape the vessel – and the clay snaked away like a living thing from under his fingers.

'Try again, and this time begin by pressing the clay inwards as though you were crushing it through the centre of the wheel; then gently, as you have mastered it, there in the centre relax your hold and draw upwards.'

Jeshua did as he was instructed and slowly a vessel rose, thick-walled and symmetrical and turning slowly on the wheel. It was the first step in making.

'Whether it's living wood or living clay, you have craft in your fingers, Jeshua.'

There were few relationships quite as generously secure as that of craftsmen together, as Jeshua had known since childhood.

Rabbi Lazar had watched with the intensest pleasure (and a pride he tried to suppress) the growing maturity of his favourite pupil. Though only in his seventeenth year, Jeshua was acknowledged as the most deft, most imaginative craftsman in Nazareth, bringing to each craft in his trade an instinctive knowledge of the growth-patterns of wood, the crystalline and granular structure of the stone he shaped, the intuitive movement of his own growing strength to the stresses, balance and counter-poise of the buildings he humbly helped to complete. His youthful superiority in his trade was not a little resented, not by the lowlier artisans, the day-labourers, but by those who for decades had pursued their craft and deemed themselves masters. For them, the youthful deference of Silas the potter or the mature friendship of Jonathan the smith, were a constant reminder that not every master-craftsman had the innate sureness of Jeshua's judgement, his ability to strip away irrelevant difficulties and strike at the heart of a problem. Reluctantly they confessed that Nazareth was a more lucid place from the presence of Jeshua.

Lazar was aware of the tensions and knew their source. He had no fear that any would proceed from arrogance or assertiveness on Jeshua's part; his ready smile, his acceptance of any task however humble or menial, the deprecating gesture if too wordy a compliment were paid him, all these assured Lazar that for the unprejudiced and to those who were themselves humble, no 'stone of stumbling' would be set in their way by this young man.

But in the busyness of life since their return from Jerusalem, that so notable Passover when Jeshua had joined the Doctors of the Law in the portico of the Temple, there had been little opportunity for their walks in the hills about Nazareth which had brought so rich a friendship between the young craftsman and the aging rabbi. True there had been the annual visit to Jerusalem (interrupted only once by the birth of the very youngest, who completed the family of five brothers and two sisters, a sevenfold blessing which Lazar took to be a happy omen); on one of these Jerusalem pilgrimages he had found the means to join the family in their Passover feast, but the closer moments had been rare and it was time to resume them.

One evening in the warm glow of sunset they sat resting beneath a sycamore which arched over the road at the entrance to the township. Jeshua had been hauling dressed blocks of limestone from the nearer quarry and was glad of the shade and of the rabbi's company. He had pulled some of the riper but ungrateful fruits from the tree (his amused comment on their toughness – 'false-figs') and in silence they savoured the breeze which came up the valley at sunset.

'Your eyes have learned consideration, there is thought in your forehead and a unique skill in your hands – how I envy them! – what a scribe you would have made!'

Jeshua from childhood had grown accustomed to the anatomising of Lazar and the old rabbi no longer troubled him in his probing. He knew that on this day the praise was a prelude to more serious talk and he waited, smiling, for the rabbi's counsel.

'I have listened to you in synagogue. You read the Haftorah with assurance and your voice has the clarity of a Temple cantor. You are now old enough to know how we, the chosen of God the Lord, His children, His family, are fenced about, cherished and protected by His arm; as one single family – like none other on earth – we are instructed by the Torah, nourished each year by the feasts, inspired by the Prophets and made joyful by the songs of Zion. These are 'family matters' and we live as one, united as an army marching together. But I, Lazar, am alone; you, Jeshua, are alone. Alone we are born, alone we die and in solitude we pursue that life which is God's and within us.'

Jeshua had never before heard these tones from the mouth of Rabbi Lazar. His memory groped back over the years to that moment in the Temple when the pharisee, the Arimathean had spoken with these echoes of a profounder voice but even those words had lacked this final, measured gravity.

'I have listened for your silences, watched for your solitariness; I have seen and heard them built round, sheltered and protected by your craft and I have been so glad to know that the life within has this protection without.'

He sought for a figure which would express more concretely what he wished to say to the young man.

'You have stood at the spring of living water which gushes out so blessedly for us in Nazareth; it is cold from the dark earth, it has been purified by its long passage through the deep rocks of the hills; it has had a long dark journey before it springs, gushing out of the mountain side. I have worked with the scribes and I have known holiness in Jerusalem. I have lived with the Hasidim and shared their ecstacy in the Divine Name. But neither learning nor ecstacy is any surety for the flowing, the gushing of the solitary, dark stream.'

For several minutes there was silence between them. A rockdove spoke almost inaudibly in the boulders above them and there was a brief stirring of the wind in the sycamore leaves. The rabbi gathered himself, with an effort of speech.

'There are no prophets in Nazareth, no Hasidim to show us ecstacy. We walk a dusty by-way, by very shallow streams – and I am glad of it. Here I know, blessedly, what it is to be wholly alone. And in those dark moments when the Torah loses its brilliance and the prophets stammer into silence, then in that dark valley I am myself alone.'

Jeshua knew, in the silence, that he too had retreated from Lazar's consciousness and momentarily he shared his loneliness, the desolation.

Lazar spoke again and this time the voice carried not only the customary words, but the overtones, the acceptance of the derelict heart:

'I will speak in the bitterness of my soul.
I will say unto God, do not condemn me.
Is it good unto thee that thou shouldest oppress
That thou shouldest despair in the work of thine hands?
Thine hands have framed me and fashioned me
Together round about; yet thou dost destroy me
Are not my days few? cease then
And let me alone, that I may take comfort a little
Before I go where I shall not return.'

The voice stopped its intoning, Lazar shook his shoulders, stood over Jeshua and looked intently at him.

'The darkness of God, His silence, is difficult to share.'

There were grey shadows on the hillside and the breeze was chill on their faces. But Lazar made to climb higher and Jeshua followed a pace behind him.

'I have shared this certainty with no one until today, that it is in the dark silence and alone that we find ourselves – and please God, that we find Him! For you the stars have sung in their courses 'and all the sons of God shouted for joy.' We have looked up at those stars, you and I, seen Orion and the Pleiades, the waxing and waning of the moon, and you have moved with a smile among those singing hosts. But for me, it has not been the stars in their brilliance, the cool, clear light of the moon that I have seen but those vast spaces between, those infinite distances where Adonai must be!'

They were walking into the rocky upper reaches of the hills and despite the cold, sat facing each other on two boulders. 'We must speak no more tonight. I have opened my heart to you, Jeshua, for you have much to do, perhaps much to learn. Think of what I have said and tomorrow we shall speak again.'

There was no sound now and in the darkness the cold struck more sharply. There was no moon and the brilliance of the stars had a clarity that seemed to sound like distant cymbals.

'As I looked out to the hills this morning the reciting of Shema seemed to need an extra Hallel. For two days now I have been in danger of wearying you with my lament. Too much have I sung:

    Out of the depths have I cried unto thee, O Lord,
      Lord hear my voice.

and this morning at the dawn I finished the Psalm with a full heart; I knew it was true that I was not derelict but waiting:

    My soul looketh for the Lord
      More than watchmen look for the morning
      Yea, more than watchmen for the morning.

and the ending sounded in my ears so securely,

For with the Lord there is mercy
And with him is plenteous redemption.
But now in this sweet daylight and in a calmer mind I must
return to the darkness of last evening.'

Jeshua was silent, not assenting but knowing that there
was more suffering to be poured out.

'It was right and proper that at the first day of creation it
is said that all was formless and void.'

He was holding his voice steady, containing his emotion
but it broke.

'Nothing but chaos! Only chaos!'

His face twisted in a spasm which was part fear, part
disgust. 'And Adonai said 'Let there be light. Let there be
light, let there be light!'

The reiteration became a prayer and Jeshua felt the
nakedness of his soul, the old man's agony after a life of
seeking for holiness and for knowledge. He withdrew from
the private sorrow; no intrusion could help the rabbi's
lone struggle, more intense now than on the previous
evening.

In the depths of Jeshua's own mind a memory seemed
to stir and the dark formlessness of the void seemed
palpable about him; he groped as if for the grasp of an act
in the far past: let there be! and there was. His mind
reached for the clear memory beyond history, beyond the
stream of time which for him and for the Jewish people
was the living present. His struggle to regain that moment,
the unconscious centre of his being, lasted many minutes
and when he came to awareness of the place about him,
Rabbi Lazar had recovered his composure.

'The chaos did not last; it was shaped, controlled, made
fitting. For six days, the Most High laboured and rested on
the seventh – the glory of the Sabbath of God!'

The young man knew that they had reached new
ground in traversing the morass in which the old rabbi

had floundered, drawing Jeshua with him. With a deliberate lightness in the question he asked, 'In what, dear Rabbi, in all his six days' labour, do you think the Lord God most gloried?'

There was laughter in the question, a hint of teasing irony. The rabbi hesitated, warned by the smile that a snare might lie in the way.

'Could God the Father show preference, an undue fondness and favour to one of his creatures?'

'I think perhaps he could! Was not man made in His own image? Isn't that in itself a gracious favour?'

'And how we mar that image, Jeshua, how we mar it! If we could see Him face to face, would the Lord of the Ages show the lines of doubt, the wrinkled senility, as I do.' The pleasure of the game was restoring his tranquillity and Jeshua pressed on, glad to occupy with him the new ground they had won.

'It has always seemed to me a bewilderment that when any creature is given being, he is given at the same time the burden of will; and where there is will there may be wilfulness.' Rabbi Lazar had not in all his years of knowing Jeshua heard in his voice that secure assurance.

'Have you seen how creatures determine their own way, mark out their path and highway? When the poet created the tale of Job' – the shocked perplexity in Lazar's face halted Jeshua's argument.

'*Tale*? a story? Isn't it truth, history, our history?'

The concept of fiction, of feigned history confounded his gentle intelligence, cast a shadow of doubt over the accepted verities.

'You are not above using tales yourself, dear Rab Lazar! We have listened for many an evening to your 'parables', like the story of that rock, so massive and so ornamental which caused such havoc to the householders. Was it any less 'true' because you or the Psalmist invented it to

61

confirm a higher truth? Whenever I hear the noble narrative of Job, I know I am present – again – at a day of creation. And each time I listen for and hear so clearly that moment when the tragic story takes on its own will, asserts its own direction, whatever the teller of the tale may wish. It is that moment when the story moves from earth and the riches of Job, our so familiar earth of our family, our flocks and our herds, and goes to the greater imaginings of heaven and the Adversary returned 'from going to and fro in the earth and from walking up and down in it.' From that point onward the writer had to work in concert with the will of the work he was making, perhaps unlocking a door here, undamming a stream or opening a new channel there. It is a wonderful thing, this harmony of the two wills, of the maker and the thing made.'

These were speculations beyond the immediate grasp of the humbler mind of the rabbi; was it perhaps for this that he had left the more arid speculations of the Jerusalem doctors?

'Do you remember you once asked me if I could make for the synagogue a 'Torah Pointer?' I think it was the first thing that fascinated me as a child at the reading of the Law, that the very parchment itself was too sacred to touch and I watched so eagerly as the carved finger moved along the line of writing. We still had the precious silver chain which fastened it to the Torah stave but the pointer itself was old, clumsy and worn. It would be a deep shame to us if one day at the reading, an old man's pressure on the handle snapped away the moving finger and his hand rested upon the sacred words. I was asked because we couldn't afford to employ a silversmith. I took a piece of olive wood, about a foot long – you know, with acacia, it is my favourite wood; it has endured so many winters and summers, so much drought and flood in its slow growth over so many generations of men, that the heartwood is ripe and warm in its colour and texture. With my sharpened knives I began to carve, paring away to make a slender forearm for the pointing hand. But as I worked the material itself made its own demands; a vein of deep red-brown wood invited the fold of a rich sleeve and as I went on, the delicate arm scarcely more than an inch in thickness, became clothed in its own finely folded sheath, as splendid in colour and pattern as a king's robe. The wood spoke more insistently when I passed to the hand. I wished it to be a learned hand. I wanted it to point imperiously to the holy words, but as I carved at the wrist and back of the hand, with its veining and the bones of the index finger, it changed under the knife blade, became as delicate as a young girl's or as the hand of an angel might point to a star. It wasn't pride I knew when I saw it first used on the Day of Atonement; it was wonder that I had shared in the power of growing timber, matured by the rain and sun of so many centuries.'

In the silence that followed, as Lazar meditated with pride on the ceremonies of his beloved synagogue, Jeshua knew that the dark shadows had been moved away, the agony deflected. They were back, rabbi and pupil, on the common ground of their daily ways; Lazar's look into the chasms of God's withdrawal from his apprehension of man, Jeshua's groping into the abyss of time before history was, these had both been set aside into a shared tranquillity. The commonplace rhythms were best restored by a pupil's exploration:

'When we began to speak of these things, as we climbed among the rocks, you seemed to tell me of two states, of our family unity, a race knit together, and of our solitude, that is man's lot. But of that loneliness you have spoken only of its terror, at those moments when we seem forsaken even by God. But that was not the only solitariness of which you would tell me?'

'You have known all your life that the symbol of our unity is the *minyan*, the quorum of ten in which we honour our prayers and the reading of the Torah. *Minyan* is our family realisation that in the gathering-together we are both strong and humble, one people before God. The prayers, the blessings, the thanksgiving and praise, these we celebrate together. But you, Jeshua, more than most, will know that there are journeys, explorations that we fulfil alone, that only then, when 'the family' of Israel has been set aside, do we face the truth of God: Moses alone on Sinai, with the thundering of the Word about him, Elijah alone on Carmel, with the majesty of 'the still small voice', David alone with his kingly authority, Elisha alone as he assumed the mantle of prophecy. And for that 'aloneness' there was to be discipline, a buckling on of the last pieces of armour. You have them to hand in the words you love: the Fifth Book of Moses, *Devarim*, the joys and sorrows of David's Psalms and above all that vision of Isaiah's prophecy that the Servant of the Lord is a servant who suffers. I have no need to teach you love of their words, no means to learn your stillness to meditate on them; this you have in yourself. But they will drive you out of the fair pastures; though your lines 'have fallen in pleasant places', it is the wilderness, the arid desert which will teach the ultimate truth, the heart of God.' The words had for Jeshua the finality of prophecy and in their austere harmony he returned to his home.

The Sea of Galilee had been a distant beckoning. Most journeys until now had been southward, Jerusalem the lodestar, across Samaria and the Judean highland ridge. But the Sea of Galilee had been for Jeshua a kind of small metaphor for the 'Promised Land', a place of abundant richness, of fields, orchards, rich fish harvests and cities with the working of precious metals – and in all this, paradoxically, it had been in some strange way forbidding, had held him at arm's length. Now it was time to catch at least a distant but searching look at the Lake and its surrounding land.

It was summer, encroaching on autumn, the olive harvest almost over, the air clear, without haze or too much cloud. Jeshua set out early, some raisins and barley bread in his pouch and walked north-east along the ridge with the snows of Hermon and Lebanon closing the horizon. A long spur of hill extended far towards Caesarea and led him to a height from which the whole panorama could be seen, the green of the fields ready for the ploughing, the enclosed vineyards and the orderly olive groves. It was all of such lush richness that Nazareth seemed almost poverty-stricken. But it was the road that gripped his attention. It was the main highway that linked Ptolemais with Tiberias, with spurs to Sepphoris and to the road south between Tabor and Moreh. To his right was the long shore of the Sea of Galilee itself, with the road joining Magdala, Gennesaret, Capernaum and Bethsaida, with another spur road to Chorazin in the lower hills. It was a fascinating pattern of activity laid out with such clarity below him: straggling wayfarers on foot, overladen mules and donkeys in crude convoys of merchandise, fruit, cloth, spices, and, a rarer sight, two or three camels accompanying a more affluent visitor to the Sea.

His eyes rested on a wedge of dust, which travelled slowly along the road; it was from the feet of a century of soldiers marching in full kit to their garrison at Caesarea. For Jeshua it was a sombre sight, the dark skins and darker accoutrements, the occasional gleam from spear-point or gladius hilt, the uniformly blank gaze ahead and, as they passed close beneath the spur on which he sat, the regular tread of two hundred feet, a soul-less rhythm unlike anything in nature. It strode through dust, gravel and stones with the exact precision of a machine. Jeshua, who knew the broken scamper of sheep or goat-hoofs over stony uplands, the drumming of wild ponies in a panic surge or the clumping tread of yoked oxen at the plough, felt he had known nothing so inexorable, so dehumanising as this regular tread, unbroken, undeflected. He had gazed in Jerusalem, with the heartache of his race, at the Antonia watching so impassively over the Temple courts, had seen soldiers, centurions and officers in far more ostentatious panoply than this century of men, but never before had he seen it in concerted movement, as deadly as a lance-thrust. He watched them march towards the Lake and out of sight, the moving wedge of dust rising and thinning, then eddying away in the evening breeze. He turned to the open hillside, grieving that something had been violated in his sense of man and of man's dignity.

He had finished his bread, stopped to drink at a spring in the hillside and settled to the last miles of walking to Nazareth. The whirring of the cicadas and grasshoppers, hypnotic at noon, had now the slower, more syncopated rhythms of dark. The birds were quiet and only the distant bark of a jackal showed that the predators had begun their work. In a small patch of scrub – briars twisted about a thorn bush – there was a tired fluttering and he crossed to see what it was. A dove had one foot tangled in the briar and its right wing hung limply to the ground, seeming dislocated. Murmuring a quiet imitation of its call, he slowly untangled the foot and leg from the thorn-trap and held the bird in his left palm, stroking back the ruffled feathers at its neck and gentling its efforts to fly from his hand. He explored the wrenched wing and thought that there was no break in bone or tendon; firmly, but sensitively responding to the wincing of the bird's limbs, he pressed the joint back into place and held the two wings fast against the dove's body. The throbbing of its throat was now almost stilled and he placed it on a mound of dry leaves beneath a young thorn. He waited a while as the bird settled and then unhooked the scrip from his belt, shaking it to find some crumbs which might have been left over from his meal; there was a small palmful and he slowly held it out in the direction of the dove. It glanced swifly from hand to crumb to Jeshua's eyes and then turned with complete assurance to its meal. The pecking into his palm as the beak took each crumb gave Jeshua a remarkable pleasure. The quick rhythm of the bird's head travelled into his fingers and wrist and, without thought, he was one with the bird and its urgent life.

The family in Nazareth was close and affectionate, though Jeshua had a special concern for Miriam and Jacob. Ruth could look after herself, an amusing, ungainly child with limbs as uncontrolled as a colt's; Simon, still the baby of the family, was in danger of being treated more like a household pet than a child, while the other two, Joses and Jude, felt themselves drawn together into an isolated partnership, conspiratorial and noisy. All these could be enjoyed or ignored; but with Jacob and Miriam his relationship was different.

Jacob, sixteen years old and already strikingly handsome, if without the delicate features of Jeshua, could be silent and withdrawn to the point of being morose. Insecure as the second son in a large family, aware of his seniority but without the authority of the heir, he withdrew from most of the boisterous activity of their leisure and feast days. He was made the more insecure in that he felt Jeshua in many ways to be growing aside from the family. He was still the first partner of his father, did at least his share of the planning and the hard work; but there were hours of silence at the hearth, where his thoughts seemed far distant, or of day-long withdrawal into the hills. Jeshua tried once or twice in recent months to share both the walking into the heights above Nazareth and the thinking which went with it. But speculation was alien to Jacob – orderly and intent on organising his share

67

of the work with neat fastidiousness, he found the movement of Jeshua's mind strange and forbidding.

Miriam was as effervescent a child as Ruth but she was now a young woman, with something of the controlled poise of her mother. She came into her own at the Feast of Purim in the month of Adar. For the days of preparation before the feast she disciplined herself by helping with the flax harvest, gathering the stalks into bundles for curing and crushing, as the first stage in their making of linen. It was bruising work for the young girl and she was content in the evening to help her mother prepare and sieve the wheat for the Purim meal.

For this was the feast of woman's steadfast triumph. The whole family went to the synagogue and Mary gathered the two girls to her side behind the lattice to listen to the story of Esther, she who defeated the machinations of Haman. She no longer rejoiced, as she did as a child, in the killing of the wicked sons but felt the steady pride of young womanhood in the heroic story. The meal on their return was her responsibility, Mary watchfully alert against the smallest catastrophe. It was wheaten bread that day, freshly baked that morning. The flour had been newly milled by Miriam and Mary, Joses and Jude standing by the grinding-stones to feed in the grains. Into the dough was placed the fragment of leavened dough from the previous baking, and here Miriam insisted on her own fastidious method. Instead of placing the whole fragment into the unleavened dough, she divided the leavening between her fingers into portions scarcely larger than a lentil grain, placed them meticulously within fold upon fold of the new dough and only then began the kneading.

'So the whole lump will have leavening,' she said pedantically and her mother who had baked, not unsuccessfully, for twenty years, smiled her assent – if that was to be Miriam's way, so be it.

Poor friends had been called in to the feast, bread with fresh fruit, three goblets of wine (tempered with water for the children) and a portion of lamb which would not have demeaned Passover. Rabbi Lazar came in time for the blessing of the third cup.

'Miriam queening it today?' Miriam was not in the least affronted by the banter and looked demurely across at her brother.

'Jeshua must not be allowed to think all feasts are his! Passover, yes; the Day of Atonement, yes (he does more happily without food and drink than the rest of us!) but Purim is mine, as it will be Ruth's; and it's always our mother's.' There was laughter as they prepared to go out with their gifts to their neighbours, and as they went out into the twilight, Miriam, now all shy humility, asked Jeshua, 'May I come with you to Hannah's? I know she looks for your gift but there is something about her that warms my heart. Please let me come.'

Hannah was not the only child of poverty in Nazareth and Jeshua had his own especial care for the shepherd-boy, Issachar, exposed to so much in the upper hill pastures. His flock was not large either in number or size and the wool was not of the finest but he had a smiling, gentle gravity, much to Jeshua's liking. They were of an age, Jeshua the junior by a year and a few months, and they spoke little as they took their occasional walk in the hills, if the sheep restlessly looked out a better pasture. Jeshua had finished a long week furnishing a new home with all its chattels and furniture, turning platters and dishes in sycamore and making one stool, especially beautiful in its plainness, out of cedar-wood. Some of his work had been peculiarly strenuous and he was glad to relax his limbs in a leisurely scramble to the upper meadows. He had now reached the new pasture and was resting on a boulder in the sun, when he heard the shepherd, evidently in a wadi around the shoulder of the hill. Jeshua listened with pleasure, for the shepherd was evidently experimenting with a pipe he had not heard before. It had the sweet, true tone of an old instrument and Jeshua listened for a melody to emerge. The notes climbed slowly, the breathiness of the pipe inaudible in the distance and then came an unusual halftone before the notes climbed to the octave. A variation, and the notes formed a melody leaping the halftone, and then plaintively descended to it; this interval he repeated like the call of a bird and then wove around it a web of notes, a delight in capturing the song. He repeated it, at first with hesitation and then with assurance and pleasure. There was now laughter in the playing, a release which Jeshua had not heard from him before.

He thought it wouldn't now be an intrusion if he walked into the shepherd's valley and he called to him as he turned the bluff into the scrub-land where the sheep sought the few grass patches. As he came up to Issachar he saw, as he had thought, that it was not his usual pipe.

'Not a new one, Jeshua. My father visited his old brother last week in their home this side of Cana. He had found this pipe which was his father's and sent it for me to play.' Jeshua saw that it had been reamed out of a dark, true-grained piece of wood which he failed to recognise. The close grain had mellowed with use and the years to a deep chestnut sheen, the finger holes surrounded by even depressions worn in the wood with much playing. Issachar gently blew each note as he climbed the scale; there, halfway in the ladder of sound, was the curious so unaccustomed interval. Issachar, meagrely articulate in words, now began another melody, strange again to Jeshua's ear and the alien interval spoke to him of another tribe in another land, a mystery of sound which spoke beyond words between the two. Tenderly, as if handling a ritual object, Issachar wrapped the pipe in a fragment of

70

linen and put it away in a fold of his tunic. He walked away, drawing the flock after him.

FIVE

Rabbi Lazar was glad to be able to ask Joseph and Jeshua to make a substantial work for the synagogue. Over the years he had copied out considerable portions of the Torah and felt that, poor as Nazareth was, they still merited a more seemly home for the scrolls than the ark which now stood there. Joseph was called in to consultation in the synagogue.

'I don't think we should use any of the old ark; it has done its turn, the wood is worn and wormed in some panels. Let it stay until the new one can replace it.'

Lazar hesitated. His frugal need to preserve anything that had further use in it joined with his reverence for all that was hallowed by synagogue worship, resisted, even resented Joseph's craftsman's need to begin again, to set a new task in motion with its own chosen materials. This ark had been opened over and over the generations. Chosen readers had come up from the congregation to receive the scrolls and generation after generation had woven Nazareth into its humble past and formed its humble future. He opened one leaf of the ark's door; his hand moved down over the panel, caressing it along the grain, with the gesture of fondling a favourite dog. Joseph knew his reluctance to abandon an object that had become a living thing, breathing with the breath of the Torah.

'It shall not be abandoned, rabbi, and certainly its wood shall never be used for any other purpose.'

Looking directly at the apex of the ark and avoiding Lazar's eyes which seemed at the point of tears, he said 'It shall be burned, with incense and with prayers. For a few moments we shall be here in Nazareth as the Temple

71

in Jerusalem. The smoke shall go up, a sweet-smelling sacrifice.'

'But Joseph, there is no precedent.'

'Affection for the Law, rabbi – you have told us this so often – needs no precedent, no argument from the doctors.'

Lazar was unconvinced but let it go for the moment.

'When will you begin the work?'

'I shall not begin it; this is to be Jeshua's work, entirely his. When you first spoke of the synagogue's need, I saw something in his eyes I had not seen before, a kind of yearning. And I watched his hands, his fingers restlessly twining, as if they would be about the wood. He has a way with wood, Rabbi Lazar, a way which reminds me of his voice as he reads the Haftorah. His voice has a vibrance then as if – forgive me if I sound too steeped in a father's pride – as if he had been there as our forefathers received the tablets graven by the fingers of Adonai.'

Lazar looked at him sharply, a rebuke hovering instinctively, until he saw that Joseph was saying exactly what he meant.

'His voice has the sureness, the command which I see in his grasp of the carving tool. He knows the wood's grain, its growth, its thrust upward and around its core. He feels for the knot and its pattern, as, when he reads, he feels for the sense and pronounces it with assurance. I have rarely had that secure command, even of wood or stone and never of the Word.'

'Nor have I, Joseph.' It was a hesitant, reluctant admission and yet with a teacher's pride, almost as a father. 'I have lived long years in the writing-chambers of the Temple. There, when Jerusalem was filled with the learned, as I heard the sharp voice of Shammai question the compassionate dogma of Hillel, and as the doctors gave their oh so sure pronouncements, I have not heard even there such a certain note of truth. Yes, let Jeshua begin his work!'

An ark requires little wood; the quantity and weight was negligible as Jeshua chose and transferred to the work-bench the most treasured balks that Joseph drew out of their store. The corners, the strong articulation of the structure, was to be oak, chosen from the russet-streaked heart-wood, to match the panels which were to be of the finest cedar. The ornaments, the handles and the finials, demanded olive wood and the especially precious acacia from the 'Oasis of the Acacia' over against Jericho and across the Jordan. Each piece of timber, when it had had its first preparation to reveal the grain and patterning, was placed againsts its fellow until the structure began to emerge in the separate flat planes of each aspect of the ark. It needed no measured drawing as the wood revealed its inevitable place – the structure and the austere pan-elled framework took its fourfold shape on the work-bench. The work began on each in turn, the back, the two sides and then, closing the structure, the frame and two leaves of the ark's entrance as it would face the synagogue congregation.

Jeshua gave it no more and no less careful craft, as he moved from plane to plane, than he devoted to a chair, a yoke, a lintel or a door-frame. All the craft of the work-shop floor engaged him with an intensity that joined hand, tool and wood in a unity that perhaps only the player on a delicate and precious instrument knows its like. And it was music's order and assurance that informed the severe austerity of the ark with a quality of lyrical intensity. The boxwood dowels were smoothed to a fit that held the structure in a coherent strength. It had needed no initial drawing and the completed work had a massive strength which responded to the Torah it would enclose.

The austerity of the ark now assumed a new vitality. Along its base was a traditional frieze of bells and pomegranates, stylized, but without any of the mechanical repetition of ornament turned out to a pattern; each motif was carved with its own inner tension, growing out of the grain. The fine edge of each bell was smoothed to a sharp, almost cutting edge, the gentle ogee-curve of its profile giving promise of a ringing tone; each pomegranate seemed delicately at the point of a different maturity, some suavely enclosed and intact, others bursting to reveal the rich seed. And yet no unit asserted its individual life at the expense of the total design; it was a lively dance of ringing tone and fruitfulness. The structure of the ark was now almost ready for its installation in the synagogue. Only the final polishing and burnishing remained. Jeshua asked of Mary a substantial measure of wax from last year's honey harvest and to the wax from the domestic hives he added a little of the darker wax from wild honeycombs. Into the kneaded lump he added enough olive oil to moisten his palms and continued kneading until he had a malleable fistful of polishing wax. This he rubbed into each surface, oak, cedar and precious hardwoods in turn, until each took a darker sheen which married each tone to its neighbour. With a blunted awl he delicately removed any surface wax from the carved line of the panel frames and from the grooved surfaces of the pomegranates. The final burnishing with a coarse rag of goat's wool gave each surface a glow and a radiance like the cut and polished facet of a patterned agate.

The ark now needed only its curtaining; Jeshua wished this to be Miriam's initiation into a more exacting use of her dexterous weaving skills. Her mother had taught her the craft of the narrow loom, the woven strips some cubit and a half in width and five cubits in length which were sewn along their edges to make garments, hangings or blankets. Miriam had an especial sensitivity to both texture and colour, setting the weft with successive groups of light and dark sheep's wool, the coarser threads of goat-fleece and even, – a bold innovation – of narrow groups of flax threads, dyed in the same muted colours as the wool. The shuttles for the weaving when the loom had been set with its full range of threads, were charged with the softest lamb's wool, a little lighter in colour than the lightest threads in the woof. The resulting strips of cloth had a delicacy and variety of patterning to the eye and a rich-ness to the touch which was quite unlike any other in Nazareth. Jeshua asked Mary if she thought Miriam would be affronted if she were asked to renounce some of these skills in order to produce a background curtaining of simple sheep and lamb's-wool in the warp and weft.

'I think she would be proud of the task; why don't you yourself ask her?'

Miriam had occasionally looked into the workroom while the ark was in the making and envied Jeshua his commission. His request for curtains overwhelmed her and her first impulse was to say no. There was a gleam of raillery in Jeshua's smile as he waited for the considered reply, which challenged Miriam's docility; almost defiantly she replied, 'Of course!'

'Good, and it's not as simple and undemanding as it sounds. For your first weaving of cloth which must be of full curtain length, is to provide a foundation for the cherubim.' The phrase sounded outrageous to Miriam; the words seemed to hover at the borderline between presumptuous arrogance and blasphemy.

'Cherubim!' Her tone was a rejection of every infini-tude, every space and creature beyond her conception. It was no sophisticated rejection of 'graven images' – and Jeshua refrained from leading her into those territories – but rather an instinctive fear of having her humble, dom-estic craft raised to a power she could not contemplate. 'Craft,' 'art,' 'to create,' these were not terms in her vocabulary – they were not customary terms for Jeshua; but she knew that to produce fine palatable bread and a good stew-pot, to construct an economical and efficient fire, to weave with tact and delicacy a fine piece of wool or linen cloth, all these were a young girl's matronly duties and skills. She knew equally intuitively that all she performed in the home, with an unobtrusive efficiency which she had learned from Mary, was in a wholly different world from the richly-woven priestly garments she had seen on those visits to the Jerusalem Temple at Passover. She had listened for the almost inaudible notes of the tiny bells, had wondered at the subtle gleam of gold and silver threads. These were worlds apart from the crafts of the home in Nazareth.

And yet her mind, without pride or self-seeking, allowed doubts. She had an almost possessive pride in the skills with which Jeshua could turn from the making of a humble table or work-bench to the ceremony of a special stool as a wedding gift or a finely ornamented yoke for that leading ox. And the new ark for the synagogue! They, the family of Joseph, to have a place in the synagogue ceremony, to see the rabbi's hands open those doors which the hands of Jeshua had fashioned, for that moment of all moments when the Torah was shown and spoken forth at the *Bimah*. And if this ark fashioned by Jeshua was a bridge between humble carpentry and the sublime, hadn't she known a small but intense pleasure when, for the last Feast of Purim, she had woven of the finest wool a *tallit* for Rabbi Lazar? These were vague, small gropings, but they halted her protests and she listened to Jeshua's plan for the work.

'We shan't really see the cherubim, but just feel their presence. They are all about us as they move between us, and the ark, and the temple, and His Throne. We can't even hear their wings, we can't even see that radiance, so much greater than the shining colours of any jewel you could think of. But there, oh yes, there! And this is what I ask you.' He unwrapped carefully a small, tightly rolled ball of gold thread; 'This I bought last Passover in Jerusalem for just such a moment as this. I want you to use it, as you could draw a pattern with your fingers in sand, a delicate pattern, almost not there, lines which a breath of wind or the little sweep of your fingertips would brush away. The curtain hangings will be in two panels, before the two leaves of the doors concealing the Torah-scrolls. You have woven them so delicately that this very finest gold thread will be like a little stream seen at sunset, a long way away, from the top of a hill. You know how the rivulet gleams, then disappears, then shows again around a further boulder; that is how I want you to draw wings in thread on each woven panel. Your cherubim will have no bodies, no faces, not even eyes. You remember the words from the prophet Isaiah you heard one Sabbath: 'With twain they covered their faces, with twain they covered their feet, and with twain they did fly.' I think your cherubim wings will be 'the twain with which they cover their faces,' don't you?'

His words gentled her on, the little hint of laughter in their under-tone throwing the solemn moment of her decision into something that recollected their childhood banter over a game. She smiled, still a little unsure of her ability to do what Jeshua asked of her, walked to the door of the workshop, turned for a last look at the completed ark, now shining darkly in the half light and went out into the full sunlight.

Jeshua's eyes followed her as she walked to the furthest corner of the sandy forecourt. Kneeling down, she gathered the sand in little heaps over the flattened area in the sunny corner, then swiftly smoothed them with the palms of her hand into a 'writing area,' of almost the same dimensions as the doors of the new ark. She seemed to hover over the blank sand and then, swiftly, with her forefinger traced in the left-hand panel the gently serrated outline of a wing, the long pointed wing of the migrating swifts which shrilled their way through the col above Nazareth and down into the vale of Jezreel. The poised wing, so delicately drawn as scarcely to be there, was more a tracing of flight than of feathers. Drawing back from it, and squatting on her heels, she looked at the outline, touched it here and there to soften its contour, and then turned to the other 'panel,' and swiftly traced in the outline. It was not precisely the outline of the left-hand panel, but its very asymmetry confirmed the impression of flight. A slight breeze ruffled the sand, sending feather-like ripples across the wing surfaces and blending them into the background.

Jeshua had moved behind her on the fore-court. 'Yes,' he said eagerly, 'yes; just that! Can you capture just that, in gold thread?'

'I must try.'

Without looking back either at the ark or her first drawing, she walked into the house to pick up and explore with her fingers the woven texture of the cloth. She had not touched the sand but left it to the breeze to turn feathers into flight and in a few moments into blank unruffled sand.

That evening Jeshua spoke aside to Mary and Joseph, telling them briefly of the task he had set Miriam and asking that they pay no attention to her work on the woven hangings, respecting any silence and reserve she would keep. Mary knew that Miriam was at an important threshold; Joseph knew in his craftsman's art that silent turbulence as an idea took shape. Miriam was left to her quiet self.

And the drawings took their own definition in the cloth. The firm curve at the 'shoulders' of the wings were a continuous line of gold, as Miriam bridged the gap, where the gold thread disappeared into the weave, with a second thread of gold, connecting the stitches. And as the wings swept down into the long curve to the sharp tip, the intermittent threads flickered and shone as they appeared on the denser surface of the woven wool. Almost furtively she gathered up the single length of cloth and ran out to the workshop, hanging the curtain from the top of the partly open door of the ark. Now the thick texture of the wool and the glowing sheen of the gold feathering, contrasted with the rich patterning of the wood; the deep auburn tones of polished cedar and oak, the patterning of olive and acacia gave another and more intense meaning to the concealing curtain, its secretive density carrying in its surface the merest suggestion of angelic flight. She saw that the work was good and returned to the other panel.

Like her drawing in the sand, this wing was not the precise reverse of its fellow but leaned to the right as if preparing to thrust the flight in a circular movement. When the gold line was completed, she took this panel also to the workshop and the whole design was now complete; the cloth-hanging lost its definition in the shadows of the workshop and the two panels, waveringly joined at the centre were framed solely in the figured oak patterns of the ark's framework and the hovering flight suggested by the wings was given definition and significance by the crowning lintel of the ark itself.

Miriam shyly called Jeshua to the workshop and his smile was sufficient confirmation of her success in realising his vision. Gently he said, 'Yes, it's worthy.'

So that the slight vertical rippling of the cloth, which would give vitality to the hangings when they were finally in the synagogue, should not be lost, Miriam had, to this end, made the hangings each a handsbreadth wider than the wood panel it concealed. Then the two cloths were laid face to face, enclosed in linen and hung up without folding. Jeshua then released the temporary dowelling of the ark and laid the pieces in order, for reconstruction in the synagogue.

Under Lazar's nervous direction he did the same to the old ark in the synagogue. The dowels had shrunk over the years and patiently, using only the pressure of his fingers (there should be no sound of hammer or other tool within the holy place) he prised away the round pegs which held the worn structure together. Beginning with the door panels, (which he left intact, removed only from their wooden hinges) he laid each element in a neat pile, topped finally by the dismembered framework. He tied the whole together with two roped strands of crude linen and it lay, no more than a bundle of faggots which they might carry for kindling from the hillside.

'I have thought of this, Rabbi Lazar;' Jeshua's gravity held the old man who heard also the quiet consideration in his voice. 'It is not good, perhaps not even seemly, that we should burn these holy things here in Nazareth. For where could we make the pyre? We can't 'sacrifice' in the synagogue and it would hurt many people – and you, rabbi? – to see it consumed here, in a public place. We shall take it next Passover to Jerusalem and there the Levites shall help us.' Lazar nodded his approval, gathered up the bundle and took it to his home.

By mid-afternoon the new structure was in place and ready for assembling. With the sure touch of one who had designed and made the whole, Jeshua fitted each part together and locked them with the boxwood pins. As each part took its place, it grew in strength and poise, seeming to expand before their eyes and to open fittingly to take the Torah scrolls. Each was placed upright in its rack by the rabbi, and the doors closed. The two stood at the entrance of the synagogue, looking towards the ark in its glow of new wood; they were conscious that they had brought into being not an inanimate object but a gesture. Silently they fetched the two hangings which fulfilled the design and they withdrew into the sunlight of late afternoon.

Some time before evening prayers in the synagogue, every family crossed the open square to its doors, pausing for a moment to absorb the change in its order and furnishings, and then, men and women severally, went to their places.

The voices rose:

I will lift up mine eyes unto the hills
From whence cometh mine aid
My help cometh even from the Lord
Who hath made heaven and earth

He shall give his angels charge over thee
To keep thee in all thy ways

They that wait upon the Lord
Shall renew their strength;
They shall mount up with wings as eagles,
They shall run and not be weary,
They shall walk, and not faint.

SIX

'I have grown up and lived here in Nazareth for nearly twenty years.' The two craftsmen sat on their customary boulders looking out in the minutes after sunset over the valley below, a purple bar of heavy mist forming the basis to the shifting gold and red of the last light of evening. Both men looked down at their hands, folded, relaxed, on the aprons which covered their tunics. The older man saw the ink-stains, brown and black with the rare streaks of red and then, as if in a tentative envy, looked at the younger hands, strong, shapely, the nails carefully pared to avoid the wood-snags, the pads of the fingers and their tips hard-skinned with callouses. Each had the hands of a prideful craft, their several skills in grain. Jeshua echoed the rabbi's unspoken comment.

'Yes, these hands have come through their tough apprenticeship. I can now do, make, form anything my father does. Together we have made a great deal.'

'There is something in your voice – perhaps in your eyes – I have not heard or seen before. I have seen boys of fifteen, restless as you now seem but never before a craftsman, settled in his craft, as you are.'

'Not restless, rabbi; I want nothing more than Nazareth can give, its peace, the harmony that long years have created. It's so like that pool you taught me to fish as a boy; the stream flows strongly but with a little eddying; that great pool lies beneath the bank, tranquil and aside from the main current. And there the little fish bask, with scarcely a flicker of their fin or tail to keep them still above the gravel.' There was a laughter and a touch of irony in his voice but a swift change in its tone as he turned fully to the rabbi.

'But mature fish need the main stream and I haven't swum in it, with or against the current.'

There was silence as the sun drew down to its last light and the purple radiance became an ashy grey-black. The smoke from the evening fires could no longer be seen but there was an after-taste, the slightly acrid flavour of green bark as the brushwood rekindled the flames for the evening meal.

'But you have seen Jerusalem.' The rabbi sounded fretful as though someone were about to snatch from him a treasured possession or deprive him of a loved activity.

'Oh yes, I have seen Jerusalem! I have seen that fortress which the years have built about and beyond the City of David, perched there on its bluff. I have seen Herod's Temple, suspect in its stone and gold and I have seen Rome poised above it. These things are there; I have seen them; they press on my flesh but I have not seen them in my mind, I have not -' his voice faltered as he looked for the word: 'I have not loved them.' The words came out

82

almost defiantly, drawn from a deep unease, a struggle.

'You should marry, Jeshua. A wife and children would settle you here and when you took them on Passover to Jerusalem, in true love you would love Jerusalem.'

'But, dear rabbi, you have not married. Forgive my boy's presumption but you haven't married and isn't that wrong for a rabbi?'

'Yes, the rabbis all say a rabbi should marry, be fruitful and multiply' – some of Jeshua's irony could now be heard in Lazar's tone – 'but somehow, something always came in its way. As a boy, becoming a young man, I was too poor, in some ways too wretched to be inflicted on any woman. Then came the manuscripts in the Temple and my growing skill with reed and ink. I grew to love the parchment, the vellum and the ink as it traced its way through the Laws – I suppose I grew married to the Torah.' The deprecating voice and the hint of laughter removed from the rabbi's staid little jest any hint of blasphemy and there was answering laughter in Jeshua's eyes.

'Then – I have told you before – the Temple brooded over me too heavily, pressed on me a vocation I couldn't face and I came to Nazareth. Humble synagogues need their Torah scrolls renewed as urgently as those of the Temple and I grew contented here. Here I truly entered a family, loving, quarrelsome, mean, brave and enduring; every boy I prepared to be a Son of the Law was my son also; every girl who heard my words and, like Miriam, grew towards comely matronhood, she was my daughter.'

'And that was enough?'

'Fully enough – a large and troublesome family! And there was another reason. I revere marriage; it could be as paradisal as the love of our first parents. But they fell; paradise was closed to them, and some of us are called by God to be free of the demands – the demands loving and onerous – of any marriage, to have the single mind to pray for all marriages.'

The last words were almost inaudible as the rabbi looked out over Nazareth with the brooding concern of all in authority. It seemed as if his look entered every home, in deep compassion.

Jeshua remained silent, accepting their unbroken but unspoken dialogue, content to let the rabbi's mind traverse the train of reminiscence, certain that when it had gone its course, his mind would veer back to its earlier subject. After some minutes came the response to his silent waiting. Very slowly and in a whisper he heards the words, 'Jerusalem is builded as a city' – 'that is at unity in itself?', the halfline fulfilling of the metric was almost angry in its explosive reply to the whispered words. 'And if not at unity, then why not? What are the rifts in the garment of God, what are the breaches in its walls, what the desecration of its holiness?'

Lazar had never before heard this acerbity, had never realised the sharp, secure authority in the young voice and he remained silent, wondering. In a fuller tone, half apologising for his outburst, 'Rabbi, I too have known the zeal of my father's house; last Passover I too was eaten up by it, torn apart by the conflicting glory and desolation of our Jerusalem. Do you know, rabbi, I confess to you that our Passover journeys have been a mysterious experience. I am here in Nazareth; some days later I am in Jerusalem and somehow I have not travelled, not known the intervening journey. Oh, it's true I have traversed Jezreel, passed through Samaria, and, greatly daring, we took the route of the ambushes, the road from Jericho to Jerusalem. But it was like a land in a dream. There was Nazareth, home, security; there was Jerusalem, the dangerous fortress enclosing the altar of God, holiness desecrated by that which preserved its holiness – and there was no land, no journey between, no way to marry the two sanctities.'

Here, as with the acid anger, the words of Jeshua explored landscapes of the mind where Lazar could not follow. He could only wait in a bemused patience for words of a maturity greater than his own.

'They have been two eddying pools, here in Galilee, there in Judah, both aside from the stream. Dear rabbi, I must test the current.'

There was no reply the rabbi could make. It was becoming chill and, drawing a fold of his tunic over his head, Lazar walked back with Jeshua to their homes.

SEVEN

A week later he set out, north-west along the spur from which he had earlier seen the Capernaum road. In lower Nazareth, before he struck out for the open country, he passed an open door and just within, an elderly man sitting on a stool and vacantly watching what little activity caught his attention.

'Leaving home, then?'

The guttural question carried more than a little contempt, the resentful recognition of another and perhaps alien, even threatening way of life.

'For a few days' was Jeshua's kindly reply, half stopping to greet the man.

'Lucky to be able to leave your business!'

'Yes, Jacob's a good brother and doesn't envy me a few days away. Work has been quite hard.'

The narrow eyes, the thin-lipped smile, showed the man quite unmollified by Jeshua's tone of friendly reserve. He spat into the dust outside the door and turned his head away in dismissal. 'He knew no Lazar when he was a boy' was Jeshua's sad reflection, as once more he strode quickly away.

He reached the main lake highway, dropping down from the escarpment, in what was still quite early morning, and in an hour or so entered the fertile slopes above the sea of Galilee. Before reaching the true cultivation, he gathered two or three of the dry and so unsatisfactory sycamore 'figs' and chewed toughly on them as he walked, taking with them a fragment or two of the barley-cakes from his wallet. Above a terraced vineyard a clear stream rushed down into an irrigation channel and before it reached the artificial banks, he scooped up a drink in his cupped hands. It was singularly cool in the increasing heat of the day.

The vineyards and olive groves were remarkably different from those he knew at Nazareth. At home and at the greater and more exposed height, refined cultivation was impossible. Some of the older vines, their trunks massy and gnarled as stunted oaks, had been allowed to send their branches like the spokes of a wheel, pruned and staked over a substantial area. The younger more productive vines were trained along stout withies held horizontally between willow posts. One of Jeshua's first insights into human labour had been to see the old workers bent almost double as they held the brown-scaled shoots, sought the bud they were to retain, and with a sharp pruning-knife severed the unwanted growth; it was patient and cruelly arduous work, demanding swift labour at the right time, if 'bleeding' was not to lose so much of the meagre strength of the shrub. Pruning had none of the communal joy of the grape-harvest which made the toil a festival. Even when the pruning was done, there was still the exacting task of gathering the discarded branches into bundles and again Jeshua remembered his childhood view at sun-down, as the peasants carried the faggots home, still bent almost double, both under the weight and from their inability to walk truly after the day's held posture along the rows.

There was no shadow of this in lakeside Galilee. There the orderly lines, an arm's-span apart and with a vivid green of luxuriant growth, seemed almost regimented in their efficient setting. As the slopes terraced downward towards the lake, the ancient stone walling weathered and lichened to an almost woven pattern of colour, seemed like well-worn and scoured cloth. At this time of the year there were few in the vineyards, but some boys with hoes and narrow mattocks stirring the rocky earth to preserve the moisture of the subsoil.

The olive trees had all the variety of Nazareth's orchards, some clearly as enduring as Capernaum, others mere decades old and at the height of their bearing. Each small grove was marked by groups and short lines of almond and pistachio trees and, in the shade against wind but in full sun, handsome bushes of nectarines. It was a luxuriant countryside, the sights and smells of rich and vigorous cultivation. Faintly disturbed at the aggressive prosperity Jeshua hurried down towards the town, the outer buildings of which he skirted as he made his way to the lakeshore. It was now late evening and three groups of fishermen were gathering their nets, with each fold picking off the weed which clung to them and noting any torn meshes which needed immediate repair. Two of the fisherman were folding together the long and narrow dragnet, while another group of three folded theirs towards the centre, as if setting for storage large cloths or blankets, a square net of considerable size, weighted around at intervals. Jeshua promised himself that the following day would see his curiosity satisfied about these new and strange activities. He approached the group of three men and asked if there might be lodging for the night. Their reserve held a breath of rebuff but the candour of his smile led to an immediate invitation to follow them. Along the shore and within a low dry-wall which enclosed both the house and the carefully-tended herb-garden, they led him into the large living room. Their young wives greeted him; he noticed and responded to the franker freedom of speech of the town-dweller, so different from the reserve, the taciturnity of so many at Nazareth – and the widowed father, Zacharias, gave the formal invitation to the evening meal, both barley and wheaten cakes with pieces of cold fish taken from its sauce of oil and herbs. These were flavours, refreshing and satisfying, which Jeshua found quite new after the plainer upland fare; and so was the wine mixed with less water than the drink to which he was accustomed. On the tongue, it seemed to him, there were elusive flavours, as if more than one vintage were mixed in the cup; it was his first experience of that overplus, which he called luxury and beneath his enjoyment of the meal and his gratitude for the unforced hospitality, there was a slight unease, as if he were trespassing on desires which he had never before conceived.

The meal was almost silent and when they had drunk the last cup of wine, they sat, relaxed, about the charcoal brazier. It was no more than a token fire, a centre point, for the night was happily cool, with no more breeze than was needed to bring an undertone of wave-lapping from the lake. Courteously, but quite directly and without preamble, Zacharias asked Jeshua, 'Business, is it business that brings you to Capernaum? by your dress and the dust you cleansed from your feet, you are from the uplands.'

'No, it isn't business that brings me here. My father, my brothers and I build and furnish houses in Nazareth. All our work is within the little town; we buy our materials from Lebanon or the mountains of the south and have little need of 'business,' trade as you know it.'

He hesitated and the others waited silently for his further words.

'I can't tell what has brought me – we are busy and, I suppose, prosperous, my brothers and I; we work within our strength, it's no grinding peasant labour and if we need time for rest or thinking, a day or two is not grudged.'

Jeshua now spoke more quickly and confidently, as if exploring a path he knew to be before him. 'There is no humiliating poverty at Nazareth – no one dies in want – but there are all the other ills of flesh, there are cripples and the blind; there are those who can't speak, not, perhaps, even to themselves but few are mean-minded.' It was now the turn of Zacharias and his sons to be disturbed at this countryman's confessional and they could anticipate no motive for his appearance at their home.

'The world is wider than Nazareth! Men have their needs, their cravings beyond the daily work, the hunger and the rest in sleep. I wanted to meet men in their greater needs, to meet joy and sorrow and the longing for something that 'day by day' doesn't give them.'

This was a language Nazareth would not have understood, though Lazar would have caught its undertone, and Zacharias and his family listened with incomprehension.

'And so I have come to you. May I share your fishing when you go out tomorrow?'

This was a request they could understand and, smiling, they agreed to treat him like the other curious travellers who wished, without effort, to 'share their toil.' It was time for rest; the elder brother took him by the outer stairway to the upper room, spread some extra quilting on the boards and left him to his sleep.

At sunrise, the morning was clear, the lake rippling in a breeze from the south, with the Gadara hills covered with long shallow banks of cloud. Two of the brothers pushed out a boat, the third taking Jeshua in their second boat. The long drag-net was gathered into a single thick strand and fastened at each end to the boat-prows. Simeon, the oarsman of the first boat, rowed in a great circular sweep into the bay, drawing the net taut, as Lemuel's boat was paddled slowly only some fathoms away from shore. Simeon rowed to his left, making back in a great arc towards the shore, while Lemuel shipped his oars, allowing the boat to drift under the weight of the net. As the first boat neared the shore, each fisherman raised his hand in a signal to lower the net, which was quickly unfurled, the weighted edge dropping towards the lake bottom. Lemuel leapt into the shallow water, taking one oar, and waded towards the centre of the wide arc defined by the net and struck sharply at the gravel of the lake bed. Jeshua saw the darting of a small shoal of fish, some even breaking the surface to get away from the blows of the oar. The two brothers now rowed into shore and having beached the boats, hauled in their net in a decreasing arc. Some of the fish they picked out of the shallow water but the fair catch was mainly of fish, trapped in the meshes of the net as they fled from the sound of the oar. The net was carefully folded from each end, the fish picked out and placed in shallow baskets, which sorted them for kind and size. They had caught twenty-three large fish and over thirty smaller fish which had been worth keeping from the mixed shoal. They were gutted immediately and before noon the four men were back at the house, Jeshua taking his part in sorting those fish which were to be salted and sun-dried – the larger and coarser species – from those which were to be their evening meal, with the remainder sold at market. It had been a morning's work, a little less successful than the average catch, so Simeon said, but sufficient to give Jeshua his insight into a new toil. As he scoured his hands with fine gravel in the bowls of lake-water in which they washed away the fish-scales and fragments of gut, the four spoke together as freely as though Jeshua had long been part of their family.

'Tomorrow, if the shoals run well, we shall try two throw-nets,' said Lemuel. Zacharias added that the cloud masses boded well for a fine but hazy day, ideal for deeper-water fishing. Jeshua was content, through the languor of the sultry heat of afternoon, to listen to the desultory talk and join in with little more than a smile or a brief word. Sleep that night was deep and satisfying, penetrated not even by the sound of the waves.

The morning Lemuel pronounced 'splendid for fishing' and, since it was to be the net thrown, they rowed some distance, Jeshua taking in all the shifting panorama of the eastern and southern lake, towards the Seven Springs. This was a prolific fishing ground with variable waters, warm from the inlets at lake bottom, mingled with the milky and cold waters which the upper Jordan brought from the snows of Hermon. Here the tench and the carp shoaled prolifically, ideally gathered together for the 'drop net.' As they reached the well-proven waters they saw the other crews who had also set out at dawn. One had already sighted a shoal and the fisher in the stern of the boat was getting ready for his cast. He stood, steadied by one hand, a massive and athletic man, whose quick smile challenged Simeon and Lemuel for the first catch. He had the broad shoulders of the swift oarsman and as he, single-handed, whirled the net about his head, Jeshua admired the muscular tautness, the trained athleticism of skilful craft, which extended through his arms to the rigid whirling of the weighted net. With a final curved thrust, the net spun level with the water and fell neatly and uniformly, the weights around its edge belling the meshes down into the water, a mobile trap for the fish.

'A good throw, Simon! Mine won't look so good – but we shall compare catches!'

Lemuel had little of Simon's skill but as they rowed towards shore, drawing the net by the cords they had retained at the stern of the boat, each little crew had secured a good day's haul, some large perch, and some smaller fish, with very few of the 'forbidden fish', the skeat, to be thrown aside for the waiting birds.

As they rowed leisurely back to the Capernaum shore, Jeshua watched closely the shifting colours and tones of the lake's surface, those darker hues from the deeper currents, the silvering of brief squalls from the mountain gaps to the north and east and the more flickering silver of the small shoals as some of the fish broke surface. It was a topography as 'readable' as the landscape of upland Nazareth, where he had learned to interpret every shimmer of the olive leaves, the wave motion of the pasturage, the massing of clouds towards Lebanon or Carmel or the drying winds from the Samarian highlands. This was a new, a sultry and more swiftly changeable terrain, the lake surface adding the unpredictable to his Nazareth weather-lore. They spoke little in the slow pull back to the shore but after the fish had been cleaned and set aside, they all sat in the vine arbour (which took Jeshua's thought back to Nazareth as he looked across at the mature and untidy fig tree); looking at the panorama of Galilee, Jeshua felt sufficiently one with the family to ask them of their friends and the economy of the town, how far taxes weighed on their earnings and with what resentment. From the reserved and ironic answers, which from Zacharias became the very articulate expression of long-held grievances, Jeshua felt sharply the contrast with the close-knit village community of the upland country, where isolation and the inter-marriage of few families made wrongs and triumphs into community matters. Here, surrounded by alien cultures, pagan, Roman and Greek, each family of fishermen was a passionately independent unit, sharing dangers and economic hardships and natural grievances with like families, but wholly conscious of their own small integrity in a single kinship family. The skills, the equipment, the accumulated wealth, were carefully inherited from father to son, the skills of catching, curing, marketing, shared by every member of the family, the women, the young girls, adding their own deftness and their knowledge of domestic needs to the preparation of the fish for market. Such close-knit units had their peculiar inherited pride and traditions, their own tricks of net-casting and weighting, their own scarcely conscious methods of plying every aspect of their trade shaped from generations who had fished these waters of Gennesaret. Even after a day or two, Jeshua sensed the differences in 'style' which made the family of Zacharias so unlike the family of Jonas, in their approach to their craft and their conduct of it. Intimate friends, assured rivals they might all be, and welded together into a community by their intuitive knowledge of shared catastrophe on a turbulent lake; but the community was made of more passionately independent family units than any Jeshua had known in Nazareth and to this he responded with affectionate recognition – for the carpentry, the brick making, the roofing and paving of his family craft, had given Joseph's home its private and unique place in Nazareth.

To another need of this new family of friends, Jeshua responded with equal warmth. It was the afternoon before Sabbath; the sultry heat was beating upon their nerves, making them either soporific or with that inner restless querulousness which hard work and the afternoon's humidity inevitably brought. From neighbouring houses came the raised voices of shrill and short-lived quarrelling. Lemuel rose and said to Jeshua, 'The lake will be quiet and cooler; Sabbath will come more gently there.' Jeshua smiled, surprised and interested by the remark. The bronzed and rugged face, the calloused hands and scarred forearms gave small promise of this delicacy of need but he followed Lemuel to the lakeside where he pushed out the smallest of the boats. Jeshua sat in the stern as, with no effort, Lemuel pulled slowly and silently towards the bay to the south and on the western shore of the lake. There they caught the occasional patch of shaded water, sheltered from the main heat of the sun. Without touching shore, Lemuel drew in the oars and allowed the boat, scarcely drifting, to rock in the waves of the afternoon breeze. They exchanged not a single word or comment; each looked out towards the hills, every moment changing in the movement of the clouds, with parched mustard-coloured wadis fissuring the shifting greens and purples of the more distant mountains. For almost half an hour Lemuel looked down at his hands, folded in the lap of his tunic, wordless and immobile, his body relaxing from the morning's work; Jeshua, in the silence, knew in this other person the complete tranquillity of the craftsman, gathering his mind from the labour of his craft. Again without a word, Lemuel pulled on the shoreward oar, drew in a wide circle into the lake and made for Capernaum.

The family gathered for the synagogue service and walked, men, women and children in successive groups along the shore and to the singularly beautiful synagogue which dominated in the radiance of its limestone, glowing above the sombre stone of the houses, the crowded city above the lake. As they approached, Jeshua marvelled at the contrast with Nazareth. There the synagogue was the home of the Torah, 'home', as their own homes contained their day-to-day living. Here was a building in Capernaum that spoke of other values. With a Roman austerity it spoke also of Roman majesty. After crossing the outer courtyard, a double colonnade enclosed an inner court which opened by a doorway into the hall of worship. In the outer courtyard, his ear established the whispered talk as Greek, a slow perambulation of Gentiles from the other coastal towns, of Hellenes from the villas of Gadara, mixed with the occasional talk of Romans, soldiery relaxed and off duty and civic officials mingling with their neighbours in the cool of the evening. Some of these were 'God-fearers', *goyim* by blood and upbringing but deeply respectful of synagogue spirituality and pressing towards the door of the prayer-hall, from which they could see the tabernacle and hear the Torah but not venturing beyond the threshold. One of these, a dark, grizzled Roman soldier, in worn leather and burnished iron trappings, his helmet in the crook of his left arm, caught Jeshua's eye as he moved towards the inner hall. Their glances had met only momentarily but Jeshua held in his mind the Roman's alert look throughout the service.

EIGHT

The last psalm had been sung, the silence held for a moment and the congregation moved out of the colonnaded courtyard. There the Roman still stood as if in relaxed guard and again his eyes held those of the young man from Nazareth, half his age. Without salutation, as though they needed no preamble between them, the centurion spoke.

'You visit Capernaum briefly? I haven't seen you before in our synagogue.'

It was a strangely possessive gesture from one who was no more than a 'God-fearer.'

'It's my first visit to your synagogue. I'm here only for a day or two, staying with some fishermen, the family of Zacharias. They have made me very welcome – I'm from Nazareth, a builder working with my family and the Lake is something very new to me, very beautiful, very fine.'

'My home is quite near, below the grove above the nearest inlet of the waters. Would an hour's refreshment please you? It will be Roman – perhaps Spartan – hospitality!' The small jest was deprecating but at the same time welcoming. Jeshua turned to Zacharias who stood waiting at the outer columns with his family. The centurion turned also, and anticipating Jeshua's explanation, 'Peace to you Zacharias,' 'and with you, Justus.' The familiarity was curious and reassuring to Jeshua for whom any Roman experience was alien.

'I shall be back before nightfall,' he said to his host, as the family moved away and he followed the centurion.

They walked beyond the outer olive grove at the southern border of the town, followed a narrow path lined irregularly with acacia until they reached another ancient and scarcely-tended olive grove. Between it and the boulders of the lakeside they reached a small house built on the Roman plan, wholly strange to Jeshua's professional scrutiny. Justus drew forward a quilted stool for Jeshua, set another for himself where they could both look out over the last of the sun on the hills of the eastern shore of the lake. Before sitting himself, he brought two goblets of wine ('this is the rough wine of Spain – you will like it') and a small platter of cakes of sweetened wheat and almond. Justus broke the silence almost abruptly.

'You journey for relaxation? – strange for a craftsman of your race.'

The gentle tones held no hint of unseemly curiosity or deprecation; nor even of an uncomfortable gulf between the races. It was a simple question as from one who desired friendship and to its tone Jeshua wholly responded.

'I do the more delicate work now in my father's workshop – my eyes are better than his and my brothers haven't yet the more taxing skills – they tell me I'm a good craftsman' – each smiled. 'I journey, no, not for relaxation; I have that in the uplands above Nazareth; not for relaxation but for men.'

It was a clumsy declaration, surprising even Jeshua and he hurried on, explaining as much to himself as to the Roman.

'Men are so different. They are of one kind in Nazareth, tied, wedded to the earth and their labour. Their burdens are so heavy that they sometimes forget even how to speak. They bend to the vines, stoop to the hoe, gather with such sweating difficulty the barley stalks. They pause for a Sabbath psalm but labour is upon them again, bending their backs before the sweat of the previous toil is dry on their skin. And so I journey for men, looking for the toil of the men of Gennesaret. The fishermen stoop to the nets, sweat at the hauling, but they speak and in two short days I have met men who have become companions and friends.'

The clumsy words were now articulate, the groping of the eyes and restless hands speaking to Justus of one who truly sought to meet other men, to share what could be spoken and that which could not be spoken. For Jeshua, – he knew this for the first time in this strange conversation with an alien – the dumbness of labour, its unremitting and inarticulate toil towards an ever-receding end, 'keeping body and soul together,' was in him, Jeshua, made articulate in the tips of his fingers, in his craftsman's art. And now, with this stranger, he was finding words, and with them, he felt, he could speak even with the alien.

'You have found men here; you will find them, I believe, elsewhere.' The courteous voice, its maturity bridging the gulf of age and race between them, invited confidence and questions.

'You are a centurion? – I have barely caught your name and not your rank.'

'I am Justus, a centurion in the occupying Legion' – the ironic word brushed aside any sting of arrogance in the defined status. 'I have fewer than a hundred men in my authority and I shall soon retire, a centurion, to the little house which reminds me of my home. My duties are light – though you volatile Galileans keep us alert! and I have time to read and to think and to visit friends, Greek friends in Gadara.'

Jeshua's eyes, still puzzled, trying to penetrate behind the words to the truth of this strange man, never wavered from the eyes of Justus who seemed to be more in soliloquy than in converse with his guest. In the silence, which seemed not about to be broken, he said quietly,

'Home? You say this reminds you of 'home'?' Justus smiled and if his face of authority could carry shyness, his eyes suggested it.

''Home' is Spain, the heat, the dry brown rock and earth of the high heartland. My father was wealthy and from interest in the law entered the Roman service, the staff of the Consul. I had a mind to follow him when the wild oats had been garnered but when I was just your age – you are not yet twenty-five?' 'I am barely twenty-one years.' 'When I was about your age a more than customary stupidity put my father's vocation beyond my reach. I was no longer welcome in my father's house and circle and, Spanish by birth and Roman by inclination, I joined the Roman Legion, serving for a while in Germania and on the Adriatic shores and then – now raised to centurion, to your Galilee, so parched, so futile – so Spanish!'

The tone was light, throwing away the narrative as an evening tale, but his eyes, as Jeshua looked into them, carried the pain and some of the humiliation of all exile.

There was nothing that Jeshua could add, by question or young comment, to this confessional; with rough tact he moved to the topic implied behind the personal history.

'And have you, the Romans who were your adopted race, brought anything to Galilee?'

Like Justus's light stress on 'occupation' earlier, Jeshua's words contained no acerbity; they simply demanded exchange of thought.

'We brought roads, we brought law, we brought peace.' Though the words were bantering, Jeshua had never before known the weight of Roman authority, the unquestioned assurance of empire. He was quite still for some minutes while he gathered himself, his eyes probing behind the banter to the source of the authority.

'In Nazareth we are a little aside from your swift highways but words reach us of your might and the ways in which you establish it. We hear of scourgings, wild beasts, crucifixion,' (the mobile, skilled fingers fell momentarily to his knees, the palms crimped in sympathetic pain) 'is this the source, the agony, of your law, your peace?'

'No – but rarely. It is a wide empire; from Britain to the Bosphorus, from the northern plains to the sands of Egypt, all the powers know that peace is balanced on that small fulcrum poised on the Tiber. Rome itself would stagger if barbarian power were not held in check. Scourges, beasts, crosses, yes, they are the final deterrents, but self interest, the necessity of trade, the absence of war, these are more persuasive. And in every corner, near or far from Rome, there are men who reverence Law, who see in the Pax Romana an image of the lawful peace, the tranquillity of the natural order which is the heart of their reverence.'

These were abstractions that Jeshua had never met and instinctively rejected; he had prayed for truth but never truth in this kind of language.

'We have a word' – he spoke slowly and broodingly, as if hesitating to pronounce. 'Shalom,' he said and, smiling, Justus responded; 'Shalom aleychem.' Their smiles were a bond and Jeshua had no need to concede the status of a 'God-fearer' – Justus commanded that status in his bearing.

''Shalom' – you have known it – is not the absence of war or even of strife; it is not thrust into people's paths; it is not enforced – and it can't be bought!'

Again laughter concealed the passion. 'I think it is just possible I might learn to respect Rome.' The young, so flexible mind was exploring strange waters – 'but I wonder if I could ever love your 'Pax Romana' as I love 'Shalom'?'

'And 'Torah'?' There was now no raillery in Justus's voice but the full, exploratory courtesy of a gentle mind, honed sharp in the humiliation of a hard-learnt authority, an authority that was ultimately alien, and to his Spanish instincts, ultimately demeaning.

''Torah'! that is another matter. The voice of my Father, heard by my people throughout the long ages, the voice patiently shaped to our tongue.' Justus was alerted, sharpened his gaze at 'my Father,' spoken with such direct conviction, as Jeshua himself had started to a new alertness at 'our synagogue.' These two friends of an evening were not only learning something of each other's secret minds, they were bringing to sharp awareness intuitions that hitherto had been below the structure of conscious thought.

Jeshua was drawn by the silence – the lake was now no more than a rippling irridescence in the near distance – to venture upon two new paths of thought and hesitated, choosing between them. He began in a low tone, with a little of synagogue formality, reciting the words.

''He hath showed thee, O man, what is good; and what doth the Lord require of thee but to do justly, to love mercy and to walk humbly with thy God?' Our prophet Micah has gathered the whole of Torah into those words, and Justus, if I hear you rightly, do you realise what he would have said if he had been a Roman? not 'do justly' but 'do justice' and that too is a different matter! We learn 'justice' only in the doing, by 'doing justly'. In the beginning, the ten words from the mouth of my Father were no more than signs, intuitions perhaps along the just way. The love of just men, the compassion for those fallen by the way, the dues paid to man and to Jahweh, these were all bred into our sinews and bones by the command to 'do justly.' It may even be that we have no 'Justice' as you know it and that perhaps is our strength and our treasure. David our shepherd knew the truth of it when he sang:

> Make me to go in the path of thy commandments;
>> For therein is my delight.
>> Behold I have longed after thy precepts;
>> Quicken me in thy righteousness.

In 'Torah' there is 'delight', there is 'longing' and there is all 'quickening.' Am I being unfair if I ask you if your Law fills you with that quickening delight?'

The laughter of Justus was frank and without restraint. 'You are unfair only in your refusal to argue, Jeshua. You speak with such sublime confidence of the words of 'your Father'.'

Jeshua was silent, for the second path had opened before him without his seeking it. Almost inaudibly, Justus leaning forward to catch the words, he murmured, 'I meet Him in the silent and lonely ways. We pray as a family in the synagogue, a family in which the maimed and the hurt and the wicked are held and cherished by the fortunate and the loving. But He is also in the silence and there I have to meet Him. As I walk towards Carmel a cloud somehow hovers in the evening. I speak silently and' – he paused shyly, looking sidelong at Justus, as though confessing a boy's foible – 'praying, for me then, has the scent of mint leaves, the rough mint I always pluck in passing a stream on the way to the heights. The scent of the crushed leaves is for me the incense of the wild and the lonely and there He answers.'

There was nothing more to be said between them. They sat, a strange friendship sealed, the breeze of evening off the lake echoing the sheen of water by lifting the glancing silver of the olive leaves. Another goblet of the dark red wine and a rough barley crust were taken in the quiet dusk.

'I will see you on your way to the lakeside, within sight of the house of Zacharias.' At the path's end, Justus turned with the briefest farewell and as he watched him striding quickly towards his home, Jeshua realised that he had not in the whole evening quite crossed the threshold of this roman house.

With rough tact the two brothers asked no questions about the evening, but Zacharias was less restrained and wanted to know of what they could have spoken for those long hours; 'Of the Torah' Jeshua replied, 'and of his strange Roman life; he is a 'God-fearer,' isn't he?'

'Yes' said Zacharias, a most unusual pride strengthening the affection in his voice for this alien soldier; 'He built us our synagogue.'

Two mornings later, after the Sabbath and before the brothers set out for their fishing grounds, Jeshua thanked them for their hospitality and made to return to Nazareth. They were insistent that he should regard them as his 'lakeside family', staying with them whenever his work allowed and Jeshua felt the adoption in their warmth, the children clambering about the knees of their young 'uncle.' Zacharias insisted on seeing Jeshua on his way and insisted also that they begin by going once more to the synagogue. He held Jeshua's arm as they crossed the outer colonnaded court and drew him a little aside from the central hall of worship. There, above the door-lintel and a few handspans to the left was a 'Menorah' deeply incised into the surface; so lively was the carving and the surface of the stone, that Jeshua almost felt the movement above the branches, as though seven candles flickered in their holders. Without comment Zacharias led him across the doorway to the corresponding space to the right of the lintel. The carving here puzzled Jeshua – a laurel wreath surrounding a scallop-shell. Zacharias replied to the puzzled look.

'It's a Gentile symbol but it doesn't offend us. It's the most coveted award of a Roman centurion, not just for bravery in battle but for saving the life of a superior officer,' and then, in an old man's flight of fancy, 'I like to think that they share the courage of Gideon and of David and that it shines in the light of the Menorah.' No further explanation was needed and here, in the Gentile court the carved award seemed like the signature of a donor, placed humbly a little aside from the main import of the building.

An hour or two later Jeshua was well on his way, first southward following the bend of the lake with its chaplet of cities and then striking westward to the high country. He planned the journey to take three days, sleeping where he could find a grove or a sycamore at night and allowing the days to unravel these experiences of five days at the lake. For in the Gentile world of business and of Roman occupation, shot through with Galilean labour in the waters of the lake, Jeshua had caught the full import, not of an alien world but of the world of Nazareth. Until now it had been the air he breathed, the earth he walked and the family he accepted without questioning. Now, in the double impact of the fisher family and the Roman, an experience which seemed to have lasted not days but years and to have penetrated his being, he stood back from Nazareth, from the labour, the worship and the solitary prayer and saw them, mint-new, with his unaccustomed, adult eyes. And through all this he marvelled each day at the fact that an alien soldier had drawn from him the conscious, humble certainty of his union with 'his Father'. Nazareth would not again be quite the same.

NINE

Jeshua was not to be allowed to settle to the old rhythm in his home.

103

Things were changing in Nazareth, indeed in Galilee, and under the alien influences there simmered under the surface a ferment of resentment, of wounded pride and livid scars of old humiliations. The people were alienated from Judah, while still feeling the tug of Jerusalem and the power of the old dream, a united people; they were more powerfully alienated from the Roman occupation, fear and disgust uniting to withdraw them from all but accidental or unavoidable contact. Each hill town and village became an emotional fortress, a place of instinctive withdrawal.

But even in these fastnesses there was a perpetual and restless insecurity; for they were not at unity among themselves. Some sought escape from their spiritual and emotional plight in dreams of another Maccabean revolt, a purging by blood of the desecrating aliens; others saw no redemption save in spiritual withdrawal, a holiness achieved in solitude, an inward vision fostered by desert memory. Whether by blood or prayer, purgation was their end and while the greater number of Galileans saw nothing but futility in both visions, their resolution, whether in strife or calm, was beyond their power; Galilee simmered in a sultry unease.

All this for Jeshua was inescapable. The spell of Capernaum remained upon him, a spell compounded of memories of a strange and exhilarating rural life, in which citrus scents, the new pungency of plants not known in the uplands, set his senses alert in ways he had never known in the quieter harmonies of Nazareth, its slopes and less fertile fields. And he was disturbed by the sights and sounds of the inland sea, the faint odour of fish-scales, the pungency of smoked and salted catches; he heard in the quiet night the strange sounds of wave-lapping, the cries of the fishermen, his new 'family' with the unfamiliar dialect. But above all Capernaum brooded over him with memories of Justus, the courteous-voiced Spaniard, his host at the lake-side, ruefully, perhaps tragically, recalling what might have been the destiny of a Roman-Iberian in the imperial service. And over all, there loomed the glory of the synagogue, splendid in a way that raised in Jeshua both assent and rejection – welcoming the glory accorded to Jahweh, withdrawing from an elaboration which accorded ill with his more austere vision. All this set his memories in turmoil and all his thoughts revolved about that enigmatic man who had fallen, reached authority, worn the insignia of heroism and 'built for us our synagogue.' The foundations of thought for Jeshua had shifted.

They were to be shaken again by two encounters in which Lazar was involved. Dusk had halted work in Nazareth one evening, when a message was brought to Jeshua from the rabbi's house: would Jeshua like to meet two of Lazar's friends who had called on him as they passed through Galilee? Jeshua walked across the space between their two homes in the last flush of sunset and wondered which of the rarely-mentioned friends of the rabbi had called upon him in this unexpected way. As he stood in the doorway, before greetings could be exchanged, Jeshua saw in the low lamp-light, three stools drawn about the table, some simple dishes for the evening meal set about a strange object, a dagger which gleamed, part-drawn from its sheath.

'This is Jacob ben Judas and his young friend, Simon.'

'Shalom.'

'Shalom aleychem.'

The dagger was explained, for Jacob son of 'Judas the Galilean' had inherited from his rebel father the leadership of the Zealot cause, a revival of the Maccabean temper and determined ends; Simon was younger and though subordinate, was clearly, by the fine-drawn athleticism of his figure and the brooding but restless eyes, also a zealot by conviction.

'Before you came, Jeshua, it seemed right that weapons should be set aside for the moment and visible under our eyes.' It was the strangest speech Jeshua had heard from the mouth of Lazar, and he swiftly probed its implication, seeking warning, trepidation, the hint of a threatened danger; but Lazar's eyes were unclouded, his mouth restless with a half-smile.

'We look for men of substance and of thought to be one with us.' Jacob was direct, even abrupt in his denial of any courteous amenity in their conversation. 'We look for those whose blood and mind are affronted by our wrongs and will take up the dagger with us.'

Simon was still and alert, looking for, but only half-expecting, a response from Jeshua.

'For whom is the dagger's point intended?' The tone had a touch of banter in the question but Jeshua's eyes were direct and still.

'For Herodians and those who deny our sacred traditions. And above all for the polluting Romans.'

Jeshua appeared in his stillness to look inward rather than at the two whose hands so restlessly spoke of their turmoil.

'And you speak of war against these enemies? Two such strangely assorted enemies; to fight the Herodians would seem to be to be hurling sticks at clouds of flies or to try to disperse a mist with dish-clouts. The Romans are another matter. I have only once seen them march, fully armed and in battle-readiness. They were more palpable than the Herodians and the daggers would scarcely get in range of the legions.'

Lazar smiled more openly as he heard for the first time a new tone, an unaccustomed authority in Jeshua's voice, an authority all the more assertive for the irony in which it was shown. About the little table in the uncertain light of evening a struggle without aggression, without even antagonism, seemed to be moving between forces who sought understanding, like wrestlers looking for a hand-hold.

'Galilee is unique.' Jacob was urgent in his plea. 'Its valleys are inaccessible in their furthest reaches, with rock-falls and caves, narrow wadis and defiles and it has remained uncontaminated, a proud people with a long history. Mountain people have always made the fighters of resistance.'

He paused to see the effect of his argument on the young Galilean; Jeshua's eyes, his quiet hands, his courteously enquiring look told Jacob nothing.

'And we command from our heights the vital roads, west to east from the coast to Capernaum, north and south to Jerusalem itself. As a handful can hold a pass, so can our men cripple those routes if we are determined.'

Jeshua's eyes were still gently questioning. 'And even these handfuls – have you them in sufficient numbers? The valleys are many to be held by few and the Romans have fought in other terrains like this one of Galilee. Have you even as many as Judas' – he paused with the briefest ironic inflection which the son of Judas picked up like an adversary – 'Judas the Maccabean led to the assault on Jerusalem?'

'As many, and as valiant.'

'And can you win a war like this? I see you strike and cripple a detachment, disconcert even a century of men and then scurry back to your fastnesses. I grant you courage and the agility of goats, where Rome sends men with towers and machines. You will disconcert the legions – singly – but legion will come upon legion, troop upon troop and still like goats you will run to your fastnesses and with your dagger-pricking draw blood. But can you win this war? Will they retreat? Will Rome give up one of its possessions and that one an important link on its way about the Great Sea? For how many years will you sustain this blood-letting?'

Jacob was moved between anger and conviction and Simon looked disconcerted by the sharp exchanges. With his heart he swayed to Jacob; with the cool argument of his mind he was moved by Jeshua's conviction, his quiet authority.

'We can be decades-long a thorn in Rome's side, a galling of her pride.' Jacob's conviction was unabated.

'And we can unite Judah and Israel by our courage; like the Maccabees we can bring hope of release. In Jahweh's own time we can truly free Jerusalem and cleanse it, from treacherous Jew and desecrating Roman.'

'There is a city called Rome at the core of our world; it is at the heart of seas, roads, laws and legions. Its rulers and servants are not – most of them – brutal and unfeeling. They, like us, have a dream of law.' The three men looked at him as at a total stranger and Lazar bewilderedly marvelled at the new Jeshua, so unlike anyone he had known from childhood.

'We are a minute part of this city's empire; as we were to Egypt, to Babylon, so we are now to Rome, a halting-place on the march east and south.'

'But Egypt gave up her slaves, Babylon loosed her grip.'

'And Egypt, Babylon are not Rome! Here we find no softness, no mere indulgence. Their very cruelty, yes, even crucifixion, has an end in view and it's not ignoble. They have no Torah but they love Justice and in Caesar's mind, to love Justice is greater than to do justly and certainly greater than to love mercy. Caesar walks humbly with no-one, not even his Gods.'

'Are you then a traitor? Would you submit to Rome and work with her, that you speak so warmly of her Justice?' Simon was breathless with unbelief, not reproaching but requiring a truth.

'I would give to Caesar perhaps less than you and Jacob. You at least grant him the dignity of an enemy, one with whom you would fight with the weapons to your hand.' Jeshua touched lightly the hilt of the dagger, turned it until its sheathed point lay idly between the two Zealots.

'And in according them the dignity of enemies, when they are but men like you, you raise them to a power they don't merit. It would be a sin against our manhood, against Torah, against Adonai, to condemn our people to massacre spread over the years. The sword can never solve dilemmas nor enforce ideas. Palpable power has no authority over the impalpable, the unseen truth. The things of God are of the spirit and the spiritual cannot be pierced and held on the sword's point.'

Resonances over the ages gave to Jeshua's words a conviction that momentarily deflected the bitter indignation of Jacob whose violence was but two generations deep. 'We need Moses, David and all who fought with Maccabaeus. Who is this man to be? Who will rise in their place, in their way?'

Simon stirred to the last beseeching plea of Jacob, held Jeshua's eyes with his own tormented demand for someone who could command his will, shape the ways of his life. The words were barely above a whisper but their agonised pleading reverberated in the little room:

'We need Elijah – Messiah!'

Heavily, and turning his eyes away, Jeshua replied: 'I am not so called; that is not my name.'

The contest of wills was over and Jeshua turned to the doorway. As he reached the lintel he turned, the gravity of his eyes softened into a smile.

'Shalom!' he said.

From Jacob and from Simon there was no response; the eyes of neither could meet Lazar's nor his theirs.

TEN

The familiar way seemed alien as Jeshua walked the old path out of Nazareth to the uplands. In the heat of the day the scents from the herbage had been overpowering and confused; now at the point of sunset the gentler heat gave each perfume its particular sharp clarity. As his feet trod the stunted sage brush and his feet found the delicate leaves of young thyme, the scent rose, not heavily but comforting. He chose a boulder which would give him his last sight of the sun, touched, bisected and then swallowed by the horizon. He needed the darkness and the stillness, for the clash with the Zealots, though his mind was fortified by his own resolution, had left his emotions in turmoil. The evening brought its comforting ritual duty but on this evening it was no formal rite:

'Hear – the Lord your God – with all your heart.'

The phrases asserted their old authority, standing out from the familiar sentences with a clarity of living things. The sky was still blue with evening, the west stained as the clouds caught light beneath, darkness above. The stars could scarcely penetrate the remnants of light when almost directly overhead a 'falling star' cut its arc through the heavens to be drowned westward in the cloud-bank.

'How art thou fallen from heaven,

O Lucifer, son of the morning.

How art thou cut down to the ground.'

Isaiah's triumph came instinctively to his lips, to be spoken aloud with a hint of self-parody. For the star had come too opportunily into the evening air, nature's too easy resolution of a conflict which was, now, for Jeshua an immediate urgency bearing in on him. The signs and symbols of the heavens were no part of his conflict; the verities which clashed in his mind after the struggle with Jacob ben Judas were immediate and earthly – Law, Power, Love, and their several weapons: was there a reconciliation of the conflict for him which Israel and Judah had failed to resolve over long ages of suffering?

Quietly gathering himself, in the familiar contemplative discipline, he called before his mind the heroic stature of those from old time who could now speak to his confused debate. Over the desert ways he was one with Abraham; at his side, as the herdsman made camp and the flocks moved to the well-heads, Jeshua grasped at his vision, the longing for a land where a deeper truth than he had known could be found and lived with. The command was one which Jeshua had already faced:

'Get thee out of thy country
    and from thy kindred,
    and thou shalt be a blessing.'

The 'new land' for the 'great nation' lay now before Jeshua's eyes. And he remembered Lot; and the descent into Egypt, and the binding of Isaac. Was this figure from old time to be the pattern of action in this present age? What fragment of Abraham was to be held and cherished?

He walked with Moses, knew the bitterness of his slavery, the darkness of the plagues; he stood before them on Sinai and with sudden clarity heard the words of the Law. And as these words faded, he stood at his side on the tragic Nebo heights, the mountain of the uncompleted vision.

And David; and Elijah; and Judas – with every recalling, at each resurrection of the heroic history, Jeshua heard the clash of arms, the vision of worship denied, its words quenched in the cries of the dying. And the hopelessness of exile, the waters of Babylon more bitter than the waters of Marah. To what end was this history? What law of growth or compassion governed its windings?

In the still depth of his meditation there was no fear and certainly no frenzy. The disciplined thought focussed with clarity on the objects sanctified by the history: the ark of the covenant, the stones of the Temple, the evening candle and the Sabbath light. As each hallow stood clear in his mind, he rose from his boulder and returned to Nazareth. Lazar stood in the doorway, beckoning, evidently waiting for his return. There was clearly to be another encounter.

Lazar's guest this time was no Zealot. The calm authority, the stature even in great old age, the garments, all proclaimed one of the Hasidim, gifted, withdrawn, yet powerful in their prophetic speech and fearless in any company.

'Jeshua! We have not met before, though Lazar has spoken so long and – shall I say? – boastingly of his 'son' that I know you in all your ways. You have walked with those of old time this night.'

Jeshua smiled his response, the prophetic insight causing him no surprise. 'But with whom should I continue to walk? Will it be to Sinai, to Nebo, to fulfil the Law? Must it be to Sion to cleanse the Temple? to Carmel to crush the lie? What mountain must I climb and to what end?'

The Hasid's reply was sonorous and disconcerting. 'I have words to tell you, not my own. Hear the words of the Lord:

> Hear the Law: 'And Aaron shall lay both his
> hands on the head of the live goat and confess
> over him all Israel's sins and shall send him
> into the wilderness.'
> Hear the prophet: 'All we like sheep have gone
> astray and the Lord hath laid on him the iniquity
> of us all."

The words echoed about Lazar's home and in the succeeding silence Jeshua held the Hasid's gaze as though commanding him to resume the prophecy. The response seemed drawn, reluctantly from the old man but it was an assured declaration, as the sentences, spaced and emphatic, laid their burden on the young man.

> He is despised and rejected of men
> He was despised and we esteemed him not

> But he was wounded for our transgressions,
> He was bruised for our iniquities;
> The chastisement of our peace was upon him;
> And with his stripes we are healed.

'Do you speak these words to me?'

'You have borne all these things in your mind, as you communed with Justus by the lakeside, as you clashed with Jacob and with Simon at this hearth. And you have walked with those of old time to seek your way in theirs. But your way is to be your way. Before Elijah, before David, before Moses, before our father Abraham, your way was clear. And one, our prophet Isaiah, has spoken so openly to you and perhaps to you alone:

> He had done no violence
> Neither was any deceit in his mouth
> Yet it pleased the Lord to bruise him.

That bruising you, Jeshua, will know, even to its end.'

The Hasid's voice fell and his hands rested lightly for a moment on the young shoulders. With no further words spoken, Jeshua returned to his own hearth.

ELEVEN

For many weeks it had been clear to the people of Nazareth that they would not long have Lazar as their rabbi. The old man had spent himself and was now increasingly torn by the rumours and fears that drifted like mists about the valleys of Galilee. He had presided for two generations over the births and deaths, the feasts and celebrations, the sins and atonements of his humble people. More than all the families of Nazareth, Jeshua was aware of the frail and tremulous clasp with which Lazar sought to hold to life.

'There will be few new scrolls from his hand,' he said to Joseph as they looked across to Lazar's home. Joseph gave no reply and in his silence he remembered the many years since he and Lazar had come together to this upland home, Lazar from the dignity of Jerusalem, Joseph from a neighbouring township where he had learnt his trade. With the death of Lazar, he anticipated the death of much that was the heart of Nazareth.

Jeshua crossed the small space that separated his home from that of Lazar, and when he had reached the threshold, Martha, who prepared his meagre meals, rose from the fireside and left them alone. Lazar was lying on rugs near the hearth and Jeshua heard the almost inaudible words he slowly spoke, the merest whisper of a synagogue chant.

'O may my death be an atonement
    for all my sins
    Make known to me the path of life;
    In thy presence is fullness of joy;
    At thy right hand, bless for evermore.'

Jeshua recognised the words, the preparation and confession at the approach of death. Lazar seemed to gather himself for a further prayer:

'Into thy hands I commend my spirit'
and in the pause, at his failing voice, Jeshua responded,

'For thou hast redeemed me,
    O Lord thou God of truth'
    'Amen.'
    'And Amen.'

Jeshua remained silent, waiting for the resumption of the healing, so blessed ritual. After some minutes and with a conscious gathering of strength, the words came:

'The Lord reigneth;
    The Lord hath reigned;
    The Lord shall reign for ever and ever.'

Jeshua took up the refrain, taking Lazar by the hand.

'Blessed be his name
    Whose glorious kingdom

Is for ever and ever.'
Lazar's breathing was now scarcely perceptible but his lips moved again:

'Hear, O Israel' and breathed like a sigh, the prayer left to be closed by Jeshua:

'The Lord our God, the Lord is One
      The Lord is our God, the Lord alone.'

Jeshua folded the gentle old hands on Lazar's breast, called quietly to Martha and walked across to his home. He knew in the quiet night that a root had been severed. Nazareth seemed to recede into the past.

Jeshua was now in his twenty-sixth year and the family was aware of a new tension in their affairs. Day by day there was little but happiness. Mary, still young and clear-eyed, preserved a domestic harmony in which Miriam, about to be married, took her quiet and competent role; the men conducted an ever more complex business; Joseph was the acknowledged patriarch of the little town, consulted on all civic matters and with a temperate judgment directing its affairs in troubled times. Jeshua saw with some concern that prosperity brought some ostentation and neighbourly competition to the town; houses were to be larger with furniture almost Roman in its luxury. Jeshua resisted in his quiet way but Jacob his brother next in age, was more prepared to go along with the fashion, accepting the commissions but uneasily aware that Jeshua, who should have been taking over the direction of affairs from the ageing Joseph, appeared on the contrary to be withdrawing from the craft and more and more into himself. The traditional pieces were still his concern, the comely furniture and the planning of some of the houses; by the balance and harmony of both, the furniture fitting the houses as though from long intention and use, his hand and eye could be detected in their complete assurance. But this was instinct over the years; his eyes were often elsewhere, brooding over a different, perhaps more disquieting landscape.

One morning a little after sunrise, he took Jacob aside into the quiet of their vine-arbour. Jacob was aware that at least a minor crisis had been reached, as Jeshua, silent and with his clasped hands tight between his knees, waited for the opening into his brother's mind.

'Jacob, you work now with all assurance and I've watched over these last months not only your own craftsman's maturity but the happy way you direct our brothers. As their father ages and leaves more and more to us, so the young ones look ever more to you for their direction.'

Jacob was uneasy and deprecating. 'Your hands have a greater skill than ours and your eye is much the most sure among us. Things grow under your hands like living things, while we struggle to perfect our skills.'

'You know I love the work. To see the grain in the wood obey my will, to feel living stone almost shape itself under the iron, few things can be more satisfying. But I am really asking you for a brief release, your assurance that if I leave Nazareth for a week or two, you won't miss me too greatly, be too burdened by the work. The weeks ahead are usually our quietest time.' There was a youthful pleading in his voice and his eyes asked more than his words. It seemed to be he who was the younger brother, as Jacob weighed the implications of Jeshua's request.

'You'll come back?' The question was peremptory, needing urgent assurance that the family was not being torn apart.

'I'll come back.'

'But for how long and with what real wish to be still one with us?'

'That must be as our Father wills, Jacob.' It was a

confounding answer for his younger brother and in Jeshua's brooding voice and quiet tone, scarcely above a whisper, he detected an ambiguity beyond his comprehension.

The next few days marked a return to their normal routine of working. They were not pressed for labouring time and they all worked steadily within themselves; Jeshua appeared to Jacob to have relaxed again into their routine. But the tranquil days were not to last. Late one afternoon, after the sun's heat and unbroken attention to a job of work had sapped his strength, Joseph found himself levering a lintel stone which was beyond his strength. The sons were not within calling and he found himself pinned to the ground, dangerously crushed by the rock. Jeshua heard his cry, raised the stone and carried his father to the warmth of the hearth, leaving him to the skill of Mary and Miriam. The days passed heavily, with little sign of returning strength and on the seventh day following Joseph died.

The mourning in Nazareth was deep and felt by everyone. There was scarcely a house which had not known the old man's labour and skill. Would Jeshua now replace him and become over the years the township's patriarch?

The answer came disconcertingly a very few weeks later. There had appeared no outward sign of disharmony in the family and indeed the tranquillity of Miriam at the well and of Jacob in his workshop denied any possibility of a rift in their relationships. It was the greater shock to his neighbours when one or two of them in the fields saw Jeshua walk swiftly away to the southerly pass in the hills, his clothes girded as for a long journey.

The way lay obliquely towards the Jordan valley. An eagle soaring in its wide arcs above Galilee might – if it cared to observe human vagaries – have wondered at the meandering course. It was to take Jeshua northward, southward, then across Jordan into desert country and

117

again southward to the strange, sculptured landscape west of Jordan. The eagle – granted contemplation – would have seen no pattern or purpose in these meanderings. At a brisk human pace they would take no more than the days between sabbath and sabbath; in Jeshua's purpose they traversed three sabbaths.

It was a set purpose, ultimately determined by dying words of Joseph, but formed as a necessity for long months before. The death of Joseph had been a little death for Jeshua, the termination of a patient apprenticeship. The family had withdrawn as if acknowledging that speech between the two had been private beyond their accustomed intimacy. Now, as he rested in the noon-day heat, on the foothpath to Nain, the words of the dying man came vividly back.

'What have I to bequeath to you, Jeshua? You are the finest craftsman in Galilee and your life lies richly before you; but you have rejected it in your soul?' It was barely a question, rather the insight of deep affection, an acceptance of an inevitable change. Jeshua needed to make no reply beyond the gentle assurance of his presence until death.

'Our names, Jeshua, Joseph, they are like trumpet-calls'; there was a wry smile as he whispered these resonances but he gathered himself in his last pride.

'My descent, so proud – listen to it. In my blood bequeathed to you runs the history of our people, the history of the acts of God. Hold that tradition, Jeshua, make it live.'

'But what if it has hardened like a husk-shell from which no root, no blade may shoot? All about us I see dry bones and I cry within myself – and with no prophet's answer, 'can these bones live?''

'You leaned on Lazar and he on you but before his death you were troubled.'

'You know that at his hearth I had two such strange meetings. Harsh men of the dagger confronted me with action, demanding the 'zeal of my father's house.' But a few days later an aged saint, tranquil in his soul, pointed the way of inward thought, the still life withdrawn. I can follow neither way, neither the bitter satisfaction of blows struck, nor the quiet of a still pool, whose current is deeply hidden.' Jeshua's voice faltered as he sought words which would penetrate the failing senses of Joseph.

'Some action I must know, but it won't be the action of the workshop; that you no longer need bequeath me, for Jacob is as capable as I of following the work.'

Joseph gathered his failing strength for one more probing test, a question he had not ventured to ask until this final moment:

'Why have you not married? Is the line, the proud tradition to be broken?'

'I have loved but without need of possession; I shall always love but in freedom from desire.'

There was little more between them; the quiet closing of Joseph's eyes, the softly drawn, last sighing breath was like an after-dinner sleep. Now, on the roadside, as Jeshua recalled and cherished the words, he knew they were not matters for mourning or tears. Without Lazar, without Joseph, Nazareth was no longer the centre.

Now the way was clear for these next days: a journey back through time to those places where life had come to a focus, where his people, in crisis, had known that history could never be denied in that place. And as he pursued each revelation, Jeshua determined to test it, question it and perhaps confirm and take it to himself – and this could be done only in the wilderness, the astringent desert. Here alone was the ancient proving-ground of prophecy the testing place of any vocation. Here the irrelevant is burned away, the excess load discarded. Men are here seen as men to be understood and God seen face to face, His words heeded.

He was not yet out of the fertile lands and as he looked at the ripening grapes at that most magical turning-point where acid green turns and flushes towards dark ruby, thoughts of the harsh hoeing and pruning which made this transformation possible, stretched his mind back to the beginning. With a curious sense of living in both eras, of the toilsome present and that paradise which is the craving at the heart of all dream, he followed his own thought of perfection, of the garden 'eastward in Eden', as though his Father had wished to isolate even the perfection of paradise and present man with its quintessence; of the vineyard truly tilled which all prophets deemed the image of the Kingdom of God; of dawn and sunset, the echo of the morning and the evening of the first day and the feeling in his own heart and mind that he had known them to be 'very good.' And Eve was there, the lovely, the fallen, the first flawed pattern of the perfect woman 'whose price is above rubies.'

Beyond Nain a sharp ridge of high ground gave him a vista north and south. They were dominated by two peaks, Tabor to the north and Gilboa to the south. After the meditation on paradise, these mountains held a sour aftertaste. The violence of Deborah, the violence of Jael and the bloody death of Sisera brooded over Tabor and its pollution became not visible but audible in the triumphant song of Deborah. Jeshua rehearsed the exultant words and his throat contracted in pain as the God of Israel was involved in the massacre.

Lord, when thou wentest out of Seir,
When thou marchest out of the field of Edom,
The earth trembled and the heavens dropped.

The chariots, the spears, the swords, the bizarre death by a nail through the temple, all those he felt in his flesh along his nerves and he turned in a rare disgust to gaze southward.

Southward his eyes halted on Gilboa, yet again a place of blood. Was no mountain to be a protective place, a refuge? For here a king had died, the first majesty of his people, God's vice-gerent on earth. And Saul was to die on Gilboa in a tragic company,

> and his three sons and his armourbearer
> and all his men, that same day together.

'Saul and all his men;' even in death they were pursued to degradation:

> And they cut off his head and stripped off his armour
> And they put his armour in the house of Ashtaroth,
> And they fastened his body to the wall of Beth-shean.

Which was the more powerful in obscenity, the triumphant poetry of Deborah or the enacted spoliation of a king? Jeshua felt the desecration in his limbs and in the shelter of a small grove composed himself to sleep, a rest broken by the nightmare knowledge of depravity in all the soil of his country.

For the next two days he made an uncomfortable journey by paths through the rankness of the Jordan valley. The heat was oppressive and dank and the flies a restless torment. But at the end of the second day he reached Bethabara and the shallow ford across the Jordan and went with relief into the Peraean desert ways.

Jeshua's aim after Bethabara was to avoid habitation, take a wide sweep through the rocky desert and approach Mount Nebo towards its eastern face. The land was for the greater part arid, with the occasional fertile valley like a ribbon of green through the red-yellow rock. Each upland was sculptured both by the fissuring of weather and by the sand-blasting of the winds from the east. Though rock edges were blunted by the wind-swept erosion, each great bluff or isolated rock mass seemed fashioned to be the ornament of a giant's landscape; it forbade any scale that was merely human. Jeshua moved, a stranger, through the forbidding country; he was now in the 'wasteland,' 'the place of desolation.' In the shadow of a wadi he saw the occasional solitary wild goat, a dark and elegant silhouette against the bare rock, but for the most part of the journey he was alone. There was no need to pause for meditation; the steady rhythm of his walking showed his purpose. For this too, even in its cheerless desolation, was his Father's land and the brief halting-places for rest or a little food were enough to recall the presence.

After the day's hard journey he was east of Nebo and looking towards the sunset saw it fiery below the mountain ridge. It was time for sleep and a stunted grove gave sufficient shelter.

With the dawn he moved towards Nebo, Moses's trail. Behind him he felt the press of the multitude, the slaves of Egypt who for forty years had made the testing journey to this arid border. Their desperation, their hope, their fear of the unknown land before them, was a palpable presence at his back and he was glad to shift his consciousness to the solitary figure on the track before him. His young manhood was at odds with the stumbling and mortified old age ahead of him. Moses, aged, the vision still burning, was stumbling to the last humiliated ascent. The sight was almost physical and Jeshua felt a son's instinct to take the patriarch's arm, put his hand about his shoulders; but this, over all the ages, would have been an intrusion, a grossness as the feeble body gathered itself for its last conquest of many.

Jeshua struck obliquely across the face of Nebo, taking wadis and defiles in his way to the summit. As he mounted to the small plateau he felt the brief breath of a westerly breeze which tempered the heat of the sun at his back. The final crest of Pisgah lay before him. He felt the presence of Moses at his side but as he reached the highest rock of the ascent, the vision faded and he carried in himself the patriarch's vision.

Confronting him was the solemn panorama. The words of the scroll which more than any other rejoiced his mind, came with an audible echo to his ears:

This is the land which I sware unto Abraham,
    unto Isaac and unto Jacob, saying:
    I will give it unto thy seed.

There before him was that land. Immediately below him and seeming within touching distance was the plain of the valley of Jericho, 'the city of palm trees' and a little to its left and in the middle distance, the slopes of Sion, the city of David. The slightest turn of his eyes southwards compassed the arid wilderness with the valley and plateau of Qumran at its border and beyond and to the far south the still and desolate beauty of the Dead Sea, its shores compassed by the gleaming salt statuary, monuments of death. A break in the rocks, tumbled but smoothed by erosion to a simulation of petrified waves, showed him the rocks and fissures which hid the caves of Engedi, David's sanctuary beyond the featureless waste.

The landscape, alive with centuries of conflict, shimmered almost into oblivion in the heat of noon and once more, palpably at his side, Jeshua felt the presence of Moses's longing. The law and the dictates of Jahweh were far behind him, the vast wanderings separating him from the times when, in a fearful glory he had walked with God. Now, facing westward to the land denied him, there was the after-glow of a radiance, a tension in the gaze, a craving in the clasped hands. What Pisgah-sight of a withheld promise could bring this glow, this transfiguration? Not for Moses the exultant cry that all was finished, brought to its epic conclusion. Death for him meant a broken artifact, a vision shattered into darkness but Jeshua felt in his own sinews and nerves the majestic beat of the law created, a people redeemed and a land open and craving fulfilment. It was right that there should be no grave at which to lament; this patriarch was beyond the reach of mourning.

TWELVE

Jeshua's return to the Jordan valley was more direct and with a new assurance in his step. The ascent of Nebo had meant the resolution of so many conflicts, the acceptance of the unfulfilled vision, tragic death on the brink of entry to the destined homeland, the final loneliness of death which could be shared with no one. Lazar had died beloved, Joseph had died in the fulness of honoured years, in the knowledge that the family about his bed were the heart of Nazareth. But Moses was of that small company of those who traversed unexplored frontiers; alone in the desert where the bush blazed with strange promise, alone on Sinai as the earth trembled with the onset of the Voice, alone in the desperate decisions of the desert, four decades of the strength-sapping exercise of authority. The loneliness of the last ascent, the conquest of Nebo as the body failed, was no new experience. Egypt and the desert had hardened his body and honed his temper to the finest edge. But Jeshua knew as he traversed the way with him, that mere endurance, the stoical determination to face the solitary end, is a bitter draught at the close of life. In fellowship with Moses the frontier of death's dominion had been approached by Jeshua and, in the sensitivity which had set him apart from so many of his fellows, he had tasted with Moses the awe of death itself. Overarching this strange encounter was another surety which came to him with familiar tones: 'Thou shalt love; thou shalt not transgress.' Torah was there to be cherished.

Throughout the return journey to Nazareth the certainty of a dual perspective, living at once in time and out of time, accompanied every turn of his way. In a calculated testing of his intuition that every place held firmly the joys and tragedies of all past history, he pursued not the shortest routes but those which took him to the sacred places and into the heart of Samaria, the suspicious and hostile country, to Sychar, where Jacob's well still yielded sweet water. Then north to Dothan, where Joseph was sold into his Egyptian captivity and became, in the providential shaping of sin, the salvation of his people.

At the eve of Sabbath he entered Nazareth, every doorway, every shadowed courtyard seen with the clarity of his new insights. The exploration had been into his people's history, into the land where blood had been as potent as rain in setting the texture of the soil; the exploration had been more poignantly into his own being, and into the years that lay ahead. That way was now clear.

The demands of the home at Nazareth became urgent. The death of Joseph had shaken Jacob's security which could be aggressive so long as the ultimate authority was in older hands. Now he turned to Jeshua, uncertain of their relationship. Jeshua, the elder both in skill and assurance, gave no sign of wishing to take over the direction exercized by Joseph. He undertook far more work than hitherto, was imaginative in the design of new homes, determining light, growing plants and the movement of air as the conditions without which his neighbours could know no joy in their homes. The furniture he fashioned had a new delicacy, a simplicity of form which gave each piece a vitality which seemed like another person in the household. Each evening saw him relaxed and spent at the hearth, the fulfilled weariness of the craftsman. But with all this creative vigour he showed no sign of wishing to direct, to command, allowing the family to shape its own being and allowing the future for them to emerge in its own time.

The years, three of them, passed in this stillness of waiting. Jacob also seemed determined to wait on his work, to pursue the daily demands of the community and to make no assertive overtures to his elder brother. But there was a latent unease in his waiting, an anxiety as of one looking over his shoulder for direction in a strange path.

The crisis came after Passover. The family had kept the feast with greater joy than they had known since the death of Joseph and it seemed to Jacob and Mary that Jeshua had a greater, more contained security than during the earlier months after his return. Then one evening, Jeshua suggested to Jacob a walk to the hill spur in the direction of Capernaum. For half an hour they went in easy silence and then sat to rest in the dying warmth of the day. A wide panorama opened before them, seemingly sketched in a near-monochrome. No detail obtruded but the pattern of hills and valleys opened out as though newly fashioned for their pleasure.

'A fair country and yet stirring like leavened dough.' Jeshua's voice was brooding, with intense unhappiness in its undertone; Jacob watched him, uncomprehending – abstraction was not the temper of his mind, more accustomed to the measuring and fitting of material things.

'There is a wildness here below the surface which threatens strife. We are so prone to strife, so accustomed to suffering. The growth about us, the rhythm of seedtime and harvest, of barn and winepress, for many it suffices and life appears ordered, so ordinary and of such happiness – of children at the hearth and old men folding their hands in the corner. But there is such truth in the prophet Joel:

Your old men shall dream dreams,
    Your young men shall see visions
and there is truth, a bitter truth in that saying of old,
    Where there is no vision the people perish.
The old men dream dreams in the autumn of their lives,
dreams of what might have been, and fear the winter of
their lives where even the dreams fade to an uneasy
memory. But the young men -' Jeshua turned to Jacob in
all the urgency of youthful manhood, to be met with the
same, almost sullen incomprehension.

'The young men have, each one, their vision and the
stirring in their blood is perilous. They want, they crave,
but don't know where the craving leads them. In my
wanderings in those weeks away from our home, I tested
in my own body some of these visions of old times. We
have so often had the brightness of great vision and what
has been its end?

'Abraham had his sight of God's will and it drove him to
the desert ways, drove him and his family with no direction but the stars to find a land. And what did he find?
Austere uplands where he and his kin were to live in
purity; and lush lowlands where Lot was to know corrupt-
ing prosperity.

'And Moses heard the Voice; it told of Torah and a
destiny which was to lead to a paradise for his people, it
led him to the bitter vision of Nebo, the shattered end of
his dream. And for his people it led to the scattering of the
tribes, to Philistine wars and a wasted land.

'And David pursued his shepherd visions, leading his
people to a sanctuary for the Most High. And on Sion he
knew his frustrated vision, his unfitness to build a Temple
for the Ark of God.

'And so down the ages. Why should I repeat them to
you, Jacob, who Sabbath after Sabbath have bowed your
head as the scroll was drawn from the Ark and then

listened to the so customary story – noble vision conceived and pursued and in the end frustrated.'

There was no response from Jacob; what response could there be, in his complete ignorance of Jeshua's passion, unmoved by the agony in his elder brother's eyes?

'Now I see and hear them again, a multitude of Abrams, longing for a new land beyond the cleansing desert; I see and hear Moses in their longing for the Law, loved not merely obeyed, and I hear David speaking in their young throats, craving for the peace of Jerusalem, for a sanctuary where God can be worshipped in truth.

'And yet not one of them knows the true desire, the longing hidden in the dumbness of their hearts.

'And I must answer them, purify their vision and fulfil their dream. My Father calls me; dare I deny His voice?'

Jacob was confounded, hearing only rhetoric where Jeshua had spoken with a longing for understanding. 'Where is this taking you, Jeshua? Are you telling me that your duty lies outside Nazareth? Is the home to be mine, the work to be mine, the burden for me alone?'

'When you are clear about me and about you, it will be no burden. You know every stone, every beam, every rush bundle in Nazareth! It will be for you a duty lightly borne.' The words were said with a smile, a total understanding of the younger brother; it was answered with bitterness and a curl of the mouth in malice.

'And you! Are you to be Esau and renounce your birthright? Are you even to be Cain, destroying yourself with your kin? Where is your wild dream to end?'

Jeshua made no reply to the taunt which threatened a break in their former understanding in craft. Without a word he laid his arm lightly about Jacob's shoulder, turned him towards Nazareth, walking swiftly himself into the quiet night.

There were the unhappy farewells; with Mary, silent and contemplative as always, wholly uncomprehending as she watched this so unusual son; with Miriam, who felt for Jeshua not only a sister's love but the intensity of dependence as she remembered over the years his leading her into a creative life; with Jacob and the other brothers who felt their world shifting its foundations.

One last courtesy call had to be made after the neighbours had said their rueful or grudging or deprecating farewells; this was to the new rabbi, Lazar's successor. He could never in fact be wholly a successor to Lazar. Lemuel was a young man, younger than Lazar had ever seemed to Jeshua and he was a diffident man, seemingly destined always to be a rabbi in hidden places. Jeshua walked the familiar path to his home and found Lemuel writing an address he was to give in synagogue at the sabbath.

'You are leaving us. We shall miss you and I especially, for I have looked for your strength and your wisdom in these first years among you. It is already two Passovers, two harvests since I came to Nazareth and I'm as far as ever from understanding this people!' His smile was tentative, wondering if the implied criticism would offend Jeshua. But it was met with a broader smile.

'They are of mankind, Rabbi Lemuel, a garnering of wheat with tares and perhaps the tares not so very many. With Lazar's memory before you, you will find the ground become ever more fruitful.'

They were now seated companionably in the shade of a vine which fell in an unkempt veil from the steps which climbed to the roof. There was silence while Jeshua waited for the question which was clearly struggling for Lemuel's words. At last it came; he spoke with his eyes averted, exploring the corner of the little courtyard.

'You are driven out, Jeshua. What is this force that drives you? It's no enmity in Nazareth; it can't be unhappiness in your work – I have never seen such craftsmanship in wood or stone, no not even in Jerusalem. But I know you are driven out and I wish I knew the compulsion.'

'You know it; you have heard it, rabbi:

Comfort ye my people saith your God.

'It is the Voice, Lemuel. It's sometimes a whisper almost below the tones we can hear; at other times it speaks with the clear voice of the synagogue Torah; and yet again it is a trumpet-call to a battle almost beyond imagining. I hear all three voices and yes, they drive me out.'

'But to what end? You have the wisdom of a pharisee – what a pharisee you would be! Another Hillel – and you have the insight and stillness of the Hasidim and their healing touch. What more can you want in this world that Nazareth can't demand of you?'

'I think perhaps I can tell you if you'll come back with me a long way to those first Days. No living man is without his memory of paradise, his longing to find a garden in Eden. For a little while man and woman lived there content, walking with God and tending without effort a rich beauty beyond the dreams of our countrymen.' For a moment Jeshua seemed remote from Nazareth, his mind moving through the freshness of that dawn, as though it were the living present.

'Then Adam sinned – and he sinned alone, sharing the guilt with but one other and her he loved. Paradise was still fair and fruitful but with this small canker in the midst, concealed. But on a fruitful branch a thorn grew; among the fruits of the meadow the thistles spread. A gentle mist which had always watered the land in stillness, was now a miasma and the two fell sick, in their souls, welcoming the devils into their very being; they were, as we say, 'possessed.'

'Your first parents were no longer alone in their sin. Adam's children sinned together; cities, even villages, became the breeding-places of wickedness, until Sodom and Gomorrah stood blatant and arrogant and the dream of the paradise-garden began to fade; only the cruel desert and the bare uplands with their sheep offered a redemption, a cleansing from these pollutions.'

Lemuel saw that these words were no harsh homily, not even a prophetic utterance; these words were active, creating before Jeshua's eyes the burden of guilt of which he spoke. The customary calm of his eyes was broken as though he were possessed with nightmare.

'You are surprised that I'm driven out? You will labour like Lazar in your chosen vineyard. You will tend and prune and the harvest will be there for the gathering and those young minds will grow, if God wills, into the wisdom of age. Of course we long to save man in the solitary places. But we have also to meet man in the cities, the towns, the hamlets. Here in Nazareth men sin almost alone, the single fall from innocence of the one Adam in paradise. But in the cities – out there in 'the world" – his arm was flung to embrace the Decapolis and southward to Jerusalem itself – 'out there they sin in droves, demented herds before the fall of Sodom. And there are those who love and cherish sin, who crave violence and don't feel besmirched; these would not savour paradise if their return were possible – but they must not be left to hell. And that tells you why I am 'driven out'.'

Lemuel was silenced, having no question that could penetrate a compulsive vision beyond his understanding. In an inherited wisdom he fell back upon ritual words, a prayer, a blessing and an aspiration:

'We will sanctify thy name in the world,
    Even as they sanctify it in the highest heaven'
and Jeshua gravely responded:
'The Lord shall reign for ever,
    Thy God, O Zion unto all generations.'

BOOK TWO

The Wilderness

THIRTEEN

Word of his cousin John ('the Baptiser' they had called him) came only rarely to Nazareth and always with overtones of embarrassment; no family was wholly comfortable in acknowledging such a member, who was an affront to all courteous and civilised behaviour. It was a shame, for were not Zacharias and Elizabeth estimable people, a little stricken in years perhaps, but he still capable of his turn in the Temple offices. And there had been strange tales of her pregnancy, Elizabeth well past the age of child-bearing but the Archangel Gabriel, no less, announcing to a sceptical father that a son would be born. That truly was something to boast about, a credit to any family.

Elizabeth was Mary's cousin and she, now pregnant also, had determined on the journey into the southern hills to see Elizabeth and when she came to the home of Zacharias, little wonder that there was warm greeting and much rejoicing between the two women, so disparate in age and station and yet both so miraculously blessed. Mary, as she reminded her family constantly, had returned to Nazareth in a glow of thanksgiving.

But the outcome had not been satisfactory. From the beginning John had been a wayward child, always odd one out in the little community. He was without pride in his father's calling, speaking (when he came of age to use such language) of the sterile ways of the established religion and advocating rather that penitence for sin be the core of spirituality and poverty its instrument. It was an unquiet household, the old and bewildered parents separated by such a gulf of years and temperament from the fiery son.

Gradually, even more disquieting tales percolated through to Nazareth. It was not just that John struck such strange attitudes in his harangues before his parents; he now began to affect the strangest garb; he not only sounded odd – he was determined to look odd as well. It was such an affectation, this posturing. For by his costume he seemed to be making a declaration of some kind, that for himself at least he had turned the clock back some eight centuries and saw himself as one of the prophets – a hairy cloak, a crude belt to preserve seemliness, rough sandals, little more than leather strips and no great concern that his body and his unkempt hair should be unduly cared for.

These bouts of unseemly holiness were whispered among the people of Nazareth who had known Elizabeth and her aged husband. The rumours were scarcely concealed from Mary who blushed and was silent when the gossip reached the well-head and women rested from their waterpots and refreshed themselves with malice.

Jeshua heard the rumours with a quite different reaction. Though John was only a few months his senior, Jeshua had always thought of him as a somewhat heroic, romantic figure, inhabiting a remote country of his own; the rumours did no more than reinforce his imaginings of John and when the rumours later hardened into precise

facts – of strange and erratic journeys of wayside preach-
ings which were largely invective and denunciation – all
this took shape and focus about a figure who was for
Jeshua increasingly credible and – yes – attractive. Now,
as Jeshua had emotionally detached himself from
Nazareth and was about to do so physically, even more
precise word came of John's activities: that he was now
established near or at the Jordan, that his preaching had a
new and sharper precision, that the enemies of Israel's
spirituality were being identified by name and, most disturbing of all, that he was declaring a revived Messianic
prophecy. This was no new phenomenon. A Messiah was
longed for, one both spiritual and militant who could
focus the twin characteristics of their people, a craving for
holiness and a violent repudiation of oppression. Since
Rome was both heathen and oppressive, a Messiah was
the leader looked for in desperation.

Now it seemed clear to Jeshua and to some of the most
acute observers of John's actions, that the old posturings
were no mere theatricality, that the habit and the words
were a declaration that the age of prophecy must come
again. Now the rumours came to Galilee with convincing
clarity; John had focussed his message upon one prophetic vision, derived from the noblest of the prophets, Isaiah's cry for a preparation towards deliverance:

Prepare ye the way of the Lord;
Make his paths straight.

Moreover the prophecy was framed in what seemed to
John (and in part to Jeshua) as a command to particular
action within an ancient setting; the new prophetic voice
was to be

The voice of one crying *in the wilderness*.

The image of John in Jeshua's mind was now complete;
the eccentric and wayward journeyings, the fearless utterance, the austere clothing and food and the dramatic

setting, the wilderness, birthplace and nurturing of the ancient revelations.

It came to Jeshua as an immediate imperative. The coincidence of their birth, framed in prophecy and in divine intervention, the long hidden years of preparation and now the two crises, Jeshua's in Nazareth and John's at the banks of Jordan, all these made their urgent demand and were the final severance from Galilee.

His route southward was this time swift and purposeful. There were no pauses for contemplation or for exploring the significances of the enshrined history about him. Taking the customary well-worn trade routes, he came in a few days to the wild country west of Jordan. There he paused, taking lodging until rumours of John should again harden into certainty. It seemed that his preaching had still further clarified to a herald's trumpet-call and all the people, baptised and those awaiting the cleansing, were sharp with expectation. 'Repent – He is at hand' – the message seemed unambiguous.

The day had been sultry; in a breathless evening the dark blue clouds with their coppery fringes had ceased their scudding, promising storm but with no refreshment. Jeshua walked towards the river bank and saw at the ford a figure frozen in contemplation. It seemed to deny the need for ease and rest, ignoring the boulders which would at least have relaxed his limbs. John looked fixedly at the nearer hills and repeated monotonously the command to himself: 'Prepare the way; prepare the way; prepare the way.' Jeshua halted some twenty or thirty paces distant. Gently, as if questioning a distraught creature, he called 'John.'

'Lord!' Kinship was blotted out in the smothered ecstasy of the cry. The ravaged face and the feverish eyes softened as he looked at Jeshua and his hands were held out, a plea for fulfilment. Jeshua clasped him by the shoulders and kissed his cheek, leading him to two boulders on which they sat facing each other. There were no greetings, no attempt at bridging gaps in their memory, no renewal of a relationship, which spiritually had never been broken.

'I would be baptised.'

John gazed in wonder and an immediate rejection.

'I baptise *you*?' Haltingly the declaration was formed, 'Unworthy to receive *your* baptism, how could I presume?'

Smiling, Jeshua took John's hand, pressed it to his forehead and made his request, the authority in his words kept to the undertone of his voice.

'Tomorrow, soon after dawn, at the ford. Until then peace be with you, John. This has been long awaited.'

The day dawned clear and fresh. Even as the sun rose over the eastern hills beyond Jordan there were many people already gathered on both banks, waiting for 'the Baptiser'. He strode down swiftly, his austere face emptied of all but the one purpose, to cleanse his people in readiness for the revelation. But some thirty paces from the bank he halted. Waiting in absolute stillness but smiling a welcome, Jeshua stood robed in a simple white tunic which reached to his ankles. John remained silent and the people expectant, waiting for the customary exhortation nonetheless moving and passionate for its daily reiteration.

'Bring forth fruits meet for repentence.
    Say not to yourselves, 'We have Abraham to our
    father;'
    God is able of these stones to raise up
    Children unto Abraham.
    And now also the axe is laid
    To the foot of the tree.'

The rhetoric of accusation had left them relatively unmoved – hadn't they heard it all before? – but the second prophecy, uttered daily as he entered the water at the opening of the ritual had aroused a more intense expectation:

'I baptise you with water unto repentance;
But He that cometh after me
Is mightier than I;
His shoes' latchet I am not worthy to unloose.
He shall baptise you with Holy Spirit and with fire.'

They waited at this dawning in an unusual quiet. The scene was set dramatically, two protagonists facing each other in such contrast – the wild prophetic figure and the still purity of his fellow, matching silence with silence – and they, the people, two choric companies with the water of Jordan flowing between them, the only sound of morning its rippling at the rocky ford. The scene was held for a long silence, almost unbearable in its expectancy; as others came down towards the river on each side, they too were drawn into the same stillness and silence. From this isolation John spoke, the harsh voice at this time almost inaudible.

'Behold the lamb of God;
He takes away the sin of this world.
This is He of whom I spoke
But I knew Him not.'

Tentatively he moved towards Jeshua as Jeshua raised his arms in welcome. When they were within a pace or two, Jeshua turned and stepped into the water up to his thighs. John followed but with hesitation;

'Lord, I am not worthy.'

Jeshua answered,

'Let it be so now – you – and I – must begin to fulfil all righteousness.'

John cupped his hands in the water and poured over the head of Jeshua; and yet it seemed to the people watching that it was not he but Jeshua who was the minister of the ritual. Softly, and with a tenderness which would have amazed the onlookers had they experienced it, John wiped away the waters of Jordan from the forehead and eyes of Jeshua and with no further word, withdrew to the river bank.

As he rose from the water, the green reflections from the bank broken by the ripples in the brilliant sun, out of the cloudless sky came the first mutter of thunder, increasing slowly to a drum-roll climax. Jeshua looked up, his eyes responding to the 'Daughter of the Voice,' and, with no emotion visible to the stricken spectators accepted the titles, 'My son;' 'My son in whom I am well pleased.'

Out of the brilliant light a bird swooped down; its gliding reached the turbulence at the rapids and, with slowing circles above the waters, moved to enclose in its flight the figure still streaming from his shoulders with the waters of baptism. The spectators and John were wholly silent as he strode to the bank, with his hands and a small towel brushed away the water, resumed his tunic and girdle, threw his cloak over his arm and without a word even to his cousin, walked across the bank of Jordan into the wilderness.

FOURTEEN

The Jordan had been crossed ('Out of Egypt, my Son' – the words reverberated) and the dove had moved on the waters and return to Nazareth seemed for the moment a remote need. But there were implications to be thought out, fears to be consulted. The wilderness, even the desert, was a familiar place, its stones, gravel and irritant sand a customary feel to the foot. But at this moment it was no longer a duty to be endured; it was an immediate,

141

an urgent need; its vastness to enclose thought like a tent.

For the first day he walked without hurry, traversing a steep wadi where it gave a little shade and, as the afternoon sun began to be less violent, beginning the ascent, through increasingly large, honey-coloured boulders, towards the distant rock escarpment. It was an arduous stretch of ground and, emotionally drained of feeling, he walked almost mechanically, with little thought and with only the barest attention to the sharper rock splinters at his sandals' fore-edge.

The sun, behind him, stood an hour above the horizon as he reached the rock-face. A herd path had marked the last mile or so and it appeared to point to a defile between two spurs of rock. The sparse wilderness vegetation had dwindled to a few stunted desert tamarisks and buckthorn with blood-droplet fruits. The rock shadows were lengthening and the still air beginning to cool as, beyond the steep defile, a steeper wadi led up to a rock-pile which promised a summit. There he sat with his back to a rock-face westward, watching the last swift minutes of sunset and, a day's march away, the last twilight glimmer of Jordan and its willows in the mist. In the barely perceptible breeze he moved around the pile of boulders, found a sheltered gap in the rock where a few dead and stunted leaves had drifted, gathered his cloak about him and slept.

The timid chirping could scarcely be called a dawn-chorus and no birds were to be seen as the east showed its first cold lemon-tinge of light. Some little distance away there sounded the faintest promise of water; tightening his girdle a little and pulling his cloak about him more securely he scrambled around the bigger boulders and saw below, a thread of water falling from a spring into an almost hidden rock pool, shadowed from the sun on all sides. He bathed his hands and feet, dashed a little water on his face and sat to see the sunrise. Beyond the rock-fall the wilderness shaded into the sand desert and below him the rock splinters threw shadows towards him, blue-tinted at the base and burning into orange as they shimmered with the surface of the sand.

As the rock about him took its first warmth from the sun, he stood to pray:

'May my prayer unto thee, O Lord,
Be in an acceptable time.
O Father, in the abundance of thy loving kindness,
Answer me in the truth of thy salvation.
Magnified and praised be the living God,
He was before all created things.
May it be thy will, O Lord our God,
To lead me in peace, to the haven of my desire.'

He then scooped up from the spring two or three draughts of water in the palms of his hands, took a fragment of barley bread from his pouch and with some half dozen of the meagre and bitter-sweet thorn-fruit, broke his fast.

The day moved quietly as he explored his retreat. The rocky outcrop stood proud of the plain at the end of the lower slopes, by some hundreds of feet. Wind and sand wore and fragmented into sculptured masses the exposed rocks, but the interior edges, where the great boulders protected each other, were sharp-edged and corniced. For some hours in the forenoon he walked the hill, exploring it like a sought tenement, returning at each quest to the waterspring. There he lightly touched his lips with the sweet water. The sun reached its full height and he faced it, seated on a narrow shelf of rock, his back to a fissured slab. The rays glistened on the sand grains in a pocket of flat stones to his left. He sifted some of the grains through his fingers, seeing the liquid fall off them and holding the last fragments in his palm. Each grain had its minute shadow on his skin, its crystalline form; the myriad grains, each its own form, its own structure. Nothing for the moment was as real as that grain of sand, its lonely identity in his hand, reflecting in its structure the boulders, large and small, which constituted his chosen world.

He shifted his position to the western side, the rocks beginning to take new shape in the lowering sun. The heat was still intense and his back seemed to feel the infinitesimal stirrings of the rock, expanding and in the immeasurably small shifting of position, almost inaudibly cracking in the heat. The vastness of the horizon seemed to contract upon him to the measure of this rock fortress and the myriad microcosmic grains.

The evening was the first day; he touched his lips again with the cool water, composed himself to prayer –

'For it is thou, Lord, only,
 That makest me dwell in safety.'

With a fold of his tunic beneath his hand and cheek, he slept as the last rays glowed in the heart of the rock.

Dawn brought a hint of breeze which freshened to a wind from the east. The desert sand at the foot of the rockfall stirred like a golden mist and was soon drilling its way in biting streams within the gullies and crannies of the summit. He drew his head-dress a little more firmly, covering his mouth and nose with a corner of it and waiting for the stillness. Towards noon the wind quietened, the rock took on its still, penetrating heat and he moved to the shelter of a north-facing boulder. A little scoop of water in his palm, a fragment of bread, barely held visible between finger and thumb, was his day's breaking of fast and in the noon-day heat he sat very still in the silting gravel of a cavity in the rock. His mind was unstirred, taking in the vast space, contemplating nothing but its immensity.

His left hand rested lightly on a ridge of stone. A stirring in the sand caught his eye and out of the cranny moved, tentatively, a scorpion. Its stillness seemed without menace and he moved his hand to caress it, lightly touching the scaly surface. With scarcely a change of posture, and with the accuracy of a lance-thrust, the scorpion's tail planted its sting in his palm.

After the initial thrust the pain was a gathered agony, concentrated in the circle of the palm. He held the hurt, cupping it, almost cherishing it, even while his muscles, in forearm and neck, crimped with the pain, nearly paralysing any movement in his limbs. He held very still in the heat, each drop of sweat glistening singly on his forehead and then streaming over his eyebrows on to the lids of his eyes. Gradually as he held himself within the circle of pain, it receded and he watched intently as the small creature withdrew into its place; he had known the scorpion in its very being.

In the cool of the evening he dipped his hand in the heart of the stream, touched his lips with the water and after his prayers –

'Not afraid for any terror by night
    Nor for the arrow that flieth by day' –
he settled to his rest.

It was the evening of the fifteenth day. The little barley cakes were almost consumed and the water, always a little sweeter on his tongue, now scarcely eased the cracked lips. The sliver of moon, still brilliant enough to dim the immediate stars, did nothing to shroud the brilliance of those in the opposite quarter of the sky. He gazed for a long time at the narrow crescent of the moon, tracing the shadowy fullness of the globe, completing the crescent form, and watching with affectionate assent, the 'rising' of the sun on the moon's surface, with the diminishing shadows within its craters. His gaze moved with a deeper wonder to the brilliance of the constellations, their light as sharp as dagger points in the clear desert air, and leaving a sharp imprint on his retina when he closed his eyes or turned them to the shadows of the rock outcrops.

They were numbered, ordered in their infinitely distanced groupings; as they swung in their courses their brilliance appeared to vibrate, not simply with their impact on his sight but with the ringing, reverberant harmony of bells and rods of metal. Across the ordered pattern, a falling star described its shallow parabola and he followed its descent to extinction, the sadness of the fall of an autumn leaf. He murmured Isaiah's words:

'All the host of heaven shall crumble into nothing...
    and the starry host fade away
    as the leaf withers from the vine.'

The Father held the heavens and, the hand withdrawn or raised in destructive anger, the very stars in their courses stagger in their immense pathways.

His eyes returned to the ordered constellations, 'The Bear, Orion and the Pleiades' and rested on the Pleiades. By that noble cluster his forefathers had measured times and seasons and in their influence fruit had ripened or withered. In the groups of the great ones he moved, and passed in his mind the procession of the lesser lights. As the sand grains had held all rocks in the palm of his hand, so now his eyes held all the infinite spaces.

The gnawing hunger, the bitterness of drying spittle, the cracked lips and the intolerably drooping eyelids, moved away from his conscious thought. He briefly slaked the bitterest thirst, prayed the heart of his vision:

The morning stars sang together
    And all the Sons of God shouted for joy

and in the tranquillity of the firmament he slept.

It was the morning of the thirtieth day. The cakes of barley had by this time left no crumb and only the bitter-sweet, blood-red fruit of the thorn, with a touch of water on his tongue, served to make the waking hours tolerable. In these last days his eyes had searched the wilderness and the desert and had seen no trace of a caravan or even a shepherd. He was more completely alone than he had ever been in Nazareth or the northern hills of Judah. The morning, noon and evening prayers were almost word-less, a withdrawn passiveness that gathered all thought to the centre and remained articulate only in the single phrase, 'Blessed be God.'

Towards evening, as he moved to one of the western gullies, he became aware of a brief stirring in the dry leaves, fallen from a stunted tamarisk. From behind the scaly trunk and brushing past the brittle twigs which formed a crude litter in the rock shelter, a shy, questing muzzle with still, gentle eyes, held his glance. Slowly, curiosity defeating its fear, the coney moved out from its shelter and paused before the still figure sitting on the rock. Jeshua moved his hands softly, his gesture inviting confidence; the coney moved forward, a momentary flash of white from the fur of his underbelly and then stood, its jaws moving silently with the memory of its last grazing. The hand moved forward to caress the brown back and then withdrew; the lonely vigil had, for a brief moment found refreshment with the beasts. Some miles away the hunting cry of the wolf was a brief gesture in the air; the coney gave a barely audible quaver of a warning 'whistle' and bolted to its refuge. In the cold stillness, sleep came among the rocks.

It was the dawning of the fortieth day. In these last days his mind, with the clarity of great hunger, had returned to the prophets and especially to the visions of Isaiah. For here, in the disorderly tumble of rock, above the infertile waste, with thorn and wild creatures declaring that chaos had again overtaken beneficent order, the words rever-berated like a denial of all prayer and meditation:

The owl and the raven shall possess it;
    He has stretched across it a measuring-line;
    Chaos and its frontiers shall be a jumble of stones.
In the sky there was the brief screech of a vulture and from the more distant rocks the single cry of a wolf. The loneliness was given over to desolation and the last pangs of hunger. He had remained bound by thought and by vision to this rocky bluff; his body, tempered by deprivation to a discipline beyond that of the desert people, was now reined to his will, with agony, but controlled. His mind turned, in the dawn meditation, to his most loved book of the law, Moses's exhortation to his people:

    You shall remember all the way which the Lord your God has led you these forty years in the wilderness, that He might humble you, testing you to know what was in your heart, whether you would keep his commandments or not.

His wilderness had been stringent and desolate, testing in its loneliness; but not evil – nature had lived by its laws, from the stars in their courses to the scorpion's aggression. Now, in the increasing heat, he knew the effluvium of evil, palpable, visible as a rancid vapour, and audible.

'Son of God? If you are indeed the Son of God, order these stones to be bread!'

The smaller rocks of the wadi had known the erosion of sudden downpour and the hot blasting of sand; rounded and flat, with a tinge of the oven, they looked like the midday barley cakes.

'Command these stones.' The voice and the craving were insistent.

'Man lives not simply by bread but by all the words of the mouth of God.'

'The words of the Law are stale loaves and the words of the prophets are drier, harder; teeth can be broken on these 'Words of the Lord."

'Whether the ravens of Kerith or the angels of heaven, the servants minister beyond our needs. His words are manna enough.'

He withdrew his attention from the testing and the need. As the sun rose he moved away towards the spring and the rock pool, touched his forehead, his lips and his tongue with the cool water and walked to the shade of the dwarf tamarisk. The brittle leaves gave only a meagre shelter and there was just one stunted spray of pale pink florets; it was a moment, a fragment of beauty as the odour of evil retreated.

At the next day's dawn he left his rock refuge and walked back towards Jordan. On a hillock beyond the ford he saw in the gold of the evening light the deeper gold of the Temple and the cold brilliance of the cliff-like wall dropping sheer beyond the valley of the Kidron. After hard walking he reached the boundary slopes and sat to absorb the beauty of David's city. As a fortress it enclosed so much and such diverse power. Dominating its defences rose the Fortress of Antonia, the barracks of the occupying Romans; within sight of it, the palace of Herod, a kind of temporal power; and giving reluctant and flawed validity to it all, the Temple itself, near-decadent in its splendour but holding as in an irrelevantly ornate casket, the simple truth at its heart, the Holy of Holies and the power of Jahweh. In its tangle of aspirations, fears, denials and profound faith, it held, fragile, the tradition of Israel. If this city was to be 'taken', it would scarcely be by a customary siege. As the sun fell an ancient olive tree gave him such comfort as he needed and he slept.

'Son of God?'

He woke to no desert voice; this was assured, a hint of sophistication.

'Son of God? If you are indeed the Son of God, follow me.'

Jeshua crossed at the causeway of the Kidron, breasted the slope and within a brief time, found himself at the south-eastern Tower. Poised on its cornice, he looked to Olivet and below him, far to his left was the suppurating stench of Hinnom, human refuse only a little less nauseating than the sickly odour of evil which struck him again like a physical blow. It was a dizzying perch but he held himself still, balanced, hands pressed at his sides, palms to the wall.

'Vertigo, Son of God? If you are, if you are in truth the Son of the Most High, pitch yourself outward and down. 'He shall give his angels, legions of angels, charge over your flight, lest you cast your foot against a stone'!'

The ironic voice was a challenge and an invitation; defiance, a miraculous descent, would be a denial of the powers of evil, an assertion of himself over the demonic. He remained still, poised, his powers collected.

'I fear no pain of fall and if I am to soar, I fly in my own strength, no angel of heaven or hell my escort.'

'No other Son of Man has flown; fly, Son of Man; try your grasp of the grace of God.'

'Sathanas, you are a lying adversary. It is written: 'You shall not put the Lord your God to the test' – no, not even the test of grace.'

Only the stench of Hinnom remained. The way lay back over Kidron, through the defiles of the Jordan valley and down to the reed beds. He walked through the night as virtue returned to his limbs and all trembling passed away. As he faced the dawn, he reached the familiar wilderness, its herb-scented austerity as welcome as home-coming. Seated at the rock face, he savoured the rising of the sun.

Some miles to the north of his rock-refuge, a steep escarpment led to a summit which over-towered the landscape. It was now time for the ascent and in the failing light he reached the base and the scree.

Within an hour or two of the dawn he was at the summit. To the north he sensed rather than saw the Sea of Gennesaret, shut in by ridge upon ridge, softening the landscape to a blue haze. To the west, the limitless deserts, the way of escape from desolation to the land of promise; to the south, the rocky, stunted wilderness and beyond, the yellowing haze of the Negev. Assyria, Babylon, Egypt and, over the inland sea, Rome in its immediate might, below him at gaze he saw all quarters of the earth, all majesty and dominion. Would it ever return to the one unfettered dominion?

In the sky at the sun's zenith two eagles wheeled. Their flight appeared like a concerted dance figure carried out with a nonchalant effortlessness. The male hovered on a thermal, in a shallow arc; his mate, with the lightest of wing beats swooped for a mock kill. They reversed their positions, wheeling and gliding to a pattern, in menacing grace. After a minute or two one swooped in a shallow dive, a feinting flight, while the other dropped for the kill, rising, a coney in its talons.

Jeshua shared the intensity, the cool efficiency of the eagles' manoeuvres, the death-agony of the coney. His eyes shared the sharp eagle gaze, his bowels writhed to the dart of the talons.

Out of the compassion he became aware of the voice. 'You share the survey of Abraham, the panorama of Moses – not simply the land of promise – all lands! They are in the grasp of your eye; you have savoured them in your imagination; take them in the grasp of your hand!'

'Your gift?' His question was without any ironic inflection, a question probing for truth.

'Yes, in my gift, all the kingdoms of the earth – kingdoms? all power, without limit, without restraint, enclosed in your single wish and idea, to grasp man and return him to what he was.'

'And is power to be without compassion?'

'In the last hour you watched two wheeling eagles; they quartered their kingdom, sweeping its boundaries with the ease of perfect flight. Almost playfully, with all the ease of play, they swooped on the coney. It was wholly in their power, wholly their prey. Was compassion relevant in that chase?'

'The eagles had none but mine was in the flesh, the sinews, the screaming nerves of the coney. If I felt the agony of a beast in the rocks, can I ignore the agony of man? What power, however wielded, will abate one moment of that suffering?'

'Take power, rid the kingdoms of tyranny, shape the body politic and you will then afford compassion. In the peace which follows, you can exercise the sympathy you so eagerly need.'

'And how do I take power, where begin? Conquer Rome, destroy the Legions? And they will not be replaced from the Imperial City? Challenge Herod and the Herodians, meet guile with forceful guile? Assimilate myself to the same weapons and know the gnawing certainty that I shall be less than I was, than I must be? Challenge the Sanhedrin? Pit the weapons of debate against the centuries of tradition? Descend to the arena of powerful argument, half-truth matched against half-truth?'

'You might try.'

The challenge was as contemptuous as a light flick of a whip. 'You might indeed call upon the legions. They are poised at heaven's bar – one word and they descend with more grace, more force than any eagle's flight.'

'Your kingdom, your leased power, lent to you for the little duration of time, is not my kingdom nor my power. You shall not put my kingdom, the kingdom of my Father, to any proof of arms. You shall not test the Lord your God.'

The encounter had lasted through the heat and the setting of the sun. As the last sweetness rose from the few stunted shrubs, the coolness of the bare mountain-top had the savour of a garden, eastward in Eden. The air was refreshing enough to draw him towards the customary refuge which was now almost 'home.' Before the evening prayer he washed his hands, his face and his feet and took his first long draught from the stream.

'I will lay me down in peace
and take my rest,
For it is thou, Lord, only
that makest me dwell in safety.'

There was no urgency in the return journey. He avoided the populous highways, avoided even the villages. For there was much to garner, much to record in his mind of these forty days. The fatigue was little, his lips no longer parched, his loins no longer twisted in the pain of approaching starvation. Every ridge of mountain had now its sharp definition; the green of a wadi was now an unique green, the water had its new translucency, its new sibilance over the stones. The dawn song was sweeter than the quieter murmur as the birds settled for the night; the slither of the viper through the grass and stunted brush was no longer a menace; it was a pattern of colour as vibrant as a rainbow and with the rainbow's grace.

The way seemed clear; his body subdued but not violently defeated, his will cleansed and his mind clarified in purpose and intention. He walked north along the by-ways, savouring the newly-found peace.

BOOK THREE

The Sea of Galilee

FIFTEEN

Where Jeshua's journey from Nazareth to Jordan had been swift and purposeful, the journey away from the river was slow and meandering. Each day passed in the quiet contemplation of a newly-found landscape. It was for the most part an inhospitable country, more wilderness than desert, and even the wadis gave little promise of fruitfulness. But Jeshua saw it with new eyes. No longer did he feel himself to inhabit more than one time-scale; all was now *present*, vivid, vibrating with light, as on the fifth day of creation and in his solitary movement through the landscape he had set aside his intuitions that Abraham, Moses, David were his contemporaries, that he moved through time with the ease of movement through Galilee. For the period of waiting, he seemed himself to be at a new 'sixth day', to be Adam new-created. The sun rose on rocks seen afresh, on streams in the little eroded valleys which fell over boulders with resonances hitherto unheard. Even the thorn bushes carried their three colours in a fresh harmony, the rust-brown of the branches giving plangency to the pure green of the thorny leaves and they according a new blood-red vividness to the meagre fruits. It was no paradise but a paradisal calm.

After a week of this seemingly purposeless movement, as he savoured the immediate past and gathered within himself the recent conflict, he climbed down from a high ridge to a small settlement in the valley below. Life there was clearly austere, the very elements of living; a few sheep and goats in the upper pastures and the scanty soil scraped into cultivation for a little grain, some scanty olives and shrivelled grapes which became raisins on the stem in the parching heat. The people watched the wayfarer with no curiosity, an almost complete indifference and he passed between the houses with no more than a hand raised in greeting and a quiet, almost whispered 'Shalom,' to which there was rarely a response. As he walked beyond the last of the dwellings, at a junction of two paths, there stood mute and wholly passive two men, each of some forty years. As Jeshua approached, one of them took two or three stumbling paces towards him, one paralysed leg behaving as little more than a crutch for the halting movement. Half behind him his companion made helpless, flailing gestures, in his blindness just aware that his prop and guide had moved away from him.

Jeshua halted before them, lifted his right hand in a silent greeting and, smiling, gestured to the maimed man to bridge the few yards' gap between them. He looked with wonder into Jeshua's eyes and then moved forward without stumbling, the swinging, halting gait forgotten, and clasped Jeshua's hand.

Together they turned to the blind man. His companion took him by the shoulder and turned him towards Jeshua, who, with a gesture like waking a child from sleep, caressed the forehead of the blind man and allowed his hand to move gently down to his eyelids. With the tips of his fingers he raised the eyelids, and smiled into the eyes. With incomprehension but with a growing joy he looked about him.

'Trees?' His companion nodded.

'Shadows? our village?' The gestures towards these mint-new perceptions were the embrace of a world until now only guessed at.

'And you walk so strongly!' The wonder was almost too much as they gazed at each other and then turned to Jeshua, as if craving an explanation. He shook his head but still smiling, he said, 'Go back now and see your families and friends. They will be glad of your wholeness.'

There was no more speech; he had not asked their names nor had they ventured to ask his. All they could tell their people, after the first wonder had died down, was that he was noble to look at and spoke with the accent of Galilee.

The little hamlets succeeded each other, nameless, but each imposing its urgency on Jeshua. Rumour was faster than his progress through this barren country and each roadway at the entrance to a village had its knot of paralysed, deaf and helpless creatures for whom their neighbours could do nothing, scarcely sparing compassion. Sometimes without words, often with hardly a gesture, Jeshua moved among them with a power they felt without understanding and in each village he left healing, a little wonder and a peace they had not known before.

The strange thing was the silence. Jeshua approached each place without urgency, savouring such beauty as the shadows of the rocks, the distorted branches of the trees gave him as the sun moved westward before him. As he approached a new habitation there was again nothing but a total silence of expectation; no cries, no importunities, but a waiting on his approach. Even the children became still, looking for a gesture and when Jeshua sat on a bank by the wayside, they clustered about him and, keeping the same stillness, clambered on his knees and burrowed into his cloak.

Those who needed, longed for his assistance, stood at some little distance away from him; sometimes with little more than a look or a gesture over the heads of the children, sometimes with a touch of the maimed bodies, he did his work of blessing and release and then moved on to the next village.

The general direction of his seemingly aimless wandering was towards Jerusalem, which he reached after some weeks. The city was hot and to him who had become used to the clear air of the desert, it left a cindery savour on the lips. On entering the city, he went to the Temple and, passing through the Court of the Gentiles, walked slowly along the colonnade. It was invariably his first visit on reaching Jerusalem and took his mind back some eighteen years to those wonderful days when he had spoken face to face with the learned rabbis and then, more intimately in the garden with the noble pharisee, Joseph of Arimathea.

But those were not the chief memories which crowded in as he sat on one of the plinths of the colonnade. He remembered a day when he was a mature young man and the bustle of Passover had driven him in to what he had hoped would be the peace of the Temple. At first he had been pursued by the sounds of the streets, the chaffering in the outer courts, the haggling over the sacrifices, the discordant voices, high-pitched city tones playing off against the deeper notes of the desert voices. For several minutes the sounds had seemed like a physical assault, with braying, bleating, lowing, emphasising the stench of blood and dung. This was the Temple!

Then, with scarcely a conscious effort on Jeshua's part, the sounds faded and gave way to a hush that he had known since first he had heard that scroll read:

160

But will God in very deed dwell with men on the
earth?
Behold, heaven and the heaven of heavens cannot
contain thee;
How much less this house which I have built.
The humility of Solomon's prayer entered Jeshua's spirit
and in its silence he heard again the command of Solomon, that the beams, the pillars and the joists of this
house should be fashioned where the trees grew; that the
stones should be sawn, hewn and made fit at the quarry
where they were taken; for there should be no sound of
hammer or chisel within the Temple site as it was in the
building, but all should be assembled in silence, that the
sanctuary be never defiled by raucous sound.

As Jeshua remained wrapped in this stillness, it seemed
to him that the Temple grew about him. He heard the soft
movement of the mason's sledges as the hewn stones were
hauled to their site, the panting of the builders as they
lifted each stone into place resting upon the merest thin
slurry of cement to make tight the joint; he heard the
metallic hiss of the trowel as it took up the oozing cement
and pointed the joint between the boulders. And all these
sounds were no more than the distant insect sounds of the
desert, the whirring of crickets.

This then was the vision of Solomon as he fulfilled the
frustrated longing of his father David, that there should be
silence in this place, a silence in which supplication could
be heard.

Hearken therefore unto the supplications of thy
servant,
And of thy people Israel, which they shall make
Towards this place.
Hear thou from thy dwelling-place,
Even from heaven,
And when thou hearest, forgive.

This was the silence which the worshipper craved, the silence at the setting of the sun, when the wind fell and the trees were still; the silence in that hour before dawn when nothing waked but the worshipping mind. This was the silence which had accompanied him from Jordan into the wilderness and which, after his testing, had filled every day of his healing journey, a silence which had stilled the suffering of all the scraps of mankind that had waited for him in every village.

He held the tranquillity for some minutes, like a precious liquid in a chalice; and then the silence was slowly invaded by the cries of animals, the insistent chaffering of merchants, the chink of coin in the outer court. He looked around for a place where the sound might be less but knew that the Temple rang with barter. His eyes half closed as if in pain, his mouth tightened in distaste, almost in disgust. He gathered his outer garment about him and turned to leave the Temple.

Only then did he see that he was not alone in this corner of the colonnade. Standing at some little distance and half hidden by a pillar from which he had observed Jeshua, was a pharisee, a man of wealth but with a dignity that came from an inner surety. With only the least of greetings he touched Jeshua's arm and together they walked out of the Temple.

They went through the narrow, crowded streets, to the more affluent quarters to the north of the city, which looked out towards the hill country. The pharisee led Jeshua to a gate in a high wall and he found himself guided to an arbour from which he could see the house. They sat in silence, the older man waiting until Jeshua should have gathered himself from his emotions in the Temple. At last he spoke.

'You are Jeshua of Nazareth of whom we have heard much in these last days. I am Nicodemus, friend to that Joseph, from Arimathea, with whom you spoke, a lost boy at Passover!'

Jeshua's smile had a touch of mischief as he acknowledged the vividly-remembered incident, but they both fell back into silence. Then Jeshua was startled at a quite different tone in Nicodemus's voice.

'Rabbi!' Jeshua's instinctive gesture seemed to repudiate the title.

'Rabbi, I know that you are of God. Never shall I forget those hours in the Temple, when I, with wise and holy men, and Joseph who always sought for truth, listened with awe and some fear to a boy from the hill-country who in his young Galilean accents asked such questions that our souls were searched. Now, as the years begin with stealth to creep upon me, I hear not the questions but such strange answers. I hear of a progress through the wilderness in which the blind see, the deaf hear and the paralysed walk. What, in this power, will you do to our tradition? what in God's name will you require of us?'

'The tradition may shatter – the sound, the smell of corruption assails you even in the Temple itself. We need re-birth; yes, man must be born again.'

Before the intensity of these words Nicodemus recoiled into a defensive raillery.

'Born again! And must I enter once more the darkness and the preparation of my mother's womb and be born again?'

'That is the answer of flesh, Rabbi. Would that man could know even that re-birth. But much more he needs the harsher birth by water and the breath of God. Adonai once sickened of the creatures he had made and in the waters of Deluge he blotted out the greater part of his creation. But man survived and by the breath of God knew the driving of the Spirit. I have known sickness of heart to-day and I fear the need of another Deluge.

'You call me Rabbi and, Rabbi, I honour you in your search.' Jeshua's gravity took away any hint of presumption in their relationship.

'Search! Yes, I search in Torah, in the customs, in the Sanhedrin! and there is no sure rock.' His voice grew louder, 'How can these things be?'

'Rabbi!' The authority was now palpable. 'You, a master in Israel, and you have no answers when your people asks, in fear and desolation?'

The two men now stood, almost in confrontation, Jeshua's compassion reaching out to the bewilderment of Nicodemus.

'We know; I speak my Father's words and I say to you a prophecy: as Moses lifted up the serpent in the wilderness, to the salvation of his people, Israel, even so must the Son of Man be lifted up.'

The closing words were scarcely audible and with no further question or answer they parted, Jeshua to walk swiftly out of the city as the moon, almost at the full, showed him his path to an olive grove.

The pull of Galilee, its hills and plains and its speech, was strong upon Jeshua and he determined to return, to the eastern portion and not at first to his home country. For Gennesaret, only half-known, now drew him like a lodestone; there in its commerce, its fishing, its day-to-day bustle, he felt his immediate work to lie. And there was another powerful memory; Justus his centurion, could now surely have settled to a peaceful retirement at the lakeside and memory of the swift, intuitive friendship drew him also.

First, however, there were duties to be fulfilled at the Jordan. Avoiding so far as he could the villages and townships on the way, he made swiftly towards Bethabara, to find a strange new atmosphere. He greeted John briefly and asked him the meaning of the restless stirring of the people about the ford.

'They make holiday.' John spoke drily but with a healer's yearning to be about his work.

'They come looking for the Messiah!'

Jeshua looked alertly from John to the crowds on the
meadow below.

'Rumours of you, your works from here to Jerusalem,
the healings, the release of those bound. And now they
want both words and signs.'

Jeshua made no reply beyond a silent shake of the head.
He looked at John, whose forehead rested on his hands,
almost bowed to his knees. They were of an age, but the
man at his side looked of a late and weary middle age, his
cheeks sunk and below the unkempt hair eyes burning
with a fever, both of mind and body. His bare arms were
wasted to shallow, rope-like muscles over the protruding
bones. Here was a man consumed with zeal and it was a
pitiable question in Jeshua's mind whether John would
first be destroyed by his own vision or by the crowding
enemies who resented his blazing condemnation.

'You say 'holiday'; they come as for a feast?'

'Far and wide they come; the babble of every tongue in
Israel and Judah may be heard at the ford each evening
and morning. They come north from the Negev and south
from the furthest reaches of Galilee towards Hermon; not
many – yet! and they are not idlers; these have left their
work and their homes to find something for themselves.
Will you answer them, Jeshua?'

'In good time, John, in the Father's good time.'

John pressed him no further and after brief prayers,
they folded their cloaks about them and slept.

At dawn they walked together towards the waters but
on sight of some stirring among the people, Jeshua halted
on the slope while John walked forward for the customary
daily baptisms. Two men detached themselves from the
crowd and came towards John as if about to question him.

He stopped and gesturing towards Jeshua spoke in tones loud enough just to carry to the two young men:

'There, before you, is God's Lamb.' It was no herald's voice with a proclamation, no prophet's declaration; it was simply the quiet statement of a truth, a truth clear and incontrovertible. Jeshua also heard it and turned away without word or gesture and walked swiftly back towards the arid hill country. After a mile or two, Jeshua turned and looked back towards Jordan and saw that the two men followed him but keeping their distance.

'Are you looking for me?'

'Rabbi, where is your home? May we come with you?'

'Come and see.'

They walked together for a further mile until Jordan and its people were hidden.

'You are Simon – and you Andrew.' It was a smiling greeting. 'We haven't spoken before but I have seen you at your fishing.'

The two brothers looked in astonishment but with a gradual recognition of the young man from Nazareth who had stayed a few days at Capernaum with their friends. It was also the recognition of a great deal more.

There was no more speech until they reached a grove of olive trees which had been abandoned when the homestead had been left and allowed to fall to ruin. Jeshua pointed to the shelter of the grove and then with a wider sweep of his hand said,

'This is my home.'

For some five days they walked northward, reaching the road which skirted the lake, through Tiberias and Magdala, to Capernaum where Jeshua left them and they returned to their homes.

SIXTEEN

The same urge which had sent Jeshua to Jordan before his return to Galilee, the urge that his life should have coherence, unfragmented, now sent him to Nazareth; for there too there was unfinished business. In these days in eastern Galilee, he had paused at wayside resting-places and quietly, with no rhetorical demand that people should listen, he spoke to small knots of wayfarers and casual day labourers; he spoke of his Father's Kingdom, of the tranquil heart and of mutual charity. He spoke to them of the degrees of love, of the love that comes from gratitude, admiration, desire, and that most difficult love of the will, the love of the unlovable, the unfriendly, the enemy. This gentle, unobtrusive teaching was made valid for those who listened by the stillness of his tranquil eyes, the controlled gestures of his craftsman's hands, hands which extended towards a child's tousled hair in blessing or to embrace a limb which was withered. Bounty seemed to flow from this man who had nothing but his presence to give them.

Now he felt driven back to his birthplace. If his presence brought gifts at Jordan or the land about the Sea of Galilee, much more should it in Nazareth, where Joseph, Mary, Lazar had taught him so much as he grew to knowledge of himself. Now the arc of his life should be completed; his knowledge of himself and of his mission should now be declared there where his Father's will had first been felt.

He entered Nazareth at evening, two days before Sabbath. The family was at their evening meal and Jeshua was received among them, seeming to complete a circle which had been broken by his absence. Little was said beyond comment on his good health; Jacob saw with a little envy that Jeshua's bearing had now a greater assurance, an authority which had no need of assertion.

For the next two days Jeshua returned to the workshop, took down the familiar tools, worn to the clasp of his hands and with scarcely a pause, returned to the fashioning of a plough. By the hour before the Sabbath service he had fixed to the share an iron shoe and the plough was ready for the field.

With Mary, Jacob and the others he walked across to the synagogue. For the first minutes of silence he seemed to hear the warm tones of Lazar's voice. Then Lemuel's voice broke through his meditation as the Psalms made their way to the congregation.

O come let us sing unto the Lord;
Let us heartily rejoice in the strength of our salvation.
Let us come before his presence with thanksgiving
And show ourselves glad in him with psalms.
For the Lord is a great God
And a great King above all Gods.

O worship the Lord in the beauty of holiness,
Let the whole earth stand in awe of him.
For he cometh, for he cometh
To judge the earth;
And with righteousness
To judge the world
And the people with his truth.

The old, customary rhythms entered Jeshua's mind with all their ancient peace; a radiance from David and along the ages filled the synagogue with the certainty of His presence. Lemuel's voice commanded their response:

Bless ye the Lord who is to be blessed

Blessed is the Lord who is to be blessed
For ever and ever.

Hear, O Israel.
The Lord our God, the Lord is one.

Blessed be his name
Whose glorious kingdom
is for ever and ever.

The liturgy welded the people into one and the moment was reached when Jeshua was called forward to read; the scroll was the prophecy of Isaiah and Jeshua found the passage:

The Spirit of the Lord is upon me, because he has annointed me to preach the gospel to the poor. He hath sent me to heal the broken-hearted; to preach deliverance to the captives, and recovery of sight to the blind, to set at liberty them that are bruised, to preach the acceptable year of the Lord.

He restored the scroll, and stood before the congregation, inviting their response. Some were clearly moved; Jacob looked with unbelief at this stranger who was his brother, and Mary hid her face in her veil. When the silence became insupportable and was clearly not to be broken even by the rabbi, Jeshua spoke slowly and quietly:

'This day is this scripture fulfilled in your ears. Hear it, for the sake of the kingdom and for the peace of Israel in the hand of the Most High.' Some wept, some pressed forward to touch his robe and behind them there was a muttering:

'Joseph's son;' 'Our carpenter-apprentice-prophet?' 'A new Hasid in our village!' 'Blasphemy!'

Jeshua resumed his place before them.

'Could I, Jeshua, expect a prophet to be accepted in his own birthplace and among his own people?'

He looked to his family but only in the eyes of Miriam was there a beseeching that he believed.

'I tell you a bitter truth; there were many widows in Israel in the days of Elias, when the heavens were shut up for three years and six months, when great famine was throughout the land. But to none of these widows of Israel was Elijah sent but to Sarepta, *a city of Sidon*, to a woman who was a widow. And many lepers were in Israel in the time of Elisha the prophet and not one of them was made clean save Naaman – *the Syrian*!'

His voice had risen to the prophetic rhythm as his words carried condemnation not only of their Nazareth security but attacked the very root of their belief that the Most High confined his bounty to his chosen. Mutterings increased to cursing and ignoring both Sabbath and the holiness of the sanctuary, they hurried him across the village to the brow of a steep hill. They were about to cast him over its brink when he turned to them. Without a word he withdrew from the clasping hands, ignored the clenched fists and the lifted boulders, raised his hand in blessing and passed among them, leaving no trace of his passage more than the keel of a ship in still waters. They remained in silence until they lost sight of him as he took the road towards the lake.

It was a bitter way, the closing of a life and the dark opening of another. He had known devils in the Decapolis, the ten cities at the Sea of Galilee, had bound them, exiled them and cleansed and renewed the bodies they had inhabited. But these were not devils; they were his people, of his household, his own familiar friends for thirty years. They lived in houses fashioned in part by him and furnished with his craftsmanship. He had walked with them, talked with them and shared their sorrows; above all he had worshipped with them, observed the high feasts and the days of penitence – and he had hitherto scarcely known them.

His mind and heart were so fashioned that hatred, even dislike or contempt, were alien to him. Now it seemed as though a thunder cloud invaded his soul and though the way ahead remained clear, all behind him was a chaos of loss.

He struck across the spur towards Tabor, then descended to the lake road and towards Arbela and Magdala, but needing greater solitude than the lakeside afforded he turned westward again into the forbidding Valley of the Doves. Here the sheer, raw cliffs of basalt showed the turbulence of earthquake; fissures left the hard, black rock exposed, the whole rift in the contour dominated by the pillared volcano at its summit. The breaks in the cliffs were too sharply rugged to be called wadis but along their sides were cave openings, dark and secret, speaking of flight and ambush; Jeshua's mind was filled with the ancient fears of En-Gedi and Adullam, of flight, massacre and ancient royal grudges.

The wrestling with these memories calmed him and when the heat of the day was tempered he returned to the opening of the valley where from its substantial height, he could see the lake and across its waters the Gadarene hills catching the last rays of the sun. He composed himself to sleep, with the evening praises:

Blessed art thou, O Lord our God,
 King of the universe,
 Who at they word bringest on the evening twilight,
 With wisdom openest the gates of the heavens,
 And with understanding
 Changest times and variest the seasons,
 And arrangest the stars in the watches of the sky,
 According to thy will.

With everlasting love thou hast loved
The house of Israel, thy people;
A Law and commandments,
Statutes and judgments
Hast thou taught us.

And mayest thou never take away thy love from us;
Blessed art thou, O Lord,
Who lovest thy people, Israel.

The morning brought its peace. The hour before dawn was uncertain, banks of cloud at the far horizon, revealing the promised radiance at once removed, great billows scudding at the zenith from the west and threatening storm, the last of the stars flickering above the rock pinnacles, to which the quarter moon gave a metallic sheen, like their emergence at first creation. Jeshua murmured 'Elohim', as, at the birth of time, Elohim had spoken, 'Let there be'; as Jeshua repeated the Name, a constellation swung free of its cloud curtain, its ordered, patterned brilliance a parable of Torah, the justice, the law of the Father emerging in the movement of creation. Wordless, Jeshua gathered the order into himself.

The light grew stronger but without direction, bleakly revealing without illumination. Jeshua drew into a more contained stillness, seeing only his hands, lightly folded at his knees. Each movement of his hands revealed his work, the hardened but sensitive tips of his fingers still aware of the movement, the growth of wood, the power of stone. He spoke more loudly: 'Adonai.' This was a cry for himself as he gathered men in their pitiful longings to his own touch and embrace; 'Adonai, Loving-kindness – send Mercy in their need.'

He climbed higher into the ravine away from the cave clefts and reached a shelf of rock below the summit. One name remained, the name no man uttered but carried, silent, in his mind and heart. A wry thought brought a flicker of bitterness to his lips: there was one exception to the silence; once in the year, at the Day of Atonement, the High Priest spoke the Name, cried it aloud to the people, who answered with joy. Jeshua fought his irony: Caiaphas to utter the name beyond uttering! Gathering himself again, shaking away any thoughts even of the Temple in its ambiguous holiness, he whispered the Name: '*JAHWEH*' and, as he took all Israel to himself, he responded for all Israel:

'Blessed be his Name
Whose glorious kingdom is for ever and ever.'

Where the waters from Hermon entered the lake between Capernaum and Bethsaida, the boats with the cast-nets were already preparing for the first catches. Jeshua made to join them. The walk of some six or seven miles took him almost until noon. In a small inlet in which some of the Capernaum fishermen were mending and folding their nets, while others sorted a meagre catch, he saw Andrew and Simon preparing to land from their craft. They paused, looking half-expectant, half-puzzled by this man whom they now saw in a double perspective. Was he the one whom John proclaimed, with whom they had travelled and conversed? Or was he the young Nazarene who had questioned them so many years before of their craft and their way of life? He stepped into the shallow, lapping water and clambered into the centre of the boat.

'Thrust out a little from the land, Simon.' Scarcely out of the shallows he halted the rowing, stood between the rowing seats and balanced himself with an oar used like a shepherd's staff.

'Friends, to what end do you work?' There was a little mockery on the faces of those on shore to whom his words were directed.

'To eat, young man, what else? A little more for clothing our youngsters and a little over for wine on the high days!'

'And this is the end of your work? To labour more earnestly than the beasts? To have less freedom than the birds of the air, less peace than the flowers of the field? Are you no more than these creatures and the herbs on which they feed?'

He left the question hanging in the air; the answer could wait – there would be weeks ahead in Capernaum and Bethsaida in which to draw from them the answer; and there was something more immediate.

'Simon, pull out further into the lake and Andrew, get ready for a cast.'

'Rabbi, we have cast and cast all night. It's a bad night for fishing and we have caught little or nothing; most of the catch we threw back!'

'Pull out and cast.'

They rowed into the little turbulence where the head waters, a creamy current from the melting snows, began to mingle with the stiller waters of the lake.

'Cast here and pull hard.' The command was needed, for the overloaded net was more like an anchor than their customary drag-net. They called to the shore where James and John worked with their father Zebedee, that the two brothers should help them with the catch. It was a struggle and they reached the shore with two overloaded boats. Simon knelt on the rough shingle.

'Master, leave us! We aren't fit men for the likes of you. Wasn't it sin that made us fail?'

'Simon, follow me and I will make you a fisher of men. Andrew, James, John, would you also catch men?' He gathered the four in one gesture and they left the little creek and took the upper path towards Capernaum.

174

When they reached the home of Simon and Andrew, Jeshua asked quietly, almost with shyness,

'Is there a little corner, an upper room – a Prophet's Room! – that I might have? I want very little and there is much work in the weeks before us. A little rest, a little thought for me; a little loving care for you, as you prepare to leave your present life; and then we shall see.'

They took him to a room above the main roof of the house. Before its door a few plants had been lovingly tended in pots, brilliant orange flowers against dark glossy leaves making a foreground for the view over the lake. Jeshua sat against the wall in the quiet of the afternoon, waiting for the time when he would join the family for their evening meal. There were no immediate cares, no hurried concerns; it was very good.

The meal was silent. Simon and Andrew seemed poised for more comment from Jeshua; the older members of the household, with Simon's wife, were apprehensive, fearful that this comparative stranger, a deeply disturbing figure, was about to disrupt the modest happiness of the household. For they had a sufficiency and a little more; they owed no man anything and were dependant on no man; they were at peace with themselves and their neighbours and now that peace was threatened as Simon told of their probable departure with Jeshua.

'To do what?' There was a satiric anger in the voice of Naomi, Simon's wife.

'You have strong shoulders for the oars and the nets; you have an eye for a squall from the hills or for a shoal of fish but what else are you good for? What use has Jeshua, a rabbi and a healer, for you?'

For Jeshua these questions were as testing as they were for Simon and he waited for Simon's answer. None came but Simon's eyes turned to Jeshua, his face clouded and embarrassed.

'Naomi, I *do* need him.' Jeshua was replying for Simon as well as himself. 'Those shoulders, which you say were strengthened at the oar and the nets, I need their strength. But I need more than that. Our Israel needs new truths; first the old truths of the prophets: the anger of Amos, the pitiful love of Hosea, the visions of Isaiah; but Israel needs even greater truths than these which will put a new heart and a new mind into this tired, suffering people – and I need Andrew's stillness and I need Simon's strength; rocklike, yes, he will be called by us The Rock. Simon, will you take the nickname Peter and be known by it?'

Naomi was silenced, knowing only that her old world was shattered and her new world not yet created. In her bewilderment she turned to Simon; he looked at her with compassion for her troubled mind but then turned to Jeshua:

'Yes, please God; a Rock let me be.'

There would be little more talk that evening, the unacknowledged tumult too great for facing on this first strange day. Jeshua withdrew to his room, his 'Prophet's Chamber', to be still with his own thoughts. He had much to face for himself; dared he commit others to the same testing.

The days went by in a strange passivity. The two brothers and their friends returned to their fishing and Jeshua remained quietly meditating in his upper room or walking along the shore. Then late one afternoon, a child came rushing to the lakeside. Naomi's mother had been taken gravely ill with a sudden fever, her old body showing no resistance to its onset. Peter must return at once to the house, for there was much to be done. Jeshua followed without hurry arriving at the house as Peter and Andrew had questioned the others and were trying to comfort the sick woman. Jeshua came in, crossed to the palette-bed and placed his hands on her forehead; there was little more than a whisper from him:

'Be well!'

She opened her eyes, smiled into his and with what appeared to be an apology for her weakness, moved to prepare the meal to set before them. Naomi and Peter urged her to rest, to try to sleep but Jeshua quietly set their anxiety aside:

'It has left her; let her go back to her life.'

The meal that evening was one of quiet happiness but with questioning wonder still in Naomi's eyes. Who and what was this man who could cure fevers and make lives whole, while apparently breaking hers like a vessel?

The following day was the Sabbath and Jeshua went with the whole family to the synagogue. His memories there were vivid and almost without thinking he searched among the God-fearers for one who had remained in his thoughts over the years but failed to find him.

The ritual went on, rich and satisfying in its measured tones and memories of all the ages.

> O Lord our God,
>> When we lie down and when we rise up
>> We will meditate on thy statutes,
>> Yea, we will rejoice in the words
>> Of thy Law and in thy commandments;
>> For they are our life and the length of our days,
>> And we will meditate on them day and night.

The service went its customary way but at the moment of the reading from the scroll, Jeshua moved to confront the congregation:

'Hear the word of Isaiah the prophet, words spoken to you, here, in this very land, the region of Zabulun and the patrimony of Naphtali; to you he speaks these words:

'The Land of Zabulun and of Naphtali,
  Toward the sea and across Jordan,
  Galilee of the Gentiles:
  The people who sat in darkness
  Have seen a great light;
  Those who sat in the land of the shadow of death,
  Upon them has the light dawned.'

'These words, he spoke to you; across the ages they ring in your ears: Darkness or a great light; the shadow of death or the glow of a new dawn. Repent, for this Kingdom, the dawn of heaven's light is at hand.'

The synagogue was filled with a great silence which no one had known there before. The rabbi gazed at his people; they looked to the elders among them, who drew their prayer shawls closer about them and in the same profound silence led their people out of the synagogue into the dark.

SEVENTEEN

The following morning Jeshua called Peter, sent Andrew to bring James and John and with the briefest farewells, the five left Capernaum.

They were not to leave without another encounter. As they left the border of the city a beggar called to him from the shade of a shrub at the side of the road.

'Jeshua! Rabbi, heal me!'

Jeshua stopped and crossed over to the beggar, seeing he was a leper. His four friends remained on the road, hesitating to get closer, from fear and disgust. Jeshua went without hesitation to the leper, took his malformed hand in his own and touched lightly the scabbed forehead and the blanched flesh of his cheeks. As though they had been bathed, the ravaged features became flushed with healing and his eyes looked back into Jeshua's, clear and full of recognition.

'Go back to Capernaum, show yourself to the rabbi for the prayer of cleansing and be at one with your family and friends again.'

It was all so very undemonstrative, without drama and without the rhetoric of healing. John and Peter, still shaken by their meeting with a leper, looked at Jeshua's hands, the calm smiling eyes and the total assurance of his bearing. This was one they had not wholly known before; they were drawn with as little will as fragments of iron to a lodestone. They had walked a mile or two on their way before they were once more at ease with their companion. For what future had they left Capernaum and their families?

The healed leper was even more troubled by his return to his neighbours than he had been by his exile from them. That had been tragic loneliness but there was no other way for it; uncleanness had to be kept out of their houses and from every family. Now he was doing the forbidden thing, re-entering, a known leper, the village from which he had been expelled. He had to go to the centre of the community, to the rabbi's house, to have the truth made plain, that he was not in fact any longer leprous. Meanwhile there were neighbours who would see him as he passed.

The first little group at the well, showed their repugnance and their fear that he was contaminating one of the sources of their life, the pure water from the deep rocks. He stood at some distance from them and spread out his hands that they might see the miraculous change, pointed to his forehead and his lips, where flesh was restored and already with a bloom of health on it. But long years of exile for the leprous had made it impossible for them to accept this reversal.

As he went further into the little township, former friends from the synagogue saw him approach and their rejection of his presence was even greater; for he was to them, not merely a source of sick infection, he was – a graver matter – ritually unclean. They stood and watched his progress with amazed distaste. He reached the rabbi's home and stood at the threshhold, keeping his distance from the rabbi as the door was opened. 'Master, I was leprous, was leprous and now I am clean.' He extended his hands and again with the gesture almost of pride, indicated the fresh health of his features. 'He cleansed me, He, Jeshua of Nazareth. He even took me by the hand, welcoming me back among men – but he sent me to you, for your prayers and for my return to the synagogue.'

'The Most High has blessed you'; taking him by the arm, the rabbi led him back to his own.

It was quickly understood by the four friends that there were to be gaps in their relationship with Jeshua, hours in each day when he needed to be alone, sometimes a day or two when he left them for some lonely valley or hillside on their seemingly random journey to and fro in Galilee. His requests that they 'remain here a while' or that they go on to the next village to wait for his coming, left them at first wholly at a loss. They had as yet no resources of their own for their times by themselves; deprived of their calling as fishermen, with an articulacy wholly dependent on their craft and the customary market trading, they were without words, without aims for these testing early days. But as the weeks passed by they learned a new strength. At an inn or in a friendly house they had simple words to say.

'We have found a man of power. He heals, he restores the outcasts – lepers and beggars and worse – to their homes.' 'He does it with a touch, a word, sometimes even a look and the devils themselves answer his commands.' 'We have never seen the like of this man.'

The simple wonder with which they spoke carried conviction and it was a smiling Jeshua who acknowledged that his entry to many villages in the Galilean hills owed much of its welcome to the rough integrity of his friends.

One such interlude had covered several days; they had now crossed half of Lower Galilee on their way towards Carmel. They were approaching Sepphoris, the administrative centre of the province and a town of some dignity, where his mother's family had their home. By this time miracle and teaching had ensured that his entry to a new district was greeted by considerable stirring of curiosity and expectation and increasingly Jeshua asked retreat and quiet withdrawal of his disciples. When he returned to them on this occasion, after an unusually long absence, he brought with him another young man who seemed reluctant to come forward to meet them. His eyes had the wariness of a scarcely tamed creature of the wilderness and, tight-lipped, he waited for his introduction to these new companions. Jeshua ignored both his unease and the half-hostile looks of the others:

'We shall now be six in our wanderings. Simon, here are your friends: your namesake and his brother Andrew and these are James and John, their friends from Capernaum. They were all fishermen but now they cast their nets wider!' Turning to the others:

'This is Simon – we have met briefly before in Nazareth. For a year or two he was of the Zealot band here in Galilee, hunted with Judas – but his mind is now changed!' Peter and the others had rarely heard this irony in Jeshua's voice and they were scarcely reassured by it; they drew together and watched the movement of Simon's hands as they seemed to fumble at his waist. Jeshua smiled; 'No,

Simon, you left your dagger when we spoke last night. You won't need it now, among friends.'

The four were scarcely reconciled to this new addition to their little company, as Jeshua, walking along between them, told of his meeting with Simon.

'He was fleeing – you see the state of his clothing – and he has eaten little for some weeks. His fellows have left him – or perhaps, Simon, you left them?' Simon looked away into the hills they were now entering and nodded grudgingly.

'You no longer believed their ways;' it was no question but an assertion.

'The dagger is a poor persuasion; it's final in its violence and so temporary in its argument! No, Simon, you will find these fishermen more comforting friends.'

The frankness of his words glossing over nothing of the fugitive's history, demanded a like candour from the others. They realised that the pattern was wholly changed; the six would never be as the five had been, for they had now drawn within themselves the remnant of a violence they had never known, a bitter zeal which could with difficulty be adopted within their more temperate company.

'You have not considered Barabbas? a violent man – we never quite trusted him in the mountains – but, we always supposed, a large heart and full of concern for Israel.' Simon Zelotes seemed unusually hesitant in his speech, wanting to be persuasive but almost stammering under Jeshua's gaze. He had not before met this steady, apparently unemotional scrutiny and his mind shifted uncertainly under its impact.

'I assumed you had left the mountain caves, the ambushes, behind you – and with them your dubious fellows.' Here was another shift in his knowledge of Jeshua, the irony.

'I have asked him to meet us here' – it was, in effect, a question.

'I meet all men.'

They walked along a gently sloping goat-track outside Cana and very soon saw the massive figure waiting at a curve in the path. Barabbas and Simon greeted each other with the most perfunctory of gestures and the stranger then turned to Jeshua.

'You have filched Simon from us.' There was the merest flicker of banter in the tone; the words were hostility, barely sheathed. Jeshua smiled without conceding ground.

'He is no bond-slave! He is free to return – if he so chooses.'

'He was bound to us, as we are slaves in this desolate land. Occupied! A Roman province, we the people of God in the land He dedicated to us.' Jeshua's smile had now gone and he held Barabbas's frenzy in a gaze whose steadiness seemed to the zealot like an affront, an insulting blow. His fingers curled to fists and Simon made to step between them as a blow from Barabbas seemed inevitable. With the slightest of gestures, Jeshua motioned him to stillness and he turned to Barabbas.

'It seems that you don't trust words? Are blows so invariably more effective?'

'I also have my dreams, rabbi.' That 'also' was the slightest of whiplash insults.

'All men dream, friend; we have only to be sure that dreams remain dreams, without souring into nightmare.'

'My dream, Jeshua, has substance. It is to bow before David's throne without the Legions looming.'

'And will the Legions withdraw at the touch of a dream?'

'No. A dagger's point is more persuasive!'

183

Jeshua turned to Simon. In these few sentences there had been the echoes – echoes with more acid overtones – of exchanges twice before; the first, inconclusive at the tranquil hearth of Lazar in Nazareth; the second in the solitary paths of upper Galilee. Now there was a third – and perhaps conclusive crisis. Barabbas stood, fists clenched and poised for violence; Jeshua stood, calm between them, his questioning look towards Simon gently demanding a choice. Simon, without a word, turned into the paths by which they had come to the encounter and without waiting for Jeshua, strode towards Cana.

Jeshua turned to Barabbas, who stood irresolute in his anger as he watched Simon retreating from his company. Jeshua's smile was full and warm and his words without a touch of dismissal:

'Peace be *always* with you, Barabbas.' The zealot turned away and strode into the upland path.

They were not long to remain a company of six. They had passed beyond Sepphoris and had come to a village within sight of the Carmel heights. They were sharing a quiet evening meal at a house in the centre of the village, when the muted light of the doorway was blocked by a tall figure of some dignity and apparent authority.

'Is Jeshua the Galilean among you?' Jeshua acknowledged the question with a brief gesture.

'I am Judas of Kerioth; I should be grateful for an hour of your time – alone.' The last word carried more than a touch of disdain as he looked at Jeshua's companions. Without a word Jeshua rose, took Judas's arm and went out into the dark night. They walked in silence; Jeshua waited for Judas's first words, sensing the urgency very precariously kept in control by the formal dignity.

'I have searched for many years, with my elders, with learned rabbis, for the truths behind Torah. Every visit to

Jerusalem has shown me the Law polluted, the nobility of our history dragged in the dust. I crave for Judah a cleansing from this filth.'

'Your life, Judas of Kerioth, how have you passed your life, your craft, your livelihood?'

Judas showed a momentary distaste at the word 'craft' and hesitatingly explained his background.

'My father owns land in Kerioth – a good deal of land – and I reckon and manage his wealth! His factors are honest and hard-working men and my task is relatively easy – it leaves me leisure for my reading, for my travelling; to know truth will be more precious to me than to reckon my father's gains.'

'And why have you come to me?'

'I have business in Sepphoris and heard word of your teaching and,' the voice hesitated as though reluctant to use immoderate words, 'and of the wonders that went with your teaching. Are you a rabbi, a Pharisee, a Hasid? What truth have you learnt and how surely do you declare it?'

'Rabbi is a title I hope I can earn; Pharisee is a title of great nobility and I admire their zeal, their reverence and their life within Torah; Hasid is a title of even greater nobility and who shall say that he is worthy of it?'

'You have already answered me.' Judas turned impulsively and took Jeshua's hand.

'I have burned with longing to know the truth that lies behind the truths. Help me, rabbi, to find it.'

Jeshua responded to both the warmth and the desperation of this appeal.

'You, Judas, would be with me and my wandering friends. Those shoes of such delicate leather; would they bear the flints of the high road? Your food, your garments, and above all your friends and family, how would they reach a harmony with those friends of mine you saw? If you wish to be of our company, you must know whom you will be adopting: four fishermen of Capernaum, hard-working, not poor, and a fugitive Zealot, sought by the legions and by the companions he has forsaken. They will receive you for my sake; can you receive them?'

'If this is the price of hearing your words, of sharing your knowledge, it will be a small price to pay.'

It was perhaps not all that Jeshua would have wished but he knew the deep springs of desire, resentment at all that denied the ideals of his race, the pride that drove him; these springs could be tapped, made living in their little community and perhaps purified from the bitterness that drove him as powerfully as the longing for the Law.

They returned to the house where Judas had found Jeshua; the meal was over and the five were seated beneath a fig tree in the courtyard.

'Judas of Kerioth wishes to join us. He, like you, has left his family, his comfort, and makes his way now as one of our company; greet him as your brother.'

This was as sharp a re-ordering of their minds as they had known at the coming of Simon. Where they had seen themselves as humble itinerants, moving to the dictates of weather and terrain and rejoicing in a friendship which transfigured their lives to a new radiance, Judas was an alien, a wealthy man of the south; Simon they could raise to their level, cherish him in charity – but this stranger?

EIGHTEEN

For the next few days Jeshua kept away from villages and hamlets, making eastward along the plateau, at no great distance from Nazareth. He remained at some little distance behind his friends, watching with pleasure the six as they broke into groups, talking with animation or walking silently along the paths that were little more than sheep-tracks. At first the four from Capernaum went steadily ahead together, while Simon and Judas walked behind with little to bring them together. Then James and John, whose temperaments gave them some affinity with the former zealot, joined him, asking him of ambushes and solitary attacks; the use of the land's configuration by Roman and Jew and of the outcome of it all. Judas felt more and more drawn towards Peter and the quieter Andrew, questioning them about trade at the lake cities, the crops of eastern Galilee, his expertise meeting theirs and leading to a growing respect. At evening Jeshua drew them all together and a psalm gave them a unity they would never have anticipated even a week before.

They were gradually approaching Cana, the village astir with unusual activity. Jeshua knew the people well, since it was a sister village to Nazareth and an old friend greeted him.

'Welcome to our wedding, Jeshua and bring your friends.'

It was good fortune for the family that this man from Nazareth should come in such a timely way. Without the prejudices of Nazareth, Cana was glad that the miracles and prophetic words of Jeshua should give a further joy to the ceremony; and Jeshua was glad to have such an occasion take a further step in the unifying of his little company.

Already it was time for the ceremony and the majesty of the rite captured them in its rhythms:

Blessed art thou, O Lord our God,
  King of the universe,
  Who createst the fruit of the vine.

Blessed art thou, O Lord our God,
King of the universe,
Who hast created all things to thy glory.

Blessed art thou, O Lord our God,
King of the universe, creator of man.

Blessed art thou, O Lord our God,
King of the universe,
Who hast made man in thine own image, thine own
likeness,
And hast prepared unto him
Out of his very self, a lifelong helpmate;

Blessed art thou, O Lord, creator of man.
May Zion who was barren be exceeding glad and
exult,
When her children are gathered within her in joy.

Blessed art thou, O Lord,
Who makest Zion joyful through her children.

Jeshua absorbed the whole rite into himself, assenting
to the words of creation and rejoicing in the little island of
peace which the ceremony produced; in its warmth he
repeated in an undertone the final thanksgiving of the
opening rite:
O make these loved companions greatly to rejoice,
Even as of old thou didst gladden thy creatures
In the garden of Eden.
He looked at Peter, the blunt features of his face softened
by memories of his marriage at Capernaum and at Judas
austerely responding to the measured rhythms of the rite.
It proceded through the ceremony of ring and canopy, to
the blessing and the closing triumph.

Praise God in his sanctuary,
>   Praise him in the firmanent of his power.
>   Let everything that has breath
>   Praise the Lord.

And so to the feast. Though the house was large, only a few of the honoured guests could actually enter the house, Jeshua standing just within the entrance, his friends behind him. Peter and Andrew assisted with the great platters of meat and bread and Judas, with ceremony, filled glasses from the large ewers of silver. When most had eaten, even the villagers in the courtyard taking their token of the food, wine continued to circulate as the greetings and talk grew more animated. Then there was unusual consternation; there was no more wine. This was not only a social catastrophe which denied the very nature of these celebrations; it was all the worse in that none could remember such a tragedy at Cana.

While the agitation grew, Mary of Nazareth was approached and she sought out Jeshua.

'They have no more wine.'

'Why should you think, Mother, that that is my concern?'

It was lightly spoken and was immediately followed by a grave repetition of the opening words of the ceremony they had that day witnessed:

>   'Blessed art thou, O Lord our God
>   Who createst the fruit of the vine.'

Mary said to the distracted servants and the master of the feast:

'Whatever he tells you to do, do it!'

At the entrance to the house stood six pitchers, capable of holding some fifty gallons of water between them. They were now empty, for all the dusty feet had been ritually cleansed before the feast began.

'Fill them with pure water.'

When the servants had hurriedly done so, he directed them again,

'Draw out now and serve the guests with wine.'

It was savoured with astonishment, to such a degree that the master of the feast whispered to the bridegroom:

'Is this quite courteous? The finest vintage should be served first when men can truly savour it and the lesser wines when they have well drunk. Never has such a wine as this been tasted at Cana and you have kept it to the end of the feast!'

The seven withdrew unobtrusively from Cana and before the last prayers of evening Jeshua was heard by them as he spoke almost wholly to himself.

'The marriage and the harmony of the Most High; how better can we celebrate it than with the fruit of the vine, the crushed and broken clusters, the outpouring as of blood?'

They listened in wonder as the images stirred in his mind and on his lips; it would have been intrusive to question him.

NINETEEN

It was now time to return to Capernaum. It was right that families be remembered and maintained and when they once more reached the sea-shore, the first object of the fishermen, after greeting their families at home, was to seek out Zebedee in whose care the boats and nets had been left. That night there was fishing again and with dawn Jeshua met them on the shore to help with sorting the catch, those for the market, those for the day's food and the larger fish for curing. The meal that day was a feast, of broiled fish, oat and wheaten bread dipped in oil, cheese with herbs and fruit at the close of the meal. Judas was taken to their hearts as he ate as though the peasant fare were of noble providing and Peter's wife glowed and the house was filled with a temper she had rarely known.

For all their need for peace, the household at Capernaum was in a continuous stir from the outside world. Not long after dawn the sick would come with their attendants, some led, some carried but all demanding the healing powers of Jeshua. On a particularly mild day the crowds had been greater than ever, not confining themselves to the courtyard but thrusting in to the living-room, making movement almost impossible. Jeshua did all they besought him, touching the eyes of the blind, the ears of the deaf and restoring strength to those whom poverty had rendered vulnerable and helpless. He seemed tireless in the healing.

A tearing and a hammering above them halted his work and all looked up in consternation to see the laths and cement of the ceiling torn apart until a hole some seven feet square had been ripped in the roof of the house. Through the aperture a bed was thrust, to which a paralysed man had been strapped; those who had brought him, finding that courteous access to Jeshua was denied them, had gone behind the house, clambered to the roof and opened their own access to the presence of the healer. It was a grotesque sight, the patient precariously lowered and swinging in such arcs as to endanger the heads of all below. Not concealing his laughter at the sight, Jeshua stepped aside and waited for the descent to be complete.

Then there was silence as he looked intently at the young man brought to him. Laughter was now behind him and his gaze had a searching gravity. Then moving to the side of the crude bed, he raised his hand over the sick man's face and said,

'My son, your sins are forgiven you.'

191

As the man remained still and unmoving, whispering spread through the room and into the courtyard – words like this had not been heard before from Jeshua, not even in his healing hours. Some scribes of the Law stood at the doorway and heard with amazement Jeshua's words of absolution.

'This man blasphemes! Who can forgive sins but God alone?'

Jeshua replied to them: 'What is the argument of your hearts? Which is the easier for me to promise: 'your sins are forgiven' or 'rise up and walk'?'

He turned in the silence to the paralysed man and said to his companions, 'Loose him from his bed' and then to the palsied, 'Rise; take up your bed yourself and return to your home.'

Immediately the paralytic rose, gathered up his bed and went from the house, his eyes wondering but no longer haunted by any fear. All about Jeshua there was marvelling and a new speculation – 'We have seen strange things!' – but Jeshua left them and pursued the outraged scribes as they hurried away from the house.

'You didn't answer me. Which *was* the real, the difficult task: to forgive or to heal?'

They were unprepared to risk an answer.

'They were one task. He could have been healed and his sins left festering in his heart. But it was that sin that was the root and cause of the palsy. Without forgiveness he would again have been paralysed. I forgave him.'

'*You* forgave him?' The outrage was palpable.

'Yes, my friends in the Law, *I* forgave him.'

So the days passed as the old routine was taken up and the seven became welded into one. Then on the morrow of the Sabbath, Jeshua left them and walked to the port of Magdala. This sophisticated city had taken over many of the formal duties of the larger city of Capernaum and even attracted trade from the regal city of Tiberias. Its custom house was therefore important, the merchants summoned there to calculate their dues, the import duties on all goods from the complex of routes from the Great Sea, from Judah and from the north and the coastlands of Tyre and Sidon. The taxes were large, even exorbitant and the tax gatherers men of substance and dignity. One of them, Matthew by name, was not the leading collector but was a man of consequence, and, for a tax-collector, was accounted a man of honesty and discretion. Jeshua approached his accounting-table and stood in silence before him. Matthew too remained silent, with no questioning of his business or purpose, no request to account for himself and his trade. The strange encounter created a pool of silence about them as the trading and bargaining ceased for a time. Then Jeshua spoke quite quietly.

'Matthew, son of Alphaeus, follow me!'

Without a word, Matthew closed his leaves of accounts, pushed the coins across to his assistant and in continued silence passed between the people to follow Jeshua into the heart of Magdala.

That evening Matthew took him to his home where he had gathered together his friends. It was in a sheltered inlet on the coast, just halfway between Magdala and Capernaum; his friends and the six friends of Jeshua had come from both cities to the feasting. Matthew greeted them all with courtesy and the due observances for all, cleansing and washing and a ceremonial ushering to their places at the tables set around. Jeshua unobtrusively saw to it that the six were separated into groups of two and that they mingled with the other guests, the tax gatherers, with some of whom they had previously done substantial business. Talk was at first constrained and with the irony that was never far from Jeshua's mind, he speculated on the memories of unjustified taxes, over-estimates and blatant cheatings which now clouded the conversation.

He confined himself to talk with Matthew, his family in Judea and, quietly and tentatively, with what lay before him as he gave up his comfortable home and the luxury his wealth had brought. Gradually the atmosphere lightened and talk became mixed with laughter as the wine circulated.

Outside in the courtyard, silhouetted against the fading light of the lake, two elders of the Pharisees stood watching the feast. After a while of deepening disapproval, they beckoned to Peter who was at a table nearest the entrance to the house.

'This is unseemly.' The deep voice expressed a personal affront.

'Your master, a rabbi, sits eating and drinking – carousing! – with these tax gatherers, sinners, giving his friendship to them, and in denial of the Law, giving his approval to their ways.'

'So he does, and we eat with him and them.' The customary briskness of Peter's voice, not much accustomed to urbane conversation, was more than usually noticeable. He appeared about to sharpen the exchange with some sea-shore witticisms, when he caught Jeshua's eye. Jeshua quietly excused himself to Matthew, rose from the table and went out to speak to the Pharisees.

'Friends, you seem dismayed. You and I have our own ways and they are good. But you say these other friends of mine are sinners, sick in their souls; you are well and need no physician, but these? Isn't it the physician that these need and do you forbid me to be with them in their need?'

The unassertive voice, the very pointedness of the question, left them silent; but still they failed to relax their grim condemnation of the feasting. Jeshua's courteous smile left his lips and his eyes held theirs in turn.

'Do you forget the words of our prophet, Hosea; 'I will have mercy and not sacrifice'? – 'Mercy', loving kindness, reconciling the broken hearted – isn't that greater than all the sacrifices? I hold to the words of Hosea, for I am not here to call the righteous; I have come to call the sinners to a new life; to abundant life.'

The claim was unambiguous and confounding, beyond the reach of formal minds, beyond the comprehension of these men who, after all, were his natural allies, men to whom he instinctively responded. Lazar came back to his memory, his passionate love of the Law and the gentle commendation of its precepts. Jeshua knew with foreboding that not all lovers of the Law had Lazar's wide charity. With a gesture of appeal he turned again to the two Pharisees; troubled and indecisive, they turned away from him and Jeshua was left to return to the feast.

Three days later Jeshua and the six returned along the shore to Matthew's home. There Jeshua told of his wish to go south to Judea and to visit Jerusalem and asked if Matthew were ready to go with him.

'I've settled my business and written to my family. They will agree with my friends here in Galilee that I'm beside myself – perhaps I am!'

Jeshua took him affectionately by the arm and after a little pause for refreshment, they all set out on the road, first bearing northward to avoid the busy 'merchant route' to Tiberias and then westward towards Cana.

This was their first comfortable stop, for they were made exuberantly welcome at the house of the wedding feast and they remained in Cana for a few days, while Matthew grew accustomed to the company and his new life. Nor was this the only adjustment to their number. Jeshua seemed to them all to have an unsatisfied quest, for what they could not determine, but after some three days in Cana, Jeshua returned with a diffident young man, a small trader from beyond Upper Galilee from the Syro-Phoenician coast towards Tyre.

'This is Thomas who wishes to join us.' There was a gauche salutation from the young man but they made room for him at the hearth.

'By your speech you come from the north?' Peter, blunt as always, burst through the young man's monosyllabic responses and indeed Thomas seemed glad to respond to the crude gesture of friendship.

'I was born in Sarepta but my father – he traded in wool and pelts and when times were good he did a little trade in precious dyes – well, my father thought we would be better off below Tyre on the coast. My mother didn't want to move – I was growing fast and she had dreams of a rabbi in the family – I was always the questioning sort – and she hated the thought of upheaval – you know how it can be!'

He smiled shyly, as though he had been too garrulous. He was clearly puzzled by the company in which he found himself. Judas he understood; he had noticed the sharpened look at the mention of a trade in dyes. Matthew also had the assurance of prosperity, the look of steady calculation rarely absent from the handling of great wealth. And the four friends from Capernaum, and especially Peter their most outspoken, these too he understood; the calloused hands and the muscular forearms – he had not been surprised when Jeshua's introduction had included mention of their craft as fishermen. But what were they as a company of men? What bond held together these so dissimilar individuals? They were not in the least like the bands that wandered with the Hasidim, men of like fervour with their leaders; nor were they in the remotest way like a group of Zealots, despite the quick wariness in Simon's eyes. How were they, in any sense that he could fathom, a company?

It was true that in the two or three meetings he had had with Jeshua, as they wandered in the environs of Cana, he had felt a power and authority beyond any he had known in synagogue or market place hitherto. It was not an arrogant authority that compelled him but the steady pull of a person beyond any he had hitherto encountered. In Jeshua's presence, as in no other, he felt the groping tentativeness which was the most obvious part of his make-up, fade away in a security that was so like 'sanctuary.' He hesitated now, in the strange companionship, as he tried to define that word. 'Sanctuary'; why had it come so constantly to his mind in these last brief days? Why was it associated in his thoughts with the Temple? For to speak truth, on the rare visits he and his family had made to Jerusalem, the very Temple itself had smacked of tawdriness, had repelled him in its echoes of dubious trading on the Syro-Phoenician coast. But Jeshua? Here was a person who carried with him the radiance of an ancient dream fulfilled, so that his quiet conversation in the heathlands about Cana carried overtones of Eden at the dawn of man, of the Ark as it led the secure way through the desert, of the dream of the Temple in David's mind and not its so partial fulfilment by Solomon – and Herod! The eyes, the voice, the secure embracing smile – if they could compass him in his groping, could they perhaps embrace four fishermen, a Zealot, a tax-gatherer and a wealthy aristocrat from the south?

The next journey raised more questions than it gave answers to Thomas. As they moved southward from Cana, into the fertile plains, Jeshua was again curious to assess the shifting friendships within his followers. For he had been engaged in no arithmetic accumulation of individuals; from the beginning there had been coherence, four relatives and friends, bound by their arduous and dangerous craft into an instinctive understanding. And as the alien individuals had been added to the number, so they had cohered in a richer, more diverse pattern, each member enabling all to shift in sensibility and understanding. Now as they went their way, three moved happily ahead of the others, Matthew, Judas and Thomas, bound together by the pure diversity of their background and experience but with a common knowledge of 'the world', the sophisticated bonds of commerce. Snatches of laughter came back from their talking, as they spoke satirically of shady deals detected, of plausible rascals and their tales, and of pleasures in shared luxury. In the evenings, as by a fire in an improvised hearth, they ate their dried or broiled fish and small barley cakes, and perhaps even shared a flask of rough country wine, the laughter would return, as with a gesture of fingers holding coarse fare they said to each other, 'That feast!' The satire was much to Jeshua's taste and he shared with them their tacit preference for the new, unfettered life.

Simon, James and John found something congenial in each other's company which drew them frequently into an animated group. James and John could be impatient, even irascible and Jeshua, on leaving a village with them one day when their conduct with surly villagers had been less than urbane, said, only half laughing, 'You Sons of Thunder must control your tongues! We can scarcely return to that village again!' 'Sons of Thunder' had stuck, an affectionate reproach and it had drawn Simon to them.

'Of course a Zealot must keep his temper. No good being too ready with the stabbing!' They had laughed uneasily at first but when they realised the seriousness with which he spoke of his old life, so recently set aside, they questioned him more closely.

'Anger won't really do. I naturally dislike the Herodians and detest the Romans, but one has to be steady, yes, steady describes it.' Momentarily it almost seemed to their disconcerted minds that Simon was about to plan with them another ambush, until they realised the glint of mischief in the quick glance aside he gave them. Jeshua had heard fragments of his account of hill-fighting and that evening at the fireside he had more gravely than usual quoted Isaiah and the prophecy of swords and ploughshares, of spears and pruning hooks, and of the choices which men must make. Peter and Andrew gazed around at these echoes of activity among their fellows and thought of calm and squalls, of great shoals and of empty nets. With a delicate intuition, Jeshua led the conversation back to Capernaum and its synagogue.

TWENTY

Their way now led them to the borders of Samaria and the group showed an unease that was clearly not shared by Jeshua. He pressed them purposefully, reaching the high plateau on their third day. Each evening they made a rough encampment near a stream or grove, Jeshua respecting the wish of the eight to ask for no hospitality of the surly or hostile Samaritans. The whole country was of great contrasts, bare, forbidding uplands but with distant views of fertile valleys and plains on either side. At length they came within sight of the twin peaks of Ebal and Gerizim. The loved and yet so tragic passages in Deuteronomy ran in Jeshua's mind and gathering the eight about him he invited their contemplation of this landscape before them.

'Our history has swirled about these mountains and valleys. There before you, Gerizim and facing it Ebal, the place of the choices. Moses was not to tread these slopes but pointing to them he challenged his people:

'Behold, I set before you this day
    A blessing and a curse.
    A blessing, if ye obey the commandments
    Of the Lord your God
    Which I command you this day
    And a curse if ye will not obey
    The commandments of the Lord your God
    But turn aside out of the way

　　　　　Which I command you this day,
　　　　　To go after other Gods.'
Jeshua's voice had risen to the rhythms of the passage and
they waited in the silence that followed.

'They turned aside, oh yes, they turned aside. Age after
age saw them forsake the Most High and age after age saw
the hope renewed. There on Ebal, Joshua built an altar to
Adonai and renewed the covenant sworn between them
and there below in the valley, Jacob dug a well, sweet,
living water for his people, his flocks and their shepherds.'

The so-familiar history, recalled from so many synagogue readings and exhortations, had an urgency, a
renewed life in the mouth of Jeshua. Moses himself spoke
tragically over the centuries, the mountains rang with the
ancient blessings and curses and Jacob's exultation in the
goodness of God passed into their blood as they sat
together in the evening stillness.

The whole of the following day was spent in a slow
approach to Sychar. It was again evening and Jeshua sent
the companions into the village to seek food and wine for
the next few days; Jeshua remained resting, seated on the
rim of the well, within sight of the village but at some little
distance from it.

A woman, handsome and poised beneath the large-
water jar she carried on her shoulder, approached the
well. Resentment at the stranger's presence flared briefly,
to be followed by a quick observation of this comely young
man. Jeshua spoke as if diffidently.

'Can you give me a drink of this water? I have no cup.'

A hostile tone masked the curiosity which she now felt;
'Why do you, a Galilean, ask a favour of me, a despised
Samaritan?'

Jeshua replied with a different challenge.

'If you understood the purposes of Jahweh and if you
knew who it is who asks of you this little drink of water,
you would have returned the request. You would have
said, 'give me living water'.'

'This water is 'living'; never have we drawn stagnant or unclean water from this well. And you – you have no vessel to draw from its depths, for Jacob our father dug deep.'

Jeshua answered, and now his voice had a new and measured solemnity.

'You draw water here each day and each day you thirst again; but if you drink the water I offer you, you shall never thirst again.'

A bitter resentment halted the reply and then desperation broke through the silence.

'Sir, give me this water in God's name, so that I thirst no more and have no need to come to this place day after day.'

'Why do you come alone and at this hour of the day? What company, what words do you fear? Call your husband and come back to me here.'

'I have no husband.' It was defiantly said, with the remnants of pride in her beauty.

'You tell me the truth. You have had four – five? – and the sixth with whom you now live, is no husband of yours.'

Long-accustomed shame and a profound dignity still maintained the woman's poise and with a deft change in their talk she set aside the accusation.

'Sir, you are perceptive! And I see by your words that you are a prophet. Answer me this question that stands, a barrier between you, a holy Galilean and me, an outcast Samaritan. Our father's worshipped in this mountain and by its holiness we live. But you say that Mount Zion is the true centre of belief, Jerusalem the centre of worship. Where lies the truth between your history and ours?'

'Believe me, the time is not far distant when Ebal, Gerizim and Zion will be of no account in the worship of the Father. You worship blindly, hoping for a truth; we know Him whom we worship. But a time comes – it is at hand when true worshippers, Jew, Samaritan and Gentile, will worship the Father in spirit and truth, for my Father seeks all men for his worship.'

There was no reply from the woman; the well, the water-pot, thirst and the 'living water' were all forgotten in the wonder of this person before her. In the silence, Jeshua caught at her vestige of understanding.

'God is a spirit; neither idol nor place, neither sanctuary nor sacrifice compasses him. He is spirit and true worship must be worship in the spirit.

'You speak wonders, Sir. Even we know that when the Messiah comes he will declare all these things to us.'

'I, here before you, am He.'

Silence lay between them as she gazed at him. This was not the woman who had come to the well, resentful and furtive. After some minutes of the silence, she left the water-pot at the well-head and ran towards Sychar, passing the companions of Jeshua as they returned.

Peter was dismayed at what he had seen and Judas feigned an elegant ignorance of the incident. All eight of them waited, appalled, for an explanation from the smiling Jeshua – he, a rabbi to be found in close converse with a woman and she a Samaritan! What washings, what scouring of souls could atone for this lapse? There was no way to frame their questions.

But there was tumult behind them. The woman had breathlessly blurted out her discovery and Sychar streamed out to see this alien for themselves. As the road to the well-head filled with the villagers, Jeshua turned to the disciples and to their unspoken question he said:

'There is your answer. The fields are ripe to harvest, a harvest richer and more precious than you will perhaps help gather in the fields in many weeks. Here are those who need the word; you are they who must speak it to them.'

The men of Sychar came to him, halted near the well and remained silent, expecting his words. Jeshua remained as silent as they but looking from face to face, gathering to himself their hopes and their fears, the narrow confines of their minds. They came nearer, answering dumbly the tranquil questioning in his eyes. Then one older than his neighbours took Jeshua by the arm.

'Come with us to Sychar. Stay with us and we will make you welcome.'

Jeshua responded immediately, walked to the little township with companions on either side, but with his eight intimate friends trailing with foreboding in the rear of the procession.

Jeshua remained in Sychar for two days. There was much to tell them again, with a new insight: of Jacob their patriarch, his treachery to his brother Esau, his wrestling with God's angel; of Jacob's sons, Joseph and his brothers and of the intended treachery, Joseph sold by his brothers into slavery in Egypt; and of reconciliation and a fulfilled old age. The ladder to heaven, with its galaxy of angels had been hard to achieve but the vision had become reality. They listened entranced, like children to a well-rehearsed tale but now brim-ful with vitality.

And he went on to tell them of their own country, of Ebal and Gerizim.

'The choices are still there for you. Do right before God and Torah and the blessings will come echoing down from Moses until now; deny God and Torah and the curses will echo like thunder down the years.'

They longed to confirm what the outcast woman had told them.

'Will Messiah bring these blessings even to us?'

'I give you these blessings, freely and with joy.'

Some days later, when the departure of Jeshua and the eight had left memories that still glowed for Sychar, the woman was no longer alone at the well. To her natural beauty had now been added the confident assurance of her return to her neighbours. There was even a touch of raillery in their laughing deflation in her pride in the coming of Jeshua and her making ready his invitation to Sychar.

'We too believe – but not because of what you told us. We have heard for ourselves and know that this is the Christ, the longed-for.'

Jerusalem continued to work its fascination, a demand on Jeshua and his friends that had as much foreboding in it as fulfilment of their worship.

They made to enter the city from the south, the Jericho road and the final ascent by way of Gethsemane. On the slope which gave a view of the whole city and of the Temple, distastefully neighboured by the Antonia, the Roman fortress, Jeshua was wholly silent, his eyes deeply troubled, and after standing irresolute among his friends he turned to them and said:

'A day or two only; a visit to the abode of Adonai, a greeting of a friend or two, our duties at the feast and then a swift return to Galilee.'

The duties they all fulfilled and then Jeshua turned to a quarter of the city which had always fascinated him. The Pool of Bethesda lay not far within the city from the Lion's Gate. Behind him as he entered was the peace of the Garden of Gethsemane, before him looming over the pool, was the Antonia, with the trumpeting of the watches as the Roman soldiery changed their guard. But within the structure of the pool there was something of the peace of the inner Temple court. The cistern with its still water was surrounded by alcoves in which grievously sick men lay on their pallets. Jeshua had celebrated the Sabbath, its lights and its ceremonious meal, with his friends in their customary 'home' on Mount Zion beyond Zion Gate. Now he could be about his business of healing.

He had early been told of the powers of the Pool. At unexpected intervals, so the belief went, the waters of Bethesda were strangely stirred by an angel of God. At the first sign of this movement of waters, the sick plunged into the cistern, the first to reach the surface of the water being healed of his sickness.

Jeshua moved among them and they remarked the comforting serenity of his look and occasional word to them. But one commanded his attention above the others. His look spoke not so much of suffering as of total dereliction and Jeshua was halted by the hopeless pleading of his eyes. It was clear by his wasted limbs that he had been there for many years, now wholly incapable of movement.

'You wish to be healed?'

'Healing can never be for me; I have no friend who will cast me, paralysed as I am, into the waters when they stir.'

Jeshua asked for no response but obedience.

'Rise, pick up your bed and take it to your home.'

The waters had remained still and the other sick men watched with astonishment the poise of the cured man as he took up his pallet and left the Pool. His way lay below the Temple in the direction of Herod's Citadel and as he walked, his pallet on his back, he was stopped by scribes from the Temple.

'What blasphemy is this? On the Sabbath you carry your bed shamelessly and openly within the very shadow of the Temple?'

'I was told to carry it away by him who restored my limbs.'

'And his name?'

'I am ashamed that I didn't ask him.'

His shame pursued him to his home and he felt impelled to make what recompense he could by going to the Temple before Sabbath was ended. There, walking at leisure in the inner colonnade he found Jeshua. As he tried incoherently to stammer his apology and his gratitude, his words were halted by Jeshua.

'You are whole in your body now and can move about with your neighbours. Don't sin again in case this sickness plagues you once more.'

The words carried no accusation, no rough condemnation, but their authority spoke directly to his condition and when he was again questioned by the scribes he said,

'This time I knew him; Jeshua the healer from Galilee.'

Jeshua was found by the scribes and the Temple guards, still quietly waiting for the closing Sabbath ritual. Roughly they accused him:

'You work on the Sabbath!'

'Yes, my Father works, even on the restful Sabbath, if His grace requires it. And I work also when the need compels me.

'Do I need to remind you of John? For a time you revered him – and he testified of me.

'Do you search the scriptures? They testify of me.

'Do you trust in Moses? – he accuses you and your denial for he wrote of me. If you don't believe in Moses who brought you Torah from the very mouth of my Father, how will you believe me?'

The challenge was final and definitive, the claim absolute. Pharisees, indeed the Sanhedrin itself, its ancient dignity and authority unambiguously questioned, were faced with a dilemma for which the centuries gave them no precedent. There were minor skirmishes as they tried to manoeuvre for ground on which they might trap and destroy Jeshua. There was a technical charge of 'reaping on the Sabbath' as they found Jeshua and his friends plucking corn grains in the field. There was a healing in the synagogue on the Sabbath and their accusations withered as he turned their own law back upon them.

'Is it lawful to do good on the Sabbath – or to do evil! to save life or to kill?'

The ambiguity of the undertone within the question was clear to their scholastic minds – 'to do evil – to kill!' It was they who withdrew from the skirmish and Jeshua was left free to return to Galilee.

But they were faced with a final discomfiture; word began to circulate in the streets and market-places that here, in this person, was a 'fulfilment,' a life 'according to the prophets.' More ominously than the general appeal to the accomplishing of prophecy was the sharply particular identification – for had not Isaiah himself spoken of Yahweh's 'Suffering Servant?':

Behold my servant whom I have chosen,
    My beloved in whom I am well pleased.
    I will put my Spirit upon him,
    And he shall show justice to the Gentiles.
    He will not strive nor cry aloud,
    Nor will any man hear his voice in the streets;
    He will not break a bruised reed,
    Nor quench a smouldering wick,
    Till he brings justice to its victory
    And in his name will the Gentiles trust.

Jerusalem stirred with rumour and with uneasy anticipation of tragic conflict. But in quiet and with determination, Jeshua withdrew from Judah and made his way to Galilee.

TWENTY-ONE

The journey north was not without incident which brought yet another critical change in the band of intimate followers. For now the eight became twelve. The four who were added were modest men and the journey to Galilee was sufficient to bring them into unity with the more seasoned disciples of Jeshua. As they walked along or rested at the evening meal, Jeshua told them of his purpose for them: they were to teach, to heal and to exorcise. That final power over devils was the seal on both teaching and healing; for were they not to fulfil his will that the world might again have the wisdom of the fathers and that men might be cleansed in their whole being? The purpose was expressed to them with simplicity, almost casually and for all of them it was a confounding change. They had heard Jeshua's words, they had seen his healing hands, known his authority which defeated the very devils themselves. But they? were they capable of inheriting those powers?

Their uneasy questioning was posed, sometimes in groups as they walked the highways, more often in solitary conversation with him, as one by one they sought to identify their particular place in his purpose for them. When time enough had been given them to identify both their problems as a coherent group of his followers and their agonised doubts of their individual fitness for their vocations, Jeshua planned his preparation of their minds. Until they had understanding, how could they resolve their hearts and wills?

Much of the teaching was for them alone; much also could be declared to them in the presence of the crowds who followed them. They were now approaching the district Gennesaret and Jeshua led his friends to the slopes of a gentle eminence and saw that the more numerous followers came to the foot of the slope, keeping their distance.

Jeshua stood in silence before them until a quiet expectation palpably united the whole multitude. His voice carried with clarity.

'Do you seek bread, a healing of your sicknesses, or do you seek a kingdom?'

They had expected no challenge of this kind.

'You remember the words of David as he sang:
> The Lord is King for ever and ever;
>> And the heathen are perished out of the land.

Is it such a mighty King that you seek? For David said of this King,
> Lord, thou hast heard the desire of the poor;
>> Thou preparest their hearts
>> And thine ear hearkeneth thereto.

Do you seek a mighty King in conquest or is the kingdom you long for a kingdom for the poor and the outcasts?'

They listened to the tone of his voice, knew that they were challenged but still could make no response. Nor were Peter and John, Judas and Matthew in any better case. They watched and waited knowing that it was not Jeshua's way to be merely a purveyor of dark sayings, of paradox. In the complete stillness that now surrounded him, Jeshua dropped his voice a little, demanding an ever greater attention.

'Let me tell you of my kingdom. It is a kingdom of blessedness, of peace beyond the imagining of Saul, of David, of Solomon, a kingdom in which you take your part.

Hear its new laws, as powerful as those of Sinai:
> Blessed are the poor in spirit,
>> For theirs is the kingdom of heaven.

> Blessed are the meek,
> For they shall inherit the earth.

> Blessed are they that mourn,
> For they shall be comforted.

> Blessed are they that hunger
> and thirst after righteousness
> For they shall be filled.

Blessed are the merciful,
For they shall obtain mercy.

Blessed are the pure in heart,
For they shall see God.

Blessed are they which are persecuted for righteousness' sake,
For theirs is the kingdom of heaven.

'Poor in spirit, meek, they that mourn, that hunger for
righteousness; do you recognise yourselves, are you
among them? For I *do* say to you, you are blessed, you
inherit the kingdom, you poor, you meek, you mourning
men.

'But how many of you can be counted merciful? How
many know loving-kindness, compassion, love? These
too are blessedly of the kingdom.

'And 'pure in heart', the simplicity and innocence of a
child – are you too old for that, too hardened?

'Persecuted for the sake of a righteous kingdom' – are
you courageous enough for that, to stand with Amos, with
Jeremiah, with Isaiah?

'Children, you are silent, and perhaps I have now said
enough to you.'

He turned to the twelve who were as silent as the
multitude. Judas said quietly to him, 'Meek, Lord?' and
Peter who was by his side, 'Merciful, Lord? to all men?'
Jeshua answered them with no more than a smile, took
each by the arm and led the way back to their lodging.

The next morning, very early, he took the twelve and
avoiding the familiar ways and so avoiding the crowds, he
took them to a barren, rocky defile where they sat about
him.

'Let us eat' he said and with them took out the bread and dried fruit which were to suffice for the day.

'I have much to tell you, you in particular. You heard me yesterday speak to the multitude of their stake in the kingdom. I could see the longing in their faces, for they truly hunger, even if they don't know the end for which they hunger. If they are to come to the kingdom, they must be led tenderly, like lambs.

'But you! For you it is quite different and so very testing. Let me tell you the necessary truths:

'You are the salt of the earth – but if salt has changed its nature, lost its savour, of what use is it. It may just as well be treated as the dust of the earth.

'You are the light of the world. Cities that are set on a hill cannot be hidden from a wayfarer's eye. Nor do our women, at evening – or at the Sabbath eve – light a candle and place it beneath a vessel to hide it! You have seen those blessed lights, those that welcome the wayfarer at dusk, at journey's end; you have seen the quiet golden beauty of the Sabbath candles –

'There then is your work in the kingdom, to be salt and purifying, and to light their minds – theirs, those who seek me so blindly.'

They had rarely before heard this range in Jeshua's voice, a ringing assurance, a quiet even tragic longing, a pleading with them for understanding. They sought to respond; they too craved to be one with him in his dream of his Kingdom and they waited for his further words.

'You have been with me in Jerusalem. You have seen and heard the bitterness, the hatred, the destructive hatred. And they accuse me, 'he breaks the law' they say, 'he denies Torah.' Jeshua's eyes were bleak as he reminded them of the anger at Jerusalem; and they were fearful, for anger could become retribution.

'They are so wrong, so tragically wrong. I came not to destroy the Law, to deny the prophets. Indeed, indeed, I

211

came not to destroy but to fulfil. It is so possible to conform to the words of Torah – and to be outside the Law! To mouth even 'Hear, O Israel' and be empty of all love of God. I tell you, till the heavens fall and the earth pass away, not one least syllable of Torah shall be denied; and I say to you that unless your love of Torah, your righteous thoughts and dealings, go far beyond the rulers of the Temple, you will not found my Father's kingdom on earth.

'For I say to you it is the will and not the deed that corrupts and destroys our hearts. We are told, 'Thou shalt not kill' but hatred, wrath in the breast of man, is a perpetual killing; we are told 'Thou shalt not commit adultery' but lust is subtle and serpent-like and has no hint of love or cherishing within it.

'We can be a violent people; the cruelty of the desert did much to shape our souls; and so we hear that word, 'An eye for an eye and a tooth for a tooth,' 'I will have vengeance, even I, the Lord.' Thus even the tradition of the Elders ties God and man in a common violence – 'I will repay!' But I say to you – and this is the Law of the Kingdom, make no resistance to violence, to evil directed against you. If a man strike you on the right cheek, turn to him the left also. If at law a man takes away your tunic, give him your cloak also; if you are compelled to go a mile with a violent man, walk with him the second mile also.'

He looked long at each of the twelve. Peter and Andrew were moved by his words; there was reserve on the faces of the 'Sons of Thunder,' while Simon, from old habit, fingered the fold of his tunic where the dagger was once hidden. Judas and Matthew had each his fastidious intensity, following the argument and reserving their judgment; the others were doing their best to assimilate the simple revolution in their idea of God's Kingdom.

'I would take you further. Who are the ones you love? Your family, your friends? Of course, you love your own, you love the lovable! But I say to you, the Kingdom cannot

212

cient for that day. Without a word they returned to their lodging.

The day following he deliberately led his disciples through the crowded highway and, turning towards the quieter uplands, allowed the multitudes to surround them on the way. When they had reached the outcrop on the summit where Jeshua had a natural seat commanding the crowd about him, he began to speak to them as if there had been no break in his discourse.

'Where do you keep the things you value? Do you grow rich, stack away your riches in barns or hidden in your closets? I say to you this: lay up your treasures in heaven; they don't rust there and moth doesn't ruin those precious garments – and there are no thieves in heaven!

'And be clear and single-minded in all you do. The light of the body is the eye; now if your eyes are clear, your whole body will be filled with light, but if your eyes are clouded or if you try to look in two directions at once, how dark your body will be!

'In the same way, be single-minded about your work, your aims in life. You know the trouble you get into if you try to do work for two masters, your loyalty split in two ways and not knowing, day after day, which way to turn to do right. So also, you can't serve God and worldly things which some of you call Mammon; some of you will try to serve God in worship but even then your mind is going back to your hidden riches.

'My little children, you are worried about so many things: where's the next meal coming from? Where the next pair of sandals for the little one, the cloak for my man as he goes to the fields in all weathers, aren't these your worries? Just think of the birds of the air; not one them sows, and so not one of them reaps, but your Father in Heaven sees to it that they don't starve! And think of those glorious flowers of the field; they don't work in the harvest nor spin and weave wool or flax for their clothing. But look about you when the fields are covered with

come until you love the unlovable, until you take your enemy to your heart. Blessing is the only answer to hate; love is the only answer to violence, for your Father in heaven makes the sun to rise, the rain to fall, on the just and the unjust, on your enemies as freely as on your friends. Be of one mind with your Father and then there will be no enmity, no hatred.'

His words, so quietly spoken but so urgently, had been like hammer blows, shattering all their accepted ways of thought. Now the tone changed.

'Of course I needn't tell you, when you give your alms, to a beggar or to the synagogue, that it's not seemly to have a trumpeter marching before you! There are some people who stand praying a little aside from others in the synagogue, or at the appointed hours, at the corners of streets – you can tell them as you approach them, by the longer fringes on their prayer shawls, by the solemn scowl on their faces! and they don't trim their beards when they fast!'

There was laughter at his satire, laughter in which he joined. Then with an equal gravity he said,

'But you, when you pray, go silently to a quiet place away from the sight of men and when you are quite alone, pray somewhat after this pattern:

Our Father in Heaven, hallowed be thy name.
Thy Kingdom come both in earth and heaven.
Give us our bread this day.
Forgive us all our wrong-doings
As we forgive those who have wronged us.
And do not tempt or try our strength too far
And protect us against all evil.

For thine is the Kingdom
And all power in heaven and earth
And all glory from men and from angels.

Instinctively they all murmured 'Amen' and it was suffi-

flowers after a rain shower. Was King Solomon in all his glory dressed as finely as one of these? So, set aside your worries about food, drink and clothes. Do you think that God the Father who cares for birds, beasts, and the plants of the field will be careless about you? Let tomorrow and its needs take care of itself.'

He broke off to walk among them and saw the whole pattern of the lakeland community. There were many who had no need to think of the morrow, their prosperity was manifest; and there were children whose tattered and meagre clothes and bare feet showed that perhaps the birds of the air were more prosperous. But for all of them he had the private word, the look, the gesture which held them like a spell.

'When you pray, be certain in your hearts that He will answer. Do you ever refuse what your children really need? No more will He, who knows your needs.

'But there is a graver matter I wish to tell you. You accuse, judge and condemn your neighbours; that moment of anger he showed at the field's boundary – but were you completely without blame? that unkind look at the well as you drew water – but had she never received an unkind word from you? Don't judge anyone, for the same standard of judgment you dole out to them will be used in judging you. But forgive, be loving, be merciful and generous, and kindness will pour back upon you.

'These are not easy things I ask you but I speak to you all of my Kingdom, of eternal life and the way to Heaven itself. The wide paths of the world are so well-paved, so tempting, but they lead nowhere. The path into the Kingdom may be narrow and harsh but it leads to life itself.

'Some will try to tell you other truths, false prophets, bleating to you with the innocence of sheep; look closely at the wolf beneath the fleece! You will know them by their fruits, the truths they try to sell you.

'Remember above all that doing is more important than much saying. Many will say to me, 'Lord', 'Rabbi',

'Learned and worthy Master'; those words won't get them into my Kingdom; but if you do the will of my Father, he will receive you to be with Him and with me for ever.'

Again there was a pause in his exhortation. So direct and so apparently simple his words had seemed that many marvelled at their own response to them. 'The Rabbis never spoke to us like this; and it's not the words alone – he talks with authority – he means what he says!'

'One more word, my people; let me tell you a story:

'There were two wealthy men who wanted to build new and very splendid houses for themselves. One of them liked to be at the sea-shore, to watch from his windows the changing waters and the skies. And he built. He began by digging down to firm rock and making his foundations like the rock itself.

The other preferred the gentle fields inland and at the side of a stream he built his grand house, the walls growing straight up from the turf; for in this gentle land what need of deep foundations?

And winter came. The waves lashed at the house at the sea-shore and the house took all their buffeting, firm still as the rock beneath.

But the tempest filled the head-waters of the stream inland and it became a torrent, which first ate away at the turf, the soil beneath it and then the house itself which collapsed in ruins.

Which house do you choose to build? If you hear my words and do them, your lives will be built on rock; but if you like my words, and perhaps be even moved by them, and then go away and do nothing, then your life will be built on sandy soil – the first winter will see its collapse.'

TWENTY-TWO

Jeshua sent the twelve back to Capernaum while he lingered for two days in the mountains, allowing the living, breathing stillness of those uplands to work its way with his spirit. On the third day he woke early while it was still very dark; there was no moon and even the brighter stars were dimmed by a veil of mist. He sat against a rock and allowed his mind to empty of all thought, of all the burden of welding the twelve into a company of friends, of the incessant, the overbearing demands of the crowds who followed him day by day. Rather he allowed the remnant of the night to capture his spirit with its tranquillity. From his resting-place he was looking directly eastward, the lake invisible below him and the hills above Gadara the merest suggestion of a shadowed silhouette. Gradually the darkness intensified to a deep blue, edged at the horizon with a pale lemon-yellow. Almost as if signalled by this faintest of light, the first dawn-chorus began, the somnolent cooing of rock-doves, the tentative three-or four-note melodies of the finches and the last hunting call of the desert owl. They were unrelated, even discordant but in that first hint of dawn they were the life of the day, a promise. Gradually the horizon became rose, orange and where a few clouds massed above the hills a red bank shadowed with grey and blue. The birds fell silent until the first edge of the sun's disk appeared, when the chorus of all the birds became a massed psalm. Jeshua drew his cloak about him as the first breezes came up from the lake and began his morning thanksgiving.

O praise the Lord of Heaven,
  Praise Him in the height.
  Praise the Lord upon earth,
  Ye dragons and all deeps.
  Fire and hail, snow and vapours,
  Wind and storm fulfilling his word.
  Mountains and all hills,
  Fruitful trees and all cedars.
  Beasts and all cattle,
  Worms and feathered fowls.

Kings of the earth and all people,
Princes and all judges of the world.
Young men and maidens,
Old men and children,
Praise the name of the Lord.
For his name only is excellent
And his praise above heaven and earth.

The tranquillity of dawn, bird-song and psalm had wholly possessed him and with memories of Lazar and the Nazareth synagogue, he whispered the morning blessing:

Blessed art thou, O Lord our God,

King of the universe,

Who crownest Israel with glory –

a glory he held before their eyes, inviting their hands to receive, to handle the word of life. Refreshed and with no thought of food, he walked swiftly on the path to Capernaum. He approached the city along the lake-shore from the south and was still a mile or two from Capernaum when he was stopped by a small group of synagogue elders, clearly in great distress. Peter and Andrew had told them his likely way of return and their relief was palpable as they saw him come. He stopped to greet them and they burst across the salutation:

'Master, our friend Justus the centurion is in great trouble. His servant from former times who served with him throughout his campaigns, is mortally sick with the palsy; he beseeches you to help him.'

Jeshua's mind moved back over the years to his first visit to Capernaum, the synagogue meeting with Justus and the evening at the lake-side. The elders of the synagogue misconstrued his grave silence and renewed their plea.

'We beseech you to come quickly. Justus truly is our friend; he fears God and of his own substance he built and adorned our synagogue.'

'Yes, I will come.'

Jeshua tempered their anxiety and hurry by the calm

218

and sure way he took towards the centurion's house but they were scarcely within sight of it when the centurion himself appeared. Gravely he looked at Jeshua, as if seeking a sympathetic memory.

'Rabbi, Lord, I am not worthy to receive you into my home but will you speak the word of healing, here where we stand?'

He drew himself up with a humble dignity, a centurion's bearing before a superior:

'For I also am a man of authority, accustomed over the years to command. I say to these men, 'do this' and at once they do it; to my servant, 'come to my bidding' and he comes. Will you now, for mercy's sake, declare your power?'

Jeshua gazed into the centurion's eyes for a moment and then turned to the people about him:

'Truly, I say to you all, faith as great as this I have not found in all Israel. I say to you now, people shall come from the north and the south, from the lands of the east and the west and shall sit down with the Fathers in my Father's Kingdom, but Israel? What shall become of Israel?'

He turned to the centurion.

'Return to your home, Justus. Your servant is healed.'

The centurion smiled briefly at the sound of his name, raised his hand in a silent greeting and farewell and returned swiftly along the shore to his house.

Jeshua and the elders walked further by the lakeside until they reached Peter's house in Capernaum. Rumours of the centurion's servant had reached the people of the city and they anxiously questioned Jeshua of his illness. He told them the words of the centurion and the outcome, and the meal following was like a celebration.

The brothers made to settle for the evening by the hearth but Jeshua excused himself.

'Forgive me if I take just an hour or two again to myself.' Disappointed they let him go and wondered at the path he took, past the harbour and out towards Magdala.

Memories were sharp and clear in Jeshua's mind as he walked the little distance towards the centurion's home. In the decade and more since he was here last, the house had become even more secluded, the shrubs and trees so thickly planted that they hid everything but the carefully kept view of the lake and the mountains beyond. Jeshua entered the gravelled path.

'Justus!'

'Rabbi! Jeshua!'

'Justus, Shalom!'

'Shalom aleychem, Master.'

There was laughter behind the formal greeting and more than the years had fallen away. The centurion had aged but there was still youth in the springing of his grizzled hair, in the sharp penetration of the eyes. With rest from duty had come also a relaxed and contemplative gaze to which Jeshua immediately responded.

'It's been a long time since that raw country boy came down to Capernaum and was captured by a real Roman centurion!'

Justus laughed with a little embarrassment.

'I can't be sure which of us was captured then – let's agree to call it an honourable neutrality. But a great deal, a very great deal has happened since then. For me, at last, retirement from the barrack-room and the command of men, with reading and thinking here in my home. Will it surprise you, Jeshua, if I tell you that I now feel more Greek than Spanish?'

'No , it doesn't, in a way – though I think it's perhaps tragic when a man loses contact with the soil from which he sprang.'

Justus looked at him with anxiety, wondering about Nazareth and certain rumours that had reached the lake.

'But in fact some other friends of mine have taught me much about the Greeks and I can see why you, a man of discipline, should be moved by the clarity of the Greek mind, its understanding of the great abstractions – of beauty, of truth, of mathematics and the laws of nature. But their ways of thought aren't mine.'

Justus was puzzled by the considered tone of Jeshua's judgment. All he had heard of the fervour of his speech to the multitudes, the vivid simplicity of his language as he met the simplest of peasants at the level of their daily work and their anxious needs, had prepared him little for this conversation. The young man was now certainly no longer the peasant boy from Nazareth, the carpenter's son. 'The great abstractions,' 'mathematics and the laws of nature,' this was another Jeshua. Perhaps there was truth in those rumours of the twelve-year-old boy from Galilee's confounding of the Temple Rabbis, merely by asking them questions.

'Do you find life hard, Jeshua? I have heard with wonder and not a little envy – I wish I could have been with you! – of your preaching, your healing miracles and of the crowds that follow you. But my greatest envy has been of 'the Twelve' as everyone in Capernaum calls them. What is your purpose and aim with them?'

'A kingdom.'

The instant and alert reaction of the Roman of authority was a wary searching in the face opposite him for signs of insurrection. Was this Jeshua, whose memory he had so long held, to turn out to be no more than one of the multitude of Zealots? They were little more than a nuisance and ended by the hundred in crucifixion.

'Yes, a kingdom, the Kingdom of God, a rule under the Most High of a kingdom before Paradise and after this world's dissolution; a kingdom without beginning or end, without decay and without suffering; a kingdom beyond the imagination of your Roman Law and indeed, if I may

221

say this without impiety, a Kingdom beyond Torah, where memory of Sinai will be no more than gratitude for paths laid down for guidelines for the weary and the erring.'

Justus could understand a little now of the hold his voice could have on the multitudes. Though this was language – concepts beyond the reach or desire of those who crowded to hear them – now, as he spoke to this sophisticated alien, the fire and passion in his quiet voice burned through the vision which he set before Justus with such conviction.

''The Twelve,' how do they take to your vision of the Kingdom? I confess' – he looked up with a satiric gleam – 'that if I wanted a dozen volunteers from my legion, for a difficult campaign manoeuvre, I would want, shall we say, a more homogeneous lot!'

Jeshua laughed with him. 'More strangely assorted than perhaps you know! When you take fishermen, a Zealot, a tax-gatherer and a man of considerable wealth you are letting yourself in for problems – I was! But what else would you have? No nation, no class of people, neither poor nor rich, learned or unlettered, has a monopoly of God. My kingdom must comprise them all and exclude none. It must be like a catch of fish, of every kind, palatable and unpalatable – and my Father throws none of them back!'

Their laughter together had now the understanding of long friendship as if the years between their meetings had been years of continuous association. Jeshua felt drawn to confide more of his intentions.

'My way with them is not simple. Two things must be accomplished at the same time: each man must fulfil himself, all that he has in him to become. If the skills are physical, or intellectual, or the impulse is to heal or to teach – so be it, every man to his calling. But my second object is at least as important for me – *that they should be one*. When the diverse, the conflicting natures of these

222

twelve men come together in unity, that will be my kingdom in miniature. With them the Kingdom will be irresistible.'

Justus did not reject the vision; his silence was brooding, considering. Jeshua broke into it.

'You remember – it seems like yesterday – that we spoke here of Law – your Roman 'Peace' and our 'Shalom'. You are still the Roman, I still the Jew but here we sit, in a quiet accord. As I had a boy's temerity to say to you then that our way was the surer, the greater, so I have a man's boldness to say to you now – my Kingdom will come and it will be a kingdom beyond Rome, Athens, Babylon, Egypt, a kingdom in history and yet beyond time, in which all 'do justly, love mercy and walk humbly,' for my Father will be there in their midst.'

'I, too, over the years, have begun to understand what you say. Would that my old limbs, wearied by the Legions, could march with you towards your Kingdom.'

There was silence for quite a while and then, as if shaking off both longing and frustration, Justus went to an inner room and came back with a flask, two beakers and a dish of wheaten cakes.

'The rough vintage of my father's country still comes my way, that full-blooded wine of Spain. Let this wine and this bread be a promise, an oath, a sacrament between us.'

The host in Justus had imperceptibly become something more. Jeshua felt certain, as they ate and drank together in silence, that never again would they meet like this. Their meal carried more power than the savour of its bread and wine and, after their farewells, Jeshua returned in the darkness of the night to the house in Capernaum. There was no sound but the lapping of the waves and the soft-withdrawing of the shingle but the words of Justus were like a refrain for all that lay before him – 'a promise, an oath, a sacrament.'

'Have you had your fill of this lake-land, this constant wash of waters; I long for the high country again!'

They were at their morning meal and Peter and the others knew the banter for what it was but realised also that beneath the laughter there was a real plea to them. They had quickly learned that the upland paths meant much to him, the thin, bracing air and the variety of colour in all about them. To him there was something forbidding about the dark basalt rock, the foundation of their cities, the black basalt pebbles of the shore and the grey tumult of waves which poured in from the freakish storms of the open lake.

'Where are we bound for, Master?' There was a little fun in Andrew's voice, a mock resignation at further wandering.

'Only as far as the nearest real mountains. You have never seen Nain with me — it will be no more than a Sabbath to Sabbath journey.'

After the simplest preparations they set off into the hill slopes, a comet-tail of people following them, eager for Jeshua's words and for the miraculous which punctuated their days. They took the journey quietly , approaching Nain in the early afternoon of the third day. Their entry to the town was blocked by a band of wailing mourners, crying and beating their breasts as they went ahead of those whose grief was silent and intense. On a simple bier a young man lay, his white grave-garments loosely about him and his face uncovered. His mother, clothed in a widow's robe, walked in a silent agony beside the bier. Jeshua went forward from the twelve, put his arm gently on hers and said, 'Do not weep.' Turning to the bier he took the hand of her son and said quietly — a parent waking a child from sleep -

'Young man, rise to your feet and walk.'

As if truly waking from sleep, the young man sat up, pulled the white robe tightly about him and went swiftly to embrace his mother. As they both looked a little wildly and with some fear at Jeshua, the people about them changed their mourning to a ritual marvelling:

'A prophet among us!' 'God has indeed visited his people.'

Jeshua and the twelve paused at the gate of Nain, not wishing to enter and when the afternoon began to become more temperate, turned to face the downward slopes to Capernaum.

The return to the Lake was a prelude to a meeting more sombre than the twelve had hitherto known. Waiting for them was a small group of John the Baptiser's followers. They had grave news of John. His outspoken attacks on Herod had led to his captivity and even in prison his mouth could not be stopped; denunciations rang in Herod's ears and retribution could not be long in coming.

But there was worse in what they had to say. Though John's prophetic words were as powerful as ever, doubts seemed to be gnawing away at his own spirit. He seemed to them to be no more now than a voice. Though still young, his body was worn by austerity and suffering – this they understood and accepted – but there were moments in their presence when his eyes reflected despair and his posture shrank in dereliction. Now he had sent them to Jeshua with a last beseeching for truth:

'Are you 'He-that-should-come' or must we still wait for another?'

Jeshua stood before them; in his silence he shared John's agony reflected in their faces and then he replied. His words were formal, his voice low:

'Return to Jordan and tell John what you have seen and heard:

The blind see,   The lame walk,
The lepers are cleansed,   The deaf hear,
The dead are raised   To the poor the gospel is preached
And blessed is he who shall not be offended in me.'

John's disciples left, troubled but with at least their minds reassured. They left behind them an apparently still more troubled knot of men about the hearth in Peter's house. Jeshua remained silent, as if gathering himself for a further declaration to them, but they were startled by the vehemence and the tenor of what he had to say.'

'John, baptising in Jordan; when you streamed there in your hundreds, what did you expect to see, a reed, shaken and whispering in the wind; was that the voice you expected to hear?

'Did you expect to see an honoured man in fine garments? Fine garments indeed! Those who are gorgeously apparelled and live delicately are to be found in kings' courts.

'What then did you expect to see? a prophet? Yes, a prophet and much more than a prophet. For a prophet, Malachi, spoke of him when he declared:

Behold I send my messenger before thy face
    Which shall prepare thy way before thee.

I say solemnly to you, John the Baptiser knows no equal among the sons of men. Nevertheless I say to you also that the least who shall enter the Kingdom of my Father will be greater than John.'

There was silence within the house and among those who had gathered as they heard the voice of Jeshua raised. He remained with bowed head and quite silent in their presence; then, as if for the first time realising the curiosity of those outside the house, he raised his voice, a rough edge to it and an unusual acerbity.

'What is this generation really like? They are like children sitting in the open market and calling one to another:

'We have piped the wedding-dances for you and you haven't danced! We have sung the mourning chants to you and you haven't lamented! What really moves you? John came, fasting and austere and they said of him, 'He's possessed by a devil!' The Son of Man came eating and drinking and they say of me, 'Look at him! a glutton and a wine-bibber, a friend of tax-gatherers and sinners!''

He was silent again and they were also, having nothing to reply. Then he lifted his face to them once more, his expression gentle and his eyes smiling:

'Yes, we must wait and be patient. The children of wisdom will be justified by their deeds.'

Once again his mood changed and the fire returned to his eyes.

'But you, Capernaum, you Bethsaida and Chorazin, splendid cities who have been witnesses to mighty works – has it changed you? Have you seen the light of God? I tell you, if Tyre and Sidon had seen what you have seen, penitence would have poured through their hearts; yes, even Sodom, even Gomorrah, it will be more tolerable in the Day of Judgment for them than for you, if you have seen and not believed.'

The prophetic voice was again stilled and Jeshua became the father of his family at the hearth, praying with them and for them.

'Father, Lord of heaven and earth, I thank Thee that thou hast hidden these things from the wise and prudent and revealed them to babes.'

The prayer ended he turned to all who remained silent about him.

'All things are entrusted to me by my Father. No one knows the Son but the Father, and none shall know the Father but the Son and those to whom the Son will reveal Him.'

Darkness had now fallen about them and Jeshua, raising his hands in the flickering light from the hearth embers, said aloud:

'Come unto me, all ye that labour and are heavy laden
And I will give you rest.
Take my yoke upon you and learn of me,
For I am meek and lowly of heart,
And ye shall find rest for your souls.
For my yoke is easy,
And my burden is light.'

Capernaum and the friends were to receive another lesson, a sharp one. The teaching of Jeshua, whether in the open fields to the multitudes or on those occasions when he was invited to address the synagogue congregation, had made him a popular figure among the discriminating and a most desirable dinner guest. One of the most prominent Pharisees invited him one evening, with a carefully chosen and small group of diners, including one or two of Jeshua's followers. The Pharisee's home was situated on a wooded slope above Capernaum and Jeshua walked in the early evening through olive groves and vineyards to reach the house. Simon the Pharisee greeted him formally and showed him to his place at table but before he went there Jeshua, silently and briefly, dipped into the surface of the water in the ceremonial water-pots and touched both his palms and his forehead with the water.

The feast was long and elaborate and the conversation general and stilted. Judas, who was among the guests, sardonically watched Simon's verbal manoeuverings as embarrassing questions of prophecy and political power were touched upon and hurriedly avoided. In one of the silences before a new course of fruit was offered the guests and fresh wine poured, there was a disturbance at the door. Mary of Magdala, known to many there and wearing her long hair about her shoulders in the prostitute fashion, thrust her way past the servants at the door and knelt behind the couch on which Jeshua reclined at table.

There was an even deeper silence as Mary wept at Jeshua's feet, her tears bathing them. Tenderly and carefully she wiped her tears away with her hair, kissed his feet and then took from her garment a delicately carved albaster flask of perfume. Deliberately leaving its stopper in place, she crushed the albaster between her hands, pouring the spilt oil over Jeshua's feet. The delicate perfume reached every guest; to some it brought uncomfortable thoughts of illicit love; to others the suggestion of myrrh among the rich odours carried even more uncomfortable omens of death and the anointing for burial.

In the silence Simon's pharisee friends could be seen in unspoken questioning and one, more austere than the rest, was heard to say in an undertone, 'Isn't this fellow reputed a prophet? The least of his skills would have revealed to him the status of this woman!'

Jeshua turned to his host. 'Simon, I have a question to put to you. A certain rich man had two debtors; one owed him five hundred pieces of silver, the other fifty. Each of them was penniless and he forgave them both their debts to him. Now, Simon, tell me: which of these debtors do you imagine loved him most?'

Simon replied, 'I suppose he who had been forgiven most.'

'You have spoken truly.' Gesturing towards the woman who still knelt at his feet, he turned again to his host and said, 'Simon, when I came to your feast, you gave me no water to cleanse the dust from my feet, but this lady has not ceased to lave them with her tears and to dry them with her hair. You gave not even the formal kiss of peace; but she has ceaselessly kissed my feet as we feasted; you omitted to anoint my head with oil but she has shattered her precious flask and prodigally poured the perfumed oil over my feet, yes, to the very last drop. And so I say to you Simon and to all your friends gathered here: her sins (which indeed are many) are forgiven her, she has loved deeply and well' – his gaze passed swiftly over the guests now gathered about Simon – 'but in those for whom little is forgiven, the love is little.' Turning to the woman, he raised her courteously to her feet and said,

'Your sins are forgiven.'

There was a stirring of repugnance and rejection both for Jeshua and the outcast from Magdala – who could this possibly be who could forgive sins, a blasphemous assumption of God's prerogative? Jeshua spoke in even more measured words:

'Your faith has saved you. Go now in peace. Love, and not sin, still waits for you.'

When Mary of Magdala had left the house, Jeshua also rose and gathered his friends about him.

'I thank you, Simon, for your invitation and for the feast. It was gracious of you. Peace be with you and with those you cherish.'

He left Simon's house in a profound silence.

TWENTY-FOUR

It was a restless, even bitter time. For some weeks, Jeshua and the twelve went to and fro in Galilee, apparently without a planned journey but healing and preaching as opportunity offered. One healing declared to Jeshua the depths of the enmity which was now set against him. It was at a village towards the north, at no great distance from Sepphoris. A dumb man was brought to him, a man in deep distress. His family stood silently behind him and Jeshua stepped forward to greet the dumb man whose face was a complex scene of emotions. At the sight of Jeshua, his eyes pleaded in agony, then were veiled and in a moment gleamed with such feral hatred that James and John stepped forward to Jeshua's side. He motioned them to return to the others and looked once more to the dumb one's beseeching. The muscles of his neck were strained and his mouth writhed with an incoherent babbling; even the calm compassion of Jeshua's gaze left him still torn with the conflict within him.

At length Jeshua stretched out his arm, raised his hand in a gesture of command:

'Leave him! Come out of him.'

The tearing of the face and the convulsion of his body was such that the man was thrown to the ground. Jeshua remained in the same posture of command until the terrible writhings ceased and the body lay still, as if dead. Jeshua stepped to his side, took him by the hand and restored him to his family.

'Tend him gently; he needs no more than food and rest. Go in peace.'

The relief of the twelve was palpable and they savoured the rejoicing about them. For voices were raised in wonder and a kind of aweful joy – 'It has never before been seen in Israel. At his touch, without a word, the devils flee.' Jeshua however was alert to other voices. In the forefront of the crowd that had gathered were three scribes; their assurance and their speech declared them of Jerusalem and the Temple hierarchy. Their mission was clear. Turning their backs on Jeshua they addressed the people.

'He is himself possessed and by the power and in the name of Beelzebub he exorcises; in the name of the prince of devils he casts out devils – from this man and throughout Galilee.'

Jeshua approached them and addressed the eldest of the three.

'Rabbi, you have a strange message and you see that the people are as astonished as I by what you say. You say that by the Prince of Devils I cast out devils; indeed, you seem to go further – I am myself the habitation of devils, you say.

'Let us reason of this. Can you truly say that Satan casts out Satan, the 'adversary' adversary to the 'adversary'? If a kingdom be divided against itself, warring against its own authority, that kingdom cannot stand. If members of a household are engaged in divisions among themselves, neither can that house stand or prosper. And if Satan be adversary to Satan – can you really be serious in saying this?

'If a thief wishes to despoil a house and the owner of the house is both rich and of great personal strength, would it not be wise to overpower the owner first, before attempting the robbery?

'I say to you that I bind devils and loose the possessed in the name and by the power of my Father. By your spirit you pervert the holy spirit of God Himself. Your sins – forgive me, Rabbi – your sins great and small, may all be forgiven, but sin against the Spirit of all holiness cannot be forgiven; its lying perversion puts it beyond the reach of forgiveness.

'Go now, reverend elders, and be of a new mind.'

Gravely he turned away and led his friends into the countryside. The second conflict had been greater than the struggle with demonic forces and Jeshua showed the strain of it. He walked alone, ahead of his followers and remained in this isolation until they reached shelter in a neighbouring village.

Here another bleakness awaited him. He had taken no note of the small crowd which followed him to this place of their over-night stay but as he sat at the evening meal, Jeshua relaxed in the presence of his twelve intimates and of the friendly host and his family, with whom Jeshua had stayed before. As the meal was near its end, a servant came in from the courtyard and said to Jeshua,

'Your mother and some of your brethren are outside and asking to speak to you.'

Jeshua remained still and as the minutes passed, John could read in his face the conflict of memories and emotions there. There was Nazareth of which he had spoken so warmly and there was Lazar, and the shepherd boy and the crippled girl; and there was planning and fashioning of homes and the synagogue. And there were other memories, their shadows clouding his eyes. At last, as the silence became unendurable, he spoke.

'Who is my mother? Who are my brethren?' He looked about him and his voice became lower and even more tender. With a gesture he encompassed the friends who were always with him and his host and his family who stood about. The gravity was still there and the remnants of pain but in the silence his voice had all its customary assurance.

'You are my mother, my brethren, all my kin. All who do the will of my Father, they are my mother, my brother, my sister.'

In the silence he raised the cup and drank. Then turning to his host he spoke the psalm from the blessings of evening:

O Lord our Lord,
> How excellent is thy name in all the earth,
> Who hast set thy glory above the heavens.

With a smile he embraced the whole gathering as he continued:

Out of the mouths of babes and sucklings
        Hast thou ordained strength
        Because of thine enemies,
        That thou mightest still the enemy and the
        avenger.
His eyes invited their response and all the company joined him in the praise:
        When I consider the heavens,
        The work of thy fingers, the moon and the stars,
        Which thou hast ordained;
        What is man
        That thou art mindful of him
        And the son of man
        That thou visitest him?
Never had Judas known such wonder as now captured him in the psalm rhythms and the fervour of the whole household drew them into one.
        O Lord our Lord,
        How excellent is thy name
        In all the earth.

   This time of peace was the proper moment for further insight.
   'You seem to fear being alone; you're happiest in twos or threes or all of you gathered about a hearth after a meal together – and, of course, that's as it should be. But man also needs loneliness, to meet himself, to walk with himself along the paths of wilderness.'
   This was to the twelve a strange teaching at the end of a time when they had enjoyed meals together in the journeyings, had known even feasting – after which he had spoken of 'the City at the heart of my Kingdom, the City of God, a new Jerusalem'. It had been a vision to which they responded with pleasure, a vision for which even Capernaum had given them no model. Only Judas, Matthew and

Thomas had looked reserved, attempting to relate their knowledge of city dealings to this unaccustomed view.

'The desert has taught our people a great deal, refined their bodies, hardened their minds; even after long toil in the desert, a trying passage through the wilderness to the land of God's promise, Abraham chose the bare heights, those pastures where a shepherd is so often alone with his flock.

'You see me leave you for days at a time – not weary with your company, indeed not! nor always much wearied even by the crowds and their demands. But there come times when I must be apart to see myself and having found myself again to meet my Father and to hear His voice.

'That precious knowledge I find most readily among the lonely goat-tracks of the hills, even in the unfriendly sand of the desert – for even there I find a Rock a shadow from the heat and a fortress for my trust.

'Moses spoke truly of that refuge in Him:

He is the Rock, His work perfect,
> For all His ways are judgement;
> A God of truth and without iniquity,
> Just and right is He.

'Does that tell you why I retreat alone to the desert ways? Tonight, before we sleep, our prayer shall be a song of David:

> From the ends of the earth will I call upon Thee,
> When my heart is in heaviness;
> O set me upon the Rock that is higher than I,
> For thou hast been my hope, and a strong tower for
> me against the enemy.

TWENTY-FIVE

Two conflicting intuitions drew the twelve in a close-knit fellowship in the succeeding weeks. The first was their growing realisation of the power of Jeshua, the uniqueness of his person. If challenged not even the most aware among them could have told what aspect of his being affected them most profoundly, his words or the deeds which daily transcended anything they had ever known or imagined. But a second perception brooded as strongly over them as the sense of triumphant union with him: they were increasingly aware that there drew in about them an enmity which was becoming palpable. It seemed to them that they were surrounded by a miasma; they felt its cold touch, the faint but sure smell of evil.

This was the more curious for their days too were radiant. They moved about the countryside to a welcome from the crowds and from the simple homes that gave them shelter; it was a radiance as great as the air which warmed towards harvest. Jeshua saw clearly the sway of their moods between foreboding and a prideful joy; he knew also the new temper which drew Judas in friendship with Peter and Andrew, which matured in the conversations of Matthew with Thomas. Now, then, was the moment for the most explicit teaching. Some would have to be privately theirs; more of it perhaps they would take to themselves as they overheard the teaching of the multitudes.

These had followed him to the very shores of the Sea of Galilee. They were a little outside the busiest inlets of Capernaum itself but they crowded upon him, obliterating even the grey shingle by their masses. Jeshua called to Peter that he should fetch one of the smaller fishing vessels and when Peter and Andrew had rowed it to shore, Jeshua stepped into it and remained standing in it while the two brothers steadied its motion on the lake's surface.

Jeshua's voice was of middle range and pitch and audible for all who were on the shore.

'You have heard me speak of the kingdom, my kingdom, the kingdom of my Father, the kingdom which you may all inherit! To-day we must think of it more deeply.

'You, from the country, and even you who live here in the cities; you have all seen a sower. He strides up and down the field, measuring his paths and casting wide the seed on to the ploughed earth.

'But, and there is the wonder of it! The seed falls, slips into the crannies of the soil and is lost to sight. The sun and the rain do their work and at length there grows where the seed fell -' Jeshua paused

'Another seed? No, something quite different, a green shoot, a growing stem, the blades about it and then, at last, the ear, and within it not a grain alone but a multitude of grains and all this wonder has been performed not by the sower – he only scattered – but secretly, a miraculous secret change.'

Again Jeshua paused, allowing the mystery of growth in secret to be received by them.

'You know the size of a mustard-seed – small as a grain of sand. And yet when it is sown, it becomes the greatest of shrubs, so tall and spreading that birds roost and build their nests in its branches. So is the Kingdom.'

There were some who nodded their heads in assent but the greater number were clearly bewildered. The words were simple enough – they knew their husbandry – but the meaning was dark.

'And again that farmer, the wheat he scattered and the tiny mustard-seed he sowed, he had been careful with them, sifting and cleaning them, seeing that they were pure wheat, pure mustard-seed and both of them healthy. Now I ask you the question which his labourers asked him; if the seed was good, where did the weeds come from? The farmer told them that it must have been an enemy of his that came stealthily by night and sowed the bad seed. So it is in the kingdom.'

They were struggling to understand. His voice had such charm, his gestures were so appealing, but still they struggled for understanding. Some there were whose faces glowed with comprehension and Jeshua's eyes caught theirs in pure pleasure.

'Will you listen again – it's still that same farmer! He went out into a large field to sow his grain. It was a field on the edge of his outer pasture and however careful he was, some of the seeds fell on the paths and the road – a meal for the birds! Some of the seed fell on stony ground which he hadn't been able properly to plough. It grew a little but the soil was so poor that it shrivelled in the sun. And some fell among weeds – the weeds that enemy had scattered the previous season! – and when those seeds grew in turn, they were choked by the stronger weeds.

'But some fell on good ground with a depth of soil. And they sprouted and grew and flourished and the ears were bursting with grain, thirty, sixty, a hundred times the number of grains he had sown! Now, that is the Kingdom; your ears have heard my words; I hope you have truly heard and understood.'

So many of them had felt unusually removed from him, as he stood poised in the boat, away from the shore; it was so unlike his preaching in the open country, where they could crowd about him, even touch him. Many of them left, disconsolate, but there were some who stood there quietly and in meditation; at length they also went away.

The twelve were almost as bewildered as the multitude; their advantage was their trust in Jeshua and their daily familiarity with his speech, its spare and often ironic quality. But 'the Kingdom' had so often been the topic of their conversation together that they were determined to know the truth of these parables. The fishermen felt uneasy at the appeal to the farmer's craft, the countrymen among them understood the husbandry but not its implications here; Judas and Matthew talked animatedly together, not of the context of the parables but of their mystery, the paradox of their simplicity and their cryptic darkness.

They both smiled with relief when Jeshua began private talk with the twelve at precisely that point.

'You wonder at the darkness of these sayings, the perhaps cruel testing which I gave to those eager, hungry people. But you have heard words like this before, and the prophets have told you of the intention behind them. Don't you remember Isaiah?:

> I will open my mouth in parables,
> I will utter what has been kept secret
> Since the foundation of the world.

and again he says

> By hearing ye shall hear –
> And shall not understand;
> And seeing ye shall see –
> And shall not perceive.

Some of you by your looks find this a cruel saying; but follow the prophet in his argument:

> For the people's heart is waxed thick
> And their ears are dull of hearing
> And their eyes they have closed.

The multitudes follow me. Why? Some plead for bread, and what else would you have the hungry do? Some ask for release from their sicknesses, and why shouldn't the sick look for a physician? Some for forgiveness of their sins and in their call to God they approach the Kingdom very nearly. And some – a very few – search for the light, they long for truth. They ask nothing for themselves in this world but they do long for the Kingdom. It is to them you will look when the Kingdom comes, and it is through them that you will lead the hungry, the thirsty, the blind, maimed and penitent into the glory of our Father's Kingdom.

'But what of you? You see and hear, and you understand?'

Diffidently they looked at one another and then away, ashamed to answer no. Jeshua gathered them more closely about him and then in the quiet tones of a rabbi instructing the very young, told them of the truths.

'The Kingdom is a living, growing thing. It is sown, by the Father, by me, by you, but the sowing is a brief thing indeed. The seed grows secretly, gathering its own life and, like the wheat, its life aims for perfection; a hundred-fold perfection.

'But there are difficulties; from Adam until now we have made our lives a strange field; we are too busy, perhaps too sinful to care for the Kingdom; and the Adversary sows weeds, even greater evils than the imaginings of our hearts.

'I have chosen you in the trust that you will be a good earth; not soil only but the husbandmen also. I have given you the good grain; it is my Father's will that you sow it and that it grows and is fruitful to all eternity.'

Their silence was filled with the awe of his words, of the burden laid on them and their probable unfitness to bear it. He allowed them to hold this tension for as long as they might, and then, in a lighter tone,

'When women bake our bread, there is a great deal of meal and a small fragment of yeast. But the yeast works throughout the dough, leavening it and making it fit for baking and our eating. You are the yeast in the dough!'

The tension was broken in their smiling and Jeshua went on.

'There is an old tale – it has been true many times – of a man walking through a field and stumbling over a hidden treasure. In his joy at the finding he goes and sells all his possessions to buy the field.

'And that other tale; the rich merchant whose sole object in trading was to have even finer and finer jewels.

One day he finds a splendid pearl, a pearl both large and of perfect colour and form; he too goes and sells all that he has, all his gathering of jewels and lands, and all to buy this one perfect pearl.

'You, my friends, know that wayfarer, that merchant. You are they! You have given up the whole of your lives, all you held dear, to have that treasure, that perfect pearl. And here it is within sight – my Father's Kingdom.' They were moved by the affection and the trust with which he spoke to them but they were also spent, weary with the testing of the day.

TWENTY-SIX

To escape into peace was never easy but now the demands of the crowds were ceaseless. Though the land was fertile and the Sea of Gennesaret gave catches in plenty, there was appalling poverty in the cities. With poverty went sickness, diseases of the flesh for those whose bodies had no resistance, diseases of the mind for those whose riches brought little but indulgence. Fears lay about all in the communities of Galilee, fears of robbery and killing, of the failure of crops and the death of herds, but much more, fear of the nameless powers, the demonic dwellers in the heights and the depths.

David might exhort them to reassurance:

Thou shalt not be afraid for the terror by night,
Nor for the arrow that flieth by day;
Nor for the pestilence that walketh in darkness,
Nor for the destruction that wasteth at noonday.

But they *were* afraid; pestilence did stalk the darkness and day failed to dispel the terrors. Often they repeated the words, in synagogue and at the hearth,

He shall give his angels charge over thee,
To keep thee in all thy ways;

241

They shall bear thee up in their hands,
Lest thou dash thy foot against a stone.
But would they truly? Were the angels present and were they always a match for the legions of devils? Fears stalked the minds of the simple and innocent, and the more sophisticated were haunted by doubts.

Gennesaret had, they believed, its own legions. They reached down in the tempests of the north, they rode on the turbulences that made the lake as dangerous as the waters of the Great Sea. This subtle, shapeless, unpredictable element, this water that took the form only of the vessel that contained it, that could be lashed to a frenzy, that appeared to carry malice within it, surely water, like the earth and skies and the heart of man, was the abode of beings who had better not be named.

Jeshua spoke little of these things. He healed, within sight of the twelve, the distraught and torn men and women who had lived with the fear of devils all their lives. One day they would be faced with these adversaries alone.

The immediate need, for him and his friends, was peace and withdrawal. There was no easier way than to take some fishing vessels and to drift, along the current that flowed through the centre of the lake – hidden Jordan – or responding to the breezes that blew, warm from the south, carrying the tang of snow from the north.

So they drifted, blessedly without purpose and after an hour or so of the afternoon sun, Jeshua folded his cloak as a pillow and fell asleep in the stern of the boat.

Over the hills in the east clouds gathered and swiftly covered the sun. The quiet breezes became winds that rushed through the ravines in the southern mountains and turned the lake to seething. Little ships about them were quickly near to swamping and their own sturdier craft was desperately buffeted and dangerously flooded. Still Jeshua slept, though his feet were covered with the swamping water. In desperation Peter shook him awake.

'Master, are you careless that we are in such danger, near death?'

Jeshua rose in the stern, gazed about him at the storm and raised his hand towards the centre of the tempest in the south.

'Peace, be still,' he cried. The waves lost their wild turbulence and passed the side of their craft in a quiet swell; they became mere ripples and the sun transformed the ripples to a new brilliance. To the disciples he said

'Why are you afraid? Have you such fragile faith?'

They could make no reply. Peter and Andrew, James and John had survived many tempests but few as severe as this. This was not now their awe; in whispers they spoke their wonder:

'Even the wind and the waves obey him!'

They were not wholly comforted in their minds when, instead of asking for a return to Capernaum, he asked that they turn the boat and row for the country of the Gadarenes.

This was alien and in part a fearful country for the fishermen. They avoided its waters when they fished and pulled away into deeper water when they drifted towards the shoals of Gadara. Indeed they scarcely felt this country to be true Galilee. Yet, so far from avoiding these shores, Jeshua asked to be landed and they all went ashore on a rocky, unwelcoming coast. Above the shoreline the rocks made a precipitous fall as though the mountains above had crumbled into massive boulders with little scree before them. From between the rocks a man appeared, wild, naked with unkempt hair and beard. No house would receive him and he made his shelter among tombs at the city and boulders on the shore.

When he saw Jeshua approaching, he fell on his knees before him. To the friends of Jeshua he did not appear to be a danger but they were puzzled by the contrast between his beseeching Jeshua with agonised gestures and the words which he spoke.

'What have I to do with thee, thou Son of God Most High? Do not tempt me!'

Jeshua replied to the words.

'Come out of him and go to your own dwelling!'

In a renewed agony the possessed man shook the broken chains on his wrists with which his neighbours had tried to restrain him. Jeshua appeared to reply to his dumb appeal.

'What is your name?' The reply was scarcely human and appeared to reverberate among the rocks.

'Legion! for we are a host within him.'

In a grotesque parody of the man's terrified gestures of pleading, the voice screamed from his throat.

'Not into the depths, Master, not into the depths. We beseech you, grant us an unclean dwelling.'

There was a herd of swine on the slope and as the possessed lay writhing on the ground, the swine rushed down the slopes, to be drowned in the waters of the lake.

The swineherds ran to the city of Gergasa above the lake and told their employers of these things and the fate of the herds. As they rushed down to see what the tumult meant, they were astonished at the sight before them: the formerly possessed sat quietly, wrapped in Peter's mantle and talking calmly with Jeshua and the others. Years appeared to have been blotted out and the abode of Legion was again a man. With a courtesy he had not forgotten over the years of his affliction, he thanked Jeshua for his release and turned to the path towards Gergasa.

For the Gergasenes however Jeshua was no welcome guest and with urgency they prayed him to leave their homeland. When the former demonic saw the discourtesy of his neighbours, he ran to Jeshua and asked that he might follow him into Galilee. Jeshua replied,

'You have much to do in your own home. Go to your people and when they wonder at your health and your quiet return, tell them of the power of God and of the great things he has done for you.'

Solitary, but with purpose, he turned towards the city.

TWENTY-SEVEN

The devout of Capernaum were again in sorrow. As Jeshua and his friends returned to the upper city they were met by the president of the synagogue, well known both to the fishermen and to Jeshua. Jairus fell down before Jeshua and begged him to heal his daughter, a child of twelve years, who seemed at the point of death. Jeshua followed him but the crowds in the narrow streets were so great that even the thrusting of Peter and Andrew could scarcely make a path for him.

In a doorway at the street corner stood a woman, her garment drawn up to veil all but her eyes. For twelve years she had suffered an incurable haemorrhage and in desperation she waited for the passing of Jeshua. As he approached she touched the skirt of his robe. Jeshua halted as though in response to a cry:

'Who touched me?'

'Master, the crowd press on you from every side; indeed Master, many touched you!'

'Power flowed from me. I ask again, who touched me?'

The trembling woman, knowing that she was healed but fearful that she had offended him who had healed her, knelt before him, silent and with her head bowed. Jeshua stooped and took her by the hand.

'Rise my daughter; your faith has made you whole. Peace be always with you.'

The wonder of this happening had stilled the crowd and Jeshua began to make his way to the synagogue precincts

but as he reached the wider streets a servant of the synagogue president came to him and said,

'Your daughter is dead; do not trouble the rabbi more.'

But Jeshua pressed to his home. When they reached the
house, the sound of ritual wailing was already loud but
Jeshua cried out at the porch of the house,

'Why this wailing? The child is not dead but asleep,' and
they mocked him. Brusquely he emptied the bed-cham-
ber of all but the child's parents and taking with him
Peter, James and John he went to the side of the child's
bed. He smiled at the still form and put out his hand to
take hers, saying,

'Get up, little lamb.' In answer to the tender familiarity
of the words the child sat up, clear-eyed and smiling.
Jeshua drew her towards her parents and said,

'She will be hungry, let her join your meal and be glad
with her.'

The next weeks were of passionate activity. The twelve
watched in wonder and not a little fearfully as Jeshua
strode ahead of them, pausing only when a village or a
wayside hamlet drew him, to preach and to heal. It was
not so much that they feared their physical ability to keep
up with him; it was his unsmiling determination to traverse the country at all speed and in all weathers that
brought in question their will to pursue the same mission
with the same intensity.

Physically they were changed men. Matthew and Judas,
townsmen bred and softened to their callings, were now
as hardy as the fishermen and proud of their weather-lore,
toughly gained.

The four fishermen themselves were even hardier than
when at their calling, for now, and for some weeks, there
had been no remission in the travelling each day and in
the emotional pressure of the seemingly unchanging multitudes. Diffident Thomas was no longer their shy fellow;

now his curiosity demanded an answer to all problems that came their way. Simon alone found the new life simply comparable to the old and he moved with a kind of easy gaiety from group to group of his companions.

But Jeshua was apart, driven onwards by what was clearly a profound need. They traversed Galilee from bound to bound, from Bethsaida to Carmel, from the border of Syro-Phoenicia and the Great Sea to Jordan. At each stopping-place the sick and the troubled were ministered to from dawn through the heat of the day until darkness drove the crowds to their homes; and then, his compassion and his need to gather the destitute and the forlorn drove him onwards at dawn to a new day.

They had reached Carmel on one of their long traverses of Galilee and had spent the night sheltered among the caves that had once known another, harsher prophet. From this vantage-point there was a wide panorama of Galilee and Jeshua, broodingly, almost to himself began to speak of his land and his people.

'These mountains have sheltered our fathers and these slopes and plains have fed them; and the valleys have guided their enemies. In the land before you, not a hill has been without its miracle, not a plain without its slaughter. So it has been through the years, from Abraham to our day and so it seems men determine that it shall be. When one tyrant falls, there is another to take his place; when one tribe returns penitently to give honour to God, another is willing to follow the prophets of Baal.

'Throughout all the history my lambs are torn, my sheep bleat for succour. Hear their cry from hamlet, village and city, how the starving, the exiled lepers, the maimed, the sick cry aloud for us, or silently look for our aid. Derelicts, they cry for help and in their tragedy is God's hour. As we minister to their bodies, their souls turn to God.'

He was silent, brooding over the ways which led eastward and over the multitudes which waited, each day

247

producing its birth that would be the hapless poor of the morrow.

'The harvest is great, rich in the fields before us but the labourers for the harvest are pitifully few.'

With direct appeal to their compassion he said

'Pray – you who have shared the need with me – that our Father, the Lord of the harvest will send out labourers to follow our way.'

They returned to eastern Galilee by a different route and when they had reached the hills behind Magdala and as they prepared a rough camp for the night, Jeshua gathered them about him. They sensed from his gravity that this was not for their evening worship before sleep. Silently he sat in their midst and gazed with affection and a pride they had rarely seen at each of them in turn. Then slowly he began to speak.

'Your learning is now over; you are no longer apprentice craftsmen performing my simple orders. For many days you will go your ways alone, without me and my demands. And you will not go as a company but alone with one companion.' He looked about at their dismayed faces.

'You are worthy of this trust. You will teach, expel devils, return the lepers to their homes, heal all the sick and – perhaps hardest of all – bring comfort to those whose spirits have been broken by the world.'

He allowed them to grasp what he had said and saw them look from one to another, beginning to choose their companions.

'Yet I have much to tell you. You will travel unencumbered, just one cloak, one staff, one pair of sandals – you will return before sandals or staff are worn! – and you will take no food for the journey; each village will provide of its charity – the labourer deserves his wages.

'Your teaching will be simple, only that the Kingdom is near at hand. Tell them of the kingdom – and if you can remember the sower, the wheat and the tares so much the better!

'Throughout Galilee there can scarcely be a village where there are no friends of ours. When you enter, seek out a host and at the door say 'Peace! peace be with you from the Father' and if he returns your greeting, stay with that man. But if he doesn't return it, then your own greeting will return upon you and you will seek another place. His loss will be great!

'Do you expect difficulties on the way?' Most eyes gave him an ironic reply.

'Yes, difficulties of course and more than difficulties. You must have the guile of desert snakes and the quiet innocence of doves. For they may not simply reject you or throw abuse at you. No, they will take you to their courts, before magistrates and kings, because you speak of me and in my name. Don't begin to plan what you will answer to these charges; the Spirit of God will give you the words when the danger stands clear before you.

'All about you will be the torment of strife and anger, brother set against brother and parent against child and all the hatred will gather and fall upon you. You will be hunted from place to place but truly I say to you, you will not have traversed the cities of Israel before the Son of Man comes.

'Don't expect better treatment than I have received – the servant is not better or more fortunate than his master – you have heard me called 'Beelzebub'; what then will they call you, of the same kin and household?

'They may indeed even destroy your bodies but have no fear of death, if they cannot destroy your souls. You have seen the poor sparrow – two are sold for a farthing – but not one feather of them is ruffled without the knowledge of your Father in Heaven. So don't be afraid; you are of more value than many sparrows!

'Are these the words you expected from me? I tell you a hard truth. When I came into the world I brought not peace but a sword. I can do no more than echo for you the words of the prophet Micah:

> A son at variance with his father,
>> The daughter against her mother,
>> The daughter-in-law against her mother-in-law
>> And a man's foes shall be they of his own household.'

The sombre tone of the final prophecy was chilling and they looked with foreboding at each other and with compassion for Jeshua. But he took up the theme.

'Yet you mustn't be despondent. To love your life more than me is to lose it and he who loses his life for my sake shall find it eternally.

'You will meet affection and charity and a welcome for the Kingdom and again I say to you, he who gives you or one of my little ones a cup of water in my name shall have his rich reward.

'And where will you go? Not now to the Gentile countries nor yet into Samaria; seek the lost sheep of the house of Israel and bring them to the fold.'

He held them in silence and they remained seated about him. Then, before dismissing them to their rest, he spoke for them the 'Travellers' Prayer.'

> May it be thy will, O Lord God of our Fathers,
>> To lead us forth in peace,
>> To direct our steps in peace,
>> To uphold us in peace
>> And to lead us in life, joy and peace
>> Unto the haven of our desire.
>> O deliver us from every enemy, ambush and hurt by the way,
>> And from all afflictions that visit and trouble the world
>> Send a blessing on the work of our hands.
>> Let us obtain grace, loving-kindness and mercy in thine eyes,
>> And in the eyes of all who behold us.

Hearken unto the voice of our supplication,
For thou art a God who hearkenest unto prayer.
They were drawn within the tranquillity of the prayer and were still, even radiant, as Jeshua ended:

The Lord bless you and keep you;
The Lord make his face to shine upon you
And be gracious unto you.
The Lord turn his face unto you
And give you peace.

They went to their rest and before dawn Jeshua saw four of the quiet disciples go off with the simplest of farewells while Peter and Andrew, James and John, Judas and Matthew made their several preparations; with pleasure he saw Simon the rash and Thomas the questioner prepare together for their journey. The future was shaping itself.

As Simon and Thomas waved their farewell, Jeshua took Judas and Matthew aside and spoke to them.

'You will have a hard task. For I want you to go to the cities and there seek out the men of wealth and of learning – for the rich also have souls! You will tell them of the Kingdom and they will question you, closely and sceptically. Speak to them in love and simplicity and if they will hear, you will have secured leaders in the Kingdom. Be tender and steadfast.'

Only Peter and Andrew were left, waiting for a last word of affection and reassurance. Peter, as craggy as the basalt rock on which his birthplace was founded, had softened in his speech and had kindlier, more sensitive eyes than when he first came to Jeshua's company. His beard – more carefully trimmed – framed a face as ruddy, rugged and scarred as ever; he would always bear the marks of his dangerous calling. But as he stood with the gentler Andrew, Jeshua knew that here was the stuff of prophecy and of suffering even to death.

'My Father will be with you on your way. When you have fulfilled your work, return to Capernaum and there we shall talk, with joy as we have always talked. Peace go with you.'

Alone for the first time for many months, Jeshua descended to the lake, on the outskirts of Tiberias and made his journey of healing by the wayside and teaching in the synagogues, through Arbela, Magdala and Gennesaret until he reached Capernaum. There he told Peter's wife of the disciples' departure to the further towns and villages of Galilee and asked if he might await their return in his old 'Prophet's Chamber.' Happily she made it ready and then called him to share their evening meal.

So the days passed tranquilly, Jeshua spending most of the hours in meditation, as he looked from his room on the roof across the lake in all its moods. A month passed in which he brought to recollection every event of the time since he left Nazareth for Capernaum, of the Kingdom's answer to the peoples' needs, of the nurture of the twelve, the powers released in face of desperate minds and bodies and finally, sombrely, of the forces massed against him, the evidence gathering of the menace he represented to the traditions, now so impotent in their formality but still so potent in their command of the learned and the holy. He was troubled by the Pharisees and the scribes trained in Jerusalem, not because their opposition to him was based on inherent wickedness but precisely because they loved holiness and loved it fanatically. This would have to be faced; they would have to be faced; what he and they must know was the possibility of transfiguring the ancient tradition by the outpouring of the power of his Kingdom. His duty was to the outcast, the down-trodden and the poor; his duty also lay with the Temple and as he contemplated this more demanding duty, he recalled the words of the first dedication:

252

The house was filled with a cloud,
> Even the house of the Lord,
> So that the priests could not stand to minister
> By reason of the cloud;
> For the glory of the Lord
> Had filled the house of God.

Was that the 'cloud', 'God's Glory' that now filled the Jerusalem Temple or was the cloud of a more terrible darkness? Jeshua was deeply troubled.

There came a day of clear brightness over the lake, burnished waters and glistening ripples following the breeze from the north. All seemed tranquil and smiling, as the fishermen of the night rowed their catches into harbour. Into the quiet, as Jeshua sat at rest, burst Peter's wife, distraught. Jeshua rose and led her to be seated on some cushions against the sunny wall and waited for her crying to be still.

'Rabbi Jeshua, the most awful rumours. One has come from the south, and he waits to tell you of the death of your cousin, John, he who baptised in Jordan.'

'Death?' Through his immediate sorrow, the news came as little surprise to Jeshua. The wonder had been that John had survived so long.

'Tell me the rumours.'

'They are no longer rumours and he, his disciple, waits below to tell you.'

It seemed prudent that John's disciple ascend to the roof, to avoid over-eager eyes and ears and it was in the light of a still and beneficent day that Jeshua heard the sordid history.

John had never ceased either his prophecies of the Kingdom or his denunciations of those who frustrated its coming. The most immediate object of his invective had been Herod, no less, who had married irregularly his brother Philip's wife, Herodias. Herod, as always, was torn with conflicting passions, of concern for the pride of Herodias, of passing lust for her daughter, Salome, and of fear

253

of John and the fire of his prophecies. There came a tragic day when those passions created a tempest which overwhelmed Herod. For Salome danced seductively; her reward should be anything she asked 'even to half my kingdom'; Herodias seized her opportunity and the reward, the head of John the Baptiser, was granted.

Servants had carried word to John's disciples and the whole of eastern Galilee seethed with the tragedy.

'And, rabbi, it deeply concerns you also. Herod has long sought for you. We know he fears you as he feared John. The fears of John's prophecies had such awful fascination for him that he could not hear enough of them; he seemed to gloat in horrors, and now he has turned to you. Your works and words have obsessed him more than John. Master, Herod is as dangerous as a beast of the wilderness.'

Jeshua kept his seclusion until, a day later, his disciples began to return from their journeyings. When Peter and John had rested and six others had come back to Capernaum, Jeshua left the city for a wilderness area within the jurisdiction of Bethsaida, leaving word that the last of the disciples were to follow him there. It was remote and wild, so inhospitable as to attract no visits even from the people of Bethsaida itself. Here in the complete solitude, Jeshua heard their accounts, of miracles performed, rejoicings in the villages, the Kingdom proclaimed, of hunger, thirst and weariness but above all, joy in all that had been their lot.

Jeshua shared with them the tragedy of John and it became for all of them a part of their destiny. For some of them there was a kind of exhilaration in the knowledge that conflict was now palpable, identifiable; for others among them there was foreboding at the personal threat to Jeshua, for to none did their own danger appear to matter. Jeshua turned their talk once more to their triumphs by the way and they were a band of thirteen, cherishing a common purpose, glorying in what was already accomplished.

The death of John the Baptiser had been personal tragedy, the break of a family tie; it also carried threats more dire than any they had known, even in their troubled province, 'Galil of the Gentiles', the melting-pot.

Philip and the 'Sons of Thunder' were talking at the lakeside, where they had asked for word in quiet with Jeshua. They were still in the heat of the sun, rising towards noon, and were grateful for the quiet lapping of waves. Jeshua came and sat between them; James was their deeply disturbed spokesman.

'How do we face this menace, Master? We of the lake towns have always thought of Rome as the greatest enemy, in power and in threat to our spirit, polluting our beliefs. But this outrage,' he choked on the words, 'this murder of your cousin John, this has uncovered a threat we have chosen to ignore. We have pretended that Herod Antipas is *not* in Caesarea, not in Machaerus, not in Jerusalem, and as he carries his filth from place to place, so we have drawn in the skirts of our robes and let him pass!'

Jeshua looked out to the eastern horizon of Gennesaret, avoiding the gaze of all four of his companions. There was a sick withdrawal about his tense mouth and half-closed eyes and Simon, more sensitive to the anger in James's voice than John — whose tone would have matched his brother's — could not tell whether it was the threat from Herod or the depth of hatred in James which caused Jeshua the greater distress. James repeated his question in a higher, sharper voice:

'How do we face this menace?' Jeshua turned from James to Philip and asked, 'And how *do* we face it, Philip?'

Unusually, the quiet, unassertive man was ready to talk and his reply seemed to set James and John aside, though his glance as he spoke included them with Jeshua.

'Some of my Greek friends are from Athens itself and they tell me strange and indeed wonderful things. A man who seemed to be a rabbi to them, perhaps even a Hasid, —

Socrates was his name, – preferred to die by a drink of hemlock rather than do violence to his belief or to his city. That man's name has echoed through my thoughts whenever I have heard of Herod's violence and been tempted to reply in kind.'

He seemed to have made his reply and John cut in at white heat – 'and let evil flourish about us, as weeds choke a pasture?'

'Which is the more powerful, John, a Hasid or a Zealot, a blessing or a dagger?' Philip's question was truly a question, unprovocative and inviting an answer.

'A blessing will not turn aside a dagger-point!'

'Are you inviting us to withdraw from battle, Philip?' Jeshua's question, in turn, wholly disconcerted Philip; he always assumed his rabbi to be more Hasid than man of politics – much less freedom-fighter! He could frame neither a reply nor a further question.

'Power is of many kinds and there are many ways of employing it. You John, you James, have Herod in yourselves, the desire for stabbing power; you Philip, have Socrates in yourself, the Hasid's longing for stillness and contemplation. And you Philip have Herod in the remote depths of your being, and you, my 'Sons of Thunder' may well be Hasids from Capernaum!' All three were confounded; were they to laugh at this portraiture or to accept it as true?

'You have heard me say to the sorely maimed, the blind, the leprous, 'be whole' and I think you have begun to learn that 'wholeness' is not simply 'well-ness' the absence of pain or suffering. To be whole is to know oneself in the depths, to know the extent of our compassion, our rejection of tyranny, our longing to withdraw to talk with our Father, our impulse to smite and to cry our maledictions. You will find all these in your 'wholeness' and, dear children, you have to live with your own particular 'wholeness'! I shall fight, have no fear; the gates of hell will not prevail – and yet, in all this battle, I shall not be guilty of one broken limb, one shedding of blood. All this you will learn in the way. Come; we must return.'

Jeshua was aware that they needed still longer to rest and suggested that they descend to the shore below Bethsaida and row across the narrow passage to the eastern shore. This they did, arriving at a place not as wild as the wilderness above Bethsaida but sufficiently remote – as they supposed – to be untroubled.

Some, however, had seen them take the boat for the journey across and it was scarcely afternoon before the crowds began to gather at the hillside where Jeshua spoke with his friends, having hurried the further distance along the lakeshore. Jeshua looked down at the multitude, all so silently gathered and gazing expectantly up at him.

'They are like sheep without a shepherd. Come; they need us more than we need rest' and he began to teach them, while the twelve, with their new-found powers of speech, moved among the others still crowding along the shore.

The day passed imperceptibly. So great was the pleasure of the crowd that they moved from the disciples to Jeshua and from Jeshua to small groups among themselves, eagerly exchanging their visions of this 'Kingdom' which should be theirs. But dusk was coming down about them and Peter, ever practical, approached Jeshua with his concern for the people.

'They will be getting hungry, more hungry as they feel the journey they have made. Send them into the villages to buy their bread and find shelter for the night.'

'No don't send them away. Why cannot you feed them?'

'Master! Even if we could get the bread it would cost us two hundred silver pieces, even to give them a little.'

'What have you yourselves got?'

'Nothing in our wallets; we had expected to return to our homes before this came upon us.'

Andrew, silent but efficient came diffidently to Jeshua and said, 'There is a lad here who tells me he has five barley cakes and two small salt fish. They won't go far in this multitude.'

'Gather the people before us and make them sit down, orderly and quietly, on the grass.'

The twelve marshalled the people while Jeshua laid the five loaves and the fishes on a napkin, on a large flat boulder within full sight of the people. Their silence was profound, not a child stirring. Jeshua took one of the barley loaves, broke it, lifted up his eyes to heaven and began the prayer:

Blessed art thou, O Lord our God,
King of the universe,
Who bringest forth bread from the earth.

In the silence, Jeshua continued:

The Lord hath done great things for us,
Whereat we rejoiced.
They that sow in tears
Shall reap in joy
Though he goeth on his way weeping
Bearing the store of seed,
He shall come back with joy
Bearing his sheaves.

Jeshua took the other four loaves and broke them into fragments and parted the fishes into tiny pieces, laying them beside the growing mound of loaf fragments.

We will bless the Lord
From this time forth and for everymore.

Jeshua looked up to the silent crowd below him, stretched out his hands and they replied in the so familiar response

Praise ye the Lord.

Again the multitude had fallen silent feeling the solemnity not of a feast but of ritual. Jeshua gestured to the twelve who, with covered hands, took the bread and the fragments of fish among the people. With awe, they gave into each raised palm, bread and a morsel of fish; their wonder grew as they saw the food they carried remain plenty in their hands. The silence grew even more profound as the people consumed each his portion and when all had taken their gift, Jeshua returned to the stone boulder before them. He once more raised his hands and his eyes to heaven and said:

Blessed be our God
Of whose bounty we have partaken,
And through whose goodness we live
and all the multitude responded
Blessed be he and blessed be his name.

The twelve were called by Jeshua to his side. At his gesture they gathered any fragments of bread and of fish, which they had retained and which the people had left as they ate. All was placed reverently on the rock. Other needy, beyond the five thousand who had feasted here, should be fed with the bounty.

As Jeshua and the twelve made their preparations to leave, so did the multitude slowly and reluctantly make their way to the shore road. The ritual spell was still upon them and while most remained silent, many said to each other, 'The prophet; indeed this must be that prophet who must come.'

The twelve also were silent, needing time to take this new act into their knowledge of Jeshua. He, realising their wonder, sent them back in their boat to their home, while he went up into the highest mountain to be still, to meditate and to pray. The disciples packed their boat and embarked in total darkness, pulling obliquely westward, to land, as they hoped, at Capernaum. When they set out to row, the breezes were light and they pulled leisurely, enjoying the stillness after the confounding events of the day.

But the wind backed northerly, sending waves across their bows and making rowing almost impossible. They shipped oars and hoped that calm would come as swiftly as the storm, as was the way with the lake. It worsened and in a very short time they were desperately bailing and crying their desperation. Then out of the darkness, shadowed in the spume and the mist, a figure appeared on the water an apparition which increased their panic fear. Across the waves came the familiar voice.

'It is I and there is no need for fear.'

As though on dry land he strode to the ship's side and took his place in the stern; immediately the wind ceased and the waves were quietened and they completed their journey to Capernaum in a silent amazement and fear. Ordinary men found it hard to assimilate so much truth.

A poor fisherman from Tiberias was making his excuses to his wife. 'I got there just too late. There they were, a huge crowd of people seated on the pasture, in great groups. There was no excitement – none of the wonders that the neighbours had talked about to you. That was the strange thing. I spoke to one who had eaten in the meal. He was quite 'over-awed' he said and really didn't want to say any more. I turned to his neighbour and he too could scarcely bear to look at me, for that would have meant turning his eyes away from Jeshua. You have seen him and know how he always keeps men's attention – but this was different. He seemed even taller than usual and those wonderful eyes of his, they saw everyone – he even looked at me – I wasn't just one of the thousand – he saw *me*. But then, slowly, as we walked away together, the men began to talk but didn't quite know how to say what they felt.

'They tell me it was just a young boy's snack, just enough to keep away hunger – and yet we all had a little – just a mouthful of fish, a small piece of bread – but it was sufficient; for we still looked at him and he at us and we were satisfied' – that was what he told me and I could believe him, for the silence was all about us still and I really felt I was bathed in it.' His wife, who had reproached him with being late for a miracle her neighbours had known and seen, now shared his awe. Their children and their grandchildren were to hear of it many times in the future.

TWENTY-EIGHT

The following day, when the twelve came together with Jeshua they watched him with unease, embarrassed to ask for some comment on the happenings of yesterday. He left them in their bewilderment but said to them instead,

'They will ask for healing, some will ask for our teaching, but many more will ask for bread. Let us cross once more to the other side.'

Still silent they took to the waters and quickly reached the other shore, to find again that the crowds were gathering. This time he distanced himself from them, Peter and Andrew so managing the craft that it was again a place from which he could, unhampered, address the people. His voice rang, challenging, across the water.

'Why have you followed me? To see more healings, to hear more truths? No! You ate with me in the place you now stand, you ate the bread and were satisfied. You follow me not for the truths of miracle but for bread! But you know that bread grows stale and lies heavy; you know that at certain seasons it fails.

'Hear me, for it is truth I speak to you. Work, spend yourselves, not for the bread that perishes and fails but for the bread of eternal life, which the Son of Man will give you.'

'What sign, what proof shall we have that you can fulfil this promise?' Some of the boldest had pressed forward to question him and now eagerly, some ironically, waited for the answer. Jeshua replied quietly, forcing their attention and gathering them more closely at the shore:

'At the beginning of time, my Father created the fruit of the field and your father Adam, your mother Eve, ate of it and were satisfied. But they sinned and won their bread with the sweat of labour. And even worse befell your forefathers. Wandering out of Egypt in the cruel desert and near to starvation, they looked to heaven and God gave them manna, sufficient for each day. That bread also perished, if they were covetous and tried to hoard it.

'But I say to you, I and my Father, we give you the bread of life: I am that bread of life; believe in me and you will neither hunger nor thirst – and at the end of time, when this creation shall cease, I will raise the man who believes in me, to eternal life in my Father's Kingdom.'

The declarations of Jeshua in the presence of his disciples had become more and more specific but in their growing profundity the more difficult to grasp. After much troubled thought and questioning among themselves they asked him:

'The Kingdom we begin to know, to feel part of it but 'the bread of life'? a hard saying, which we find too difficult to understand. And when you told those others who are not of our company that that 'bread of life' was your 'flesh and blood', that is frightening and beyond our reach.'

'Are you offended by these sayings and troubled in your minds? Will you be more convinced or more confounded if you see the Son of Man ascend to the place whence he came? Your usual ways of thinking will not reach the answer to these questions I put to you; it is the Spirit of God alone who can bring life to your minds, fire to your hearts. Indeed, the words I speak to you, they are themselves Spirit and it is my Father's Spirit that has brought you to me and to my love for you.'

With this they had to be content but with deep expectation and the shadows of foreboding, they awaited all that the next months would bring.

These forebodings were made the bleaker when yet another company of Pharisees came to Galilee from

Jerusalem. Like all who had come before them, they had questions to ask, questions of debate within the Law and of Jeshua's response. They faced Jeshua directly with, as they thought, an easy matter of accusation:

'Why do you and your disciples break bread with unclean, unwashed hands?'

'Are we the only transgressors of the Law? Aren't you in the same case? I would put a greater question to you: which do you choose to keep, the Law in its purity or the traditions which you and your elders have woven about it over the ages?'

They were silent, suspecting a trap and all too aware from their many encounters, of the quick and subtle movement of Jeshua's mind.

'I will be more precise with you. Torah says that we should honour our father and mother and we have always supposed that that command from Sinai embraced our love, our concern, our cherishing of father and mother.

'But you, what do your laws and traditions say? An unloving and covetous son, perhaps in a moment's wrath, swears an oath that all his possessions are dedicated to the Temple. 'It is Corban', he says, sworn to the Temple alone, when his parents need the succour of his goods. An oath must be observed, you say – an oath of that intent, when it denies the very command of Torah?'

This was to shatter the heart of their profession, the casuistry which debated so delicately of the conflicting meanings of the Law; it was prudent to remain silent.

'But far worse than this – the splendid simplicity of Jahweh's words, 'Hallow God, honour men, be merciful', these words you clutter and obscure with a mass of petty laws, with rules of washing of pots, the tithing of herbs, the touching of graves, the swearing of oaths! Your webs seem fragile as your people looks at each strand, but the mass of them, the tangled mass of them! Truly did Isaiah tell of your elders:

This people honoureth me with their lips,
But their heart is far from me.

Have you listened to that cry from the prophet? Have you heard its echo as you debate yet another subtle regulation? You pile a burden of guilt on those who haven't your leisure or your skill in maintaining every minute turn of meaning. And I say to you that all your ritual washings, your cries of 'unclean' are vain cries. Pollution doesn't come from without, from the food you eat, the wine you drink, nor from the vessels that contain them; the uncleanliness comes from within, from the evil thoughts of minds and the evil promptings of a sick heart.

'The multitudes look to you for truth, for the opening of their eyes to see the way of life. But you are blind, blind leaders of the blind and when you lead, you and they stumble in ditches.'

Once more his longing to see more of his simple people drove Jeshua into the depths of Galilee and beyond. Thomas had long hoped that they would be led by him into the coastlands of the Great Sea, his home country in Syro-Phoenicia. It seemed that this time his hope would be answered.

They went along the coast almost to the outskirts of Tyre and at the wayside they were stopped by a woman of the country, a Greek by birth. As they walked, she pursued them with the cry, constantly repeated, 'Have mercy on me, Lord, thou Son of David. Heal my daughter who is sorely beset by a devil.'

Jeshua ignored her cries and walked steadily ahead of the twelve but his silence failed to silence the woman. The twelve found the cries intolerable and Thomas was deep in embarrassment as he caught up with Jeshua.

'Master, answer her prayers and send her away, that we may know some little peace!'

Jeshua turned to the woman and spoke to her with a formality his friends had not heard before.

'I am sent only to the lost sheep of the house of Israel.'

Her prayers to him became more intense, simply crying, 'Lord, help me!' With an even sterner formality he replied,

'It is not meet to take the children's bread and throw it to the dogs.' She replied,

'True, Lord; but the dogs do eat the crumbs that fall from their master's table.'

Jeshua's mood was transformed and with the tones to which his disciples had become long accustomed, he said,

'O woman, your faith is very great. It shall be exactly as you wish,' and her daughter was cured of her possession at that very hour.

TWENTY-NINE

The journey south-eastward from the alien coast was swift, for Galilee made its irresistible demand on his compassion. Once more his people called on him for wholeness and the lame, blind, dumb and maimed were strewn at his feet as he made to teach the crowds before him. As the days passed, the twelve began to realise more and more clearly that these 'acted parables' of sickness turned to wholeness were as powerful as his very words to the multitude. One of these moments had its peculiar force. A man was brought before him who was dumb; Jeshua took him by the hand and looked into his eyes, where his speech was palpable, a craving to talk to Jeshua. He took him a little apart from the crowds and put his fingers in the dumb man's ears, moistened his fore-finger with spittle and touched his tongue. Looking up to heaven he said,

'*Ephphatha*, be opened,' and at once the dumb man opened his mouth in wonder and spoke,

'Master!'

Once more the multitude crowded about him and this time they ignored their hunger for as long as three days.

And once more Jeshua's compassion was aroused and once more he answered their need, creating bread that was enough for them and more than enough.

There were days, however, when his creative powers seemed spent; Peter, James and John looked at his eyes, heavy with lack of sleep and at the drooped shoulders; their compassion was helpless and they could only watch his attempts to withdraw and renew his strength.

One of these retreats into solitude was invaded by yet another group of Jerusalem elders.

'Your reputation, Rabbi, is great and widespread. Will you honour us by allowing us to observe these powers? Show us a sign!'

These invasions on his integrity were more sapping of his strength than all the demands of the derelict for healing. He gathered himself for his reply and in a tone of quiet authority which destroyed their irony, he said,

'You look at the skies and observe their signs. In the evening you look westward and say, 'Tomorrow will bring fine weather for the sky is red'; and in the morning you look eastward and say, 'foul weather this day, for again it is red within the lowering clouds.' You hypocrites! you are able to translate the weather signs into predictions – but you are helpless in face of the signs of the times!'

He turned from them, submitting again to his weariness but when he returned to Capernaum he told his friends of the renewed assault upon him.

'They ask for a sign! They have only to traverse Galilee in our wake; no city, town or hamlet is without its 'signs.' But the depraved will ignore these signs until they are confronted with 'the sign of the prophet Jonah'.'

They looked their bewilderment.

'You wonder at this 'sign of the prophet Jonah'? It should be manifest after these generations: Jonah, after three days buried in darkness, rose from the belly of the whale and lived again.'

Their eyes were still perplexed and Jeshua responded to their questioning.

'You must be patient, my little ones! You have seen 'signs and wonders' but the day will come when I, dead, will rise again.'

They stirred in fear and remained perplexed when he said,

'And then will be fulfilled the 'sign of the prophet Jonah',' and with that mystery they had, for the time, to be content.

Bethsaida now made its demands, a never-ending stream of tragic humanity. One of the sick men made a specially powerful appeal to him and greatly moved the disciples. Stumblingly, a blind man followed his guide who asked that Jeshua might touch his friend's eyes to restore his sight. Jeshua took the blind man out of the town, touched the lids of his eyes with spittle, pressed the tips of his fingers to the eye-sockets and asked him to look around and tell them what he saw. Peter, James and John moved from behind Jeshua, looking closely at the blind man, who smiled hesitantly and said to Jeshua,

'Master, I see men, yes I see men but they seem to me – forgive me, Master! – like trees, walking.'

Jeshua returned his smile and this time pressed the palms of his hands to the blind eyes. When he withdrew them he told the man once more to look up and about him.

'Master! I see men as men, smiling at me and holding out their hands!' There was wonder in his voice and Jeshua was content to send him on his way.

'Tomorrow we leave these familiar places and go northward towards Hermon.'

His friends were aware of a new gravity in the urgent tones of Jeshua's voice. The months at the Sea of Gennesaret, and in the uplands of Galilee had given them, as individuals and as a company, a warm sense of assurance and power. Each of the twelve had now found his secure place in the economy of their daily work and they had begun to feel a permanence in their way of life, an habitual answering of dire need which, they felt, should never end. In their private conversations they expressed this by borrowing Jeshua's own words, 'the kingdom has truly come,' they said. They were of course aware of thunder-clouds. They knew that the small groups of elders who came to visit them from Jerusalem were but the fragmentary indications of storms that brooded over Judah. But they had seen the powers of Jeshua triumphantly at work. If he could control demonic powers, what were the powers of mere man, even backed by the tradition of the Temple, to stand against him. In their buoyant sureness and in their affection for Jeshua, they looked at him and saw the truth they craved.

Yet there was unease. As they looked, they saw their loved Rabbi in the still beauty of his face, the powerful and gentle hands and the easy grace with which he walked with them or among importunate men. But Peter and John saw more. In the dark eyes they saw prophecy, something of what lay before him and which clouded with deep shadow the triumph of these months and the adoration of those whose lives were transfigured. Their delicacy, learned at his side, inhibited their questioning him but there were moments when the bleakness in his eyes chilled them as they walked.

But these days northward from Bethsaida and along the banks of the upper Jordan, were warm and spoke of harvest. It was a wider prospect and more varied than any they had known in recent weeks. The Jordan, for all its infant size, had its defiles and rocky places; the fields, vineyards and olive groves on either side, were rich to their eyes. Directly before them, some miles to the north, were the snow slopes of Hermon, while further to the north-west were the dark shoulders of the Lebanon mountains, its cedars seen at this distance as massed shadows and the crests brilliantly outlined above the snowline. Soon Galilee, with all its pleas for help and its clutching hands, was a memory behind them and Jerusalem, further still, a distant and shadowy threat, safely ignored.

They were approaching the outskirts of Caesarea Philippi and they sat for their meal at the entrance to an olive grove overlooking the city. When they had finished the meal and its grace, Jeshua turned to them and abruptly and wholly unexpectedly asked,

'Who do people say I am?'

There was an excited little babble of suggestions and among the voices, the brooding of Thomas, 'They say all things, Master,' and each of them contributed the rumoured title as it had most forcibly struck him:

'Some say John the Baptiser, come to life again,' 'Some say Elijah -' 'Jeremiah' 'or at least one of the prophets.'

'And you, who do you say that I am?'

Who should speak for them? The adulation of the crowds had been so great as to be incoherent. They themselves, the twelve, had been content to bask in this reflected praise without considering titles and identities. Wasn't he quite simply 'Jeshua', the fulfilment of all they had ever sought or longed for? As the intimates of a royal person are barely aware of his royalty, so they were content to see Jeshua as himself, unique and loving.

But Peter found his ease with the person of Jeshua fall away. More than the others, more than he had expressed before, he had been moved by the restoration to sight of the blind man of Bethsaida. He, Peter, had been one of the 'trees, walking.' He had stood, more awed than ever before, as the hands of Jeshua brought full sight to the blind. He looked intently at Jeshua, seeing as if for the first time a being behind the features, a wonder beyond the words. Impulsively, as if in response to new vision, he said,

'You are the Anointed, the Christ, Son of the living God.'

The twelve scarcely breathed, eager to prolong the vision; most moved was Judas, in whose eyes a new and sharp light sprang to life; James and John caught glimpses of a splendid life before them; Thomas brooded on the sudden shifting of all the pieces of his world.

'Simon Bar-Jona, flesh and blood alone have not given you this revelation but my Father in heaven. And Simon, you are Peter,' Jeshua paused, having united the old name, not used for so many months, with the new, which was now confirmed; he went on,

'You have so often heard the words of Isaiah,

Look to the rock from which you were hewn,
And the quarry from which you were digged.
Look to Abraham your father
And to Sarah who bore you.

You, Peter, Rock, second Abraham to whom God declared,

I have found a rock on which I can build
And found the world.

On this rock my Kingdom is built and the gates of hell shall not prevail against it.'

Silence lay profoundly about them. As each had found his place in the wandering band who had changed Galilee, so now they anxiously sought their place in this new and greater destiny.

'You shall have the keys of the Kingdom; eternal life will be in your hands, to bind and to loose. You shall have authority on earth which will be fulfilled in heaven.'

Again he looked about them, gathering them into one.

'This is the mystery I confide to you. The seed is sown; it will grow in secret; and when the time is fit, it will reveal itself to all mankind.'

Dusk had now closed in on them and Caesarea had withdrawn beyond the twilight. Together, before composing themselves to sleep, they sang the psalm of entry to the glory of Zion:

Behold now, praise the Lord,
All ye servants of the Lord,
Ye that by night stand in the house of the Lord,
Even in the courts of the house of our God.
Lift up your hands in the sanctuary
And praise the Lord.
The Lord that made heaven and earth
Give thee blessing out of Sion.

The following morning they refrained from entering Caesarea Philippi, choosing rather to leave the valley of the upper Jordan and take a more circuitous route back to Galilee. For Jeshua had much more to tell them but allowed for the moment the fair countryside to give them time to absorb their words and his on the previous day; until late afternoon he walked ahead of them, allowing them to drift in such groups as they chose.

Towards evening they saw that a deeper gravity had overtaken him. Again he gathered them closely about him and began in the manner they had so long cherished.

'You have from your infancy held fast the words of the prophet Isaiah and gloried in them. You have shared his vision of Jerusalem and prayed to see it in your day:

O Jerusalem that bringest good tidings,
Lift up thy voice with strength,
Lift it up, be not afraid.
Say unto the cities of Judah,
Behold your God.

Perhaps in these last days while Jerusalem has seemed so far off, you have comforted yourselves with the words,

He shall feed his flock like a shepherd,
He shall gather the lambs with his arm
And carry them in his bosom
And shall gently lead those that are with young.

The flocks have indeed been cherished.

271

'But I have now to lead you further into Isaiah's prophecy. After all this joy, he tells another matter, speaking of God's Servant. These are his words:

> He hath no form nor comeliness,
> And when we shall see him
> There is no beauty that we should desire him.'

Jeshua's face had taken on the full weight of the tragic words and his friends waited with anxiety for the conclusion of his speech.

'Isaiah drew this portrait with a fearless hand. God's Servant had to suffer to the uttermost.

> He is despised and rejected of men,
> A man of sorrows and acquainted with grief,
> And we hid as it were our faces from him.
> He was despised
> And we esteemed him not.'

Jeshua's voice fell and the twelve before him were absorbed as the Servant took form before them.

'To what end was all this sorrow? To what end did the Father permit his Servant to be despised? Isaiah tells us.

> Surely he hath borne our griefs
> And carried our sorrows,
> Yet we did esteem him stricken,
> Smitten of God and afflicted,

And this burden of sorrow and despair, to what end?

> But he was wounded for our transgressions
> He was bruised for our iniquities,
> The chastisement of our peace was upon him,
> And with his stripes we are healed.

'It is a heavy debt that Judah and Israel carry: 'our transgressions,' 'our iniquities,' 'our peace,' but you hear throughout that they were 'his stripes.' Have you yet learned the truth of these words? Do you yet know the destiny that waits in Jerusalem?'

Their faces had now taken on some of his tragic form. Fearfully they looked away from him, their cherished and loved one, as he sat among them.

'Soon I must go up to Jerusalem; there I must suffer many things at the hands of men and they will lift me up to my death. And only so can I rise again.'

Peter was stirred to a loving rage:

'This will be far from your fate, Lord, this shall never happen to you!'

Jeshua rose before them, seeming to tower above them as he spoke.

'Get behind me Sathanas, my Adversary! Peter, the words of your mouth, whether yours or Another's, are an offence to me; they savour not of the things of God but of men.'

The rebuke was crushing and yet Peter was not quelled. He stood before Jeshua, pleading silently for understanding. Jeshua responded instantly, took him by the arm and led him back to his friends. Jeshua now sat among them and the tragic conclusion was spoken with the assurance of fulfilment.

'If any man will come after me, let him deny his own life, take up his cross and follow me.'

At the words 'cross' their faces were convulsed in rejection. Judas took his kerchief and with horror in his eyes wiped his mouth as though after a bitter drink. But Jeshua's words were hesitant:

'For whosoever wishes to save his life shall lose it and whosover will lose his life for my sake shall find it.'

His voice changed to the gentle persuasion he used when speaking to his 'little ones.'

'Tell me, what profit is it to a man, if he gain the whole world and lose his soul? Indeed what can he give in exchange for his soul?'

And with an ecstacy in the words:

'For the Son of Man shall come in the glory of his Father with his angels.

'Truly, I say to you, there will be some of you who shall not taste death until they see the Son of Man entering his Kingdom.'

'Sathanas, Master?' The pain in the question was matched by the desolation about them. Jeshua knew that the words at Caesarea Philippi had done more than disconcert the sturdy fisherman; something within him had been crushed, malformed by a judgment he could neither understand nor assimilate to himself. His eyes had the frustrated, defeated look of the child who feels parental judgment to be 'not fair.'

Jeshua knew the sickness of his mind and led him, by gesture rather than invitation, a mile or two outside Capernaum to a ravine of basalt lava, unresolved by time and weather to a congenial valley. There, pursuing the silence, they sat side by side.

'Sathanas, Master, truly *your* 'Adversary'?'

'It was you and yet not you, Peter. Do you remember your words, 'You are the Christ'? They were unconsidered words –'

'But meant with all my heart!'

'I am not doubting that, Peter – but still unconsidered, unmeditated. They welled up as a spring wells up in a dry place.'

This was unaccustomed thinking to the fishermen and he looked up beneath his brows, wondering if this was reconciliation.

'But other words well up also – words of anger, of resentment, of disappointed longing – you have felt their sour taste as they pass along the tongue, that so unruly tongue – and unconsidered as they are, they leave a sad remorse – just as your words left joy and a light in the eyes about you.'

'But can I be at once your friend and your enemy?' Peter was in deeper waters than he had ever navigated on the Sea of Gennesareth and Jeshua was determined that he should find his own depth.

'There is in man an abyss of darkness; in those deep places you meet strange beings, some kind and good, with whom man walks in peace; others of such evil that every man rebels at the company he keeps within him. Do you dream deeply, Peter?'

He smiled; 'A tired fisherman sleeps well' – a pause and then a troubled consideration – 'there are some nightmares, Master, not of dangers, of tempests and foundering boats but' – seeking words for the inarticulate things – 'faces, words which leave a stain of shame.' Peter's eyes were troubled, for nothing had made him explore these paths before.

'Dreams can be warnings for the ways ahead. You have seen those desperate men fall and writhe before us, harsh and evil voices coming from their throats which have never owned them. Not one of us is beyond the reach of those dangers, these visitors to the shrine of your body. These impulses in the depths of your being open the way to the demons at your side. At that moment they come, not as ordered legions but as single invaders, spying the land.'

'And so Sathanas? I, the Enemy!' It was an incredulous rejection, an unspeakable betrayal of friendship achieved.

'For a moment only – and there was, dear Peter, as much generosity as enmity to me and my purpose in your words. I had spoken of reviling, of a shameful death, of me, your lord and friend, despatched like a scapegoat in the wilderness. And as your soul rebelled, sickened at the thought of execution, so in a waking nightmare the demon spoke in your throat – 'Not to you; that cannot happen to you!' – and at that moment it was the demon in your throat that I rebuked, not Simon the Rock.' The smile was an embracing gesture, but Peter, bruised and insecure, could turn only questioning eyes towards Jeshua.

'Come, friend; I must tell you more.' They walked slowly along the path strewn with rubble, Peter still floundering in the new mental and spiritual terrain to which he was invited. They reached a shelf of rock from which, seated, they could look back towards the Sea of Galilee, a fractured mirror in the noon sun. Jeshua's hand went to a fold in his tunic and drew out what appeared to be a small sandstone boulder; it rested within the open palm of his right hand. Peter tentatively stretched out his.

'No, Peter, not in your hand!'

Peter looked more closely, for it was an object wholly alien to him. It seemed human in shape, its legs and arms broken away; narrow-waisted, its hips swelled outwards and beneath the spread of the shoulders a suggestion of breasts; the head, eroded, it seemed, by sand and time, was poised arrogantly and Peter sought for an expression within the worn features. Jeshua tilted his hand so that the light glanced obliquely across the face, enhancing its contours. Now in the shadowed planes could be seen a smile, inhuman and taunting; instinctively Peter's hand withdrew from the taint of corruption.

'I found it on Carmel, within the threshold of a cave, where I was waiting for peace and returning strength.' Peter knew these solitary withdrawals in their Galilean ways.

'This idol in Carmel would have been acceptable to Baal – and Elijah would have thundered!'

Peter, withdrawn from even the remotest contact with the object which seemed to him to vibrate with life, looked at Jeshua in bewilderment; he responded to the unspoken question:

'It was safer with me than in the hands of a passing shepherd.'

'Sacred, rabbi?'

'Oh, yes, sacred; sacred, as the fallen angels are sacred, as Beelzebul is sacred, powerful as demons in a torn body. It has served its purpose, Peter, as I speak to you.'

Jeshua balanced the carved figure in his hand and then flung it into the ravine; there it shattered, debris in the basalt scree.

BOOK FOUR

Views of Bethany

THIRTY

Jeshua knew that a critical time was upon him and upon the twelve. There was so much that they knew, so much they now hoped and how pitifully small their understanding. One thing was becoming daily clearer: they had no single vision at this time, which united them in one living hope. And how could their purpose, their goal be one, if their imaginings sent them seeking in so many diverse ways? Peter, James and John had a certain fellowship together and Andrew was content to go humbly along with them; but the sturdy humility of Peter was a different – and perhaps a finer – thing than the latent longing for power that sometimes glinted in the eyes of James and John. Judas and Matthew stood somewhat apart. They knew the ways of the world, knew the shifts and stratagems of power, 'the sinews of war' in the perpetual struggle for mastery that every society experienced; they understood the meaning of compromise, the subtle moral bargaining that made life in community, and most potently in cities, possible and tolerable; their very assurance spoke of this mastery – could it be translated into terms of the Kingdom? And dear, puzzled Philip, his gentle sophistication with its veneer of Greek! For him the very transition of language from the Greek he spoke with his old friends to the crude demotic of the twelve, would these tensions ever be resolved? And would he see the Kingdom in any other terms than those of his ideal *polis*? and the friend to whom he was ever more closely drawn, Thomas, for whom every word, every gesture had to be unravelled, dissected and accounted for; their conversation a hybrid of the *stoa* and the colonnade of the Temple; the rabbis translated into the Greek of Athens! *That* might be a power in the kingdom. They were as disparate, all of them, as the Twelve Tribes and no one, not David nor the Maccabees, had suceeded in welding them into a unity.

A new beginning had now to be faced, a core of disciples prepared in a new way. Over the past weeks friendships had crystallised into closer fellowship and the three, Peter, John and James, had instinctively drawn nearer to Jeshua, in a questioning or a silent communication, which palpably strengthened their insights and their resolve as the days passed.

It was a day in late spring. Even after an hour of sunshine the dew lay like rain on the grass and there was promise of heat and of haze in the next hours. Jeshua sent nine of the band on errands for the company, that dispersed them between four villages, and taking Peter and the two brothers, set off silently into the country. They knew now, of settled custom, that silence was the only fellowship that morning, that Jeshua was contained and withdrawn, calling on matters beyond their understanding. They came to the slope of a high hill and still in silence began the ascent. Jeshua moved slowly and every few minutes stopped to look back as the panorama became ever more without concrete detail below them. They felt they were moving into a world of abstraction, the world of busy commerce, of fretful work, lying removed and below them. Gradually as the heat-haze traversed the plain below, the only focussed reality became the boulders, the scree, the stunted shrubs of the upland tracts.

After two hours of steady climbing they reached a plateau summit. The rock was hard, volcanic debris, fissured into slabs and boulders in a wild parody of a shattered city. They walked among the rocks, at last finding a small amphitheatre in which some slabs reared like monoliths, a protective wall, while others gave them the familiar setting of Jeshua's discourses. They kept their silence until he was ready to speak.

'In such a place the ancients 'walked with God', walked with such humble purpose that some of them walked out of life into His presence.'

The three waited in silence; no discourse had begun before in this brooding fashion.

'One of the Fathers asked of God, 'Grant me this mountain.' It was a demand for the difficult, for the conquest of the summit. Abraham your father knew this urgency of the spirit. Lot chose the rich and fertile plains but Abraham the summits where he and his flocks were tempered to the hardness of God's testing.

'But Sinai, Nebo and Carmel were the final testing places, the summits of all the summits. On Sinai Moses almost saw God, a glimpse of the hem of His garment. But he heard the voice, a voice of thunder and the voice spoke Law. In the echoes of the rocks, Moses heard 'Thou shalt!', 'Thou shalt not!''

'But Moses ascended another mountain, a mountain of triumph and of bitter tragedy.'

As Jeshua spoke, rose from his rock-seat and stood before them, they were awed to see the intensity of his eyes, the brilliance of his look. The sun had risen high behind him, but it was easier for them to bear its rays than the radiance which shone from Jeshua's face and garments; these were, as they were so many times to tell their friends, 'as white as snow, far whiter than any garment fresh from the fuller'.'

'Nebo is the symbol of all our lives among men. From the heights of Nebo we see all dreams, all longings for fulfilment, all ending of our struggles. There from Nebo, Moses saw the promise of God, a land for his people.

'And there on Nebo is all our tragic life, the unfinished business, the dream frustrated.' Jeshua's voice fell to depths which brought the tragedy of Moses to their very grasp.

'And there, because he had sinned in the sight of God, Moses died, his dreams unfulfilled, his work unaccomplished, his grave unknown.' The heat-haze had now gathered into a thick but brilliant cloud, incandescent, with an inner light, and from the cloud they heard a voice as from ancient sorrow:

'Would to God – would to God. One moment only!' It seemed to the three that in that voice from Nebo there was gathered every tragic frustration of man.

'Carmel is a mountain as dark as Nebo, where a bitterness as great as that of Moses was outfaced by Elijah. He was the pattern of all lonely, passionate men who long that their people should see their vision and share it. It was to a cave on Carmel that Elijah brought his derelict life before God, the desecrated altars, the forsaken and wayward people, the powerful prophets of alien Gods. And in anguish he cried aloud,

'I have been very jealous
For the Lord God of Hosts,
For the children of Israel have forsaken thy covenant,
Thrown down thine altars
And slain thy prophets.
And I, even I, only am left -
And they seek my life, they seek my life
To take it away.'

'And the Most High heard that voice, the desolate voice of failure.' And as he spoke, Peter looked in amazement from John and James to the brilliant form of Jeshua; for it seemed to all three that out of the cloud there loomed a rough-hewn being, tall above the stature of men, dressed in the crudest of robes, such a man as they had seen only at Jordan. The voice of Jeshua shaped him there before their eyes.

'And Elijah was not left to his desolation. To his sombre cry there came an answer from the crags of Carmel. They were shaken and even rent by a wind, a mighty wind which man could not withstand – but the voice of God was not in the wind. And once more the mountain shook and the rocks stirred in the conflict of an earthquake – but the voice of God was not in the earthquake.'

The three looked only at the face of Jeshua, with no eyes for the mountain-top and its strange visitants. The narrative held them like children.

'Then there came a still, small voice. It offered Elijah no violence, no harsh commands but only the same promise of God the Most High. The vision of Carmel was beyond the vision of Nebo, the assurance that in all generations there are the multitudes who have not embraced Baal nor worshipped false Gods.'

Throughout the vision and the words of Jeshua, Peter, James and John said no word. Breathless and over-awed, they waited simply on the transfigured friend who stood before them. Answering their silence, from high above the cloud which still wrapped them in its brilliant light, came a voice, quiet and with all authority.

'My Son, my Beloved, in whom I rejoice.'

The radiance of Jeshua's face intensified and the cloud about him moved away from the summit as a gentle mid-day breeze blew from the east.

To the three friends, the swiftly-passing moment left them with a feeling of utter loss, of dereliction. They had a

285

vision past man's comprehension and they grasped at its relics, its vesture.

'Master, it is good to be here, to remain here. Let us build here in this mountain three tabernacle booths, one for you, one for Moses and one for Elijah; and we may remain with you, an everlasting Feast of Tabernacles!'

Peter's voice faltered as he reached the end of his prayer. For there was no response from Jeshua but far above them, as though fading into the heavens, there came an echo of the Voice,

'My beloved, my beloved Son.'

Jeshua extended his hands to them, took Peter and John within the fold of his arms and smiling, as if in welcome after a long journey, took James into the same enfolding embrace and led them to the descent.

When they had walked in silence a mile or so down the mountain path, Jeshua paused, as though for rest, and gathered the three before him. 'Has the wonder so overcome you that even you, Peter, even you, John and James, so ready of tongue, are silent?' There was laughter in his words, an entering of the commonplace after the wonder. They could not respond to the smiling words and Jeshua went on:

'You are shaken because Heaven burst in on you, that I seemed to belong to 'another land'? But it should be as natural as the walking of God in Eden, 'in the cool of the evening'. You remember what Moses tells us, that Adonai walked in Paradise and talked with Adam and with Eve in that most perfect of gardens, 'eastward in Eden'. You saw me transfigured, my face brilliant with the light of my Father, even as the face of Moses glowed with the radiance of the Most High on Sinai. And as I looked at you, your faces were transfigured with the same radiance.'

The three looked at each other, wondering that they had again sunk into the commonplace as they saw nothing but the customary faces before them.

'There was even more transfiguring. That cloud was not to hide but to *reveal*, to blot out the unreality in which 'day-to-day' envelops you and to give you ears to hear the wonder of the Voice.'

This was still a language beyond comprehension and Jeshua, at their entry into a degree of maturity took them firmly onto this new ground.

'You saw the figure of Moses, great of stature and radiant with the power of Sinai. But you heard from his lips not the words of the Law but its heart, its essence. And you saw the might of Elijah, the power of his wrath and his compassion, but from his lips you heard not the words of prophecy but its heart, its essence.' He looked with tenderness at their bewilderment.

'And that was why you wanted to stay there, 'a perpetual Feast of Tabernacles'.'

In a cleft between three small rocks there had silted down sufficient earth to nourish a plant, the delicate mountain saxifrage. Jeshua plucked a flower and held it out before them, placing beside it in his palm a fragment of the rock, a quartz vein shining along its length. 'The petals last a day in the sun and lose their beauty by evening. This stone glints in the sun's ray but a cloud dims it to a kind of death. But all these living things, the creatures of God, they can be transfigured too, when we truly look at them – but you rarely look!'

'And now we return to the plain.'

THIRTY-ONE

When Jeshua and his friends reached the plain, they found the nine returned and gathered in a confused and defensive knot, surrounded by a disturbed crowd of people with, at their centre, two smaller groups. One was of

Temple officials, sombre and questioning but with a hint of malicious triumph, the other a father and son, supported by a small group of friends. As Jeshua and the three approached, there was a babble of questions and explanations and then the anxious voice of the father. Supporting his wildly-staring son by the shoulders, he said to Jeshua,

'I have brought you my son, my son lunatic and possessed. Days come when he is beside himself, hurling himself into water and into fire, and truly, Master, I'm afraid for his life.'

Jeshua looked from the father to the son, the latter torn and bleeding from the violence of his possession. The father responded to his questioning look.

'I brought him to your followers, asking them that they should cast out the devil which held him – and they failed. He is now in worse case than when I brought him.'

Jeshua looked about him, almost in disbelief. 'You people without faith; how long must I be among you? Bring him to me.'

At that moment the young man was again convulsed and fell at Jeshua's feet. Jeshua stood above him and asked the father how long the sickness had afflicted his son; 'From childhood; if there is anything you can do for him, please do it!' Jeshua replied,

'Everything is possible, if you believe.'

'Master, I do believe but please remove these shadows of unbelief that come over me.'

Jeshua raised his hands above the young man's prostrate body.

'Dumb and deaf spirit, come out of him and trouble him no more.' There was a still more terrible convulsion that tore at the young man and when it was over, Jeshua took him by the hand and restored him to his father.

It was a sombre twelve who walked back to Capernaum, for Peter, John and James shared the discomfiture of the nine, feeling, for all the rapture of the visions which they had shared, that they too would have failed with the nine. Thomas spoke their humiliation.

'How was it that we could do nothing with this boy?'

'You thought in your unbelief that there would be a time when the devils themselves would prevail. They will not prevail. And I tell you, truly, if you have as much faith as a grain of mustard seed, you can say to this mountain, 'Remove yourself from this place and set down elsewhere' and it would move its very foundations. Indeed, I truly tell you, faith will make all things possible to you. But this powerful evil can be defeated only by much prayer and by fasting.'

Peter and the 'Sons of Thunder' had been more deeply shocked by the failure before the demoniac than the nine who had been personally involved. Jeshua took the three aside and led them again out into the open country. They were east of Bethsaida, in the foothills, out of sight of the Lake.

'They ask for signs and wonders, miracles day by day – and you can't always respond to their needs. Do you ever wonder what they mean by miracle?' They looked their total ignorance. 'I will tell you what *I* understand by miracle.' His smile made the extraordinary promise in some sort acceptable.

'But first, look higher up the valley. There, on the sunny slope is a vineyard, carefully tended, well-watered and fruitful, while here –' he turned to a rough copse at the road-side, 'here is a wild vine, tangled and smothered in its own leaves and those grape bunches, starved, dry and almost fleshless. That vineyard looks to you like a miracle, a wonder, but it is no more than man's work, with, not against this little corner of creation.'

He drew out a branch of the tangled vine and snapped it below a leaf bud. 'You see it oozes its sap – it bleeds as man bleeds when he is wounded. But see –' He stooped to a burnt out fire, where the farmer had tried in vain to clear some of the tangle. Picking out a fragment of charred branch, he scraped it with his thumb-nail, revealing the clean charcoal. Delicately he rubbed the cut end of the vine with the charcoal and held it out to the three. 'See, it has stopped bleeding, the vine-dressers' miracle of healing – working with, not against the living thing.' His look and his voice darkened.

'There are men, and demons, who work against life, and it is then that we need – as I told you – 'prayers and fasting' – a life as perfect as you can make it. Then, and only then, can life flow again, the paralysed once more to leap, the blind to see, the deaf to hear and the leper to be cleansed. That is my Kingdom and the Kingdom of my Father and that is the perpetual dream of men, that, healed and filled with life, they return to Paradise, the Garden in Eden.'

The three were captured by the vision held before their eyes. They looked from the rapt face of Jeshua to the mountain landscape before them and as the clouds in the burning sky sent shadows racing across the slopes, the land breathed and moved with a new vitality.

Jeshua had long felt that the last lesson his friends would learn about his Kingdom was that its consummation would involve tragedy. When their hopes soared unduly or with false expectation, he took yet another way to show them the bitter truth that 'the Son shall be betrayed and slain and the third day be raised again.' Crucifixion and Resurrection were two aspects of the same raising up and then – and only then – would the kingdom come in full power. There would be glimpses of its reign, even intuitions of its presence; but Jerusalem was the arena in which the final conflict of its inauguration would be fought out.

It was therefore with one of his rare moments of bitter insight that a revelation of their blunt and defective understanding came from the very heart of the little company. They had all been moving from one village to another, preceded by cries of suffering and pursued by the joy of release. They were resting by the wayside when James and John spoke to him, clearly expressing much discussion that had gone before.

'Master, our Kingdom, every kingdom has its ranks and officers who take their part in the ruling. In your Kingdom, who will be the greatest and what rank shall we all have?'

Jeshua looked at each of them in a profound silence. Thomas looked away; Peter clenched his hands as though his body recollected its former toil; Simon became even more taut in his posture than Judas, who looked piercingly back into Jeshua's eyes, waiting for the critical answer. After holding his scrutiny for several moments, Jeshua called to a boy of some seven years who had stopped in his play in the road and was watching them intently; Jeshua held out his hands with a smile and the child rushed over to him, clambering on to his knees and burying his head in his shoulder. For a longer silence, Jeshua held the child, lightly stroking his back until his shyness ceased and he looked around with quick curiosity at their whole company.

'This is the Kingdom of Heaven, this child – his candour, his quick life, his knowledge of friendship and care and his trust in it, his joy in other people – *that* is the Kingdom of my Father. And truly, my friends, unless you become like little children you will never enter there.' The last words had a heavy finality and the whole company was stilled.

Jeshua sought in his wallet, took out a barley cake, broke it and gave half to the child. As he ate, so Jeshua ate his portion and with complete understanding they laughed together. With a little slap at his back, Jeshua sent him off to play with his companions.

'Come, let us go about our work while the day lasts.'

For some days the whole company was subdued and Jeshua divided them into three groups, sent away in three directions to minister to the people. After their return, he looked to them for their account at the end of the day of all that had happened. He saw that John was agitated and soon to burst out with his grievance.

'Master, we saw and heard one casting out devils in your name! He was not one of us and we forbade him.'

'John! 'One of us' – there is no one who shall perform a miracle in my name who can ever speak lightly, with malice, of me and of mine. A cup of water given you to drink because you are one of my company, will truly earn its reward.

'But if one of my little ones is offended, woe to the offender. And if your body offend, by sight, by hearing, by walking in iniquity, better to be blind, deaf or maimed than to lose the Kingdom.'

They were bewildered by the earnestness, whose meaning they failed to share and John was even affronted in his frustrated zeal. Jeshua went on.

'Never despise the humble little ones. Think of the shepherd. When his flock is safe and he lacks only the one little sheep, does he ignore its loss? Doesn't he rather secure the flock in its fold and go seeking the lost until he find it? So it is your Father's will that you seek the lost little ones.'

The parable had caught at their imagination and Jeshua seized the chance for further charity.

'We have much to forgive – we have all so much to forgive.' Peter spoke out of his rough kindliness:

'How often shall my brother sin against me and I forgive him – seven times?' – it was clearly a charity beyond computation and his face creased in an ironic smile.

'No, Peter, not seven times but for seven times seventy!'
Irony was met with irony.

'There was a certain great ruler who wanted to know
how his accounts stood. One of his servants was brought
before him who owed him a thousand talents. He fell
before his lord and told him that he was destitute and
could not repay. His lord forgave him.

Now that very same servant went out into the courtyard
and there was one of his fellows who owed him a hundred
pence. And he took him by the throat and demanded
payment. His fellow besought him for time to pay but he
refused and threw him into prison. Now the other servants saw all this; they were horrified and told their lord
all that had happened. He was filled with anger and gave
him over to the tormentors until he should pay every
penny.

'My heavenly Father will be like that lord, expecting
mercy of all men and rejecting from his presence all who
cannot show compassion.'

THIRTY-TWO

The joy of the Feast of Tabernacles was in the air. Every
house had its booth in the courtyard and Jeshua was
drawn by childhood memories to return to Nazareth. The
booth was prepared and Jeshua noticed with pleasure
how, in the months of his absence, the extensions to their
home had matured in colour and taken on a new harmony
from the mature vines that now clothed the walls. The
younger members of the family, who had experienced the
joy of Tabernacles so few times, were full of the excitement of garlands and miniature sheaves and of the rejoicings in the course of the feast.

One evening, two days before the feast was to begin,
Jacob and Joses were sitting with Jeshua just outside the
arbour within the courtyard. Jacob, who had never wholly

recovered from the departure of Jeshua from the household, which he still obscurely felt to be a betrayal, said as tonelessly as he could,

'Your fame is widespread but remains solely in Galilee. Jerusalem is the centre where fame and a prophet's powers are tested. Why not go up to the feast in Jerusalem and there declare yourself?'

Jeshua turned to him with a look of love almost overborne by compassion and replied quietly,

'Not yet; it isn't yet my time.'

The ambiguity was no answer to Jacob and he seemed to be about to pursue his questioning further, when Jeshua cut into his words,

'You and the others go up to the feast, if Jerusalem draws you at this time'; he paused and then as if gravely balancing two ways of life,

'The world need never hate you, for you never confront the world in its ways. But it deeply hates me, even perhaps to the death. I remain in Galilee awhile, and you go in my place to the feast.'

There could be no reply to this nor did their faces show any clearer understanding of his need, his deep need for their fellowship in the approaching crisis. The following morning he moved out of Nazareth into the village where his friends were teaching and healing, and sent them ahead to prepare lodging on the road to Jerusalem. The swiftest route was by way of Samaria and later the following afternoon he overtook James and John as they waited for him at the outskirts of a village, their faces transfigured with anger.

'They refused lodging, even refreshment! Shall we do to them the way of Elijah and call down fire from heaven to consume them with their houses?'

'You cannot know what you are saying nor the temper that has possessed you. Forgiveness is all. Come, let us go to the next village and take our shelter there – or be with the beasts for whom the rocks are shelter enough.'

Moving swiftly along the pilgrim route they approached the outskirts of Jerusalem and a young scribe approached Jeshua, saluting him gravely.

'Rabbi, I wish to follow you, to follow you wherever you go.' Jeshua replied,

'The foxes have their earths and the birds their nests but the Son of Man has nowhere to lay his head.'

As they moved further towards the northern gate of the city, Jeshua saw a man whose passionate look had followed their progress for some miles. He turned to him and said,

'Follow me, if you will.'

'Master, my parents are old – near to death – and I feel their hold on me. Let me first attend to their burial; it cannot be long before I follow you.'

Jeshua looked at him with understanding and no little compassion and replied,

'No man who has put his hand to the plough and then looks back is ready for the Kingdom of God.'

It was at this time that he sent out seventy of his most tried and faithful followers, just as he had sent the twelve, to carry the power of God throughout the country, while he went on alone to the feast in Jerusalem.

For the opening days of the feast he moved about the city, with no contact with friends or strangers, aloof even from the joy of the people. But they had not forgotten him and rumour passed from man to man, from family to family. They sought him in the Temple, in the synagogues and at the ancient holy places but for all their seeking he was not found. Removed from the power of his presence they swayed in their opinion – 'He is a good man' – 'He deceives the people, promising a kingdom' – 'At least he heals as no physician has healed' – and so the debate went on.

Then, with no flourish or announcement, Jeshua was found in the quiet, innermost court of the Temple, speaking, reasoning with the knots of people who gathered about him.

'How do you see the Kingdom? how work for it? how long to enter it? Is it to be Saul's kingdom, David's or Solomon's? Their kingdoms withered and however men sought for power, they died and power slipped from the grasp of their children. Have you heard and sung with understanding

> By the rivers of Babylon
> There we sat down,
> Yea we wept when we remembered Zion.
> How shall we sing the Lord's song
> In a strange land?

That is the fate of all who long for earthly kingdoms, to hang up their harps and fail to sing! And even Babylon the mighty, even proud Babylon fell to the dust.'

The people uneasily looked towards the Antonia and the armour which glistened there; could Rome also fall? Others looked in doubtful wonder at Jeshua; he seemed not to be of the scribes and though he spoke with simplicity, it was with an assured authority that they had not met elsewhere. 'Is this man unlearned? How did he come upon this authority, beyond even that of the Pharisees themselves?'

Jeshua heard few of these words but answered the questioning in their eyes.

'My teaching is not mine but His who sent me. If any man wishes to do the will of God, he will know the truth of the teaching, whether it be of God or whether I speak from myself alone.

'Moses gave you the Law yet none of you keeps it! Because I heal on the Sabbath, do you go about to find reason and opportunity to kill me?'

Some thought him beside himself; others more shrewdly asked why he was allowed to speak so openly and in the Temple if the authorities sought him to silence him. 'Can they perhaps believe that he is in fact the Christ, the Messiah, anointed of God?'

The impasse frustrated the authorities; to all their attempts at arresting or silencing him, when they had heard what the people conjectured about the person of Jeshua, he replied openly to them and to their agents,

'I am among you only a little while and then I return to Him who sent me. You will still seek me but you will not find, for where I go, you cannot come.'

It was a confounding answer and the impasse persisted.

As the feast drew to its close, the ceremony of the waters, the fountains and libations, became ever more prominent. This became the occasion for Jeshua's last exhortation to the people in the Temple.

'If any man thirst, let him come to me and drink. He who believes in me, from within him shall flow rivers of living water.'

Was he then the consummation of the feast, the final fruit of the harvest of God? Was this 'the prophet', or even the Christ Himself?

The debate in the Sanhedrin became critical, some demanding the immediate silencing of these destructive sayings. But into the frenzied argument one voice demanded a pause; Nicodemus, who knew Jeshua's integrity, said to them,

'Our law judges no man nor condemns him until it has heard his testimony and scrutinised his works.'

Their sole reply to Nicodemus was to accuse him of being 'Galilean' in his thinking and loyalty; but for the while the Sanhedrin was halted in its search for a solution.

The quiet nights were spent either on the Mount of Olives or in a nearby village and when the gates were opened in the morning, Jeshua returned to the Temple to teach. He had a group about him and was beginning to speak of forgiveness and the enlightening of the soul when there was a commotion beyond the pillars of the portico. A dishevelled woman was being dragged before him and the Pharisees blurted out,

'This woman was taken in the very act of adultery; what shall be done with her?'

The woman was unable to hide her shame, for they dragged her by her outer garments; Jeshua's disciples and those who where gathered for his teaching shared his appalled embarrassment, which Jeshua showed only by his heightened colour and averted eyes. At length, when his silence had begun to trouble the group who held the woman before him, Jeshua stooped down and wrote with his fingers in the dust of the pavement. The foremost Pharisee craned forward and then started back as though violently struck; in the dust; plain for them to see was, the central phrase of the Shema:

'Thou shalt love.'

The command stopped with those words but there was no one among them who had not recited the words daily. Jeshua looked up from the stones below his eyes,

'Is there any here without sin?'

Their silence became even more intense. 'If there is one among you without sin, let him first take up one of these stones' – his gesture embraced the Temple – 'and cast it at her, and let the others among you follow him in the stoning.'

And again he resumed his writing with his forefinger in the dust of that place. Quietly, even stealthily, those who had brought the woman before him crept away, beginning with the eldest among them. The woman now stood alone before Jeshua and his friends, her face almost hidden by the garment she had caught about her.

'Woman, where are those who accused you? Has no man condemned you?'

'No man, Lord.'

'Neither do I condemn you. Go in God's peace and sin no more.'

Later in the day Jeshua was passing the entrance to the Temple and saw, leaning against the wall, extending his hands for alms, a man who had been blind from birth. He paused at some little distance and one of his friends whispered, 'Is it this man's own sin or that of his parents that caused the blindness?'

'Neither,' answered Jeshua 'It was not caused by sin but it is now an occasion for showing the compassionate works of my Father. As long as I am in the world, I am the light of the world; it is my will and my Father's that none should be blind.'

He gathered dust in his palm, and with his spittle made clay. He called the blind man to him and he was led before Jeshua, who then anointed his eye-lids with the clay and told him,

'Go now and wash in the pool of Siloam.' There he was led by his friends and Jeshua turned away from the Temple gate.

The man who was blind performed Jeshua's command and at once saw clearly, both the pool itself and his friends he had never before seen, and in his joy asked that he might be taken with all speed to his home. His neighbours said to each other, 'Isn't this he who sat and begged at the Temple?' and others, confounded by his seeing them said, 'It *is* like him.' But the man who was formerly blind said,

'I am he who was blind' and to their questioning, replied, 'A man I did not know made clay, anointed my eyes, bade me go to the pool of Siloam to wash and now I see.' They asked him where Jeshua was and he replied that he knew not.

He was brought to the Pharisees that they might see the miracle and he repeated to them the means of his receiving sight. They said to him,

'This man is not of God; he heals on the Sabbath:' Others in confusion asked, 'How can a mere sinner do these things?'

They therefore approached his parents for more confirmation but to all their questions they replied, 'He is of age; ask him!'

This they did but got no satisfaction; to all their derogatory questions concerning Jeshua, he replied, 'I have already told you; why ask me again? Do you also wish to be his disciples?' They replied in anger, 'We are the disciples of Moses. As for this fellow, we can't tell who he is or what his origins.'

To this he replied with even greater and more dangerous irony, 'Now this truly is a marvel! You know nothing of his background and yet he opened my eyes! Since the beginning of the world it was never known that any could open the eyes of one born blind. If this man were not of God he could do nothing.'

Their anger was such that they expelled him from their worshipping community. Jeshua heard of this expulsion and sought him out and asked him,

'Do you believe in the Son of God?' He replied, 'Who is he, Lord, that I may believe in him?' Jeshua then said to him, 'You have seen him already and it is he who now talks with you.' Seeing him now plainly and with recognition, he cried in adoration,

'Lord, I believe.'

Jeshua gathered him with a gesture into the company of his friends and as they walked across the Temple court said to them, 'My very presence here is a judgment. They all see me but some remain inly blind while others see me for what I am. This is indeed the judgment.'

When they had reached the customary place of teaching he began to speak to them of sight and of blindness. Looking from him to the man born blind, they were confused as to his real meaning and Jeshua spoke more formally.

'I am the light of the world. He that follows me shall not walk in darkness but shall have the light of life.'

Those who opposed him stood at the fringes of the group he was teaching; they cried over the heads of the disciples,

'You are your own witness only and it is false testimony you speak.' Jeshua replied, 'My witness is true, for I know whence I come and when I return, you cannot follow me. You belong to this world and remain bound to it. I am from above.'

Some were moved, others shaken and yet others sceptical; to them all Jeshua addressed himself,

'When you have lifted up the Son of Man then you shall know that I am he and that the Father has never left me bereft. If you believe my words, you will be truly my disciples and the truth will make you free.'

'Do you dare speak to us of bondage? We are sons of Abraham and were never slaves to any man.' Jeshua turned away their angry accusations and with words that might draw them into the company of those who believed him, said,

'Truly, I say to you truly, if a man believe me and keep my teachings, he shall never see death.'

Their anger was only the greater and they ridiculed him.

'Abraham is dead; the prophets are dead and you say, if a man keep my sayings, he shall never taste death! To whom do you compare yourself?' Jeshua replied,

'If I honour myself, my honour is nothing; it is my Father that honoureth me. Your father Abraham rejoiced to see my day; he saw it and was glad.'

'You are not yet fifty years old and you have seen Abraham?'

Jeshua looked about him, his eyes gathered those about his feet who followed his words and he then gazed at his detractors. Solemnly and with words that struck to the very core of their belief, he said,

'Before Abraham was, I am.'

THIRTY-THREE

The turmoil of Jerusalem was not the conflict of a battlefield where two identifiable opponents clash in clear opposition. Rather it was a maelstrom in which innumerable currents whirled, sometimes almost halted as forces matched each other. There were moments when natural enemies became temporary allies, united in a common resentment of a third more bitter foe. So it was with the Pharisees and Sadducees, opposites in their view of the significance of this life and the next; united in their detestation of the Herodians and their equivocal and ultimately fatal political actions.

Nor were the pharisees themselves at unity. Most were a holy, scrupulous and God-seeking body of men, passionate in their attachment to the Law and fearful of any attack upon its authority. As with so many bodies of this kind, great learning could occasionally go with essentially trivial minds and there were those among them, few but aggressive, for whom the jots and tittles of the Law were of equal significance with its eternal commands; scruples, pursued with relentless casuistry became the end of their disciplined search. Within the Sanhedrin the contrasts would be startling, between those for whom minutiae were foremost and those of the quality of Nicodemus, for whom God the Most High was the end of all seeking. In the two decades which spanned Jeshua's adult life the power of Jerusalem's holiness had united the searching debates of the school of Hillel and the school of Shammai with those equally close and solitary searchings which tore the debates of the Pharisee counsels. To them, from his boyhood, Jeshua had been drawn; this was the Israel to which he had come.

Carried out of their tranquil lives by the frantic declarations of Zealots, the people found no hold within the subtler arguments of their leaders. Most – though this could not be perceived by their rulers – were content with the round of the seasons, the glorious punctuation of the feasts, the quiet contemplation of Torah under the guidance of humble rabbis, the safe anchorage of the synagogue; within their homes was the daily confirmation of their tranquil trust in the tradition of their fathers.

Over all there brooded the constant menace of Rome, which found its ultimate safeguard in ringing Jerusalem with the stench of crucifixion. Rome itself was ultimately concerned only with its Pax Romana; it was well if a subject people regarded absence from strife to be a grateful peace; it was but a passing nuisance if they rebelled. Meanwhile the legions marched and the sentries watched and beneath the exterior calm, there seethed the complex turmoil.

Into the heart of this tragic city Jeshua brought a new tranquillity. The appalling irony lay in the fact that this tranquillity was an affront to every faction and became itself the current which pressed forward authority's wrath. But that was still before them; meanwhile he taught. His presence was now as familiar as that of the earlier prophetic figures of his boyhood and day after day there came to sit at his feet a faithful group, with others changing daily, drawn by curiosity to hear his words. As in Galilee, the confounding fact for them all, believers and sceptics, was the world of contrast between the simplicity of his words and the overpowering meaning which they felt to lie behind them. For a child could follow and enjoy the parables – indeed they did, clambering about him to hear them when he left the Temple for the villages – but the most learned among them paused in their attempt to relate all the implications of his teaching to the traditions they had so passively inherited.

Much had been said and learned in his days among them but there came a morning when Jeshua had an air of departure, as though there was to be one discourse before he left them, at least for a while.

'Truly I say to you the sheepfold can be entered by many – by the gateway where the sheep and the shepherd have their safe passage, morning and evening; and by the walls, clambered or broken through – this is the way of the thieves and robbers.

'You will know the shepherd without difficulty; he it is who comes to the entrance gate; those within, the sheep and the other shepherds, all know his voice and the sheep will follow him as he leads them to pasture. But the stranger and the robber have no voice that the sheep recognise and trust.'

He paused and as so many times before they heard and followed the words but understood little of what he said.

'Truly I say to you, I am the door of that sheepfold. The deceivers that came before me the sheep did not follow. If by this door you enter in, you will be saved and move through life, finding green pastures. I am the good shepherd; my flocks shall have life, abundant life and if necessary I give my life, like the good shepherd and his sheep and not as the mere hireling who flees from the wolf.

'As the Father knows me, even so I know the Father and he loves me because I am ready to lay down my life for my own people. No man takes my life from me; I lay it down of my own will. And I say to you, I have power to take my life again to be with my own.'

He then left the courts of the Temple as they still debated the meaning of his words. Never had they heard him speak so richly and so darkly.

Jeshua went out into the villages neighbouring upon Jerusalem to wait for the return of the Seventy. They came back to him in small groups, all with the same triumphant joy and at length he gathered them together in one solitary place, hearing of their victory over evil spirits and the sicknesses and the needs of men.

'My friends, I too have seen the Adversary fall like a star from heaven and I have given you power to tread upon all evil. But that is not the matter of your rejoicing but rather that your names are inscribed in the scrolls of heaven.'

And as he spoke to them they were confirmed in their steadfast mission; raising his eyes to heaven, he began to pray in their presence.

'My Father, Lord of heaven and earth, I thank thee that these things have been shown not to the wise and the prudently careful but to the babes of the faith.'

Jeshua spoke a final word of private encouragement to the Seventy:

'Blessed are the eyes which see the things that you see; many prophets and kings have desired to see those things which you now see, and have not seen them and to hear those things that you hear and have not heard them.'

He returned with some of them to Jerusalem and before he could resume his teaching, a lawyer approached, asking,

'What shall I do to inherit eternal life?' Jeshua replied, 'What do you, a lawyer, consider to be the heart of the Law?'

''Thou shalt love the Lord thy God with all thy heart, all thy soul, all thy strength and all thy mind; and thy neighbour as thyself'.'

And Jeshua replied, 'That is a proper answer; now all that is needed is that you fulfil this Law; do it and you shall live eternally.'

The lawyer, hoping to justify himself and mitigate the demands, protested, 'But who is my neighbour?'

Jeshua now raised his voice a little, for some of his disciples had gathered, hoping to profit by the disputation.

'A certain man took that notorious road from Jerusalem to Jericho and – like many another – he fell into a thieves' ambush, who stripped him of his clothing, wounded him and left him half dead.

'Now a priest passed on his way, perhaps to his duties in Jerusalem, paused at the wounded man and then hurried on. In the same way a Levite came to the same place, looked askance at his wounds and hurried by on the other side.

'But a Samaritan passed through that gorge as he journeyed to Jericho and he saw the wounded man; and he had compassion on him, bound up his wounds with a dressing of oil and wine and set him on his own mount, brought him to an inn and placed him in the care of the innkeeper. And the next day, when he left the inn he took money and gave it to the innkeeper and said,

'Take good care him; spend what you need to make him well and the next time I pass through again, I will repay you.'

'Now tell me, which of these three was, in your judgment, neighbour to the man who had fallen among thieves?'

'I suppose it was he who showed compassion on him.'

'Go then, you should do likewise, for in the doing you will know your neighbour.'

His friends and those who came to learn at his feet, applauded the parable, for they understood almost all its implications. Jeshua pursued it one step further.

'You will do kindness and courtesy to all who demand it of you, by their poverty or misfortune. And you will do this in the present world, even before the coming of the Kingdom.

'For such is the eternal compassion of the Father. You see to the welfare of your children; would one of you dream of giving a child a stone when he asks for bread, or a serpent when he begs a fish? If you, being men, fallen men, know from your hearts how you give good gifts to your children, how much more will your heavenly father give to them that ask him.'

It was now necessary that his lodging should be further than the shelter of the Jerusalem olive groves and he chose Bethany, a village within easy walking distance of Jerusalem. There he sought out a home for himself and found welcome at the hands of Lazarus, Martha and Mary. They were a reserved, contained family; Lazarus, the eldest was a quiet, studious man who said little; Martha was a consciously busy housewife, perhaps inclined to be garrulous, while Mary, the youngest, was a contemplative, thinking much about the present condition of Jewry and brooding on the prophecies. Jeshua went there at dusk on many evenings and while Lazarus sat silently at the hearth, listening to whatever Jeshua had to say; it was Mary, by her eager questioning, who drew from him an account of his mission and that of the Twelve and the Seventy. It was clear from her questions and her brief rapt answers that she was growing in understanding of his concept of the Kingdom and longed to be part of it. Women of her comparative affluence were among those who saw to the day-to-day well-being of Jeshua's company as they journeyed through the villages: Susanna, Salome, Mary of Magdala and Joanna, the wife of Chuza, Herod's steward. These were at the heart of Judah's society and on the fringes of its power. Mary's contemplative cast of mind kept her a little apart from these active participants in Jeshua's ministry but she knew instinctively that action in his Kingdom required the mind and the heart at least as much as daily activity. And so, at the hearth, she questioned him and evening by evening her sensibility moved with her understanding.

Martha, in the more tedious chores of the household neither understood her sister's explorations nor sympathised with them and at last burst out in protest.

'Master, don't you think ill of my sister that she allows me to do all the housework alone? Do please tell her to help me!' Jeshua replied gently,

'Martha, our dear Martha, you allow yourself to be cumbered and clogged by the work you give yourself. Only one thing is truly needed in our life and Mary has chosen that good and essential part. Neither you nor I should try to take it away from her.'

In the household, Jeshua found his new centre and from it he could go swiftly to Jerusalem to add fragment upon fragment of his teaching, concerning eternal life and his Father's Kingdom. Winter was drawing on and Jerusalem was about to celebrate the Feast of Dedication. It was a moving but sensitive occasion while the politics of Jerusalem were so delicately poised, for this was the feast which the Maccabees had been able to institute when their military triumphs had enabled them to purify and rededicate the Temple after its pollution and desecration by Antiochus Epiphanes. To the Temple Jeshua came as always to take its history beyond its mere restoration. There, in the shadow of the Roman occupation he made to teach.

He was, however, interrupted by another of the testing questions:

'Why do you keep us in suspense by your ambiguities? If you are the Christ, He-who-should-come, tell us plainly.'

'I have told you and indeed shown you. The work which I perform in my Father's name, this must bear witness, but you still will not believe.

'Not one of mine shall perish, for I and my Father are one – in compassion and power.'

Stoning was the sole appropriate answer to such blasphemy but – with bitter memories of another such occasion – Jeshua escaped from their hands.

THIRTY-FOUR

Some of the Pharisees had a concern for Jeshua's safety and, to avoid what seemed to them to be inevitable turmoil, they said to him, 'Leave Jerusalem, for Herod is determined to kill you.'

Jeshua replied to them, 'Go and tell that fox that this day I cast out devils, and equally on the morrow – and the third day I shall be made perfect. Whatever the threat, at this time I must walk in the full light of day, for it cannot be the fate of a prophet to die outside Jerusalem.'

Then, in full prophetic utterance to the whole city, he cried,

'O Jerusalem, Jerusalem, which killest the prophets
And stonest them that are sent unto thee,
How oft would I have gathered thy children together,
As a hen gathers her brood under her wings
And ye would not.'

Tensions increased as the days passed and the old conflicts with the Doctors of the Law were renewed. One of these occasions was within the house of a Pharisee, where he had gone to join his host in the Sabbath meal, and the Pharisee's friends watched him closely, for there was present a man grievously ill with dropsy. Jeshua observed their observation and answered the unspoken question:

'Tell me, lawyers, is it lawful to heal on a Sabbath day?' and they kept silent, watching for the outcome. Jeshua approached the dropsical man and raised him to his feet, at his touch curing him, blessed him and bade him depart to his home. And he then turned to the lawyers.

'Which of you shall have an ox or an ass fall into a pit on the Sabbath and will not immediately pull it out of its peril? You know – both in your minds and hearts – that the action would be lawful. Why then ask me these false questions concerning men in need? Is their need the less on the Sabbath?

'Nor is this your only sin. I have observed you at feasts; you seek out the chief and most honourable places but take advice from me; when you are invited to a wedding, do not sit down in the chief places, lest a more honourable man than you be invited also and when he comes, the host will have the discomfort of inviting you to take a lower place! Rather, when you first arrive, look for a lowly seat and then the host will come to you and say ''Friend, go up higher!' and you will then have honour among all the guests.

'I have more to tell you of this feasting. A certain man prepared a great feast and invited a large number of guests. When the time of the feast arrived he sent his servants to welcome his guests to his home – and each began to make excuses. One said, 'I have bought a parcel of land and I must go to inspect my purchase; I pray you, give my excuses to your lord.' The second said to the servant, 'I have bought a team of oxen and I must yoke them and try them at the plough, to see if they are well matched; I pray you, ask your lord to forgive my absence.' And a third said, 'I have married a wife and I cannot come to a feast, leaving her at this time' – and he failed even to excuse himself! Then the master of the house, being angry, said to his servants, 'Go out quickly into the streets and lanes of the city and invite to my home the poor and the maimed, the halt and the blind;' they did so and the servant said to his lord, 'Master, there is still room for others.' And the lord said, 'Go out into the highways and the byeways and among the hedged lanes and bring them urgently in, so that my house be filled, for I say to you, there shall be no room vacant for those who were invited and failed to come'.

'From the days of the patriarchs until this day, Israel and Judah have been invited to the feast of my Father; now the invitation is renewed; will you heed the invitation?'

Jeshua's fullest happiness was when he and his disciples sat down for a feast of stale bread and dried figs. To them he began to speak of 'losing and finding.'

'Which of you having a hundred sheep' – there was delighted laughter as they contemplated such incredible wealth and Jeshua joined them in their mirth – 'if he lose one, doesn't leave the ninety-nine in safety and searches the wilderness until he finds it? Or consider a woman who has a dowry-circlet of silver coins – an heirloom. One day she sees that one of the coins is missing, so she sweeps out her house and searches in every corner until she finds it and she, like the shepherd, calls her neighbours, saying to them, 'Be glad with me – I have found the coin.'

'It's even more serious when one of the family is lost.' He looked about the company where many (who had joined the twelve to hear his words) turned their eyes from his and looked at the ground in sorrow and some in shame. Jeshua respected their embarrassment and went on quietly,

'There was once a family of three, a father and two sons, who between them cultivated a small farm. The younger son was a restless, ambitious boy who found the little home irksome and asked that his portion of their property should be given him now, while his father still lived; and it was given him.

'As he had longed to do, he went abroad to seek his fortune but instead he lost the little he had among those who were only too glad to rob him. In desperation, he attached himself as a serf to a farmer of that country and he had descended so low that he became a mere swineherd, and in his hunger eating husks intended for their trough.

'When life had seemed to him wholly worthless, he began to think with longing of his home and said, 'How many hired servants of my father fare so much better than I. I will go now to my father and I will say to him, 'Father I have sinned against heaven and wronged you and have lost the right to be called your son; take me back as one of your hired servants.'

'And he made ready and returned and while he was still a long way from his home, his father saw him, ran to him and embraced and kissed him. He told his father all he had determined to say but his father's reply was to call his servants and command that the best robe be put upon him, a ring on his finger and shoes on his feet, 'and prepare the fatted calf for a feast where we can rejoice. For my son was dead and is alive again; he was lost and now he is found'.'

Never had a narrative of Jeshua's been listened to with such attention. On some faces there was the shining of a new hope, in others tears of despair but all the desolate company clung to his words as to a last hope in their lives.

But at the fringes of the group were some of his more affluent acquaintances, who looked with bitter disapproval at this ragged audience and Jeshua continued,

'But sadly that is not the end of the story. The elder brother was in the field at work and as he made for home he heard the rejoicing and the music of the feast and was told the reason for it. He refused to go in and when his father went out to him he burst out, 'All these years I have worked faithfully – twice the work and with less resources – while that wastrel has spent on harlots what should have been ours in common. Yet all this time you have not so much as prepared a kid as a feast for me!' – and his father said to him, 'Son, you are always with me and all I have – my love and my possessions – is yours. It was proper this night that we should feast and make merry, for this brother of yours was dead and is now alive again, was lost and is found.'

All were now equally silent and Jeshua felt no need to speak, either comfort to the dispossessed or reproach to the affluent. He was content that the Kingdom should make its way.

This was not the last occasion when such a group gathered about him to hear his words. They had been questioning him with anxiety about riches and poverty in this life and about the nature of their future life, its rewards or its punishments. He answered again, obliquely, with a little narrative:

'There was a rich man whose clothing was linen and a garment dyed with the richest purple and for him every day was a feast day. And at his door, a beggar named Lazarus, diseased and covered with sores, had set himself to beg. After some years, the beggar died and was taken to heaven, to the very presence of Abraham. And Dives also died and was buried – and in hell he lifted his eyes from his torments and cried, 'Father Abraham, have mercy! Send Lazarus that he may at least dip his finger in water to cool my tongue.'

'But Abraham replied to him, 'My son, remember that in your life on earth you received all the good things and

Lazarus nothing but suffering and sorrow. And beside all this, between you and us is set a great gulf, a chasm unpassable.' Dives then cried, 'At least then, father, send him to my home, for I have five brothers, that he may tell them the truths concerning them and us, so that they may avoid this place of torment.' But Abraham said, 'They have Moses and the prophets; let them hear them.' And he said, 'Father Abraham, if they heard one risen from the dead, they would listen indeed!' but Abraham replied, 'If they refuse to hear Moses and the prophets, they will not be persuaded even if one rose from the dead to convince them'.'

All of them present heard the deeper tones of these narratives and the brooding sombreness of Jeshua's voice and they wondered what should become of him and of themselves.

THIRTY-FIVE

It had been a day of sunshine tempered by haze and a cooling breeze and as the sun declined, Jeshua took Judas by the arm and led him out into the countryside.

'We have had too little talk, you and I; the poverty and sickness about us has demanded every waking moment and there has been all too little time for my friends. But this evening shall be quiet to ourselves.'

They walked on in silence until the olive groves and vineyards had given way to some withered fig trees and then to open wilderness in which the prevailing parched soil and stones were relieved by juniper and some stunted bushes with brilliant accents of red against the drab background. At last they reached Jeshua's favourite kind of rock corner and they sat to talk.

'Kerioth is strange to me – I have never been so far south – but I should like to hear about it.'

314

'There's very little to tell and in any case we lived well outside it. My grandfather had inherited a small, rather arid parcel of land which he tilled with little reward for many years. But he was a good husbandman and worked without sparing himself. After some time of ceaseless striving he was able to afford two more fertile pieces of land adjoining his; one was an upland stretch which he made into a much more fertile grassland for a flock of sheep; the other, on a southern slope, was perfect for vines and for olives, though of course in planting olives he was preparing for future generations.

'My father was his sole heir but he had three sons, two elder brothers and myself. Since my mother had died when I was four years old, it was a hard, male household with little softness for a growing boy. There was much laughter but never a smile. My brothers' wives were brood-women, there for the next generation, themselves unloved and unlovable, with no flicker of kindness for me or their own children. It was a joyless household but rich, very rich.

'I had been brought up in the legends of warfare, of the battles to and fro in Judah and of the heroes who had saved our people and of those who would come again. We were too well-placed to be much troubled by oppression from our own people or by the Romans who cared only to subdue the land south of Jerusalem.

'Then comes word of John and of him whom John announced. I was held by the words which spread southward – 'He who should come' – and I gladly gave up my inheritance – unlike your prodigal, I asked for nothing of my father! – and so came north to Galilee to seek you out.'

Jeshua listened intently and without interruption, not even to encourage more confiding. Judas held the silence, looking out over the barren land and occasionally glancing at Jeshua, as though to confirm certain brooding thoughts.

'As you know, I have been brought up in plenty and used to command and obedience. The other eleven of your intimate friends I found strange, ill-assorted. I knew that Messiah, when he came, would bring not only deliverance from our present bondage but a new kingdom. I felt in my heart that the present serfdom was worse than Babylon, for here we are enslaved, insulted in our own country.' For a moment his face was transfigured by disgust and hatred, so that Jeshua was impelled to look away.

'Gradually I became convinced of other things. I heard you speak much of your Kingdom and I warmed to the life we should find within it; but how was it to be achieved? Were these eleven, even the seventy chosen who followed them, the forces that would overthrow Rome? And when her power was overthrown, her Procurator expelled and the Sanhedrin – and Herod! – convinced of our power and right to rule, were these people, your friends, truly those who would exercise power in the new Israel of God?'

'As you speak to me, Judas, you speak the whole time of 'your friends' as though they were exclusively mine; they are your friends also, as by this time you well know.'

'Of course, and with all of them I have known a fellowship and a tenderness that Kerioth never showed me. But I still ask the same two questions of myself – are they sufficiently powerful forces to take rule upon them? And when they take rule, can they sustain it?'

'Through the ages, from Joshua to David, from David to the Maccabees, we have assumed that the kingdom of Israel is to be won and maintained by the sword. That I have never believed nor did our greatest prophets. Isaiah saw pruning-hooks rather than spears, and ploughshares rather than swords. In the time of God's own mind, Rome will wither and die; but make no mistake, another empire will come in her place, as so many came before her. And it will be a hard task to distinguish one from another in the suffering and humiliation they shower upon man. I would never have Israel in such a case. Not by the sword will the Kingdom of God's intention for Israel come to pass and it will not be maintained by the sword.'

'I have known this throughout these months, from the moment I first heard you speak of 'the meek of the earth' and of the poor in their inheritance. And my whole nature rebels at it! I can feel Simon's frustration as he still feels instinctively for his dagger when insults are poured on you. I know of the anger of James and John when they long to thunder at injustice and even on Peter's face I see the blood rising when arrogance is all that your words and wonders draw upon you. Is your whole aim for us that we should lose our courage, our manhood and inherit in their place only meekness?'

Judas's voice had risen in frustration. The well-born fastidiousness of his bearing, the inherited will to command, rejected the very central core of Jeshua's teaching. For the moment Jeshua met the arrogant response with just the slightest lifting of his hand and a smile that demanded silence.

'Judas my son, what the years and the generations have bred in Israel's bones can't be removed at a word and in a moment. You have been with me for so very short a time; have patience, watch and listen and you will know your place in my Kingdom. When I shall be no longer with you – and my time approaches – then you and the others will have such different tasks. Yours will not be the least, if you trust me and yourself. The stern resolve your father bred in you, the very forbearance you had to show in your childhood, the courage of your decision to give up all to follow me – all these things will find an honourable place, an essential office in my Kingdom.'

Judas was gradually stilled by Jeshua's words and got up as if to return to their company in the villages.

'There is no more that we should say now, but Judas, truly, truly, my peace I give to you, my peace in all its

317

fulness, and my Father will confirm that peace if you ask Him, even to your life's end.'

Tensions were palpably growing as Jeshua and Judas rejoined their friends. Peter was in desperate agitation to have word with Jeshua.

'We have heard from Bethany that Lazarus is sick; his sisters have sent messengers to beg your coming to them, for Lazarus is sick almost to death.'

'Death will not be the end of this sickness but rather the glory of God.'

Peter and the others marvelled at his calm, for they knew the love he had for the family in Bethany; and still he stayed near Bethabara performing his works of healing and teaching all who would hear; and they moved from place to place, still keeping their distance from Jerusalem. Then, as if in sudden resolve, he said to his disciples, 'Let us go into Jerusalem once more.' 'But master,' they protested, 'only recently they tried to stone you and they still seek to kill you.' Jeshua replied, 'There are no more than twelve hours in each day and we must work while we still have light – we shall stumble in the night! We shall indeed not go into the city but to Bethany on our way. Our friend Lazarus sleeps.'

The disciples were glad at his word and said, 'Sleep will be his best cure' but Jeshua then spoke plainly,

'Lazarus is indeed dead but we must go up to his home, that you may believe in me.'

They were fearful even of the journey to Bethany, for it was within striking distance of Jerusalem. And Thomas said, when he saw the resolve of Jeshua, 'Let us go with him also, so that we may die with him.'

When they came to Bethany they found that Lazarus had already been in the grave four days and many people from Jerusalem had come to comfort Martha and Mary. When Martha heard that Jeshua was coming she ran to meet him; she burst out at greeting him,

'Lord, if only you had been here! Then my brother would not have died. But I know that even now, anything you ask of God will be granted you.' Jeshua said,

'Your brother will rise again.'

'I know that he must rise again at the resurrection in the last day.'

'I am the resurrection and eternal life. He who believes in me, even though dead, he shall live and whosoever lives by my word shall never die. Do you believe this?'

'Yes, Lord; I believe that you are the Christ, the Son of God who has been promised to the world.'

Martha ran quickly and told Mary that the Master had come. Both then ran back to the place outside Bethany where Jeshua waited for them. When Mary came to him she fell at his feet and cried,

'Lord, if you had been here with us, Lazarus would not have died.' Jeshua saw that their neighbours and those from Jerusalem had followed and were watching the little group, and he sighed and said,

'Where have you laid him?' and they led him to the place and he mourned there with them.

The grave had been cut into a rock-face and had a stone placed over the entrance. Jeshua commanded that the stone be rolled away and Martha protested, 'Lord, he has been dead four days; there will be the stench of putrifying.' Jeshua replied,

'Did I not say that if you believed, you would see the glory of God?' and they took away the stone.

Jeshua stood before the cave entrance, Martha, Mary and Jeshua's disciples behind him, with the neighbours and strangers encircling them at some distance. Jeshua raised his eyes and said,

'Father, I thank thee that thou hast heard me in this; as thou dost always hear my prayers but now all these about me may believe that thou hast sent me.' And stepping nearer the grave, he cried aloud,

'Lazarus, come forth!'

There was complete silence, then a quiet stirring and a movement of feet. Lazarus, hampered by the grave-wrappings which bound him from his face to his feet, stood motionless, framed in the cave entrance. Jeshua said quietly to the servants standing by,

'Release him from his bondage.'

Hesitant and overawed, they approached Lazarus and beginning at his head, they delicately unwound the grave-bands until his feet were released and he stood before them, still without movement and gazing at Jeshua. Over his inner tunic the servants threw a cloak and gently fastened it and as they stirred about him, the scent of myrrh and the burial spices came from within the cave.

Martha and Mary moved one on each side of Lazarus and touching his hands for guidance, walked in complete silence to their house. Behind them, the crowd observing, said in whispers that Jeshua went beyond all wonder-workers, for who before this had seen the dead raised?

Within the house, which no one entered except Jeshua and two or three of his friends who remained quietly standing at the doorway, Jeshua sat opposite Lazarus at the hearth, with Mary at their feet. After a long silence, Lazarus whispered,

'Why? Why have you done this thing to me?'

Jeshua waited in silence until he had gathered himself and in a stronger voice, Lazarus said,

'I have thought much about death and have feared its pain and the severing of all bonds. I had never thought of death as tender and compassionate, a longed-for quiet. But that was how it was with me. Out of my sickness came a great peace, a gentle giving-up, a surrender – and this I have never expected.' He smiled tentatively, asking for Jeshua's response, but he gave no reply but a quiet, assenting smile, waiting for his further vision.

'It was a great quiet. Why, Jeshua, why did you bring me back?' In the voice of Lazarus there was now a shade of desperation and an infinite regret.

'It was Bethany transfigured! Each blade of grass, each flower and each tree had its own clear being. The colours were without blemish or shade. And music; I have heard the pipe on the hillside, the music of a wedding party, but in my childish thought, I had dreamed of angelic voices! This I was not to hear – but this was sound I had never conceived, harmony of perfect purity.' He broke off in a sudden shyness.

'I'm speaking too much; I've never spoken much here at the fireside. I have pondered a great deal and Mary has known my thinking. But why have you drawn me back? *This* is death's kingdom, death's *only* kingdom and I had escaped it.'

Mary looked in bewilderment from Lazarus to Jeshua and again at each of them. She could understand the agony in the voice of Lazarus and it bore down upon the joy of his restoration to her. At Jeshua's feet and listening to his teaching of the Kingdom she had never – as Lazarus evidently had – faced the ambiguous meaning of death. The last four days had been suffering beyond anything she had known; to receive her loved brother back had been all her hope. Now she, with Lazarus, was learning a profounder truth, and the learning was bitter.

'Lazarus, the border between what men call life and death is only a breath, a moment's pause. All our hopes and dreams, from childhood until our maturity, are wrapped in life and its longings. But you have known how easy it is at the last to give up these dreams, to move tranquilly through death to this fulfilment of dreams.

'Mary, you do well to have your hopes and your longings, your rich dreams of earth – they are memories of the six days at the opening of time, and they were very good! Life is full of the joy of dreaming, the visions of your lost

Eden. It is one of the saddest moments in all prophecy, in the prophecy of Ezekiel, when he says that 'time runs on and visions die away.'

'Be content, Lazarus, you have known what Mary has longed to know and what Martha struggles to achieve in her orderly household; you have seen the achieving of hope, and you will see it again. Live your life now, in peace.'

Jeshua rose from the fireside, leaving the brother and the sister there in their silence. Martha came to them and looked tenderly at each, waiting until a meal should bring them together again.

Jeshua gathered his friends about him; Jerusalem lay before him.

THIRTY-SIX

A critical conflict was now unavoidable and with it almost certain tragedy. For the elders and doctors of the Law gathered in deep perturbation when news reached Jerusalem of the raising of Lazarus.

'He performs all wonders, even raising from the dead,'
'All will follow him if we take no steps against him.'

The real power among them was Caiaphas, the High Priest, one of whose dominant concerns was maintaining their neutrality with Rome; an astute politician, he was wholly impatient at the Council's scrupulous arguments.

'You speak like ignorant children! It is simply expedient that one man should die for the people, rather than that the whole nation should perish.'

Jeshua had word of this council and for a while retired north to the town of Ephraim, but maintained his healing among the remoter villages on the borders of the wilderness. At the outskirts of one of these villages, maintaining their distance from its inhabitants, stood ten lepers who begged Jeshua that they might be healed and return to their kindred and friends. Jeshua did no more than command them to show themselves to their rabbi. As they went to seek him out their leprosy fell away and they knew themselves to be clean and they went confidently to have themselves declared fit to return to their people.

As Jeshua lingered at the place of their healing, he saw one of the ten (a Samaritan by his garments) who fell at his feet, glorifying God and declaring aloud his gratitude to Jeshua. He turned to his disciples and asked, 'Were there not ten cleansed?; where then are the nine?' and to the Samaritan he said, 'You were healed as you went your way; now your faith has made you whole.'

With this miracle Jeshua began to direct his way towards Jerusalem and certain Pharisees and others of Jerusalem learned of his determination and walked with him on the way, questioning him. He said to them,

'I exhort you not to think yourselves righteous because of your outward observances. Hear the parable of the Pharisee and the Tax-Gatherer.

'They went, these two men, to the Temple to pray. The Pharisee (and of course there was justice in his claim) prayed in these words: 'I thank you God, that I am not as other men, extortioners, unjust, adulterers or even like this tax-gatherer in your courts. I fast twice each week, I tithe all my possessions, and so I worship Thee.' The tax-gatherer, half-concealed from the other worshippers, would not even raise his eyes as he prayed. But his prayer was heart-felt, as he smote his breast.

'God be merciful to me, a sinner.'

'I tell you he went to his home justified more fully than the other, for he who exalts himself shall be cast down but the humble shall be raised up.'

In the same temper he received the numerous children who were brought for his blessing. The disciples were disturbed at their number and pressure upon Jeshua, but he rebuked them.

323

'Allow all the little ones to come to me, for the innocent are the heart of the Kingdom. Indeed I tell you, anyone who cannot accept the Kingdom with the innocence of a little child cannot enter.'

What was the nature of this 'innocence'? Even the friends about him were not wholly sure. At this time, they saw approaching Jeshua a young man in whose bearing they saw both authority and wealth. To their joy, he questioned Jeshua.

'Good Master, what shall I do to inherit eternal life?' Jeshua tested him. 'Why do you call me 'good'? There is none good but one and that is God the Father. But if you would indeed inherit eternal life, keep the commandments.'

'Which of them must I keep?'

"Thou shalt not murder, nor commit adultery, nor steal, nor bear false witness. Honour your father and mother; and' – here Jeshua paused, gazing at him searchingly – 'and thou shalt love thy neighbour as thyself'.'

'All these things I have always kept, from my childhood.'

'That is well, but you lack one thing. If you wish for perfection, sell all your possessions, give them to the poor (for you shall have treasure in heaven!) and then come and follow me.'

Jeshua still gazed into his face and had deep compassion on him as he read the struggle in his eyes. At length, with an embarrassed and helpless gesture, the young man turned away, for he was very rich.

Jeshua turned to the twelve.

'Have pity on those like this young man, who are very wealthy; they have much to hold them fast and only with great difficulty enter the Kingdom.' Peter said,

'And what of us? We were not poor and we tried to give all for your sake.' Jeshua replied,

'You who have followed me through all this time in the world, when the Kingdom comes, shall sit on twelve thrones, judging the twelve tribes of Israel. No-one who left all, family, friends, possessions, for my sake shall fail to inherit eternal life.

'But judgment then shall be very different from judgment in the world, where wealth, lands, power, bring respect and worship; not so in my kingdom where the last in the world's esteem shall be first in honour. Let me tell you of this kind of reckoning.

'There was a wealthy landowner who needed extra workers for the harvest in his vineyards and he went out at dawn and made a bargain with labourers for so much a day. But the work was defeating them and he went out again at noon and in the afternoon, telling them to trust him to give a just wage for their work. An hour before sundown, the work was still not done and again he took on more men on the same terms.

'When the work was over and it came to payment he called those who had worked for an hour and gave them their payment; then those who had worked three, and six hours and they all received the same payment. Then came those who had worked throughout the day and they, though expecting more, received the same sum of money. 'What' they said, 'we who have laboured in the strong sun, to have the same as these who have done so little?' Then the lord turned to them all,

'Did I not agree with you for a just payment? Do you doubt my right to give to all of you what I think to be right?'

The twelve shuffled uneasily, Judas and Matthew looking at each other with some dismay and Peter and Andrew, who had in their time employed day-labour looked askance at Jeshua. He smiled at their perturbed looks.

'You don't understand? In the vineyards of Galilee that would have seemed unjust but you know of old that when I speak in these parables, the vineyard is my Father's Kingdom and I speak not of measured rewards, carefully and justly calculated but of eternal joy. Can you give that a reckoning? Can you earn by long labour a more intense joy in heaven? These outcasts, the driftwood of our people, they will come when they hear my voice and will get into heaven as the doors of their lives are about to close. And there they will mingle with the glorious prophets, the just and noble Pharisees, the Hasidim of Galilee – yes, and even with those Sadducees who will be surprised to find that there *is* an eternal life after all!'

For the moment they were prepared to laugh with him but the following morning he was up in the cold light before dawn and they were awakened by his preparation for the journey. They took their meal standing and they had scarcely made their thanksgiving when he set out, his face unmoved and his steps swift and firm, outpacing theirs. At noon he rested to wait for them to overtake him. They were doubly fearful, first because of the determined speed with which he led the way, and even more because they knew that way to end in Jerusalem. It seemed to them that he had determined on yet another revelation to them of his purpose.

'My children. You see we press to Jerusalem and I prepare for my end. For I shall be betrayed, delivered up to the Roman power and mocked and reviled. Then will come the scourging and the crucifying and in three days I shall rise again and be with you.'

They stood speechless before him, their minds trying to clutch at all they had heard in the long wanderings in his company. At last, after deep silence in which they had not even looked at each other, each wrapped in his own private tragedy, Peter said tentatively,

'But, the Kingdom?'

'The Kingdom is here among you and there in God's eternity. It is here, before death and will be there when that door has opened and closed. Above all, you remember all I told you of God's Servant, who was 'despised and rejected' but 'by whose stripes we are healed'? Remember that, cling to that, my children and through all suffering you will believe.'

They gathered themselves, not even venturing even tentative speech together. Their lives through all the long months had appeared to point to a consummation in great joy, perhaps, in some of their minds, in great triumph. Now the dreams were fractured, the pieces they had so painstakingly tried to fashion into coherence now scattered without relation. The one secure fact in the dissolution of their minds and wills was the steadfast figure of Jeshua, striding forward towards Jerusalem.

The hours passed in this resolute march, apparently towards enmity and final tragedy. But one by one they gathered the fragments of their private visions together and began to foster a resolve once more. Two of them, James and John, walked the way with their mother who had joined the other women of Galilee. They were earnestly in talk and the three of them hurried forward to overtake Jeshua. Their mother burst out in eager request to him:

'Rabbi, your kingdom, when it comes to pass – it will need officers, counsellors of state. These, my two sons, strong wills and good minds both of them; grant me this, my Lord, that they may be your nearest in the kingdom, even on your right and left hand.' Jeshua replied to James and John,

'You don't know what you are asking. Can you drink the cup that I shall drink and be baptised with my baptism?' They replied, 'We can, indeed.' Jeshua said to them,

'You will indeed drink that bitter cup and know that baptism but to sit on my right hand and on my left is not for me to grant; it shall be given to those for whom my Father has prepared it.'

By this time the other ten had caught up with them and understood the implication of the brothers' request and they were understandably angry – for they all shared ambitions of varying degrees. Then Jeshua gathered them again about him.

'You know how it fares in the Gentile world: princes rule and those beneath them wield their own authority; but it shall not be so among you. If any one of you wishes to be great, let him be your servant and if he presumes to be chief among you, let him be your slave. Remember, the Son of Man came not to wield authority but to minister to his people – and to give his life as a ransom for all who need to be redeemed.'

They were now descending through the hill country and approaching the defiles north of Jericho, and by the wayside, among the multitude that gathered to hear Jeshua, was a well-known blind beggar, Bartimaeus by name. Long accustomed boldly to cry for alms, he now shouted above the tumult of the thronging people,

'Jeshua, Son of David, have mercy!' Many tried to silence him but he cried the more loudly,

'Son of David, have mercy on me!'

Jeshua halted and commanded that Bartimaeus be brought to stand before him. And his friends said to him, 'Be glad; he's calling for you!' In his haste Bartimaeus threw away his outer garment and fell down before Jeshua, who said to him,

'What do you ask of me?'

'Lord, that I may see again!' And Jeshua said to him, 'Go on your way; your faith has made you whole' and Bartimaeus received his sight again and followed Jeshua with his praises.

They were now very near to Jericho in the highway before its gate and a rich tax-gatherer called Zachaeus, longing simply to catch sight of Jeshua, had climbed a sycamore tree in order to see him. As Jeshua came that way he stopped and looked up at the eager face of Zachaeus, and said to him,

'Come down to my side, I wish to stay at your house.' Zachaeus hurried down and as they walked he said to Jeshua,

'Rabbi, I wish to give, even now, half my property to the poor, and if in my business I have defrauded any one, I will give him fourfold what I took from him.'

There was astonished merriment in Jericho; Zachaeus, of all people, had prepared a feast. All his friends were there, of course – they were mainly tax-gatherers like him and were best avoided. But the next set of invitations left Jericho astounded, for Zachaeus was inviting to the feast all whom he had defrauded and was going to recompence them four-fold! Strange how these small men always seem to do exaggerated things; and what a human mix it would be – and would the other tax-gatherers follow suit and approach Zachaeus in generosity? – three-fold, four-fold even perhaps five-fold. Jericho was to know some changes of fortune.

Astonishingly, nothing untoward happened. Jeshua arrived at the handsome, so well-appointed home with most of his disciples and somehow the atmosphere of feasting was like a tranquil family meal. Zachaeus moved diffidently but with radiance to Jeshua's side; there was no ostentation, no demanding of rights but a sense of burdens lifted, of harmony restored.

At least for a while. At the gate there were untoward outcries. Many had heard the shouting earlier in the day – Son of David, Son of David' – and they knew of old experiences that that skilful beggar, blind Bartimaeus was difficult to silence when he was in full cry. And it had always paid. His alms dish was always fuller than any other and this day the gift had been unique, his sight restored. So, why now this renewed outcry, 'Son of David'?

Part of Bartimaeus's success in the past had been the pawky determination to admit no conventions, to conform to no demands of propriety. He was unkempt and yes, dirty. Where others besought charity, he raucously demanded charity – and took it as his due. His present appearance at Zachaeus's gate was a nuisance but might have been anticipated.

He burst into the feast itself. 'Jeshua, Master, Son of David, forgive me! Sight was such a shock, I ran before my thanks were out! Forgive me.' Jeshua smiled his delight in this strange, eccentric scrap of humanity – Bartimaeus was so essentially Bartimaeus! Jeshua's smile emboldened him. In other settings he would have been a 'Lord of Misrule'; 'Ah, Zachaeus, you see he has cured my blindness and I hear he has cured you!' There was general laughter in which both Zachaeus and Jeshua joined. His satire become broader and some guests looked uneasy.

'Your hopeful parents named you Zachaeus, 'the pure one'. It's true today, I hear!' Zachaeus, his laughter softening the retort, took up the verbal contest: 'Bar-Timaeus, 'Son of Uncleanness' – you determine to fulfil your name also?' In the laughter – none of it malicious – Jeshua took Bartimaeus by the sleeve and drew him down to his side. 'He invites you; eat, so that we too may share a little silence!'

As the guests were stilled by the courteous gravity of Jeshua's voice, Bartimaeus crossed to the doorway, removed his tattered outer cloak and with silent care bathed his hands and face and, with a gravity they had not before seen in him, took his place at Jeshua's side.

The feasting was a happy interlude but the following morning Jeshua resumed his progress to Jerusalem, climbing through the tortuous Jericho gorge to the open country beyond and so to the township of Bethany. Already Jerusalem was agog with rumours, as the people prepared for Passover; 'will he come?', 'will he dare venture to the Temple, even dare to teach there?' 'What will the powerful ones say?'

But Jeshua rested at Bethany and in the evening was invited to a feast at a house in the little town. Lazarus had also been invited with Jeshua and the twelve, while Martha, ever industrious, waited at the tables.

When the feast had progressed a while, Mary entered silently, carrying a simple vessel of translucent alabaster of great delicacy, filled with a costly ointment of spikenard. She crushed the fragile alabaster between the palms of her hands and poured the whole contents over Jeshua's head and body.

The drama of the action stilled the whole company and as Jeshua sat in their midst, the perfume of the spikenard spread and penetrated the whole house. To all of them it brought a powerful mixture of emotions, of incalculable luxury, of prodigal outpouring of a precious heirloom and, on the face of Lazarus, a spasm of agony as the embalmer's hands seemed once more to traverse his flesh and the perfume of the cave returned again to be his first sensation of renewed life. Some saw the pain of Lazarus's half-blind look about him; others saw only the shattered fragments of delicate alabaster; and yet others, less sensitive, were aware only of extravagance, a squandering by this silent and adoring woman. Jeshua broke into their thoughts and murmurings:

'Do not trouble Mary, for she has done a good work. You speak truth when you say that this ointment, sold, could have succoured the poor – but the poor you have always about you and do you always remember them? But you

331

will not always have my presence with you and Mary has this night anointed my body for its burying.'

There was a hushed awareness of an event beyond their understanding and it was some time before the silence was broken, while the perfume still lingered.

BOOK FIVE

View of Jerusalem

THIRTY-SEVEN

Jeshua and the twelve stayed at Bethany before the week of the Passover and Jeshua was much on his own, walking in the villages and the countryside and on to the Mount of Olives where he could see the whole city of Jerusalem laid out before him. On the morning after the Sabbath Jeshua took aside two of his disciples and gave them directions.

'Across the valley before us is the village of Bethphage and at the crossroads before you enter the village, you will see an ass tied, with its foal. Go there and untie the two beasts to bring them to me. You will be stopped by the owner who lives nearby, who will say to you,

'Why do you loose the ass?' And you will answer, 'The Lord has need of it,' and immediately he will allow you to take it away. Bring it to me and we shall make all ready.'

The disciples did as Jeshua had instructed and they found the ass and, having given the required answer, they brought it to Jeshua at Bethany.

On it they placed a folded cloth (for the ass had never before been saddled) and Jeshua rode on it, along the way to Jerusalem, his disciples with him, two leading his mount and the others behind. As they went their way, other Passover pilgrims on their journey to Jerusalem looked curiously at the little gathering with the solemn and noble bearing of Jeshua on his humble mount. Some of them were from Galilee and recognised him; others had heard of his miracles and of his teaching; all realised that here was no ordinary pilgrims' entry to Jerusalem.

Then some of them ran ahead and strewed branches ceremonially by the wayside and as Jeshua approached them, they laid their cloaks in the road before him; and as he progressed, the cries before him and about him grew gradually louder until it became a chant of triumph;

Hosanna!

Blessed is he that cometh
In the name of the Lord
Blessed be the Kingdom of our father David
That cometh in the Name of the Lord.
Blessed be the King that cometh
In the Name of the Lord
Peace in heaven and glory in the highest.
Hosanna in the highest.

Among the onlookers were some of the Temple lawyers and as the triumphant shouts began to take on the quality of a regal welcome for a holy king, they approached Jeshua and his disciples and said,

'Rabbi, rebuke your disciples for this blasphemy!'

Jeshua replied,

'I tell you that if these should hold their peace, the very stones themselves would cry out.'

It was not the lawyers alone, however, who were troubled at the quality of ovation which Jeshua was accorded and the transformation which had overtaken what most of them had expected to be a customary approach to the holy places. Thomas brooded as he walked alone in the procession and Simon looked about him, the old instincts fearing ambush at every turn or a direct assault from Temple guards, Herodian soldiers or a detachment of Romans, fearing insurrection before the feast. With Judas, it was wholly otherwise, a seething but indeterminate conviction that all was not well; this he kept to himself until a time came when he could talk to Jeshua privately. Meanwhile he found it difficult to conceal his contempt for Jeshua's lowly and unsuitable mount and for the rabble's shouting, which he thought hysterical. Was anything in the future of the Kingdom to be gained by this uncouth demonstration?

By this time a hundred or so men and their families were eddying about Jeshua and as they approached the city, there were cries from those who had already arrived for the feast:

'Who is this?' 'Is it insurrection?' The reply on all sides was clear:

'This is he, the prophet of Nazareth in Galilee' and in a hopeless resignation the Temple officers returned to their people, saying,

'You can do nothing at this time. The whole world follows him!'

Jeshua, however, halted as he came to the last rising ground before the city entrance, dismounted and stood alone before the whole company of his followers. He looked long and tragically at the city spread out before him and raised his arms in prophecy.

'If thou hadst known, even thou,
At least in this thy day,
The things which belong unto thy peace,
But now they are hid from thine eyes.
For the days shall come upon thee
That thine enemies shall cast a trench about thee
And compass thee around
And keep thee in on every side,
And shall lay thee even with the ground
And thy children within thee.
And they shall not leave in thee one stone upon
   another
Because thou knewest not the time of thy
   visitation.

The cries of 'Hosanna' were silenced and those about

Jeshua were sobered as they saw the grief which ravaged his face. With no more word, Jeshua and the twelve walked in an island of silence, made the greater by the tumultuous cries and counter-cries of those who ran before and who followed them.

Within the narrow streets of the city, as Jeshua walked swiftly through and into the Temple, as though to reassure himself that all the holy places were there intact, the crowds gradually fell away, pursuing their business of preparation for the feast.

In the late afternoon, Jeshua made to return to Bethany where it was his purpose to spend each night until the eve of the feast itself, and the twelve walked with him. Judas soon made occasion to detach Jeshua from the others and to walk more slowly alone with him.

'You are still troubled, my son, as you were at our entry; you were troubled by the palm branches, the cloaks on the way and the cries?'

'These were troubling, Lord, and we may have to pay too dearly for a mere passing show. But my trouble was deeper than that.' He paused and he wiped his mouth – a customary gesture – as though a bitterly distasteful thing had touched his lips; and he then burst out like an affronted young man, indeed in his shaken dignity he had all the appearance of a young nobleman deeply insulted and Jeshua stopped and turned to hear more clearly what he had to say. When the words came there was a touch of the ridiculous in them:

'That ass! It wasn't seemly; a donkey and not even saddled!'

'What would you have had, Judas, which would be more fitting?'

'The moment seemed to have come, the people were like tinder ready for the blaze which should bring down

Rome and all your enemies. And you should have been gloriously mounted. There is not a stallion at my home in Kerioth which should not have pranced in pride to carry the King, the Son of David. You could have won the city!'

'Dear Judas, I did win the city, in the only way I could have won it. Come, let us sit down a while and reason together about all this.'

They sat facing each other on the stony bank of the wayside. The sun was near to setting over the Jerusalem countryside and a few solitary birds flew eastward towards Bethany which the other eleven companions had already reached. Jeshua waited to gather Judas's quieter attention.

'I must remind you first of the prophecies which I came to fulfil. You remember the words of comfort which Isaiah spoke to the troubled people of Jerusalem:

> Say ye to the daughters of Zion,
> Behold thy salvation cometh,
> Behold his reward is with him
> And his work before him
> And they shall be called
> The holy people
> The redeemed of the Lord
> And thou shalt be called 'sought out',
> A city not forsaken.

'Do you understand the truth of these words, Judas? – their splendid truth, even for today's Jerusalem – 'A city not forsaken' and moreover one 'sought out' by all the peoples of this world. Don't you understand that, my son?'

'I do, indeed I do, for you have promised us no less in all these weary months we have learnt from your mouth. But 'a city not forsaken' is occupied by Roman legions, seduced by Herodians and betrayed by its own rulers, those who should lead them into their kingdom, which is truly your Kingdom. And if that victory is to be theirs –

339

'not forsaken!' – they need a king regally mounted and entering with pride to command his people as they rise against their enemies. And what did they see as they cried their 'Hosannas'? You, entering humbly and riding on an ass! It was a betrayal – forgive me, Master, I have to say it!'

'You must speak your mind and do your will, Judas, but pause a moment in your judgment. I promised you as we sat here, not a prophecy but prophecies and I must now give you the second of them. You must now recall Zechariah. His is truly a triumph-song and watch closely for his description of the king's entry:

Rejoice, Rejoice, daughter of Zion,
Shout aloud, daughters of Jerusalem.
For see, your King is coming to you,
His cause won,
His victory gained,
Humble, and mounted on an ass,
On a foal, the young of a she-ass.

Do you think now that I was wholly forgetful of my duty, my destiny, the triumph I was to bring to the daughters of Jerusalem? No, Judas, the scriptures must be fulfilled.

'But the prophecy doesn't end there; Zechariah has more to tell. When the king has come to Zion,

He shall banish chariots from Ephraim
And war-horses from Jerusalem,
The warrior's bow shall be banished.
He shall speak peaceably to every nation
And his rule shall extend from sea to sea,
From the River to the ends of the earth.

There is our triumph, Judas, there alone is our way.'

'And by that way you will die, Rabbi, for nothing but force, sword and chariot, will subdue Rome.'

'And by that death I shall triumph, Judas, and only by that death. 'Despised', 'rejected' and killed in Zion for Zion.'

'But, Rabbi, we have heard from your very lips – and we

have trusted and believed your word – that while Rome has its legions of men, you have your Father's legions of angels. What an escort they would have made for your entry!'

'The legions of angels will be there, Judas, their swords drawn but unsullied by blood, their cries heard above all the tumult, but cries of adoration not of exultation; have no fear, my son.'

Judas was unwillingly silenced and walked with Jeshua to Bethany in the golden light of the risen moon, that in a few days in its full brilliance would mark Passover. Judas longed for the Kingdom as passionately as the other eleven, perhaps more passionately because it would fulfil a deep craving in his nature. His vision of the end and of the means to achieve it was clearer than theirs, because more deeply brooded upon and argued in solitude. Better perhaps that his imagination had been as unformed and blunted as theirs.

THIRTY-EIGHT

The next day they returned to Jerusalem and it was clear both to Judas and the others that, whatever the attitudes of the pilgrims to the feast or of the lawyers and rulers of the Temple, Jeshua was in no mood to avoid any kind of confrontation. Indeed, as that day and the days immediately following were to show ever more clearly, Jeshua now took control of events; his opponents, both declared and potential, did little more than react to his initiatives. Sometimes the reactions were blindly violent, the blundering and flailing blows of those who felt them-selves threatened in the dark; at other times they were the reaction of subtle minds, careful and devious attempts to trap him intellectually. Unfortunately for their subtlest attempts, they had forgotten that in rabbinic argument he was more than their equal, indeed had been from their very first encounters with him.

341

On this day, then, his determination was set and was made clear in his striding from Bethany. As always as he reached the Mount of Olives, his steps slowed and he gazed with anguish at the city where so many of his people's hopes had for generations been centred. Time and again it had borne the vision of God's supreme residence among men; in generation after generation it had been sacked, despoiled and desecrated, its stones the mute relics of a nation's dream; over and over again it had been restored, purified and become once more the holy centre, the very heart of the visible universe. Now, as Jeshua descended within sight of the noble gate which would give access to the sacred places, he grieved as one who bore precious gifts and had had them spurned.

By the time Jeshua reached the entrance to the Temple itself he had outpaced the twelve, whose foreboding increased as they saw more clearly his fixed determination. He entered the Temple and stood quite still, apparently hearing nothing and seeing only the colonnades where the teaching of the rabbis had traversed the generations and where he had himself gathered so many about him. He seemed slowly to become aware of the hubbub, the chink of coinage and the chaffering of exchange, as coins from all over the Jewish world were exchanged for the only coinage legitimate in the Temple for the purchase of sacrificial victims, the coinage of Tyre. Occupying much of the space within this Court of the Gentiles were the beasts to be offered; the cacophany of lowing, bleating and the rituals of barter had their lower tones of doves' cooing, the lowly offering of a poor man. The whole busyness was a double affront; it crowded out those Gentiles and even the 'God-fearers', who, attracted by the historic glory and sanctity of the Temple, might well have been even more drawn to the prophetic power of His worship; even more, the trafficking, the cheating and above all the sheer noise was an affront to the God who desired to be contemplated with silent awe.

Jeshua became rigid, still and expressionless, as he looked at all the offensive scene. As John looked with deep understanding and compassion at his beloved Rabbi, Jeshua seemed to him to be a figure of frozen anger, that pure anger which is one of the sources of justice; and John repeated, as though by ritual to still the tempest in his Lord, the psalm of cruel affliction:

> Save me, O God, for the waters are come in,
> Even unto my soul.

John looked about him and wherever his eye's rested, there were the adversaries.

> They that hate me without a cause
> Are more than the hairs of my head.
> They that are mine enemies
> And would destroy me guiltless,
> Are mighty.

Then Jeshua marched towards the tables of the money-changers and with a sweep of his right hand, brushed all coinage to the floor, whether the Temple Tyrian or the many pilgrim offerings. John continued his whispering prayer.

> For the zeal of thine house
> Hath even eaten me;
> And the rebukes of them that rebuked thee
> Are fallen upon me.

Jeshua stood with the coins about his feet and the hysterical abuse of the traders assailing him; Jeshua seemed to hear nothing but cried above the din,
'You have heard it said by the prophet,

> 'My house shall be a house of prayer
> For all nations'

but you have made it a den of thieves, even here where the Gentiles might worship.' Turning to the cages where the doves were kept and with his gesture negating the whole offensive marketing, he cried,

'Have you not heard my Father's command, 'I desire mercy not sacrifice'? If you have heard Him, take these things away.'

The Temple officers and the priests heard him with abhorrence. Where would the teaching and exhortation cease? – with the destruction of the Temple worship itself?

For the moment they remained silent, with the hope that the traders and their friends would arouse sufficient anger against Jeshua. They were the more dismayed when Jeshua turned to the people, from his familiar place in the shadows of the colonnade, and began to teach them.

'Your father David, King of Israel, so it is said by Samuel the prophet 'hated the lame and the blind in his soul.' I would not have it so. The blind among you, let them see and the lame among you, may they walk without stumbling.'

And they were brought to him, as they always had been and as was his custom, he healed them and sent them away rejoicing.

This was of course to compound the offences which Jeshua had commited and there was consternation among the authorities who were even more angered when one among them, Joseph of Arimathea, spoke as though to himself but with a carrying note to ensure that members of the Sanhedrin heard:

'Indeed we may be seeing and hearing the prophecy fulfilled' and in rhythms which became ever more disconcerting to those who heard them, he went on:

'Behold I will send my messenger
And he shall prepare the way before me
And the Lord whom ye seek
Shall suddenly come to his Temple,

Even the messenger of the covenant
Whom ye delight in.'

As he spoke the last phrase there was a flicker of irony in the glance he gave towards the older members of the Sanhedrin. There was silence among them, as he went on, still as if in private meditation:

'But who may abide the day of his coming?
And who shall stand when he appeareth?
For he is like a refiner's fire -'

He broke off as if for a moment conscious of his listeners; and looking more directly at the priests among them, he continued in a lower, more tragic tone, as if despairing of the prophecy's fulfilment:

'And he shall sit as a refiner
And purifier of silver
And he shall purify the sons of Levi
And purge them as gold and silver
That they may offer unto the Lord
An offering in righteousness'

This was far too near the tone of those events in the Court of the Gentiles to be tolerable. Joseph of Arimathea had never, in any event, been admitted to their more secret conclaves and ignoring him now, they determined on an intellectual skirmish with Jeshua.

Returning to the outer courtyard a small group of them approached Jeshua at his healing.

'By what authority do you do these things? And who gave you this authority?'

Jeshua smiled, for this was a question to delight that part of his mind that reverenced the scholarship of the Rabbis – as it would have delighted Hillel.

'I will ask you one question and if you answer me well and honestly, I will also reply to your question, telling you the source of my authority: The baptism of John, whence was its power, from heaven or simply from men?'

They recognised at once the subtlety of the dilemma

posed by Jeshua. If they answered, 'From heaven', Jeshua could justifiably reply, 'Why then not believe him and his whole prophecy?' And if they should say 'Of men', then they feared the wrath of the people who universally held John to be a prophet. They helplessly cut through the dilemma:

'We cannot tell.'

'Neither will I tell you by what authority I do these things.'

They wished to retreat from the contest, for the people standing by saw their discomfiture and many of them rejoiced at it. The stakes were now getting higher. Jeshua had proclaimed his aims, a purification of the Temple, its ritual and its authority and as he won more of the assent and worship of the people, so his very being was the more greatly adored. For them, and especially the holiest among them, the very Law itself, which they reverenced was now under threat. Mere office and officialdom they set aside. Here, menaced before their eyes, was that tradition of the Fathers, handed down, protected from pollution and worshipped as the very word of Adonai. And yet to be silenced by a prophet of Galilee!

Jeshua respected their silence, the intensity of their grief and the affront which his very presence gave to them and all they cherished. Then in the silence and in no way raising his voice he said,

'I will tell you of two sons. Their father came to one of them and said, 'Son, go to work this day in my vineyard' and he said 'I will not go' but afterwards, deeply repenting, he went and did his father's bidding. And the father went to the other son and made the same request; he replied, 'I go, Sir' but yet he did not go. Which now of these two did the will of his father?'

They replied, 'The first.'

Jeshua replied to them gravely and firmly, 'And I truly say to you that the tax-gatherers and the harlots go into

346

the Kingdom of God before you. For John came to you, pointing the way to righteousness and yet you did not believe him. But the tax-gatherers and harlots believed him and you, when you saw the truth of the prophecy acted out before you, failed to repent, that you might believe his truth.'

They were silent but in his compassion for those among them for whom truth and holiness was the core of their being, he still spoke in a low voice, a tone addressed solely to them. But as he looked among them, he saw the hard minority whose eyes glowed with frustrated hate and speaking directly to them he said:

'Listen to me once more. A householder established a vineyard, hedged it about, built a winepress within its bounds and built a watch-tower at its gate. He then let it out to tenants who should cultivate it and he went into a far country. When the time to harvest the fruit drew near, he sent to his tenants, requesting his part of the fruits of the vineyard. And they took his servants, beat one of them, killed another and stoned the third. Again he sent more servants and again they behaved as before.

'But then at last he sent his son to them, saying to himself, 'They will reverence my son'. But when the tenants saw the son, they said among themselves, 'This is the heir; let us kill him and seize his inheritance for ourselves.' And they took him, cast him out of the vineyard and slew him.

'When the Lord of the vineyard returns, what will he do to those tenants?'

The whole company was confounded, for they saw very clearly the meaning and purpose of the parable; but they could scarcely remain silent before his question. One of the oldest among them, whose bent back and brooding eyes showed years-long wrestling with the truth, replied heavily,

'He will mercilessly destroy those wicked men and let

his vineyard to better tenants who will give him honestly his due.'

Jeshua looked at each of them, the contrite and the hardened, and said, 'You have been present throughout your lives at the feasts and have sung the Great Hosanna at the Feast of Tabernacles:

O give thanks unto the Lord,

For he is gracious,

Because his mercy endureth for ever

and yet in this great Hosanna you have also sung, from your bitter experience – which I share,

It is better to trust in the Lord

Than to put any confidence in princes.

'But the Psalmist goes even further than this and speaks now to you across the ages,

The stone which the builders rejected

Is become the head-stone at the corner.

This is the Lord's doing

And it is marvellous in our eyes.

'You have a great trust reposing in you, you rulers of the Temple and leaders of the nation; have a great care that you do not refuse the way of salvation, for yourselves and for your people. I say most solemnly to you, if you betray this trust, the Kingdom of God will be taken from you and given to those more worthy to bring forth its fruits.

'If you stumble at this corner-stone, you will be broken, but if in judgment it falls upon you, it will grind you even to powder.'

There were eyes that kindled among those who heard him and not with anger. This was a voice of authority which they had not heard in their generation but only echoes of it as the Law and the prophets had been read. Those Pharisees, and they the majority, for whom right-eousness was a consuming passion, heard Jeshua with longing that it might indeed be He for whom their soul waited. Their gaze and his locked in understanding and a profound hope was raised in Jeshua.

'I have one more thing to say to you and let it test you, as silver is tried.

'A king prepared a great marriage-feast for his son and invited many guests but they refused to come; and again he sent to those who were invited, saying that the feast was prepared and bidding them welcome. But they refused with false excuses, of husbandry or trade and others among them took his servants, handled them roughly and even killed them. And he took steps to punish those murderers.

'Finally he said to his servants, 'The wedding-feast is ready, go therefore into the highways and bid to the feast all whom you find.' They did as he commanded and they gathered in a multitude, the worthy and the seemingly unworthy and the feast was fully furnished with guests.

'Then the king came in to greet his guests and he saw one who had not troubled to dress in a courteous way for the wedding and he said to him, 'Friend, how did it happen that you came to my feast in your soiled, workaday garments?' and the man was speechless and the king ordered his expulsion from the feast.

'There is truly a great feast, a greater than any king may give. The multitude of men is called but each has to be prepared. Woe to him who is unprepared, for there will be great wailing and sorrow at his rejection.'

The silence was held unbearably in the Temple court. Many of his hearers would gladly have heard more and spoken with him but some tempers were at breaking point and many others were still debating in their minds the seemingly simple demands that Jeshua made.

THIRTY-NINE

Pharisees and Herodians had always differed profoundly about the propriety of submitting to Roman taxation. The Herodians looked for political accommodation in all things and pointed to the impracticality of refusing to be taxed; more could be lost than gained by recalcitrance. The Pharisees found the whole Roman occupation an insult and the payment of taxes abhorrent. It appeared to the more devious among both parties – each deploring the conduct of Jeshua – that they should both at once challenge him with the problem.

They found him again with his disciples in the Temple and their spokesman put the question to him bluntly,

'Rabbi, we know your regard for truth and in worshipping God you have no care for the opinion of man. Tell us, therefore, is it lawful to give tribute to Caesar or not?'

'Why do you test me in this way, you hypocrites? Show me a piece of the tribute money.' And they brought him a coin.

'Whose is the image and superscription?'

'It is Caesar's portrait.'

'Render therefore to Caesar that which is Caesar's and to God that which is His.' He paused and then with finality said,

'For man was created in God's image and in all Torah we are stamped with His superscription.'

Very soon the third great party of the state, the Sadducees approached him, with a question about life beyond death, in which they did not believe. Using his own method of parable teaching, they put to him a testing instance.

'Rabbi, you know the law of Moses that if a man die childless his brother shall marry the widow and raise up a family in his stead. Now consider! A man dies childless and his brother marries the widow; he in turn dies childless and a second brother marries her and so with the third until at length seven brothers had married this widow. Now – at the resurrection – if there be a resurrection – which of those brothers is husband to her who was married to seven of them?'

'Your error, Masters, is manifold! In heaven they neither marry nor are given in marriage, for their relations one with another are like those of the angels of God. By your ridiculous instance you desire to mock the fact of resurrection from the dead but I say to you, read the scriptures and learn what God says:

I am the God of Abraham
And the God Isaac,
And the God of Jacob.

'God is not the God of the dead but of the living, who in life and beyond life are in His hands.' And they were silenced.

There was muted rejoicing among the Pharisees at the discomfiture of the Sadducees but Jeshua had stirred many of them to profounder speculation. To all of them Torah was the centre of reverence and a favourite and frequent topic of disputation among them was the primacy of certain Laws, and the relative greatness of all the Mosaic commands. One of them came alone to Jeshua, wishing for grave talk with him, and said,

'Rabbi, which is the first and greatest commandment of all?' Jeshua replied, in the words which were daily on all their tongues,

"Hear, O Israel, the Lord our God is one Lord; and thou shalt love the Lord thy God with all thy heart and with all thy soul and with all thy mind and with all thy strength,' this is the first commandment.

'And the second is like to it, namely, 'Thou shalt love thy neighbour as thyself'.' He answered,

351

'Rabbi, you have said truth and I would say to you that there is but one God and that to love him with all the heart, the understanding, the soul and the strength and to love my neighbour as myself, is more than all the burnt offerings and sacrifices.'

Jeshua looked at him in a warm understanding, for here was the heart of noble Pharisaism and with a yearning in his voice he said to him,

'You are indeed not far from the Kingdom of God.'

The conflict for the moment was intellectual, a duel of adversaries who, tragically, had so much in common. At every turn of the deft struggle, of which Jeshua held such brilliant command, he left the way of escape open. Memories of Hillel and Shammai and his boyhood reverence for their dedicated minds, preserved for him a love for all who kept the Law alive in the hearts of the people. His enmity was all the more fierce for those who placed stumbling blocks before the feet of the untutored poor.

There came an hour in the Temple, while the doctors of the Law meditated their next assault on Jeshua's authority when he opened the argument against them.

'The Christ, what standing do you give to Him and whose Son is He?' They replied with the traditional title,

'The Son of David.'

'How then does David call him 'Lord' and, in the spirit of prophecy, say of him,

'The Lord said unto my Lord,
Sit thou on my right hand
Until I make thine enemies thy footstool'

If David calls him 'Lord', how then is he David's Son?'

This was the last skirmish between them and no more questions were asked of Jeshua; the Pharisees, the doctors of the Law and the rulers of the Temple withdrew, seeking another mode of attack.

Jeshua however still held the attention of the visitors to the Temple and in the comparative peace that followed the great debate, he began to teach them of spiritual values and how they, in their humility must discriminate.

'Children, when you are taught in synagogue or Temple, there will be those who sit in 'Moses's Seat', and from that prophetic place they teach truth; listen to their words and follow them, and also watch their actions and, where they hallow God by their conduct, then follow them; but if they are mere play-actors, do not join them in hypocrisy.'

And he began to declare a dire fate on those shepherds of the people who betrayed their flocks and to the Pharisees and Rabbis who denied grace to their people, he cried a refrain of 'Woe':

'Woe to you that shut the doors of the Kingdom against the poor seeker.

'Woe to you who corrupt your converts like yourselves.

'Woe to you, blind guides, whose eyes should be opened.

'Woe to you who exalt the trivial, the tithes of anise, mint and cummin and neglect judgment and mercy.

'Woe to you who cleanse the outside of your cups but within are full of corruption.

'Woe to you who honour the tombs of the righteous and the prophets but take no part of their sufferings.

'Woe to you who will scourge and persecute, kill and crucify the prophets who shall come to you.

> 'O Jerusalem, Jerusalem who killest the prophets,
> How often I would have gathered thy children
> Even as a hen gathereth her chicks under her wings
> And ye would not.
> Behold, your house is left unto you desolate.
> For I say unto you,
> Ye shall not see me henceforth
> Till ye shall say,

'Blessed is he that cometh
In the name of the Lord'

The diatribe and the prophecy were as confounding to the twelve as they were to the strangers gathered there. The maledictions against treacherous religious leaders carried for them the appalling authority which Jeshua had always shown against demonic powers; but the reiteration of the 'Woes' had for them also the greater force in that they carried a desolate negative echo of the benedictions he had uttered at the opening of his mission. For them, the lips of Jeshua ought always to carry the tenderness of 'Blessed are ye!' Indeed they had some fear of this Jeshua who was now revealed to them, who demanded perfection even in small matters. As they heard Jerusalem and its rulers, who betrayed their holy traditions, reviled in the very Temple, they silently called to mind their return three days before, to Bethany. They were tired and hungry and Jeshua turned to a fig-tree, almost arrogant in the surfeit of its leaves, and parted the branches. It was not the time for the ripe fruit and Jeshua sought the small, green 'false fruit', the size of a pigeon's egg, with which the poor often sought to refresh themselves. It was bare even of these. Jeshua turned to the twelve and in the tones they knew from his Temple utterances he said,

'This tree shall never henceforth bear fruit',
and the following morning, as they returned that way, the fig-tree was withered and dying. They were fearful, and few of them took comfort from Jeshua's assurance that with faith they would do greater things than this, even to the moving of mountains. His power had hitherto almost always been shown in their presence as an instrument of his compassion; now they remembered only the commands uttered to demons and the authority he exercised even over the waves of Galilee. This Jeshua, keen as a steel blade, was the obverse side of their compassionate master and they found it difficult to come to terms with this new revelation.

And yet the compassion broke through, even on occasion when judgment was pronounced. They were seated near the Treasury where money was cast into boxes for the maintenance of the Temple. The rich came by and ostentatiously, with broad gestures and a flourishing of sleeves, threw in large sums in gold. But a poor widow drew from her garment two of the very smallest coins and slipped them into the alms box.

'Do you see these gifts? I say to you truly, this poor woman has given far more than all the others together, for she, out of all her poverty and need, has given her whole means of living.'

Jeshua was rarely alone with Matthew or indeed with any of the twelve. But this was a day to leave Jerusalem, a day for the bleak but refreshing countryside. The two set out northwestward in silence, tacitly avoiding the loved and familiar road to Bethany. The hills were of no great height and the valley strips of cultivation were a refreshing green. Talk at the Temple treasury had sent Matthew back to his memories of dues and taxes at the lakeside.

'For me, a tax was a tax, extortionate perhaps but never, in prudence, squeezed beyond the limit – they had to be there to be taxed again! But that widow you pointed out to us – prodigal surely, beyond the limit – her all.'

They had, all of them, and more especially the sophisticated Matthew, learned that a bantering irony was always a short cut to the brilliance of Jeshua's teaching. Joining, with a smile, in the conversational game, he responded to Matthew's challenge.

'Yes, her all. With the awful patience of the poor there also goes a kind of heroic desperation: a mother gives – not shares – her last crust; a friend gives – not shares – his last silver piece; and that widow threw at the feet of God the last coin which might have bought the loaf so desperately needed. Hunger is no bar for their final, despairing generosity, the recognition of a need, a demand, greater than the pinched cry of their starving bodies. They give their all to a starving neighbour or a loving God. We may hope the neighbour will one day respond; we *know* that the love of God will never desert them.'

Matthew had not expected this response, so different in kind from Jeshua's sharp rabbinic exchanges with legalist minds. He was silent as they walked on into the hills, seeing for the first time, a shekel, a denarius, a 'farthing', not as a crude medium of exchange, but a living thing, a potential sacrifice; even taxes ceased to be metal.

They stopped at a very small and isolated village and sought an inn for a brief meal. At the only likely dwelling, Matthew asked for a little refreshment to see them on their way. The master of the house looked at the bearing of Matthew and Jeshua, the quiet assurance of their greeting, and replied,

'We have nothing that wouldn't insult such as you.' Jeshua's smile grew broader: 'May we not share what satisfies your hunger and thirst?'

Dubiously he responded, inviting them directly to the board on which were a wooden platter of bread, two beakers and a jug of wine, which seemed by its colour to be liberally slaked with spring water. Two more beakers were placed on the table and hesitantly the man and his wife sat facing Jeshua and Matthew. At first there were no words but the prayers at the breaking of bread and at the pouring of wine but as the meal progressed, no more than the grey rough bread and the thin wine, the talk moved between them, the commonplaces of crops, flocks, drought and flood, drawing them together within the warmth of Jeshua's look from one to another.

The time came to leave and Matthew drew out his purse. With the utmost courtesy and swiftly halting even the gesture of payment:

'This last hour has been beyond price' and no word of Jeshua's was needed to fulfil the peasant courtesy.

FORTY

Because of Philip's Greek connections through his friends in his hometown of Bethsaida, he was the natural channel for any Greek Gentile's approach to Jeshua. But these approaches were rare and it seemed of peculiar significance that one came to him now, at this time of crisis. Certain worshippers from the Greek-speaking northern coasts came to Philip with the request,

'Sir, we would see the Messiah.' Philip told Andrew of their desire and they both came to Jeshua. He granted their request and in the presence of his disciples greeted them prophetically.

'The hour is come for the glorifying of the Son of Man. Truly I say to you, unless a grain of wheat fall into the ground and die, it remains unfruitful. But if it die, it brings forth much fruit. He who loves his life shall lose it, but he that sets aside life in this world shall keep it eternally. If any man wishes to serve me, let him follow me; where I am, there will my servant be; and if any man serve me, him will my Father honour.'

Jeshua turned from the Greeks and stood aside praying within the hearing only of his intimate friends.

'Now is my soul troubled. What shall I say? 'Father, save me from this hour'? but for this I came into the world. 'Father, glorify thy name'.'

There came a sound from heaven which filled them all with awe, and to some the sound was revealed as words,

'I have both glorified it and will glorify it again.'

Jeshua now addressed them firmly but with a sobriety which overawed them.

'Now is the time of the judgment of this world. Now shall the Prince and Power of this world be cast down. I, if I be lifted up from the earth, will draw all men unto me.'

Some of them answered this prophecy,

'We have heard in the Law that Christ lives for ever.

How then do you say that the 'Son of Man' shall be 'lifted up' in death? Who is this 'Son of Man'?'

Jeshua answered them, 'The light is with you but a short while. Walk in it while you have the light, lest you be overwhelmed by darkness. Believe in that light that you be known as its children.'

The people about him were puzzled by his oblique reply and despite his miracles and the authority of his words, drifted away, uncomprehending.

Jeshua turned in sorrow to his intimate disciples, saying tragically,

'Now we see indeed Isaiah's prophecy revealed:
    Who hath believed our report,
    And to whom is the arm of the Lord revealed?
    For he shall grow up before the Lord
    As a tender plant
    And as a root out of dry ground.
and those who have not listened shall most terribly fulfil his prophecy,
    He hath blinded their eyes
    And hardened their heart
    That they should not see with their eyes
    Nor understand with their heart
    And be converted and healed.

'You, my little ones whom I have loved, now it is to you only that I speak and I say to you: Judgment has come into the world and the world is judged; but I come not to judge the world but to save it.'

The feast was approaching, the faster because of the many preparations to be made; and beneath the bustle and the anticipation there was brooding distrust and increasing tension. The twelve were glad that Jeshua had withdrawn from immediate contact with the crowds of pilgrims and sat more with them, withdrawn on the slopes of the Mount of Olives. In the shade of an ancient olive tree they looked in the blaze of noon at the Temple building, the limestone blocks and the gold leaf radiant with the heat they had absorbed. There were murmurs from the twelve of 'Splendid', 'Most wonderful!'

Jeshua turned to them and wholly silenced their admiration by saying quietly,

'Look at those buildings in their splendour. There will come a day in which not one stone shall be left upon another, for the Temple, the Temple itself shall be thrown down!'

They were appalled, for this could be none other than the end of their world. Their looks demanded Jeshua's response.

'Do not be deceived when you hear the cries, 'Here is Christ!' – or 'I am Christ!' for, before that end comes when Christ shall again be in your midst, much shall happen, in famines, pestilence and earthquakes, wars and rumours of wars. But this will be no more than a beginning!

'First, all nations shall hear my words taught to them. And then will come the persecutions when they shall seek you, to persecute and kill you. But he who endures to the end shall be saved.

'Then the thousands shall flee in fear and pray that their flight be not in winter or on the Sabbath, for there shall be great terror and sorrow.

'Then shall the world itself be troubled and shattered, the sun and moon shall shed no light, the stars shall fall from heaven.

'Then shall the Son of Man come in power and great glory and shall gather his own with his angels from the four corners of the broken world.

'But of the hour when this shall happen no man, no angel, nor even the Son has knowledge, but only the Father.

'Watch, therefore, for you do not know the hour in which your Lord will return.

'Learn of me one last time in parables.

'Ten young women took their lamps and went out before a marriage to meet the bridegroom; five of them were wise and five foolish, and the wise took vessels of oil to replenish the lamps but the foolish took only their lamps. They all slept. And at midnight there was a general cry 'The bridegroom is on his way and near!' and the young women rose and trimmed their lamps but the foolish ones found their oil all burned away and went to the wise to ask for oil. The wise young women said 'If we give you ours then our lamps also may fail. Go to the dealers and buy for yourselves'. So they went.

'Then the bridegroom came and with the wise young women went into the feast and the hall was closed. Then the foolish ones came and cried 'Lord, open the door for us!' and the Lord said, 'Indeed, I say to you, I do not know you.'

'Watch therefore, for the Son of Man comes like that to your presence, unexpectedly.

'And remember, also, you bring yourselves, all that you are to that meeting at the last with the Son of Man. I tell you again in a parable:

'A man determined to travel far abroad and he called his chief servants to him and to one he gave five talents, to another two and to another one. Then those that had received the five and the two talents traded with them and doubled their value; but he who had received one, hid it away by burying it in the earth.

'Then the lord returned and asked an account of his servants. Then he who had received five talents came bringing it and with it five more. His lord said to him, 'Well done, you are a good and diligent man; you have been faithful with this small charge; I shall give you rule over much – come and share the joy of your lord.' So it also happened to him who had made increase of the two talents.

'But then the third came and said to his lord, 'I knew you were a hard man, reaping where you had not sown, and I was afraid and hid your talent in the earth – here it is, safely back to you.' And his lord was angry. 'You knew my expectations and that I looked to have them fulfilled. Why then did you fail to take the talent to the market place? Then I should have received my money with interest.' In anger the lord turned to the other servants and commanded, 'Take the talent from him and give it to him who has ten, but cast this useless servant out from my presence and service. All like him shall weep and gnash their teeth.'

'For you have seen that judgment has in part come to the world, but when the Son of Man shall come in his full glory then he will make the final judgment. He will say to the wise and blessed ones, 'I was hungry and you fed me, thirsty and you gave me water; I was a stranger and you welcomed me, naked and you clothed me; I was sick and you visited me, I was in prison and you came to me.' And these good people will say, 'When did we see you hungry, or thirsty, naked or bereft, sick or imprisoned?' And he will say, 'In so much as you did any of these things for one of my little ones, you did it for me; come into the Kingdom prepared for you by my Father from the very foundation of the world.'

'Then will he turn to those on his left hand and will say to them, 'Neither to me nor to my beloved little ones did you give any succour or relief; depart from me and be for eternity deprived of the joy of my Father's Kingdom.'

Sombrely, the twelve themselves brooded on this judgment and went in silence to their lodging.

After the conflicts and the threats, it was incongruous to see Jeshua walking away from the Temple with a pharisee who spoke to him eagerly. Joseph, who divided his life with uneasy loyalties, between Jerusalem and his estate in Arimathea, had detached himself from the disputes and pursued Jeshua who was walking alone, from the Temple precincts.

'Rabbi, would an hour spent in talk with me inconvenience you?' Though Joseph was some ten years older than Jeshua and – though never wholly assimilated by his fellows – had an assured place in the Great Council, his deference to Jeshua was no formal courtesy. They walked together in an easy silence until they reached the outer confines of the city. Through a gateway surrounded by a carefully trained vine whose buds promised spring, Joseph guided Jeshua to an inner arbour.

'You inhabit a paradise-garden, carefully tended.' The pharisee's smile was a response to a welcomed compliment. 'The work is a deeply pleasant duty and the garden greets me and my friends at all seasons and Festivals.' There was silence between them for some minutes and then – a touch of fun in his voice – Jeshua spoke with a near-rabbinic formality:

'The words of Moses in his first Book have always seemed to me remarkable: 'And God planted a garden eastward in Eden.' This was graciously perceptive of our father Moses. Adonai could withhold no gift from man whom he had made, no bounty was too great to pour upon him. Man would have supposed Eden to be glory enough in its pure beauty, but God went further – isolated, fenced about the very quintessence of Eden in a garden eastward! And you take hints from the bounty of God the Lord! Jerusalem is a holy city, the seat of our father David, glorious in majesty – though it has its noisome bye-ways. And you, northward in Zion, plant a garden – I would almost have it in my heart to envy you!'

Joseph's pleasure in Jeshua's tone was very great but embarrassed and he excused himself to fetch for their refreshment a light wine from the vineyard slopes of Arimathea. When he returned to the courtyard, Jeshua was sleepily watching the movement of the shadows from the shrubs on the wall opposite. 'The scents from the herbs are so delicate and refreshing. You must find this a haven from the stormy Sanhedrin – and with Eve's serpent kept firmly beyond the garden bounds.'

Joseph's reply was quiet, almost as though guilt shadowed the words. 'The sibilant whisper of that serpent is heard within this peace and beauty.' A silence fell like a curtain between them.

'Rabbi, the hatred is like a mist about you. We pharisees are deeply divided among ourselves. The great majority, decent men of substance, go about their business before men, their prayers and fasting before God, and look to the blessing and redemption of Israel; a small but virulent minority fears all that your words and deeds do to 'the tradition' and they seek your life. A still smaller minority – I among them – watch appalled as this poison works its way into the hearts of good and holy men.' He stopped to receive Jeshua's response but he remained still, his hands lightly folded and without tension.

'Even at the height of this Feast of Dedication, even as we rejoiced before the Most High that his Temple had been cleansed and reconsecrated by the Maccabees, an approach was made to my friend Nicodemus – to Nicodemus of all men! The most meditative of those longing for the peace of Israel – to consult him about the traps the Law might set to entangle your feet in the way.' The wry twist of his mouth showed the words to be gall.

'Nicodemus stood aside; no answer could be adequate that didn't besmirch his tongue. But the danger is real, its shadow upon you wherever you walk. There is safety only beyond Jordan, with the wilderness a barrier between you and them.'

'Joseph, your words have been spoken in grace, whatever the pain they will have cost you in the uttering. They will not be ignored and the love within them will not be forgotten.'

Fear still lay heavily upon Joseph and his eyes were hidden as they remained gazing, unseeing, at the cobbled surface of the courtyard.

'Joseph, the law and the prophets have been your meat and drink since you were one in the synagogue *minyan* at Arimathea. Allow me, in this place of such beauty, such peace, to remind you of the blessed words of our prophet Jeremiah. They begin with such forebodding – turning to joy:

> It shall comes to pass, that like as I have watched;
> over Israel, to pick up and to break down, and to
> destroy and to afflict; So will I watch over them,
> to build and to plant, saith the Lord.'

At the words 'to plant', Jeshua looked with a smile at the trained vine, the espaliered peach tree and the garden of herbs and said, 'It would seem that fulfilment of prophecy is your longing. But Jeremiah has more to say and a burden of knowledge is not shifted:

> In those days they shall say no more,
> 'The fathers have eaten a sour grape
> And the children's teeth are set on edge'
> But rather –
> Every one shall die for his own iniquity;
> Every man that eateth the sour grape,
> His teeth shall be set on edge'.'

There was no a tragic awareness in Joseph's alert attention to the familiar words, given a new validity in the authority of Jeshua's voice. 'But, in the Mercy, there is yet more:

I will make a new covenant with Israel:
After those days, saith the Lord,
I will put my law in their inward parts,
And write it in their hearts;
I will be their God,
And they shall be my people.

And they shall teach no more
Every man his neighbour and every man his brother
Saying, 'Know the Lord';
For they shall all know me,
From the least of them unto the greatest;
For I will forgive their iniquity
And I will remember their sin no more'

Jeshua rose from his seat in the courtyard, with a gesture inviting Joseph to remain seated there.

"I will remember their sin no more' – hold that promise in your heart, Joseph. I go beyond Jordan.'

FORTY-ONE

It was now only two days to the Passover itself and Jeshua, with his twelve, was in Bethany; he, with Peter and John, was at the house of Lazarus, while the other ten were with their friends among the villagers. Martha had prepared their simple meal, bread, a little broiled flesh, some fresh herbs and dried fruit, with sparingly, a rough red wine from friends in the south. They were now seated about a fire of brushwood, for the evenings were chill after sundown; they were glad of its few flames and the glow of the embers among the grey ash; the hearth formed a living focus for the six friends.

They had been wholly silent for nearly an hour after the meal, each differently occupied with troubling thoughts. Unusually, it was Mary who broke the silence.

'At the home of Simon the Leper,' she began and then paused, while Lazarus became more alert and with shadowed eyes watched her closely. Jeshua looked up gravely at Mary.

'I did without thought what I had to do and was glad to pour out what was left from the burial of Lazarus.' She drew in her breath sharply at the sheer incongruity of her sentence and she looked with a troubled apology at her brother; with a strange and constrained movement he pressed his hands to his thighs as he sat opposite her at the hearth and his face became closed, as if in a bitter memory. Jeshua remained silent, knowing this to be but an opening sentence.

'You said then to the others who were at Simon's meal and protested at the waste of the ointment, 'She has anointed my body for its burying'; the words have racked my mind every day and night since you spoke them.' This was a tacit question and both Peter and John in their several ways waited tensely for Jeshua's reply.

'We have been much away from Bethany in these last days' – with a smile he drew Martha into the conversation – 'we have perhaps too readily used your home like an inn!' Lazarus replied, 'It is perhaps no more than an inn, Master, an inn which the hostess furnishes with love and her sister with grace.'

There was a deeply affectionate courtesy in the words and Jeshua responded warmly to them; but to Peter and John they struck chill. Mary put her hand gently on Martha's arm and then turned to Jeshua again.

'It's an inn whose door will never be closed to you and yours, but, Master, for how long? You said, 'For my body's burying' but Master, that surely is many many winters away?'

Jeshua replied as though to Lazarus alone. 'For most men and women, death is like an afternoon's sleep and through its gentleness they step out of time. For how long were you asleep, Lazarus?'

'It was no time and yet all time, Master; no time, for I waited for nothing; it was simply 'the Presence' and all

366

peace.' His eyes fell before the deep and compassionate understanding in the eyes of Jeshua, who immediately turned to the two women.

'I said we have not been much with you in these days but have simply returned, tired, to the peace of your meal and your hearth. All day we have been with others in Jerusalem.' There was a brief pause at the word 'others' and a silence.

'Peter here, and John have heard the love and gratitude in the streets and in the Temple and they have heard the murmurs, the questions and the hate. They have also heard my words in reply to the hatred and now you must hear them, my so dearly-loved kin.'

John and Peter were fearful of this promised intimacy of confession of that which had hitherto been spoken in the conflict of crowds. In Jerusalem the searing words had been in a sense sustained and made almost tolerable by the palpable antagonism of those who pressed in on him; Jerusalem was the place which made dire prophecy bearable. The home at Bethany was different. They had held death in their hands like a shroud, and had transcended it. Their peace – and its offshoot, their simple hospitality – had been won in pain but had returned to its former unaffected simplicity. Here resounding prophecy, judgment and the pronouncing of woe, and the declaration of redeeming suffering, were all in too loud a key, intrusive and improper. What tone could Jeshua use here? How draw these gentle people into the inevitable tragedy?

'You have always called me 'Master', you, Mary, have twice called me 'Lord' but I have always returned here to you simply as 'Jeshua.' Peter, John and the others have learned a harder lesson; in the face of my enemies they have heard me say that I am 'the Way' and 'the Light on the Way.' But our people are deeply torn; to teach them and to heal them, even to show them the power of the Son of Man, these are not enough. It has taken many months

and much toil along the paths and highways for the twelve
to learn that these are not enough. You must learn it in
one brief hour.'

Peter and John sat still, their eyes on the burning logs.
Lazarus was alert as he had not been since his coming
from the dark cave; Mary and Martha were still as a
balance is still, precariously poised.

'One man of old time has known the heart of the truth,
Isaiah the prophet. For more than twenty generations we
have heard his words and our people have scarcely
opened their ears. His truth has rung out like a gong
struck and it has been for deaf ears. Who indeed has
believed his report?

'And this – you know his words – is what he said:
  'Behold my servant, whom I uphold,
  Mine elect, in whom my soul delighteth.'
The words in Jeshua's mouth seemed for all their quiet
tones to swell throughout the house and his listeners
heard with awe as though they stood in vast reverberant
spaces.

  'I have put my spirit upon him
  He shall bring forth judgment to the Gentiles.
  A bruised reed shall he not break,
  And the smoking flax shall he not quench;
  He shall bring forth judgment unto truth.'
His voice fell almost to the tones of meditation, as of one
reciting his night prayers.

  'He is despised and rejected of men,
  A man of sorrows and acquainted with grief;
  We hid our faces from him;
  He was despised
  And we esteemed him not.'
In the silence, even the flames had ceased their
whispering.

  'He was wounded for our transgressions,
  He was bruised for our iniquities,

The chastisement of our peace was upon him,
 And with his stripes we are healed.'
'Mary, Martha, Lazarus, I am that Servant. In days, indeed in not many hours, you shall see the prophecy fulfilled and justified.' He looked directly at Lazarus.

'You, Lazarus, you will know part of the truth which will be hidden awhile from the others. But before you all, and to your sorrow and your joy, I shall descend and come forth again and my peace will be upon any of my children who call upon it.'

For Peter and John the words were unequivocal. This was not, as they had perhaps hoped, the form of rhetoric of a prophet expounding another's prophecy. This was the quiet statement of truth at the hearth. For the three friends who heard the words for the first time, it was the reverberation of death without its redemption. And yet as they looked at the calm dignity of Jeshua, as he now stood before them, they hoped they would more fully understand. Jeshua looked at all of them in turn, then said quietly,

'Come; we must take our rest while we can.'

On the following morning all twelve gathered at the home of Lazarus and Jeshua said to them,

'In two days we have Passover, the slaying of the lamb and the deliverance of Israel; we must prepare for our feasting together – for the Son of Man goes now to be crucified. Have no fear; it is to be as I told you.'

Slowly and reluctantly they made ready for the journey to Jerusalem and for all the duties to be carried out there. They had walked half the distance to the city and were climbing the slope to the Mount of Olives when they realised that Judas was not with them.

Timing had become critical in Jerusalem. All the plans of Caiaphas and his associates had gone awry, as if, so they conjectured among themselves, a power they could neither name nor handle was pitted against them. It was, they felt, absurd. Behind them stretched all the ages, the tradition and power of the Law. Now, in their righteous concern for the welfare of the people and with fear that their uneasy concordat with Rome might be broken, all their subtlety was threatened by a mere Galilean, from pitiful Nazareth. One decision was critical. Could Jeshua's arrest and destruction be effected before the feast itself, and effected in such a way that the partisan-ship of the multitudes should not be aroused; or was the game to be deliberately played for delay, until after the feast? So went the debate in the palace of the High Priest, Caiaphas. The arguments on either side were delicately poised, for there were at least two imponderables, the volatile people of Jerusalem and the devious Roman Pro-curator, Pontius Pilate. And wasn't there a third, perhaps even greater imponderable, Jeshua himself? Charlatan, Prophet, Hasid, deluded peasant? What in fact was their adversary?

To this irresolute, seemingly insoluble debate came a wholly unexpected interruption. A well-born and hand-some young man with the accent of southern Judah came into the company, announced by the servant as 'Judas of Kerioth'. Caiaphas greeted him with a puzzled courtesy, while others of the company who had had more day-to-day contact with Jerusalem affairs, seemed to recog-nise in this man a figure they had seen both in the Temple and in the streets of the city.

Judas addressed Caiaphas with courteous reverence.

'Most holy Master, I am Judas of Kerioth and I have been for many months a listener to the words of Jeshua of Nazareth.'

'A follower and one of the inner twelve who form his fellowship,' – it was shaped as an accusation and spoken harshly by one of the Sadducees who had seen the twelve in the Temple. With courtesy directed wholly towards Caiaphas and ignoring the interruption, Judas went on:

'Many of the people regard him, openly proclaim him, as the Messiah. You will need to force him to declare his intentions and before the feast. At the feast you may find only tumult which may gain nothing and lose much.'

'And so?' Caiaphas was reserving judgment of this confident young man.

'I know both his mind and his movements before and during the feast. Would it not be prudent to be led privily to him at nightfall and make all sure?'

Caiaphas paused only the briefest time before closing with this suggestion.

'On the eve of the feast we shall meet at the Beautiful Gate. From there, I shall lead you in all security to the place of his retreat. Be ready with what force you need.'

'Judas, young man, we are indebted to you and will meet you as you suggest.' He sought his pouch within the skirt of his robe and counted out a quantity of silver.

'Your hand, Judas of Kerioth. Receive the price of this slave, this servant whom you have served.'

Mechanically Judas put out his right hand and the small stream of silver poured into it. With a kind of fastidious contempt – of them or of himself? – Judas closed his hand on the silver. He put it quickly into his purse and as he backed away from the high seat of Caiaphas, he wiped his right hand in the cloth of his tunic. He had seen his father pay more for a menial at the home farm, more indeed for having drawn blood in a merited thrashing of a slave. With no further word spoken and followed by the eyes of a silently questioning council, he walked alone to the outer court of the palace and through its entrance into the city.

FORTY-TWO

'There are now just the last preparations. Three of you, go ahead of us and as you go into the city you will see a man carrying a water-pot on his shoulder; he will be lingering there by the well, but as he makes his way within the city, follow him until he reaches his house. When he turns to see if you have followed, say to him, 'The Master asks where we may find the guest-chamber where he may eat the Passover with us, his disciples' and he will show you the room.'

Peter and Andrew went quickly on to Jerusalem, while the other disciples took their leisurely time, in twos and threes, leaving Jeshua alone in Bethany.

Matthew had traversed alone about half the distance to the city, his mind in considerable turmoil. For the first time since joining Jeshua, he felt rootless and without a clear idea of his future. His austere and practical mind, having accepted Jeshua's warnings of the next days and weeks, saw more clearly than most of the twelve what the consequences of Jeshua's death would be. He had been to them first a magnetic teacher and worker of wonders; then a revelation of the truth of their lives and the richness hidden within each soul; Matthew had heard the solemnity behind the promise made to so many healed men and women – 'hath made thee whole' – and he had begun to know what that wholeness meant. In his case, it had meant at first renunciation, the abandonment of wealth and all the comfort it had brought; but soon he knew the change within him as his mind became attuned to the rhythms of the Law and the truths sunk in the ancient prophecies; and the voice of Jeshua, which brought these words to life, was the voice also that opened his ears to the beauty of sound, his eyes to the glory of sun and stars, of the desert austerity which, at a shower of rain, burst into a beauty he had never before conceived. Yes, Matthew acknowledged the 'wholeness' but would it survive the absence of Jeshua? If only there were more time; if only the withdrawal were more gradual.

He had fallen further behind the others and was rounding a gap between tall and fractured rocks when he saw Judas approaching his road by a side path, which surely came *from* Jerusalem. Yet Judas, with easy friendship, fell into step with Matthew, affectionately, for a moment, pressing his upper arm. They walked on silently for a while, Matthew still uneasily wondering not only at Judas's unexpected appearance from a strange direction but troubled also by the contrast between his hectic eyes and heightened colour and the dark contraction of his brows. What could now be causing conflict in this strange and lonely man who had found in him the only friendly confidant among the twelve?

'This will be a testing time, but what matter?' The words were scarcely addressed to Matthew, who kept silence.

'He is daring all on this move to the city but what is really his aim – what is really his aim, Matthew?'

Matthew still kept silence, for the debate was clearly Judas's and not his.

'Will he really at this time declare himself? Will he at last redeem Israel? This issue's clear enough; if he be the Son of Man, the Christ, then nothing can withstand the majesty of his claim and action; whatever force is there against him, we know, Matthew, surely we know – the legions of angels are there to command – and if not, then, Matthew, we are of all men most desolate!'

The former brooding look had now been replaced with a face of such total desolation that Matthew feared to look into his eyes.

Peter waited at the gate of the city and led the scattered disciples along the city streets to the house of Jeshua's friend. There in the upper guest-chamber, with its little view of the huddled houses about them and a glimpse of the Temple above them, they made their preparations. There were stools and couches to be set about the table, the lamb to be dressed and given to the care of the women in the house, to make ready, with theirs, for the ceremonial meal. There were the four dishes of the unleavened bread, the flasks of wine, the goblets for the drinking and the prayers and, a reminder to them of the tone and flavour which lay beneath the solemnity of the feast, the three bowls of bitter herbs. At low stools at the entrance to the room was a large bowl and a tall earthenware jar of water at its side, and neatly folded on another stool, towels for the ceremonial cleansing before the meal began.

Peter stood at one end of the room, facing John at the other. Gravely their eyes travelled around the preparations, checking in their minds, from long years of the ceremonial, each item that would be needed for its accomplishing. They looked at each other and Peter said, in a heavy tone that surprised even John, 'All is now ready.'

Jeshua reached the western slope of the Mount of Olives in the early afternoon, the yearning over Jerusalem tearing him as it always did. He turned for a few minutes into the relative shade of Gethsemane and remained very still beneath the gnarled branches of an old olive tree, scarcely removing his eyes from the city across the valley. He gathered himself as though for a final decision and walked swiftly to the city gate and went immediately to the outer court of the Temple. The memories crowded in, of disputation from his maturing childhood, through to the innumerable people who had hung on his words in this place and for whom Torah became a living flame in the power of his words.

The palace of the High Priest had an atmosphere of swift preparation. The Passover was a high moment in the year and Caiaphas took his duties seriously. His chief advisers moved about gravely, preparing with especial care the ceremonial vessels and vestures.

Beneath this orderly and grave memory of redemption out of the hands of Egypt, there lay darker and more immediate concerns. The nation was in peril. Its safety lay heavy on the shoulders of Caiaphas and time pressed.

With his most senior adviser he spoke alone and in tones scarcely above a whisper.

'Time drags at us, Samuel. We cannot move before dark and all events must meet together: the Temple guards assembled swiftly and in secret, the route to the city, if the Nazarene is taken outside the walls, secured and with no rabble aroused; the Council assembled here but with no hint of its purpose and – Samuel, the most delicate matter of all! – the Lord Pilate secured in our favour. That is to be your task. You have entry, you have the wisdom and the tact.'

There followed the subtle weighing of arguments that would sway, flatter and if necessary delicately threaten the Procurator, to secure his assent to the swift condemnation and execution of the Nazarene. The younger mind of Samuel pursued the old wisdom of Caiaphas, schooled in a bitter diplomacy for more than a decade of coping with Roman power. In mid-afternoon Samuel was fully briefed for his assignment and left for the Procurator's residence.

'Is there any posting in the imperial service more trying than this appalling Jerusalem? Claudia Procula' – he savoured the name as he looked across at his troubled wife – 'Claudia, this would be intolerable, even Caesarea, where there is at least air to breath, would be unbearable without you! For more than three years now I have been bent, dried out, burnt by these superstitious festivals which bring us to this city. Your patience is beyond price, Claudia.'

Claudia understood the impatience which racked her fastidious, quick-tempered and ambitious young husband. She, the blood of the Imperial house giving her authority, the instinctive wisdom of Rome with its subject peoples, tried with her calm to still the turbulence of her rash husband.

'And now this, this Galilean!'

Claudia concealed her alert interest, for she had heard much both from her own women and the Herodian court of this extraordinary man.

'The wily Samuel, the High Priest's diplomat' – there was a world of Roman contempt for the very idea – 'has been with me within the hour. This Jeshua of Nazareth, heir to a long line of prophetic trouble-makers, will be taken tonight, questioned, charged and in the morning brought to me for condemnation. It seems they have not seen enough crucifixions!'

Claudia knew that behind the sardonic bitterness, Pilate was troubled. For all his rash contempt for Jewry there still remained his intuitive Roman concern for the forces of Law and – more potent than that – the generations had instilled in him the knowledge that without Roman justice its imperial power was nothing.

'The effrontery of it! They use me as a mere seal on documents they dare not sign! They make of me, the Procurator, an assistant executioner!'

Claudia foresaw the seething anger which might well issue in an action as crude as any he had been guilty of in the past.

'Come, you lack sleep in this sultry time.'

In the garden of his house at the northern border of Jerusalem, Joseph walked the paths among the herbs and craved for Arimathea. Stooping, he plucked a sprig of mint and crushed its leaves between his fingers and brushed his forehead with the sap. Why was the Council summoned and why the Sanhedrin in the morning? It was unseemly when they should all have been gathering themselves for the glory of the Passover. Couldn't they see, these busy people, that in stillness alone could the ages lay their blessing on the soul?

Deeply troubled, he descended the garden slope to its rocky confines below him. To still his mind, he repeated the prayer:

> 'Blessed art thou, O Lord our God,
> King of the universe,
> Who hast kept us in life
> And hast preserved us,
> And enabled us to reach this season.'

The twelve had assembled in their upper room, hands had been laved at their entrance and all now looked to him who in such gravity presided at the feast. At first there had been some unobtrusive movements in an attempt by some of them to secure more honourable places at the low table, on the divan and the stools on which they were to be seated. Jeshua noticed their wishes and, while they were still standing, said to them,

'The Gentile rulers wield authority and their ministers are called benefactors, even as they lord it over them! But not so among you. Let the greatest among you be as the younger, and each be servant of all. For I have prepared for you a Kingdom and there you will eat and drink at my table and sit on the judges' thrones, judging the twelve tribes of Israel. Now, we worship together.'

377

'O Lord, open thou our lips,
And our mouths shall declare thy praise.

Blessed art thou, O Lord our God,
God of our fathers,
God of Abraham, God of Isaac, God of Jacob,
The great, mighty and revered God,
The most high God
Who bestowest loving-kindness
And possessest all things
Who rememberest the pious deeds of the patriarchs
And in love wilt bring a redeemer
To their children's children
For thy name's sake.

Thou hast given us in love
O Lord our God,
Appointed times for gladness,
Festivals and seasons for joy.
The Feast of Unleavened Bread,
The season of our Freedom.

The wine was drunk, the unleavened bread eaten with the bitter herbs and there was a pause in the order of the meal. Jeshua rose and went to the water-jar and the bowl at the entrance to the room and, sitting on a stool, girded his waist and thighs with a towel and poured water into the bowl. He beckoned to the youngest among them and in silence washed his feet and placing each foot in turn on the towel, wiped them dry. When it became Peter's turn he drew back and said,

'You shall never wash my feet, Lord!'

'If I do not wash you, you have no part in me.'

'Master, not my feet only, but also my hands and my head!'

'He whose feet are washed is clean every whit.'

When he had finished, he returned to his place at the

feast and said, 'Do you understand this ceremony? You call me 'Rabbi' and 'Lord' and you do well – I am your Lord. If then I, your Lord and Master, have washed your feet, so ought you to do for one another.

'Truly, I say to you, the servant is not greater than his lord, nor he that is sent greater than he who sent him; if you understand these things you are indeed happy if you follow them.

'Truly, he who receives my friends receives me; and he who receives me receives Him who sent me.'

While they murmured among themselves, each interpreting Jeshua's words in his own way, Jeshua looked about him and said sombrely,

'One of you will betray me.'

The simple, unemphatic statement carried truth but directed at whom? In deep humiliation, each of them asked,

'Is it I, Lord, is it I?'

Jeshua looked about him, knowing their weaknesses and the point at which the will of each might break and he answered,

'He dips in the dish with me, even he, my own familiar friend.'

It was no answer to their heart-searchings but Jeshua then turned to Judas, who was indeed in a place of honour at his side and gently and with no emphasis which raised the command above the conduct of their daily affairs, said,

'What you have to do, do quickly!'

and Judas went out into the night.

Jeshua again gathered their attention and said to them, 'Now is the Son of Man glorified and God glorified in him. My little ones, I am with you for a little while. Then you will seek me but where I go you cannot come. But I give you a new commandment, that you love one another as I have loved you.'

Peter said impulsively, 'Lord, where are you going?' Jeshua replied, 'Where I go, you cannot follow now but you shall indeed follow me.' Peter replied,

'Lord, surely I may follow you – I would lay down my life for you!'

'Indeed, Peter, will you lay down your life for me? Truly, Peter, I tell you the truth, the cock will not crow this night before you have denied me three times.'

Peter had known such a rebuff only once before in the words of Jeshua. Dumbly he looked from one friend to another but there could be no comfort, for each was absorbed in his own fear. Into this chill came the unexpected words of Jeshua. Taking one of the loaves of unleavened bread, he looked up to heaven and said,

'Blessed art thou, O Lord our God,

King of the universe,

Who bringest forth bread from the earth.'

He broke the bread, piece by piece, giving a fragment to each and commanded them,

'Take and eat; this is my Body.'

Each of them took the morsel of bread and ate it. Jeshua poured wine into the cup, raised his eyes to heaven and said the thanksgiving:

'Blessed are thou, O Lord our God,

King of the universe,

Who createst the fruit of the vine.'

He raised the cup and drank from it, and then, holding it before them, commanded,

'Take and drink; this is my Blood

Of the new Covenant

Which is shed for many.'

They each received the cup at his hands and drank, and when it had been laid down, he said to them,

'I say to you, I will drink no more of the fruit of the vine until I drink it new in the Kingdom of God.'

The silence was profound as the eleven tried to bring these words 'my Body', 'my Blood', into relation with all they had heard. In every sense this was the darkest, most incomprehensible moment in all their knowledge of Jeshua, and their fellowship with him. Over all their meditation hung now the certainty of his death, his imminent death; this fact they could no longer evade, for the past weeks had led inevitably to the clear statements of the last few days. There was the shadow over these words of Egypt and the sacrifice, the lamb as victim; and yet for all their sombre thought, as Jeshua stood among them, there was no shadow or trace of the victim in his bearing. They were aware as never before of overpowering authority, of a security in his words and his poise before them, that if sacrifice there was, he was more priest than victim.

Yet they were aware of darkness looming. This was for none of them the simple grief at the possible departure of a friend; this was more than deprivation. To all of them came the sense of mighty issues and in particular to John in his especially loving relation with his Master; and to Peter with his growing and yet constantly rejected sense of leadership. And through the darkness – even enhanced by it, like the pure fire of a jewel in a dark setting – there glowed the certainty that another mighty issue had been revealed to them in the very simplicity of a domestic command, 'Eat', 'Drink.' They failed, all of them, to fathom its truth but such was the authority of the command that they were assured that understanding would come.

Jeshua knew the turmoil at the heart of their silence and responded to it with all the compassion to which they were accustomed.

'Let not your hearts be troubled. You believe in God – believe also in me. In my Father's house there are many places to abide; if it were not so, I would have told you. I go now to prepare a place for you, for all of you. As I go, so I

381

will come again and shall receive you to myself, that you may be with me always.

'Where I go you know and the way you know.'

Thomas, the most ready to voice the bewilderment of them all, said,

'Lord we do not know where you are going, so how can we know the way?'

Jeshua replied,

'I am the Way, the Truth and the Life. No one comes to the Father but by me; if you have truly known me, you have known the Father and from this time onward you know Him and have seen Him.' Philip besought him,

'Let us have one glimpse of the Father and it will truly suffice.'

'Philip, have I been so long with you and still you have not known me? He who has seen me has seen the Father; why then your request now that I should show you the Father? I am in the Father and the Father in me. The *words* I speak are the *actions* of my Father.

'Whatsoever you ask in my name, I will do, that the Father may be glorified in the Son.'

It seemed to them all at that moment that his authority was not confronting them as something outside and beyond themselves. He stood before them, radiant, and in those moments they were filled, engulfed in the power of his presence. They were not yet in a state to assent to it but they knew its strength.

Answering the doubts and the fears that still hovered, Jeshua went on:

'If you love me, keep my commandments, and I will pray the Father to send you a Comforter, even the Spirit of Truth. He will be with you always. In a little while the world will see me no more, but you see me. Because I live, you shall live also. There will come a time when you will surely know that I am in my Father, and you in me, and I in you.

'The Comforter, the Spirit of my Father, will lead you into the truth of all that I have said to you.

'Peace I leave with you, my peace I give to you. I give not as the world gives. Let your hearts be neither troubled nor afraid. If you loved me, you would rejoice that I go to my Father, for my Father is greater than I. Let us arise and go from this place.'

They stood and sang together,

O come let us sing unto the Lord,
Let us heartily rejoice in the rock of our salvation.
Let us come before his presence with thanksgiving
And make a joyful noise unto him with psalms.
O come let us worship and bow down,
Let us kneel before the Lord our Maker,
For he is our God,
We are the people of his pasture
And the sheep of his hand.

FORTY-THREE

They came down from the upper room and in the dark stillness of the almost deserted streets, made their way past the portals of the Temple. They quickly passed out of the city gate and began the ascent to the Mount of Olives. At the entrance to the Garden of Gethsemane, Jeshua paused and gathered the eleven about him.

'I have now little more to tell you. You are already like the branches of a vine tree, a living part of my life. Every branch, cleansed and pruned, which remains part of me, will bear much fruit and in my love for you and yours for me, my Father is glorified.

'All the words I have spoken to you were to fulfil your joy. This is my last commandment to you, that you love one another as I have loved you.

'In life in this world you will know hatred, as I have known it – but I have promised you the Comforter and he will lead you, through persecution into truth. They will reject you in the synagogues and to kill you will seem to them the service of God. But then will come to you the Spirit of God and he will give to you the fullness of knowledge: of sin because they do not believe in me, of righteousness because I go to my Father, and of judgment, because the Prince of this world is finally judged.

'I have indeed many things to say and to reveal to you but you cannot bear them yet. But when He comes, the Spirit of Truth, he will fulfil my teaching and lead you into all truth.

'A little while you see me; yet a little while and you will not see me, and then you will truly see me, for I go to my Father. You will sorrow like a woman in travail at your loss of my presence; but then your joy also will be like hers as she brings forth – for you will be with me always.'

Gethsemane was very still in the moonlight and the eleven and Jeshua looked out in this quiet light towards Jerusalem.

'These things I have said to you because you have believed that I come from God. But you must now hear my words the more closely, for the hour is approaching – yes, even now it is upon us – when you shall all be scattered, each one of you alone and abandoning me. But I shall not be alone, for my Father is with me.

'My warning and my blessing – you need them both. In the world you will suffer tribulation but lift up your hearts – I have overcome the world.'

Jeshua turned from them and moved into the shadows of the Garden. There, as they stood in an uncertain knot at the entrance, he moved away from them, raised his hands and his eyes and prayed:

'Father, the hour is come, glorify thy Son that thy Son may glorify Thee.

For my own I pray, that they may have the eternal life

which is to know Thee and Thy Son. I have given them the Word. The world has hated them because they are not of the world. I do not pray that Thou shouldest take them out of the world but to keep them from evil.

'For them and for all who will believe because of their word, I pray that they all may be one; as Thou, Father, art in me and I in Thee, that they may be one in us; that the world may know that Thou hast sent me, and hast loved them, as thou hast loved me.'

Turning to the eleven, Jeshua told them to rest a while as he wished to go apart to pray. He beckoned to him Peter, James and John and went with them into a darkly secluded part of Gethsemane. There was silence between them as Jeshua appeared to them more and more torn in distress. At length, as the agony was more than they could sustain, he said,

'My soul is deep in sorrow, even to my death. Wait here and watch with me a while.'

He went a little apart and fell like a suppliant before a throne.

'Father, the evil, the wanton sin, it is about me like a vapour, a stench of corruption!' The words were but a part of the agony as his body was wrenched by the reality of evil, every nerve and fibre and the whole of his mind responding to its loathed presence. In the struggle, the sweat poured from him, falling like blood about him. Then came silence and the struggle ceased as he turned to the three; but they were asleep. He touched Peter's arm and his stirring awakened the brothers.

'One hour only, I ask that you watch but one brief hour.'

He returned to his place of prayer but the struggle had shifted.

'Father, must the world always corrupt itself? Your word, and the power of your servants, are they the way of peace?'

385

Like Jacob at the brook, the struggle was now with the angel, the longing that purity might conquer. The wrestling was greater than with the evil itself and again the agony overwhelmed him like a torrent.

Once more he turned to his three friends and again found them sleeping. This time he left them to their rest and returned to his lonely prayer. The conflict was now at its climax. His prophetic mind saw clearly the inevitable events before him; every fibre in his being shrank from the torturing certainty, and the prayer was like the agony of a child.

'Abba, if it be possible, let this cup pass from me.' The struggle had lost its frenzy and, as the passion spent itself, he prayed again.

'Father, if this cup may not pass away unless I drink it, Thy will be done.'

The agony was stilled and after a long silence, Jeshua again turned to the three and again found them sleeping.

'Sleep on, now, and take your rest' and he stood in a gap between the olive trees, giving him a view of the rough path which approached the Garden. His watch was broken by a confused pattern of torches and shadows at the gate of Jerusalem. He returned to the three, gathered them together with the others, and quietly prepared them.

'Rise! the hour is now at hand and the Son of Man is betrayed into the hand of sinners.'

It was a strangely assorted crowd that burst through the entrance to the Garden of Gethsemane: torch bearers at front and rear, a detachment of the Temple Guard, and huddled behind them, an ill-clad knot of those who must act as 'witnesses'. Alone, behind the first torches, strode Judas, his face impassive. He walked swiftly forward, placed his hands on Jeshua's shoulders and kissed his cheek, saying, 'Greetings, Master!' Jeshua held him by the forearm and replied,

'Judas, my friend, why have you come?' but Judas had turned and was mingled with the witnesses. Jeshua moved forward, standing isolated between the eleven behind him and the Guard which faced him. Jeshua spoke in a tone that all could hear,

'Whom do you seek?'

The Guard replied,

'The Nazarene!' Jeshua replied

'I am he.'

At the words 'I am', it seemed to the eleven as though a blow had struck each one of the guards who all stumbled and fell backward. When they had resumed their arms, he asked them again,

'Whom do you seek?' Defiantly they again replied, 'The Nazarene!' Jeshua replied,

'I have told you that I am he; if you seek me, let these, my friends, go their way. I would have none of them harmed.'

Peter had watched with despair the hopelessness in which Jeshua appeared to stand before the crowd. From its concealment in the folds of his cloak he drew a short stabbing sword and clumsily swept at the head of one of the attendants, cutting his ear. Jeshua turned to Peter.

'Put up your sword; all they that take the sword will perish by the sword. Do you think that I could not, even now, pray for my Father's legions of angels? But in this way only will the prophecies be fulfilled' and he stretched out his hand and healed the ear of the servant, whose name was Malchus.

Jeshua turned again to the Guard and in tones which his followers had heard as he taught and reasoned in the Temple, asked them,

'Have you come now, as if you were arresting a thief, with swords and staves to take me? Why? I sat daily among you, teaching openly in the Temple, and you stretched out no hands against me then. But this is your hour and the hour of the powers of darkness.'

Then the officer of the guard commanded that his wrists be bound to lead him away for trial. They looked about, seeking Jeshua's followers, but they were not to be seen.

The residence of Annas was greatly disturbed. The servants hurriedly made ready for the hastily-called tribunal and their curiosity had been aroused by rumours that the person to be questioned was Jeshua of Nazareth. It was a name of which they had heard much in recent days and one or two of them had taken brief opportunities to listen to him in the Temple. They all had a profound respect for the power and shrewdness of their master – they regarded Annas as the superior of Caiaphas, his successor as High Priest – but they had also experienced the authority and the brilliance in controversy of this strange man from Galilee. It would be a notable contest, of which, if they were astute, they might catch echoes.

It was very late when the great doors opened and the guards brought in the calm prisoner. They saw him briefly as he was taken to the inner chamber where Annas and his retinue waited to question him.

Annas still bore the unmistakable marks of high office and responsibility. A heavy man, he sat heavily, his bulk filling his chair like a throne, his forearms relaxed across its arms. He looked at the prisoner before him. Jeshua stood upright, his tall figure enhanced by the simplicity of the white robe falling to his ankles. Though his hands were bound at the wrists, his dignity was wholly unimpaired and Annas sourly reflected, 'This fellow is worth any three of our Council!'

From Jeshua there was no protest, no word of any kind as he waited for Annas to speak. He had the calm nobility of bearing of one who had looked at death and was waiting to cross its threshold and his eyes told Annas that this time, for Jeshua, was but an interim, a waiting.

'You know the charge?'

'There is none, Lord Annas.'

'Have you anything to say to me before your trial?'

'Nothing, Lord Annas.'

Annas paused before deciding on any action. This was his first contact with Jeshua and, accustomed as he was to quiet authority, he was the more disconcerted by the calm courtesy in Jeshua's words and stance. There was no more to say and Annas gave command that he be taken before the court of Caiaphas, his son-in-law and successor.

Here were all the trappings of rule and dignity; the outer door led into a large courtyard at the far end of which was a brazier with a substantial fire, for the nights were cold. There was far greater expectation here than in the house of Annas, for these servants and officials constituted a court and there could be none of the frustrated expectations of Annas's servants. In the outer courtyard, then, was all the bustling preparation to receive the Council, the guards and their prisoner. And there were refreshments to prepare for the dignitaries, if the hearing were prolonged.

To the outer gate with its constant trafficking came two weary men, one with the assurance of old acquaintance in this place, the other with the furtive stance of a fugitive, but a fugitive determined to face the worst. The first of them called to one within the courtyard whom he knew, and asked that he and his friend should enter and await events. They were allowed to the far end of the courtyard, where Peter held out his hands for the warmth of the fire. He spoke little but his accent, carried on his resonant voice, declared him a Galilean. The woman at the gate crossed to him and said, 'You were one of the Nazarene's followers.' Peter roughly answered, 'I was not.'

The gates were now opened with ceremony and into the courtyard came the guard, with Jeshua in their midst, the last of the Council of Caiaphas and one or two Sadducees from the house of Annas. All went into the main hall of the palace, where Caiaphas waited for the assembly.

Here was a personality of wholly different quality, a shrewd statesman capable of tacking to any wind of policy, Roman or Sadducean but in himself almost wholly dependent on the status of his office, which in integrity he barely matched.

His chief officer called the witnesses and there followed a confusion of testimony, that this fellow taught blasphemous doctrine, that he subverted the people, that he used demonic powers; through it all there was no measure of agreement.

Jeshua stood impassive, his calm undisturbed but in the silence after the bogus testimonies, his eyes met those of Caiaphas. There was no need for words. Each knew that the trial was over; each knew the clear, the unambiguous clemency of their Law, that all guilt or innocence turned on the unqualified agreement of two or more witnesses – and none was forthcoming here. The very stillness of Jeshua's gaze was itself a challenging question, 'Will you release your prisoner as guiltless?' Nor was Jeshua's gaze the only one troubled in that close-knit assembly. All present had rabbinic discipline, the integrity fine-honed through ages of mediating Torah. They waited in profound unease the outcome of this silent questioning.

Caiaphas was the first to break the silence. 'I have two things to ask you: who and of what quality are your disciples? and what is the doctrine that you teach them?'

'I have throughout spoken openly to all the world. I have taught in synagogues, here and in Galilee, and in the court of the Temple itself. There has been nothing secret in my words or actions. Why then do you ask me? Ask them who heard me, for indeed they know what I taught them.'

One of the officers standing by gave Jeshua the insulting blow with the open palm, saying, 'Do you answer the High Priest thus?' Jeshua replied to him,

'If I have spoken evil, then declare that evil; but if I have spoken truth, why did you strike me?'

Again there was the silence of impasse but this time it was broken from outside; through the door of the council chamber burst two witnesses who blurted out their testimony that Jeshua had declared that 'he would destroy the Temple of God and in three days raise it up again' but closer questioning again revealed inconsistency. One of them was repeating hearsay and pressed by one of the rabbis could not say 'of his own knowledge' whether 'the temple' he spoke of was Herod's Temple in their city or that 'temple of the soul', the cherished body of every man.

Again the duel was a silent one, Caiaphas aware that the night and his time for decisive action were wasting away, Jeshua conscious that upon himself alone his fate depended. Caiaphas had only one weapon, the sacred oath, with which to trap the prisoner, and this he now administered.

'I adjure you, by the living God; tell us whether or not you are the Christ, the Son of the Blessed.'

All present, including Jeshua, knew that there was no evading this question and the council marvelled at the calm with which he gathered all eyes to him and held silence before his measured answer. He began with the courteously oblique answer,

'Thou hast said'

and as all held their breath at his quiet assurance he spoke with the authority that had held men at the Temple,

'I am. And hereafter you shall see the Son of Man sitting on the right hand of the power of God and coming in the clouds of heaven.'

The High Priest stood and tore the hem of his garment. 'What need we any further witnesses? You have heard his blasphemy; what judgment to you pronounce?'

The voices varied in their assurance. Some had been moved by the prisoner's closing words, spoken with an authority they could never summon; others knew that momentous issues turned on this conflict, which they had explored with much self-searching. Then the answer came,

'Death!'

The stirring in the council chamber caused more movement in the outer courtyard and another of the servants crossed to the fire and said to Peter,

'You are also one of them.' and Peter answered violently, 'Man! I am not.'

One or two of the rabbis began to leave the inner chamber and the group of men near the fire again said firmly, 'Really, this fellow is one of that man's followers, his accent gives him away as a Galilean.'

With a rising hysteria, Peter began to blaspheme and swear and then burst out,

'I have no knowledge of this man at all!'

As he spoke, the door of the council chamber was thrown wide open and Jeshua walked out, his guards remaining at a distance, leaving him solitary. He paused on the threshold and looked at Peter and as his eyes held those of his friend, there came the single piercing note of cockcrow. There was a startled silence and pause in everyone's activity, for it was still many hours to dawn.

But there was no repetition and Jeshua moved across the courtyard with the guard and some of the council.

Peter left the courtyard, weeping bitterly.

At the first light of dawn they took Jeshua to the Procurator's residence and he met them in the outer court, for they could not enter this Gentile residence, having no time before the feast to cleanse themselves of defilement. Pilate gave a sign that Jeshua be brought alone and without guard into his private quarters. There the exchange was brief.

'You are the Jeshua of whom they speak?'

'I am.'

Pilate, for all his impetuous nature, was a Roman patrician and married into the imperial house. He recognised gravity when he encountered it and the complete absence of pleading, much less of servility in this man drew his wondering admiration. For the first time, at this unique encounter, he understood the troubled silence of Claudia Procula and the murmurings he heard among his court officers and their wives. They faced each other as equals in dignified authority.

Pilate left him standing at his hearth and went out to the courtyard.

'What accusation do you bring against this man?'

It was an ominous question to the officials of the Sanhedrin. Was the Procurator about to re-open a trial they regarded as concluded, requiring only a formal Roman endorsement? With threatening effrontery, they answered,

'If he were not a malefactor we would not have brought him before you for sentence.'

Pilate was alert enough to place another snare in their way.

'You must take him and judge him according to your law.'

This drew from them the pre-judgment for which he had sought;

'It is not lawful for us to put any man to death.'

Impassively, Pilate waited for them to elaborate their charge and blunderingly they blurted out their accusations,

'We found him perverting the nation – He forbade giving tribute to Caesar – he declares himself the Christ, a King!'

Pilate left them and returned to Jeshua.

'Tell me; are you the King of the Jews?' Again the courteously oblique answer,

'Thou sayest it. And, Lord Procurator, will you then answer me? This title you give me – did you pronounce it of your own will or did others tell it of me?' Pilate was affronted but something in Jeshua's bearing suppressed his anger and he contented himself with a sardonic reply,

'Am I a Jew? Your own nation and the chief priests have delivered you to me; what have you done to deserve these charges?'

'My Kingdom is not of this world. If it were, then my servants would fight, that I should not be delivered to my enemies. But my Kingdom is from elsewhere.'

'Are you then a King?'

'You say that I am a King. Indeed, to this end was I born and for this cause I came into the world, that I should bear witness to the truth. Everyone who has the truth, hears my voice.'

Pilate, a pragmatic politician was not accustomed to dealing in abstractions and again came the dismissive tone,

'What is truth?'

There was no common blood, tradition or word that could bridge the chasm this question opened between them. Jeshua waited courteously for any speech Pilate might have with him but after uneasy silence, Pilate gestured impatiently and strode out again to the waiting elders.

'I find no fault in him.'

The hysteria increased as they cast about for accusations that would convince this sceptical Roman.

'He stirs up the people throughout your whole territory beginning in Galilee and extending to Jerusalem.'

This gave Pilate yet another devious move. If Jeshua were a Galilean then he was judicially under the rule of Herod and to Herod he promptly sent him.

FORTY-FOUR

By full dawn, word of the arrest and the devious charges before Caiaphas, Pilate and Herod, had passed through the city and there was already rumour abroad that the dignified bearing of the accused had affected all his accusers, some to deeper anger, others to a reluctant admiration.

One now hurried to the Temple, crossed the outer courtyard and burst into the presence of Caiaphas and some of the elders; he held out his hand and with disgust looked at the silver lying in it, a slave's ransom.

'I have sinned; I have betrayed innocent blood.'

'What is that to us? The consequences are yours.' He flung the pieces of silver across the pavement of the Temple and made his way blindly through the city. In a desolate field, beyond the southern precincts, he hanged himself. There, in the field bought with the price of blood, in after-years they buried aliens and strangers.

The court of Herod Antipas stood apart from the residences of the High Priest and the Procurator. Antipas himself, the second son of Herod 'the Great' was the characteristic jaded and corrupt son of a ruthless father. Herod's long rule had culminated in the majestic extravagance of the Temple. His eldest son, Archelaus, succeeded to the 'kingship' of Judaea until his sordid incompetence forced Rome to replace him with a Procurator; Herod Antipas inherited Galilee and adjacent portions of land, a lesser if turbulent charge which he ruled with a flippant arrogance. His father's corruption burgeoned in him, with none of his father's force in statecraft. He had a residence in Jerusalem which he visited when he was not in his administrative centre of Caesarea.

Self-indulgent corruption would have destroyed his rule as quickly as that of his brother, Archelaus, had he not administrative officers of sufficient competence. Chief of these was the high steward, Chuza, a wealthy man whose gravity appealed to his Roman fellows in administration. His pre-eminence in Herod's court stilled the tattling tongues in the potential scandal that his wife, Joanna, was so impressed by 'the Galilean' that she and her friend Mary of the neighbouring town of Magdala, were chief among the women who ministered to Jeshua and the twelve in their Galilean wanderings. Chuza was perplexed by her loyalty to this disquieting preacher and wonder-worker and spoke of it in a troubled way to his few friendly colleagues.

They were now in Jerusalem for the feast, Antipas, Chuza and Joanna. The sober considerations of the steward and his wife, their admiration for the nobility which Jeshua showed in all circumstances, led to more general talk in the court, talk which soured down into dismissive jesting when it reached the ears of Herod Antipas. But to Antipas and his sycophants, Jeshua was at least more interesting than a troupe of acrobats or of performing animals; his presence at the Court would be a relief from the dismal seriousness of the Jewish festival; he might even perform a wonder for the titillation of jaded appetites.

It was therefore a most fortunate matter that it suited Pilate's interests, in the early morning of Passover Day, to transfer Jeshua, as a Galilean, to the formal jurisdiction of Herod Antipas, who could treat the case with appropriate jest or gravity, as it demanded. To Joanna it was a matter of most tragic foreboding.

For the fourth time in less than twelve hours, Jeshua was brought into the presence of a courtly authority. This time the setting was dramatically different from those at the homes of Annas, Caiaphas and Pilate. Here Herod Antipas was immediately surrounded by his courtiers, corrupt jesters and grave officials, who waited in their several ways for a lead from Antipas. Behind the courtiers stood a group of the officials' wives, Joanna the centre of concern and interest. Half encircling this whole company were a detachment of Herod's soldiery, the token force which Rome permitted as the personal bodyguard of Galilee's tetrarch.

Facing Herod's court was a small but voluble group of priests and their servants who held Jeshua's bonds and presented him, with near-hysteria before Herod. For time was slipping away; they now had less than ten hours to complete the trial and execution before the sacred hours of Passover itself. Their accusations were therefore voluble and well-nigh incoherent.

Herod, with malicious laughter, waved them back, leaving Jeshua isolated in his own dignity, mid-way between the two forces. Jeshua's face held the same courteous waiting upon events which had been his since the agony of Gethsemane had been stilled; but as he caught the eyes of Joanna, painfully silent as she suffered in his humiliation, there was a momentary lightening of his grave dignity and a compassion in his eyes which she had so frequently seen when he spoke with lepers and outcasts. It was a look which lasted over the years as her pride and certainty grew.

Herod silenced the accusations and he proposed to enjoy the next hour, playing a malicious parody of a trial.

'Galilean – my subject! We have heard much of your powerful words – another prophet, we are told! – and of the wonders you perform' – there was a cruel satire in the half-glance he threw at Chuza over his right shoulder – 'and we would have you perform one of your wonders, for our pleasure.'

There was no change in the quiet courteousy of Jeshua's stance, no response in the steady look he gave to Antipas.

'Cures will be difficult here; we have no lepers, cripples or the deaf or blind here' – there was pleased laughter from the courtiers – 'they would not do at court.'

Jeshua looked at the assembled courtiers, saw with pity the corruption that disfigured them and some of the eyes fell before his gaze.

'But at least we can give you a rod; you, like Moses before you, may perform at least a wonder or two?'

Herod still received no response and with a sudden blazing change from jest to anger, he shouted at Jeshua,

'King! and King of the Jews! King of *all* Jews, my superior and Lord over the Procurator Pontius Pilate himself! This is your claim? From carpenter's bench to the Throne of Moses is indeed a leap! Will you now give me your commands, my Lord King?'

His fury was almost beyond control and increased by the complete stillness of the white-robed figure before him. Never before had his sadistic rages failed to quell any victim brought before him. But this figure was patrician, as none of his courtiers were, as very rarely he had met in the high-born Romans with whom he hoped for fellowship. This prisoner was in all things invulnerable.

'King of the Jews! most unsuitably arrayed! Untie his wrists, hold the thong about his left arm, give him a sceptre and robe him!'

An officer stepped forward from the soldiery, threw a ceremonial cloak of deep purple about Jeshua's shoulders and thrust a simple rod into his right hand. The soldiers and the sycophants among the courtiers, laughed and jeered and some pretended obeisances before the robed 'king.' Joanna stepped forward to Chuza's side, taking his arm; for her the satire fell away and the robe and the sceptre became a fitting truth.

By the time the little company reached again the outer courtyard of Pilate's palace, Jeshua's captors realised that the judicial farce was reaching no tangible conclusion. Pilate, with increasing impatience, was forced once more to meet their delegation, with Jeshua, in the open space of the courtyard. As he reached the seat prepared for him, a servant of Claudia Procula hurried to his side and thrust a message into his hand. He gestured for silence and read the tablet, so hurriedly written by his wife.

'Have nothing, I beseech you, to do in the cause of this just man, for I have suffered much in a dream concerning him.'

Pilate respected Claudia's inherited wisdom, knew of her greater insight into Jewry than he had ever reached and was now in a deeper dilemma than before. Herod and his soldiers confronted him with a visible parody of the High Priest's charge, and all parodies contain some truth. Here was indeed an acrid truth; the very jest itself declared, 'King of the Jews.'

There was still one devious turn he could try, a legal fiction characteristic of his tortuous mind. He addressed the priestly delegation and the few crude 'witnesses' they had assembled.

'You will know, Sirs, that I have a prerogative, that at the feast I release a prisoner, a celebration of clemency on this high day.' The deliberate and many-sided irony was not lost on them as they prepared for the blow he proposed to their hopes. But at the last moment the conflict turned their way:

'What would you then? We have two notable prisoners, your heroic rebel, Barabbas and this Galilean who appears to be entitled 'Christ'; which of them shall I release?' They cried at once,

'Barabbas!'

'And what of this man? I have examined him closely and find no fault in him. I will chastise him and release him.' And again they cried,

'Release Barabbas!' Pilate appealed again,

'But this man?'

'Crucify him!'

Pilate saw that this contained uproar might become riotous if it spread beyond his residence. He therefore commanded that water be brought and a towel; he washed his hands before them and said,

'I am innocent of the blood of this just man; see you to it.' The uncouth little rabble of paid 'witnesses' replied with malicious cruelty, 'Crucify him.'

Pilate then gave command; Barabbas was released and Jeshua was handed over to the soldiers. They led him within the palace to their quarters and there scourged him, put a robe about him, made a crown of thorns for his head and a reed in his hand. Pilate then led him out to the waiting group in the courtyard and declared,

'Your King – behold your King!' They still cried,

'Crucify him, crucify him!' Pilate commanded them, 'Take him and crucify him yourselves!' They replied, 'We have a law and by our law he must die because he declared himself the Son of God.'

Pilate had himself been moved by the nobility of Jeshua's bearing even under scourging and mockery, and was still disturbed by the message from Claudia Procula.

He therefore yet again took Jeshua alone into the judgment hall and in all gravity asked him,

'Whence are you?' Jeshua remained silent.

'Do you not answer me? Do you not know that I have power to crucify you and power to set you free?'

'You could have no power of any kind against me unless it were granted from above. Therefore their sin is the greater who delivered me over to your authority.'

Again Pilate sought to reason with the priests but desperately they used their final argument:

'If you let this man go, you are not Caesar's friend!'

Pilate came down and sat formally on his judgment seat and said to them,

'Behold your King.' They shouted their reply,

'We have no King but Caesar. Crucify this man.' And Jeshua was led away.

Strength was ebbing but the regality unimpaired. With a kind of rough compassion, the centurion who commanded the execution party arranged the cross-piece across Jeshua's shoulder so that, balanced, it could be supported by his left hand. Even so, Jeshua stumbled under its weight and with a courtesy the centurion had never before encountered, Jeshua thanked him for his assistance. But the weight of the balk of wood was too great for Jeshua's failing strength and the centurion halted the whole party. Calling roughly into the crowd in the street, he selected one from among them, a sturdy countryman, to carry the wood. He shrank with repugnance from the task but the centurion cut through his protests:

'Your name?'

'Simon.'

'A citizen of Jerusalem and a Roman?'

'Neither; of Cyrene in Libya.'

The soldiers balanced the wood across Simon's shoulder and he made to move on; but he paused, as Jeshua stretched out his hand and with no word, thanked him with such a depth of yearning in his expression that Simon felt as if a great and unexpected privilege had been accorded him.

As they moved away from the halting-place, a group of women began the ritual lament. Jeshua looked at the centurion and again with no word of command spoken, the party halted. Jeshua drew on all his strength and turned to the women and the others who stood by.

'Daughters of Jerusalem, weep not for me but for yourselves. For the days are coming in which they shall say, 'Blessed are the barren wombs and the breasts that never gave suck.' Then shall they begin to say to the mountains, 'Fall upon us' and to the hills, 'Cover us', for if they do these things in a green tree, what shall be done in the dry?'

They came to Golgotha, the 'Place of a Skull', where the execution was to take place, of Jeshua and two with him. The uprights were taken from their holes in the rock, the crosspieces attached and the three nailed to the crosses. They were lifted into position and the stone wedges hammered about the base. Each stage and each movement was a separate agony, which Jeshua bore in silence and the others with the relief of cursing their executioners. Then briefly, Jeshua's silence was broken and the centurion was startled at the import of the words:

'Father, forgive them. They know not what they do.'

The people about the foot of the crosses were a bitter contrast among each other. As near as they dared approach were John and Mary, Jeshua's mother. In a sneering and reviling circle about them were the ruffian witnesses who had tried to speed the trial; and beyond them, mingling with the merely curious crowd, were a handful of the disciples and the women who had assisted them in their mission. Behind the crosses was the execution party, busily dicing for the meagre property of those executed and the one man, alertly watchful, the centurion whose eyes travelled from Jeshua to those about his cross and back to Jeshua. Though helpless and pinned to the wood, Jeshua seemed to him to have transfigured the posture of his arms into a regal gesture of acceptance.

The cursing and reviling became partly stilled as the storm-clouds gathered in the west. Slowly they covered the sun and all about Golgotha the landscape seemed stained with a sulphur mask, like the breathless pause before an earthquake. Despite the clouds, there was no hint of rain through the oppressive dusk. And then for two hours, Golgotha was struck to silence, broken only by the antiphony of muffled curses and subdued weeping.

One of the High Priest's retinue had been sent to Golgotha to assure the Sanhedrin that all was over. To his affronted dismay he saw that above Jeshua's head his 'accusation' had been nailed and, unambiguously, in the three languages, Hebrew, Latin and Greek, it read starkly:

Jesus of Nazareth
King of the Jews.

Pilate was to be disturbed once more on that feast-day. A deputation from the Sanhedrin demanded,

'Write not that he is 'King of the Jews' but that he claimed of himself, 'I am King of the Jews'.'

Pilate was in no mood for further debate with them; his day had been sombre with recollection of the morning and Claudia's brooding gaze kept the tragedy and his avoidance of it starkly before him. At least he would remove some of his bitterness and throw it back at them. There was no argument and imperiously waving them away, he replied,

'What I have written I have written.'

The afternoon passed in the stifling murk and out of the near silence came the wholly unexpected. One of those crucified at his side gave a bitter acknowledgment of his power:

'If you really are the Christ, save yourself and us,' but the other silenced him:

'Don't you fear God, as you hang here with him? We are punished justly but he has done no wrong.'

Again there was silence and at last, gathering his strength, he turned his head to Jeshua,

'Lord, remember me when you come to your kingdom.' Jeshua replied,

'Indeed, I say to you, this day you shall be with me in paradise.'

John had had to support Mary in his arms throughout the silent watching and at length Jeshua looked down on them and, in a brief phrase disposing of their whole future, said

'Woman, see your son at your side.' 'My son, this is your mother.'

John looked at Mary Magdalene and Mary the wife of Cleophas who was standing near, and seeing their silent assent, he quickly took Mary away from Golgotha.

As the darkness intensified, many fled from the place but others drew nearer to the crosses; with a renewed access of strength, Jeshua cried:

'*Eloi, Eloi, lama sabachthani*?'

'My God, my God, why hast thou forsaken me?'

One of the soldiers, wishing to reduce his suffering, took a reed and placed on it a sponge soaked in sour wine and pressed it to his lips and though Jeshua turned his head away from the drink, in the torture of his body he burst out,

'I thirst.'

The centurion had now moved to the front of Jeshua's cross waiting for a truth he could not identify. It came, as the crucifixion had lasted for three hours; Jeshua opened his eyes as if seeing before him with the utmost clarity; his pinioned wrists allowed the slightest movement of his hands, which he raised as if beginning a prayer of thanksgiving and of blessing. In a voice of his former clarity, he said,

'It is finished, fulfilled to the uttermost. Father, into Thy hands I commend my spirit.'

With the briefest inclination of his head, he relinquished his life.

No one who had experienced Golgotha that Passover day, ever forgot it. Not the routine – they were accustomed to that: the soldier, leaving his prize of Jeshua's garment woven without seam, in order to give the killing blows to the two dying malefactors; the arresting hand of the centurion, who permitted no blows but a single spear-thrust, releasing water and blood from Jeshua's side; these were indeed routine, hurried actions to save the sanctity of the Sabbath which would be polluted by dead or dying men on Golgotha.

The memorable things to the onlookers were quite different: the rending of rocks, the shaking of all foundations in Passover Jerusalem – and the rumours that the Temple had not escaped, that the curtain before the Holy of Holies had been torn from top to bottom; – the dead walked the streets, sheeted and bound figures, and spoke, to the discomfiture of those who heard. And yet this was not the culmination of their wonder on that afternoon. They had looked with curiosity at those who had loved him, at Mary Magdalene and Mary the mother of James and Joses, and Salome – their grief had been transfixing –

but that which had given all this its indelible quality in their minds was the speech of the centurion at the cross, that figure of their customary derision. Through all the final acts of crucifixion he had remained silent, standing as if on watch at the foot of the cross. Then, with no thought for those about him, he had pronounced the one judgment that on that tragic day had validity:

'Truly this was a righteous man; truly, Son of God.'

Even the inner court of the High Priest's dwelling could not escape the oppression. The warmth of the cedar-panelled walls vibrated to the stifling heat of the after-noon. though the sun was obscured.

Malchus stood at the entrance, between the outer and inner court, holding back the heavy curtain in order to talk to his fellow at the threshold. His words were light but his eyes betrayed his continued state of shock.

'Who would have thought it of that absurd Peter and his waving, slashing sword!' He fingered the lobe of his ear, as though dubious of its continued existence. 'It was no practised stroke and I was lucky; an inch or two further and I should have lost more than my ear!'

'You lost nothing, Malchus, not a drain of blood.' He resented the scepticism with which his account of the arrest had been met and now replied, with an edge to his voice, 'I've mopped up the blood and changed my tunic but the pain was sharp and I thought I had lost my ear! It was humiliating and the more so as the prisoner turned from the grip of the guards and with a strange courtesy ('Suffer only thus far', he said) he touched my ear and all was well. I felt more than a little ridiculous – even you're smiling now – I suppose I shall always be a little ridiculous, the High Priest's personal servant!'

The resentment was cut off as the pavement appeared subtly to heave under their feet and the walls to shift from the vertical. Malchus's hand grasped desperately for the curtain of the doorway and his fellow stumbled back a pace or two into the outer court. They had barely recovered some kind of poise when a slave ran in from the outer gate. 'Three were crucified together. I saw them pass and I heard the curses, smelt the fear. I had thought to run to Golgotha but couldn't. And then people ran past me to the inner city and as the way seemed to rock under my feet – the more frightening because you were not even sure of the movement – people began to dash past with absurd shouts – 'the graves are open', they said, 'the sheeted dead', or some such words. And then there was all about me the stench, the shuffling of feet and most awful of all, the sweet scent of the grave-clothes.'

Malchus looked from one to the other, appalled. 'He seemed so gentle, and now, I suppose, he's dead.'

FORTY-FIVE

It was indeed to be an unforgettable day for Pilate. At his dismissal of the deputation from the Sanhedrin, he had retired to his apartments in the sure knowledge that no more would be heard of regal claimants, the clamour of the priests or of restless crowds seething towards insurrection; his soldiers were disciplined and trained and he would take such ease as he could summon.

Still there was interruption but this time it was welcome; for his servant announced that there waited for him in the ante-room, Joseph, a wealthy landowner from Arimathea and a distinguished member of the Sanhedrin – Pilate sourly commented to himself that this courtly and dignified man was the only member of that august body with whom he could have friendly and courteous dealings. He went himself to the door of the ante-room.

'Joseph! welcome to you. I have not yet repaid that meal I so much enjoyed amongst the scents of your garden. The next must be here, giving pleasure to Claudia Procula, as to me. But – your pardon – you seem in haste.'

'Lord Procurator, your guards have this day crucified one, Jeshua of Nazareth, for whom I had an ever-growing regard. No, Lord Pilate' – he responded to Pilate's gesture, compounded of apology and distaste – 'I bear no reproach. But the Sabbath is at hand; it is inconceivable that Jeshua should be cast into a common grave – may I beg his torn body, that I may give it honourable burial?'

'Burial, where?'

'In my own grave, Pilate. I had thought to be buried on my lands in Arimathea, to return to the resting-places of my fathers. But Jerusalem – this holy and hateful city, this seat of the Most High, blessed be He, and this seething place of dispute and sin – all this has held me, made me captive. Here, one day, I shall die and to this end I caused a grave to be hollowed in the rock which closes off my garden. There I would lay him – and another cave shall be hewn, not too far away.'

Pilate was silenced. It was of course a solution to an administrative dilemma – how secure a burial which should not be a focus of uproar? But this was more than that. 'Have nothing to do with this just man' – Claudia's words had haunted the day. Now, the one man he wholly respected in Jerusalem asked for the body of 'this just man.'

'Surely, Joseph.' He hesitated before making his own request:

'Tell me more, when we meet over our wine.'

Golgotha was almost deserted; it was barely an hour until the Sabbath lights should be kindled and Joseph noted with surprise, as he approached the cross with two of his friends, that some yards away there still stood a small group of women. Would the Sabbath candles not be lit by them at this quiet dusk?

408

The body was swiftly lowered from the cross and laid on the rock before it. Reverently, Joseph and his servants wrapped it in the long winding-cloth and lifted it on to the bier. They had some half mile to carry Jeshua to the lower gate of Joseph's garden, which led in a very few yards to the rock-face. The stone was already standing aside in its groove; the body of Jeshua was placed within and before the stone was rolled back to cover the entrance, Joseph and his friends spoke their farewell:

'May there be abundant peace from heaven,
And life for us and for all Israel.
He who maketh peace in His high places
May he make peace for us and for all Israel.'

From the gate of the garden, where all had been observed, there came from the women who had followed, a whispered 'Amen.' With an impulse he could not explain, Joseph drew them into the liturgy:

'My help cometh from the Lord.'

and the reply came with dignified assurance,

'Who hath made heaven and earth.'

The women turned away towards the city and Joseph climbed heavily through his fragrant garden to his own home.

The morning was still and cool, the refreshment of spring in the breeze from the west. Pilate, after a restless night, hoped for an untroubled day – it was not to be. Quite early, earlier than he judged proper, came yet another deputation from the High Priest. Debate after the execution had aroused a fear, based on certain words of the Galilean and the bold intransigence of some of his followers; these might well attempt to 'fulfil' his claim that the temple of his body, destroyed, would in three days, 'rise again', by stealing that body and spreading malicious rumours; would Lord Pilate prevent such a potential disaster by setting watch on the tomb? No, Lord Pilate would not!

'You yourselves have guards, see to it yourselves. Indeed, it is your responsibility, not mine; one of your own number – with my permission – took possession and charge of the body.'

This reminder stung. The absence of Joseph from their debate of the previous day still rankled; who knew what consequences might follow from this break in their ranks? for Joseph was a man of stature and mature wisdom. They hurried away, entered the rocky area of the garden by the lower gate and did their best. Seals were placed at the outer edges of the circular stone at the tomb's entrance and guards from the Temple were set on watch. They had done what they could.

The Sabbath passed and the third day dawned in a special calm. Mists lay over the west and south of the city which doubtless an hour's sun would burn away. To the lower gate of Joseph's garden three women hurried before the rising of the sun. Their minds were on the spices, the ointments and the clean linen they carried but there were troubling doubts about their ability to roll the stone in its groove away from the cave entrance.

Mary of Magdala was to the fore and walked swiftly along the curved and stony path to the tomb. She stopped, amazed; the stone was rolled away and in place of the shrouded and recumbent form she had expected, there stood a white-robed young man. Gently halting her at the entrance he said,

'You seek Jeshua of Nazareth who was crucified. He is risen. See, he is not here in the place they laid him. Go and tell his disciples and especially Peter that he will go before you into Galilee.'

Mary ran past the other women and so to the house where the eleven were staying in fear.

'They have taken the Lord from the sepulchre.' At once Peter and John ran to the place and John outran Peter and rushed to the entrance, stooping down and seeing the linen cloths lying in the place of burial. Then Peter brushed past him into the cave and both knew that Jeshua was not there.

Mary Magdalene had followed them slowly and knelt weeping among the flowering bushes that lined the paths to the upper garden. She heard footsteps on the path below her, the approach, she supposed, of the gardener. She remained silent and half-hidden but he said,

'Woman, why are you grieving? Whom do you seek?'

'Sir, if you have removed his body, tell me where you have laid him and I will take him away.'

'Mary!'

'Rabboni!' It was a cry that banished all grief and looking up, she saw him about whom all her world turned. Eagerly, as she had done an age away from this moment, she sought to embrace his feet. He said to her,

'Do not be afraid nor must you cling to me now. I have not yet ascended to my Father; but go to our brethren and tell them, 'I ascend to my Father and to your Father, to my God and to your God.'

Mary ran back to the eleven and shared her joy with them.

Meanwhile the guards were in great confusion. As they incoherently told their masters, they had not been asleep, indeed not! But an hour before the dawn, there was a stirring in the rock beneath their feet – 'Your reverences will remember the earthquake just two days ago!' – and under their eyes the stone before the grave entrance tilted, tore away the seals and rolled to the left of the entrance; they could see nothing, for the darkness outside and the glory of light in the cave.

'No, Sirs, no one passed us and we feared to look into that dazzling light. We have come to report all we know.'

'You have done faithfully; here is money beyond your wages and when you are asked of this thing, report that the followers of this Galilean overpowered you and stole his body.'

The bewildered guard blundered away and told their story in the guard-room, to mixed derision and belief.

The knocking at the gate was answered reluctantly. It was a spacious property, an outer courtyard, with a locked and barred gate, leading to the porch before the main door of the house – itself locked in these troubled times. Jeshua, at each visit, had been reminded of the home at Nazareth as he climbed the steep stairway to the large upper chamber at roof level, the steps protected by the trellis which sustained, seemingly, the Nazareth vine, which in turn softened the contours of the balustrade protecting the open roof space.

But all this graciousness, even if they had not been wholly familiar with it, would have been lost on John Mark's family and those friends of Jeshua who were in semi-hiding as Jerusalem steadied itself after the crucifixion.

The two who now half-ran across the courtyard after the gate had been hurriedly opened for them and equally hurriedly closed, went not to the lower door of the house but to the steps of the upper room. There they burst in on the despondent eleven, the women clustered about Mary of Nazareth and John Mark, the energetic son of the head of the household.

'We have seen and heard marvellous things.' There was no time for greetings, as Cleopas and his neighbour from Emmaus, burst out with their news. Their ambiguous expressions, torn between bewildered fear – a kind of wild awe – and exultation, matched too readily the fears and hopes of those already in the upper chamber.

'There was nothing to keep us in the city and I had work waiting for me at Emmaus' – Cleopas was struggling to give his story as much normality as he could summon – 'but we had been battered by the three days and I had no taste for Emmaus and my duties. Sunk in the crowd on Golgotha, torn by the murder of our Lord, sick with the earth's swaying and frightened by the soldiery, we were in no state to hear word of the empty tomb.' It was the attempt at coolness of the provincial man of affairs who had been grasped by events beyond his control.

'We were trying to resolve these things – had he truly been the Christ? Was it possible that he suffered death? Had the women truly seen what they declared or rather, not seen what they had expected? In what kind of truth would these things fulfil our minds, answer our hopes?

'We were climbing the last hill before Emmaus – after all it's no great distance – and were pausing to catch our breath, when we realised we had been quietly joined by a stranger.

'Your talk is earnest', he said, 'and I can't truly tell whether you speak of joyful things or of sorrow.'

''You come from Jerusalem, it seems, and yet you must have been merely passing through if you heard so little of these things.' He seemed not to understand and I went on – 'these things concerning Jeshua, our prophet and healer. We had hoped – but how can such hope be held fast when so many have come and gone who might have redeemed Israel?' He held us there before we moved on to Emmaus and, like a learned and skilful rabbi, told us of truths we had hoped and guessed at – that the Servant of God must suffer but the suffering was not the end and climax of it all; that the Servant indeed by his suffering redeemed Israel. In the lucid wonder of his words we asked nothing of him, who he could be and of what family and town.

'We reached Emmaus and it was not possible that we could let him pass the village; we pressed him to join us at our meal – and there it happened!

'We sat in silence at the table, said the opening prayers and he reached for the bread. Breaking it before the wine-cup, he raised his eyes and we knew; it was he! We had seen that gesture at the lakeside when the five thousand were fed; again when the four thousand had their needs fulfilled after the same gesture. But this night was different. As the bread broke and the hands turned upward, there, at the wrist, we saw it, the raw wounds of the torn flesh. It was he!'

To the eleven themselves he appeared. They had instinctively sought the friendly host of their last meal with Jeshua on the eve of his death. The upper room now seemed bleak and empty of life and then Jeshua stood before them. Despite the words of the women, they were dismayed at this 'apparition.'

'Why are you so disturbed? You believe you see a spirit? Look at my hands and feet – touch them and feel their flesh.'

Tentatively they put out their hands which were clasped by his.

'Have you anything to eat?'

They motioned him to sit and silently brought him a portion of fish, which he blessed and ate; and they brought barley cakes and the remains of a honey-comb which he also ate; for them, recollection and a great peace returned. Jeshua rose from his meal, gathered them all about him and said,

'Peace be with you. As my Father sent me, so send I you.' He embraced them, each one severally, and said,

'Receive the Spirit of God. You have power to remit and to retain sins. Make peace and joy in your world.'

Thomas the Twin was not with them when Jeshua had appeared and he rejected all they told him.

'I must see with my eyes. Unless I see the print of the nails in his hands and feet and feel the wound in his side, I will not believe.'

Days passed and the eleven were once more together and Jeshua again appeared to them. He drew Thomas forward before them all and said to him,

'Touch my hands, Thomas, and feel the wound in my side.' And Thomas fell before him in a shamed adoration.

'My Lord and my God.' Jeshua replied,

'Thomas, you believe because you have seen me; blessed are they who have not seen me and yet believe.'

FORTY-SIX

The instinctive fisherman's search for a secure haven from a troubled sea had brought Peter, alone, to Bethany. He had the gait and bearing of a man in late middle age and after the evening meal, almost silent but for perfunctory talk, he sat by the embers on the hearth, Lazarus opposite him and Mary between them. Martha was busied with a warm spiced drink which should send their wearied guest comforted to his bed.

Lazarus was alertly aware that the swift journey southwards from Galilee to Bethany carried news of significance for them all but his quiet tact and the watchful silence of Mary kept the questions unasked.

'He didn't mask the pain.' The words when they came were so seemingly irrelevant that the brother and sister gave no response.

415

'Three times he asked me; three times! 'Simon son of Jonah, *do* you love me?' He asked me that, three times. Shall I ever forget that fire, that courtyard, the courtyard of Caiaphas and the cockcrow?' Peter's voice had intensified to a pitch that Mary thought of as a quiet hysteria, and still they waited on his words.

'Three times he asked me and three times commanded, 'Feed my sheep; tend my flock.' The other ten all heard the words, knew my guilt but couldn't share it, couldn't lighten my burden. Denial, treachery, betrayal, all can be forgiven but' – he extended his hands and bare arms into the glow of the fire, showing the old scars of rope, sail and oar which had cut deep into the flesh – 'forgiveness yes, but the branding is there, burnt into my body. The scars will be there at my death – like these' he shook his arms in the light of the flames.

Lazarus shifted in unease and Mary looked across with concern for her brother. Peter resumed, almost as though unaware of his friends: 'Three times I have seen – always three times! – those hands take food and break it.' Quickly he answered Mary's puzzled gesture. 'Of course, many times more we have eaten together, day after day in our wanderings – but three times, first at the lake shore, when bread amd fish seemed strangely created as if at the beginning of time; then in Jerusalem at the Passover, when he said those words which I shall obey but without understanding them: 'Bread, Wine, my Body, my Blood; Eat, drink'.' The brooding gaze returned again to the embers at the hearth and he extended his hands to the few small flames.

'But now, once more at the lake shore; he was there before us; a rock-slab, large enough to be our table, extended from the grey pebbles, outward to be lapped by the waves' – he smiled for the first time at the seeming triviality of his memory – 'and there it happened once more. He had broiled fish at a little fire, he had brought

416

bread and – you know his gestures and that quick glance upward 'to my Father'. And we ate – four small portions were a feast, a fullness. It would be his blessing I think.'

Again there was silence and in the silence the wonder grew, drawing Martha into the listening group.

'I had hoped that my two lives would now be knitted in one; that fishing would be my skill and livelihood, with healing and teaching – and learning in his blessed presence – as a world-without-end joy and glory! But it was not to be.'

Peter's voice was now more confident and he looked from one to another of his friends for assent to his narrative.

'You remember we have often told you that we could never guess the pace at which he would walk. There were times when he strode the hill paths from village to town as though 'today' was all we had; and there were other times when blessedly he would linger between gentle walking from place to place, as though a flower or a wayside creature was of more importance than tomorrow or the day after. That was how we journeyed from the Sea of Galilee to the hills above Ephraim, only a day's journey from Bethany. We would walk a mile or two and then, sitting by the wayside, he would gather us about him; he would talk to us – and how he talked! He called it 'opening to us the scriptures' as though the Arks in all synagogues everywhere were all open and empty, the scrolls permanently unrolled to our gaze. And we understood – that was the new miracle – we understood what had before been so dark. One day we walked with Abraham, the long, thirsty, trusting journey from the Great River to our land; the next day the Voice would resound through Moses, we would dream with him of order and prayer and the Temple – and, to our believing wonder, we understood Torah! and we sat with David, built with Solomon, suffered and believed with Job and – final wonder of all – we knew at last what Isaiah had truly spoken of 'his Servant' and how Jeshua was he – despised and rejected and killed and for our iniquities and our salvation.'

Never had Lazarus heard Peter in this manner. It was the cry of a herald and yet pitched confidently to the tones of a hearth, the discourse of friends.

'In all his joy there were burdens he laid on us. 'You will lift the weight of men's sins' he said ' but where they cherish their sins you will retain them on their shoulders. You will bless my people and eat and drink with them – my Body, my Blood – and in you will the kingdom be fulfilled.' There were days when even the glory of the vision seemed to be too weighty, too heavy to bear – but a smile, a gesture, set all well again and we walked on – to an end we had not expected.'

The four about the hearth were now one, the speaker and his listeners held in a single quiet awe.

'We had rested in a shade in the greatest heat of the day. He had led us – it was a modest slope – to the top of a hill. You have seen it countless times; though it's not high, it commands a view of valley and plain about it. As we climbed, a mist lay about us and, higher, we entered thick cloud. John and James and I had memories, moments to which we always hold, of Jeshua's body glowing with a light we had never seen before; and voices, declaring his wonder, Son of the Most High. In joy we looked at each other and thought we were to have such a revelation again.

'But that was not his intention. He embraced us and turned away. We had not thought of farewell and the cloud was a merciful veil – over us and over him. And then' – Peter was now struggling for words for the inexpressible – 'and then came the greeting, echoing ever higher and higher:

"Peace be with you'; 'Peace be always with you' and

those words seemed to echo like the glorious song of angels and yet, more vision than sound.'

No understanding was possible but simple acceptance. Jeshua would rest in Bethany never again.

'So I'm with you once more, to gather myself before I go to Jerusalem with the ten.'

'And we shall be here, waiting.'

FORTY SEVEN

To return to the Temple required a girding of the mind. Its precincts held glorious memories, of profound truths explored and exchanged, of miracle and compassion, of a tranquil and noble figure, walking in quiet dignity those courts where rabbis had always held Torah in their minds. And those same precincts held clouded and tragic memories, the savour of which was like the after-taste of a bitter draught; of burning eyes that belied the dignity of the priestly vocation, of searing words that denied the truths of prophecy, of actions that more nearly resembled the trapping of wild beasts than the opposition of deeply-held convictions.

Peter and Thomas kept their turmoil in their minds as they descended the familiar path from Gethsemane to the Jerusalem gate. There was the Temple and its incongruous neighbour, the fortress, Antonia. The weeks were too few to have blunted their sense of deprivation; but they walked steadfastly in the familiar way.

'I can almost find it in my heart to be glad that I doubted, questioned his renewed life among us.' Thomas's belief, burned deep by humiliation and his touching of wounds, was too much for Peter. Every stone of the way, every dark alley and hidden courtyard in the tortuous city was for him a renewal of the sordid moment of denial – thrice forgiven but its wounds still burning.

What for the future would they find in the 'Cloister of Solomon', that secluded area where Jeshua had taught day by day? They walked its full length among the knots of disputants, meditative individuals, rabbis with their attentive scholars, and they moved among them, bereft. There were some questioning glances from those who remembered the little company; but in the absence of Jeshua, recollections were not sharpened to overt hostility. They spoke scarcely a word and they were about to leave the Temple when they were approached, obliquely across the line of the colonnade, by a man in late middle age, whose bearing and habit declared him a pharisee.

'We have neither met nor spoken but I listened intently and at length to Rabbi Jeshua. I am Gamaliel, grandson of that Hillel who won the admiration of your rabbi and master.'

'Rabban!' The reverential title was drawn from Peter, as he stood before the dignified pharisee; 'Rabban, we have no right to your time. Forgive us if we withdraw.' Gamaliel smiled. 'Humility is always seemly in those who aspire to wisdom. You were long with Jeshua, you loved him, a Master in Israel, and that alone would give you 'a right to my time'.' The smile continued to deny any hint of irony or condescension.

'Come, let us sit and talk about these things.' He led them to a small alcove, three sides of which had stone benches let into the wall, the fourth side open to the 'Cloister.'

'These have been troubled weeks and I am perhaps too old now to take much change to my heart.' He was admitting Peter and Thomas to his private meditation. 'The death was terrible – and not desired by most of us; indeed, I take pride in that gesture by Joseph, my friend from Arimathea.' He turned to Peter on his right hand: 'There will be more deaths, much persecution – would that I could contain it – but if your King lives, there will be life for all.' Peter and Thomas were held by the words; this was no rabbinic speculation on possibilities, probabilities; this was quietly-spoken prophecy, such as they had heard from only one, in the Galilee hills and here in these courts. Gamaliel's prophetic voice changed, his smile softening in welcome:

'Here are two friends, who have been with me in these last days.'

Peter rose to his feet, an embarrassed disbelief in his look from the pharisee to the two brothers who approached them. Weren't these of the Nazareth family, of the kin of Joseph and Mary – and of Jeshua? Gamaliel greeted them, drew them into the group with formal courtesy:

'You have, of course, known Peter and Thomas, intimate friends of Jeshua' and to Peter and Thomas; 'This is James – Jacob of Nazareth – and Jude his brother.' They now filled the little alcove, the two friends on the pharisee's right hand, the brothers on his left; all four were pupils again, at the feet of a rabbi.

'Your ways will be far dispersed – but, if truth be with you, you will be one in the Unity of the Most High. You, Peter, in your rugged strength, a rock at the heart of things? but a rock hidden and reviled?' Peter looked in his eyes, tense with foreboding and then – a kind of submission – down at his clasped hands. 'And you Thomas of the doubting, questing mind! taking wisdom, a magus even, to the east?' Could there be jesting in prophecy, banter at the heart of the future? – the questions crowded upon Thomas.

'You, Jude; you have spoken little. Nazareth has tenderness and sweetness for you, only occasional shadows crossing your memory; for you there will be 'mercy, and peace and love – multiplied to eternity by him who will keep you from falling'.' The last words faded, as the pharisee looked intently at James, his eyes tragically clouded.

'You, James, your memories are darker. Jeshua for you could be a 'stone of stumbling'.' James's arm stirred as though to ward off a blow. 'Your thoughts by day and in the stillness of the sleepless night are overcast by shamed memories; that steep place, James, at the outskirts of Nazareth.' Gamaliel's eyes held his, steadily; there was no escaping the shame. 'But Jeshua returned and you spoke together, brother to brother and he took you in memory to another steep place, here, where these walls plunge down to Hinnom; and here he was poised, with the voice of Beelzebul in his ears – 'cast yourself down – legions of angels wait!'' James was enmeshed in memory, in prophecy and in deep fear.

'James, my son; Adonai, blessed be His Name, has throughout time, been content to use flawed vessels. Your voice, James, will be strong in Jerusalem, strong to establish, strong to direct and if you, like Jeshua, look over the abyss, even to the depths of Hinnom Valley, he in his mercy will perhaps not 'keep you from falling' but will present you faultless before the presence of His glory – and there will be great joy.'

There could be no more words. The four stood silent before the nobility of the pharisee, and they turned and went their several ways. Each of them knew in his own fashion that the future had been gathered there, sent out in grace from those precincts where Jeshua had walked.

EPILOGUE

'Have we destroyed our lives?' The question sounded both impious and melodramatic, even to Joseph's own ear in his heaviness of spirit. It was some six weeks after the Passover. In the full heat of noon, even in the shaded court, the herbs smelt heavy on the air. The old irony still lurked in the eyes and about the mouth of Nicodemus and there was something near banter in his reply:

'It was your grave, Joseph. You found it untenanted, neatly vacant. You rejoiced in the dawn, as they did, the eleven and the women; and I was glad with you – 'after much heaviness, joy in the morning.' Is there more to say or to do?'

The two pharisees went through the courtyard arch and sat on a worn stone seat above the narrow copse-filled valley. The path below them disappeared into the dark laurel thickets. There was much to talk about and they fell quickly into their customary rhythms of thought.

'The Unity, always the Unity: 'thou shalt have none other.' One – and ever One.'

'True. But the prophecy has been bitterly alive in these last weeks: 'My servant – treading the winepress alone.' That servant – the Son? – what does that do to the Unity?'

Joseph took the irony like a sword-point thrust. This was the very breath of life, the stroke and parry of mind with mind. But the learned play had darkened in the air of the recent months and the next feint was no longer merely of the mind.

'He was crucified – cursed on the Tree.'

'And what does that do to your clean, new-swept grave?'

There was no answer; none was possible in the sombre, rabbinic exchange. From the shallow valley a light breeze brought a suspicion of thyme, a faint odour of acacia blossom. It carried to them also something of the astringency of the desert air.

There was a long silence between them and again the disciplined minds stirred, out of the warmth and the scents of the day, into the testing of their hearts.

'But Jeshua?'

The question was diffident, exploring, as though Joseph's dignity was forced to bend to a hapless search.

'I never knew him.'

No answer could have been less expected and Joseph waited silently.

'When he first spoke to me, he was almost unknown, an articulate but unremarkable Galilean – well, perhaps, not quite unremarkable. Less than half my age, he spoke with an assurance beyond my authority, and I listened as I had waited on the words of my rabbi as a boy! He spoke only of the wind that blows, breathes where it will. We rabbis are used enough to that word-play; we have explored it often enough in synagogue: *Ruah*, wind, breath, the breath of God. But his was no Sabbath address before the Ark; when he spoke of 'the Spirit' – 'born of the Spirit', he said – he spoke of 'Spirit' as of a person he knew, a well-loved being.'

The two learned friends were used to exploration, whether alone or in rabbinic debate; but this was no pitting of wit against wit, the exercise, the honing of professional skills.

'I met him once again, after that first encounter. Alone, away from his friends and followers, he spoke so vividly.

'Of his Kingdom and the gathering of his people?'

'No; of music!'

Joseph suspected a joke and for a moment looked affronted.

'He virtually took me back to Galilee, to his little by-way of Nazareth.'

'There must have been little music there!'

'No; but it was a remarkable story he told, of a shepherd's pipe which he had heard a hundred times in the hills, calling the sheep to the fold. But this was a different pipe, an old one which the shepherd boy had inherited. Jeshua seemed to be telling me of a strange scale of notes, an interval between notes which he had not heard before. And it brought a new melody and a new rhythm to the shepherd's playing, as though the music of a distant tribe, from a distant world had been brought to Nazareth. But it was still a tender world of the hills about his home, the world of sheep and their lambs and the caring shepherd.'

Joseph had never before in all their years of friendship, heard the ironic and sophisticated voice of Nicodemus take on these tones of wonder and puzzled tenderness. His words were now still lower, exploring an experience unique in his life of contemplative learning in the Temple precincts.

'The music of the great simplicities – though his words left me defeated, the gentle smile and the glow in his eyes told me of his secret, a depth of harmony that our Sanhedrin, the Romans, and most of the people – even his followers – knew nothing. But that was the secret at his heart. The harmony of things, from the humblest flower in the field to the furthest star; harmony; and peace; and the withdrawn life of the spirit, that was what he craved for all men; that, I believe, was what he meant by his 'Kingdom'.'

'And yet he was entangled in Rome.'

'That was his secret too; his 'withdrawn life of the heart' was no retreat. He had known the world of trade and of the tax-gatherer; he had moved with poor farmers and prosperous fishermen; he could face the court of Herod, of the Procurator Pilate himself and never feared being, as you say, 'entangled' – his truths were as much for the market-place, the Sanhedrin, the courts – and the Temple – as they were for the heart in its stillness.'

Again Joseph looked at his friend, as though he had scarcely known him before. For Nicodemus was now exploring his own mind, scarcely aware of the presence of the younger pharisee. Joseph tentatively drew Nicodemus back to the harshest realities:

'And then – crucifixion?'

'I have never known death so faced, as though the agony, the very tearing of the body was in his control. His last words were as still, as assured as the peaceful death of a patriarch.'

The two friends fell once more into silence, each pursuing his own questing into the mysteries. The evening breeze was little more than a sigh.

'He walked with God.' Nicodemus could pass no greater judgment; few men of old time had received that accolade.

'As an equal?'

Joseph's temerity had taken him far, to the brink of an abyss and an instinctive denial burnt in the eyes of Nicodemus. In the uneasy silence, he responded:

'In the Unity; in the Unity.' The assertion from the ages now held for Joseph all the searching ambiguity of an inconceivable idea conceived and explored.

Jerusalem murmured its tumults in the distance, as the two friends were silent, savouring the rich scents on the evening breeze.